Silently they drifted over the Tijuana enclave. G'kaan kept one eye on the map, whe icon, and the other on below them. It was disorie was below, but she coul

"That's it," G'kaa

Rose was compl e you sure?"

"There they are." With a touch, G'kaan refocused the monitor.

A shadowy image appeared. A man was standing near the shed on the roof. His back was to them, and his head was bent. As their angle changed, Rose saw someone kneeling in front of him. It was Shard!

The grav sled lowered. Bolt must have heard something, because at the last moment before they touched down, his head went up and turned. The white-blond hair and chiseled profile were exactly as Rose remembered.

G'kaan popped the door open and Rose was out like a flash. Chad had come up the stairs behind them and was wrestling with Bolt, holding both of his arms. Chad outmassed and outmuscled Bolt, but for a moment it looked close.

"I got him!" Chad exclaimed as G'kaan brandished a stun-wand. To Rose, he added, "It's on the back of my belt."

Bolt was fighting him, but Chad had the edge and drove him to his knees. She reached around Chad and pulled a very large knife from its sheath. "Nice. . . ."

"Just what you asked for." Shard was out of breath from hanging on to Bolt until Chad could subdue him.

"You worthless bitch!" Bolt spat at Shard, trying to wrest out of Chad's arms. "Setting me up—"

Rose stuck the knife in his face. "Shut up!"

The knife had exactly the effect she wanted. Bolt's eyes fastened on the long silver blade with a dramatic hook at the end. It was honed to sharpness, but had a worn grip, as though someone had used it for a long time.

"Don't you remember me, Bolt?" Rose asked sweetly.

SLAVES
UNCHAINED

SUSAN WRIGHT

POCKET **STAR** BOOKS
New York   London   Toronto   Sydney

An *Original* Publication of POCKET BOOKS

A Pocket Star Book published by
POCKET BOOKS, a division of Simon & Schuster, Inc.
1230 Avenue of the Americas, New York, NY 10020

Copyright © 2005 by Susan Wright

ISBN: 0-7434-5765-X

First Pocket Books printing March 2005

10 9 8 7 6 5 4 3 2 1

POCKET STAR BOOKS and colophon are registered trademarks of Simon & Schuster, Inc.

Cover design and illustration by David Stevenson; photos © Erica Lennard/Nonstock

Manufactured in the United States of America

For information regarding special discounts for bulk purchases, please contact Simon & Schuster Special Sales at 1-800-456-6798 or business@simonandschuster.com

1

Rose Rico checked the flashing red display to be sure their automated distress signal was running. She was at the helm of the *Relevance*, the powerful Fleet patrolship that her crew had hijacked from Archernar shipyard two decnights before. They had long ago crossed the border of the Domain, leaving the Procyon sector far behind.

Another Fleet patrolship was holding steady up ahead, sitting stubbornly on the mouth of the gravity slip leading into the Sol system. This slip was one of three ever-shifting doorways to Earth, the homeworld of pleasure slaves. The patrolship *Fortitude* clearly wasn't going to budge even for a sister Fleet ship flashing its distress signal.

Rose grinned at her crew on the sleek command deck. They were biting their nails at the sight of their ship bearing down on the *Fortitude*. The *Relevance* was a match in hardware, but the former pleasure slaves were panicked about going up against a trained Fleet crew.

"I don't know about this, Rose," Chad warned. The big Solian was at the auxiliary helm, backing her up in case she needed to concentrate on weapons. The systems on the patrolship were much more complex than the systems on the old freighter she used to command. Yet she could tell that everything was running smoothly by the hum of machinery in the air and the subtle vibrations of the deck plating. Her old freighter had usually felt loose at the seams, with hitches in the helm response and sudden episodes of deceleration. She felt much more secure in the powerful *Relevance.*

"We talked this out in conclave," Rose reminded them, as she secured her curly dark hair into a messy coil. "This is the only way to get in close enough to capture the *Fortitude.*"

Stub's usually sunny expression was worried. "I don't know . . . the Qin are more than three hours behind us. That's awfully far away."

Rose rolled her eyes. She had picked Stub as her regular bed partner for his sense of fun. The negative attitude didn't suit him. "Three hours or three minutes, who cares? We crush them or we die."

"That's not exactly reassuring," Chad pointed out. "What if they've heard about Archernar shipyard? With the damage you did, it's bound to get talked about. There's already been too much buzz about the Qin battleship inside the Domain."

"We're way ahead of the rumors." Rose gestured to the gleaming silver-and-black displays of the terminals and the strong curves of the double-thick bulkheads. "Look at our ship! It's brand-new with the best of everything. Who could get here faster than us?"

Chad was verging on rebellion, which was typical. Yet Shard, seated at the comm, also looked uneasy. She was a curvaceous Solian-Yllia hybrid, not the type to fret over anything. Which was probably why Stub was so upset. The anxiety was contagious—and annoying.

It was times like this that Rose missed Ash. The poor herme was safely back on the Qin battleship, receiving brain treatment to restore hir memory. For Rose it was a bitter thing that Ash wasn't by her side. Ash had helped her seize control of the cargoship *Purpose*. Rose knew that the old Ash would have loved the fact that she was taking her revolt into Sol. She could certainly use Ash's help right now, but she wouldn't let even her friend's absence stop her. Ash had told her to return to Earth: Rose was going to throw the Fleet out of Sol with or without hir.

"You can leave any time you want," she told her command crew. "There are lifepods for everyone, and the Qin will pick you up in a few hours. But you better jump now, because we'll be in weapons range soon."

No one moved as the stars silently passed in the imager. None of them would bail out; it was just opening-night jitters. Everyone would settle down as soon as they engaged the patrolship. Rose was looking forward to showing the Qin that Solians could kick butt along with the best of them.

The patrolship at the slip couldn't see the *Endurance*, which was still safely beyond scanner range. The Fleet captain must have detected the gravity burst from the battleship when it entered the pocket the day before. They probably thought a Fleet battleship was approaching and were scrubbing down their ship for inspection. The Fleet had a bad reputation for eating its own.

Rose had used their patrolship's security decoder to strip the anchored beacons in every gravity pocket on their way to Sol. She had gathered a lot of useful information, but there was nothing about their attack on Archernar shipyard or the hijacking of the *Relevance*.

That was good because their ship's ID had already been triggered during their approach. The *Fortitude*'s shields were raised and they were in a defensive posture at the slip as per procedure.

Rose couldn't possibly pretend to be an Alpha-captain, so the deception was necessary. Kwort and Nip had unbalanced the power feeds and disconnected two transducer units to create the impression that their comm was off-line, which explained why they didn't respond to the *Fortitude*'s repeated hails. Kwort Delta was a former Fleet bot tech, so he knew how to make it look real. Rose trusted Kwort, despite the fact that the little ridged-headed Deneb was a complete coward, because when things got dirty Kwort always came through.

To make their malfunctions look even more convincing, G'kaan's battleship had blasted a few scorch marks strategically across their hull. Even though G'kaan had done it to help them, Rose's fingers had itched to fire the missile-activation sequence right back at him. Now their port weapons hatches appeared to be twisted off, which left them conveniently open. Their comm unit sported a charred stripe, curling a section of the outer edge of the parabolic dish from the heat of the lasers. The damage optically distorted comm and scanner relays, making random bits break up in the imager, but Rose didn't care as long as it lulled the suspicions of the *Fortitude*.

"I'm receiving a message from the patrolship," Shard announced. The gorgeous woman was almost as good at the comm as she was in bed. Though her long, silver-white hair was held back and she wore a plain brown flightsuit, nothing could spoil her transcendent beauty. "They're demanding that we disengage shields and stand down for inspection since we've refused to answer their hails."

"Can't they see we're damaged and can't hear them?" Rose asked gleefully. "Make sure Kwort is ready with the transducers. We won't have much time if we need weapons."

Shard keyed her terminal, speaking into the comm link slung around her neck. Every motion was graceful. Stub's eyes lingered on Shard as she reported the bot tech's readiness, until Rose gave him a frown. She didn't care if Stub drooled over their resident sex queen, as long as he didn't do it while he was on duty.

"We're entering weapons range," Rose announced.

"The *Fortitude* is shifting," Shard warned. "They're on an intercept course."

Rose could see it with her navigational scanners. The *Fortitude* was advancing to keep them from getting near the gravity slip—standard procedure for the Fleet, as Rose had learned from long hours of studying the database on board. She thought that the manuals made for some pretty dull reading, but now she was glad she had invested the time. Rose felt as if this ambush would be a piece of cake.

"Slowing to one-quarter power," Rose said. That was also according to procedure when approaching another Fleet ship. It would help put the captain of the *Fortitude* at ease. The subliminal thrumming of the engines eased as they slowed, which would give her more power when she activated the attractor. "Send the waveband message now."

"Aye, Captain," Shard agreed, triggering their prepared waveband message. The text claimed they had been attacked by a Qin battleship and needed to dock with the *Fortitude* to receive technical assistance.

Waveband took much longer, because the message

was carried by ordinary EM waves, while the comm relayed instantly through the subspace grav field. Rose was no engineer, so she didn't know why the comm had a limited range while grav slips could transport them instantly across light-years. All she knew was how close they needed to get to use their attractor field on the *Fortitude*. Once the restraining energy was wrapped around that ship, with missiles aimed at such close range, the Fleet crew would have no choice but to surrender.

"They're arming weapons!" Shard exclaimed.

That was *not* standard procedure. "Weapons and shields on-line!" Rose's voice rang throughout the ship. She couldn't afford to risk her crew, not even to win another Fleet patrolship.

They were so close that Rose could see the missile hatches on the *Fortitude* begin to open. In response, her own weapons instantly blinked on-line, thanks to good old reliable Kwort.

"Firing port tubes!" Rose hit the buttons, firing missiles in rapid succession through the two open portals.

There was a breathless moment as the missiles streaked across the imager, while Stub worked frantically at ops to get their own defenses up.

The first salvo of missiles impacted against the shielded *Fortitude* and rocked it with a white-hot explosion. Rose spun the ship to fire both tubes on the starboard side. Reloading took time between each launch, so firing an alternating pattern gave maximum coverage. Again, straight out of the Fleet weapons manual.

"Our shields are up!" Stub sounded frazzled.

Rose finished a complete turn, firing the port missiles again. She had to trust the automated targeting scanner, since they couldn't see the patrolship behind the flashing rainbow arc of its shields.

Shard started to speak. "There's a hull breach in their aft section—"

Rose skewed just in time, putting their burners between them and the doomed patrolship. The *Fortitude* blew up as direct impact on the exposed fuel cells spewed a fury of irradiated atoms into space.

For one weightless moment, Rose felt as if she were salvaging back on Spacepost T-3. But she was stuck to her chair by the microgravity field. Then her magnificent ship bucked underneath her as the stars spun in the imager. Through the semitransparent image, she could see Stub and Shard trying to hang on to their terminals.

Shaking her head and nursing a bit tongue, Rose got her bearings. The *Fortitude* was nothing but expanding wreckage floating dangerously in front of the gravity slip. It would make a nice obstacle course for any other ships that approached the slip.

"We did it!" Stub stood up and raised both arms into the air, crying out again, "We did it!"

After a stunned moment, the others joined in, jumping up and down and hugging each other as Chad shouted out in relief. Sounds from the slaves they had saved from Archernar shipyard came from deeper within the ship.

Rose kicked back in her chair with a smug grin on her face. It was about time they learned to never doubt her!

As Captain G'kaan neared the Centauri-Sol slip, he regretted the loss of life on board the Fleet patrolship. But it was Rose's decision whether to take the *Fortitude* intact or destroy it. He only wished there were less blood-thirsty satisfaction in her description of the ambush. He had not taken the point because the *Fortitude* could have identified them by scanner and escaped through the gravity slip to warn the intrasolar patrols that a Qin battleship was attacking Sol.

"After you." Rose gestured toward the grav slip, grinning through the imager.

The approach to the gravity slip was cluttered with debris, but G'kaan set his course. "Please hold back and allow us to clear the area on the other side," he told Rose sternly.

"Yeah, sure," Rose drawled, as she closed the channel.

His ops corpsman, L'pash, glared at the now-empty imager. "Who does she think she is?"

M'ke at the comm answered for him, "Rose thinks she is the liberator of her people."

"She isn't going to back down without a fight," G'kaan agreed. At least Rose was not fanatical like S'jen, his former Qin mate. S'jen would have already jumped through the slip and tried to single-handedly overpower any ship on the other side, regardless of whether that was the optimum course of action. G'kaan was determined to make smarter choices during the next impending lust. L'pash had amply proven she was ready and waiting for him.

G'kaan engaged thrusters on his enormous battleship, gracefully diving around the debris at the speed of the gravitational constant. He prepared himself for the disorientation of being transported four light-years away. As the *Endurance* entered the slip, they blinked out of existence in that part of space and were instantly brought to the pocket just outside the Sol system, more than three billion miles away from the primary sun. It looked like any other bright star in the field, nearly indistinguishable from the rest.

"Powering up the converter." G'kaan tried to ignore the light-headedness he always felt after traveling through a slip.

"Patrolship dead to starboard!" M'ke announced, relaying the coordinates.

The patrolship hesitated, as if its crew was caught by surprise. Clearly the *Endurance* wasn't Fleet. The patrolship sped away.

After decades of piloting, G'kaan's reflexes obeyed at a thought. His systems were already running hot and they began to gain on the patrolship.

"It's the *Devotion*," M'ke informed them, reading the ID. "According to the files Rose gave us, it's one of the three patrolships assigned to guard the Sol system."

"Attractor beam ready," L'pash eagerly put in. Her eyes sparkled, and a jaunty, white hourglass blaze marked her dainty nose. "Shields at maximum."

"They're targeting us with their missiles." M'ke sounded exactly the same as usual, as if he had seen it before. G'kaan once again thanked the foresight of his grandfather who had anticipated his need for an elder, experienced advisor. M'ke had been by his side since he first gained command of an Armada warship.

G'kaan stretched his lips to reveal his cuspar fangs. "We've got them!"

The *Devotion* fired a round of six missiles. They were so close that his point defense lasers could hardly react in time, destroying only two. The other four missiles impacted against their shields, shaking the *Endurance*.

G'kaan ignored it. They could handle every one of the

patrolship's missiles with their immense shield generators.

The patrolship frantically discharged another six missiles. The explosions jolted the battleship, but G'kaan stayed on course.

"Systems are holding," L'pash declared steadily.

"Closing to intercept." G'kaan increased speed, maneuvering up and over the patrolship, cutting it off.

The patrolship tried to turn away, swinging wide as it reversed course.

The tricky part was in L'pash's hands. She cast the attractor field, trying to get exactly the right angle to capture the patrolship. But it slipped off, deflected by a sudden shift. Biting her lip in concentration, L'pash adjusted the angle and tried again. "I've got a lock!" she exclaimed.

The patrolship seemed to surge forward, then swung back as the attractor field killed their momentum. Under the field, the patrolship's converter cycled off-line causing them to lose all mobility. Now they were under the *Endurance*'s control.

"Hail them," G'kaan ordered.

There was a long wait. No doubt the Fleet captain was trying to figure out something heroic to do that would save his ship and crew.

"Send the following message." G'kaan narrowed his eyes, thinking of the useful information he had gleaned about Fleet psychology from the *Relevance*'s database. Rose had acquired a treasure beyond compare when she had captured that patrolship. "I am Captain G'kaan of the Qin battleship *Endurance*. You have nothing to save but yourselves. Evacuate to your lifepods or we will begin immediate decompression of your ship."

To back up his threat, G'kaan carefully targeted the command deck and sent a low level laser bolt directly into the hull. The patrolship shuddered in their grasp.

A blackened crater in the polytanium plating showed how close he had come to piercing the hull. A slightly harder strike would neatly punch through the unshielded plating even though it was armored.

"One lifepod has ejected," M'ke announced.

"There go another two," L'pash pointed.

M'ke scanned the lifepods as they popped off. "They're full of Fleet officers."

"Good." G'kaan glanced back at a smiling R'yeb, his second. "Are you ready to take command of your new ship, Captain R'yeb?"

It was Armada tradition for the second to receive a promotion in the field in order to command a war prize. Even though the practice hadn't been carried out in nearly a century, G'kaan knew that Chief Commander T'ment would confirm R'yeb's rank of captain. G'kaan's only regret was losing the services of one of the best corpsmen in the Armada. But he couldn't let that hold R'yeb back from what she had rightfully earned during their campaign against the Domain. In fact, he had alerted R'yeb to the possibility so she could study the Fleet manuals Rose had downloaded for them.

R'yeb's smoky brown skin showed her proud heritage in one of the earliest spacefaring clans. "Aye, Captain!"

R'yeb left the command deck while G'kaan carefully docked with the *Devotion*. When the *Relevance* came through the grav slip, Rose sent her congratulations.

G'kaan had agreed to help Rose liberate Earth because no other blow against the Domain would be as devastating as an invasion of Sol. Even if G'kaan could destroy Canopus Regional Headquarters, that wouldn't reverberate throughout the Domain the way shutting down their supply of raw pleasure slaves would. The Alpha regents wouldn't stand for it, and battleships destined to savage Qin would be diverted to Sol. G'kaan would buy time for the clans to prepare to defend their territory against the Fleet.

Yet G'kaan wasn't thinking only about Qin. He took pride in freeing the Solian people and righting the terrible wrong Qin had done to them so long ago. Since G'kaan's mother had been Solian, that made it personal for him. He had barely known her, because she had died when he was a young child, but he liked to think she would be glad to see her son fighting for Solian freedom.

Nip couldn't believe they were actually in Sol. Rose had done it again! She had led them out of the Domain, and was bringing them home to Earth.

Nip was at the helm of the *Relevance*, but he wasn't alone. The command deck was crowded with Solians who longed to see Earth. None of them, except for native Rose, had ever been there, but they all felt the same way. They were coming home.

It took more than a full day to get to the planet from the gravity pocket on the outer edge of the Sol system. They had downloaded the latest Fleet navigational charts from the beacons inside the Domain. Luckily, *Relevance* had the right codes in its processors to access the data for Sol. At the moment there weren't any intrasolar slips to Earth close to their grav pocket, so they blasted through the system on a straight run. The only planet they passed near was Neptune, which looked like a bright lime disc hanging against the stars.

Rose and the senior crew returned to the command deck as they neared Earth. Nip gratefully gave up his post to the captain. He didn't want to be in command if the Fleet counterattacked. Instead, he stood against a bulkhead, trying to keep out of the way. The deck was packed with crew members who, like Nip, weren't going to miss their arrival at Earth. Nip had gone through too much to get here: partial dismemberment and near death. He was then cast away on a derelict space station, forced to hide out as a renegade slave before he finally got a chance to help his friends escape slavery again.

"Magnifying image of Earth," Shard announced in her sultry voice. For a moment, Nip was distracted by visions of sexual delight with Shard. His daydream was halted as a gasp rose when their home planet appeared in the imager.

A vast blue orb with swirls of pure white hung in the imager, glinting with light. Nip could even see the thin coating of atmosphere blurring the edges and thought that it seemed too fragile for the towering sky Rose had described. But that jewel-toned blue was exactly right. It was more intensely blue than anything he'd ever seen. He felt tears coming to his eyes.

The others kept staring at Rose as if unable to believe, even at this moment, that she had brought them to Earth. Only Chad was the voice of doom, as usual. He kept reminding them that two more patrolships were somewhere inside Sol. Rose finally had to threaten to kick him off the command deck. Chad shot daggers at her for a while after that, but everyone was too engrossed by the sight of Earth to care.

Nip was going home. He didn't care that he had

never been to Earth. He could feel it in his bones that this was where he belonged. He only wished that Trace could be with them. After all the risks they had taken together, she deserved to be here, too. Not for the first time, Nip regretted that he hadn't urged Trace to come along. But he had been so excited about seeing Shard and Chad that he hadn't really thought about what was happening. Then Trace was gone with the *Solace*, and he didn't have a chance for a proper good-bye. It was too bad, but Trace was in love with Gandre Li, not him.

It made Nip feel better to know that he was doing something good for Trace, as well as for every other pleasure slave still stuck in the Domain. He was helping Rose take back Sol. He wasn't much when it came to brains or brawn, but he knew that he could run the helm of this ship. He didn't care about the danger. He would do it for them.

"The *Devotion* and *Relevance* are pulling up," M'ke announced.

G'kaan checked his navigational scanners. To the port, the *Relevance* stopped at their predesignated coordinates, letting the battleship move ahead. He hadn't heard from Rose during their inward journey, because they had agreed to maintain comm silence. Scanners had picked up no sign of the other patrolships. Perhaps they had seen the Qin battleship and were fleeing back to Canopus Regional Headquarters to fetch reinforcements. His crew would be particularly vulnerable in a few decnights when their lust hit. But M'ke agreed they had to take this opportunity to distract the Fleet from Qin. If necessary, they could retreat from Sol and travel into deep space outside the grav pocket where they would be safe during their lust.

R'yeb pulled up the *Devotion* near Rose's ship. R'yeb's patrolship was dragging the cache of lifepods that served as self-contained jail cells for the Fleet crew, complete with waste facilities and food packs. At the first sign of trouble, she had orders to detach the pods.

"Entering weapons range of Earth's moon," M'ke announced.

M'ke had performed a scan of the extensive Fleet base situated on the shadow meridian of the large moon. The base was heavily shielded, because the moon's orbit exposed it to the full glare of the sun. Most of the base was buried deep under the basalt rock shield, which was pocked with craters. The laser array was positioned near the moonbase, while an automated laser platform orbited Earth opposite the moon. Both arrays had their mighty cannon muzzles trained on space. Between the two lasers, the Fleet could take out any raider foolish enough to approach Earth.

G'kaan sent in eight long-range missiles, but the lasers on the moonbase expertly destroyed every one. His battleship rapidly closed the distance.

"We're being targeted!" M'ke warned.

Though their shields were at maximum, the moonbase's lasers were more powerful than Fleet missiles. They used solar power, which was in abundant supply, to fuel their multi-head beams.

The lurid purple lasers leapt from the rotating heads. G'kaan maneuvered to deflect the strikes off his shields into space. The *Endurance* vibrated as if riding over rough terrain.

"Firing lasers," G'kaan announced.

Streaks of ruby red fire slashed into the laser array. Purple bolts tried to respond, but were cut off by their sustained fire.

G'kaan switched to their secondary lasers before the primary heads overloaded. He hit the laser array on the moonbase again, sustaining the beam.

Although the moonbase was used to repelling raiders with their missiles and short-range lasers, they had not been designed to withstand an attack by a battleship. The only other battleships in this arm of the galaxy belonged to the Kund, and they were over a thousand light-years away. After word of this got out, every senior Alpha in the neighboring regions would scream for a weapons upgrade. Yet any stationary weapon was inherently vulnerable to a powerful battleship.

Outgunned, the laser array on the moon overloaded and sent feedback into the power generator. G'kaan cursed under his breath as the power generator also exploded, taking out a chunk of the moon along with it. The array was concealed behind a blooming cloud of debris. It began to drift toward the moonbase.

"Unfortunate," he muttered. They had hoped to be able to repair the laser array to use it for their own defense.

"The orbital laser platform is still intact," L'pash hastily reminded him.

"We didn't expect to take the moon without some damage," M'ke agreed.

G'kaan wasn't ready to declare victory yet. According to Rose's Fleet database, nearly one hundred personnel were stationed on that moonbase. "Order the combat teams to the pinnaces."

* * *

The hand-to-hand laser combat in the moonbase reminded G'kaan of the bloody battles on board the Fleet mining stations that he had helped liberate. But here the upper ranks were in no mood to sacrifice themselves. They surrendered in harried groups to the Qin combat teams, who moved efficiently through the sprawling underground complex.

The moonbase offered plenty of hiding places for people who refused to surrender. The levels meshed at odd angles, since the base had been built up over millennia of use. Even the maps they had downloaded from the control center covered only the first few levels. G'kaan, like the other Qin, knew the long, bloody history of this base. It would be difficult to search every part of its ever-deepening layers. The danger of escaped Fleet personnel was enough for G'kaan to order the moonbase off-limits to the Solians.

When it became apparent that the situation was under control in the vicinity of the control center, G'kaan brought Rose down to the moonbase. L'pash was irritated by that, though she didn't protest. G'kaan knew they would need help freeing the abducted Solians who were being held in the warehouse.

Rose arrived at the moonbase with Chad and Clay. She didn't like Chad, but he had been trained by G'kaan and was good at seeing things she missed, much as she hated to admit it. Though Clay was mute, he was as steady and reliable as a rock. He had been the first to support her plans of escape from Archernar shipyard.

When they walked into the long room with rows of tables, Rose felt as if she were about to blow up. The arched ceiling was exactly as she remembered, supported by beams that looked like molded green plastic. It stank to high heaven from the waste that had been expelled in the Solians' panic when they realized they had been abducted. Rose had never smelled anything quite so foul, despite the fact that the galaxy was a pretty disgusting place. It made her lungs seize, and she couldn't draw a breath.

"Are you sick?" G'kaan asked in concern.

"I remember it like it was yesterday." Rose looked at the straps that were used to hold down the people during the inductions. "Where are the handlers?"

"The combat teams took the base personnel to one of the supply warehouses," G'kaan replied. "It's the only place big enough to hold them all."

Rose walked through the door into the adjacent bay, followed by Clay and an uncharacteristically silent Chad. Inside the huge bay were two stacks of transparent slave cubes. One stack was empty. The other one had a naked Solian inside each of the clear boxes. There were at least a hundred abductees.

"They're frightened," G'kaan said.

Rose stared up at the cubes. Their shouts and cries were muffled, echoing weirdly through the air tubes. Their mouths moved and they reached out with their hands, banging against the clear walls to get out. Some were huddled into a corner, trying to hide themselves.

"These poor people!" Chad exclaimed. "We have to get them out."

"What do we do with them all?" G'kaan asked.

"They'll be our shock troops," Rose said. The others didn't seem to understand. "Nobody on Earth knows that Solians are used as pleasure slaves, except for the underground. These people can tell everyone what they've seen."

"There could be underground members in these cubes," Chad realized.

Rose nodded. "We'll give them all datarods with pictures of this base, including these cubes, so everyone on Earth can see what the Domain is doing to us."

"We've already got images of this stack," G'kaan agreed. "And there are logs in the database of the handlers doing the inductions and injecting the translators."

Clay let out a low whistle that was easy for everyone to interpret. Rose grinned at him. "You're right. That should scare the hell out of them!"

"Then let's get these people out of the cubes." G'kaan showed his fangs. "We'll load the base personnel and the Fleet crew from the *Devotion* into them once we're done."

Rose thought that was too good for them, but it would do for now. "Strip them first. That will show them how it feels to be a slave."

2

Ash sat on the padded jumpseat in the medical bay of the battleship *Endurance,* waiting for biotech D'nar to arrive. Ash had run to the bay when the alarms went off and the battleship was jolted around. It awoke a memory that was so vivid and detailed, it had driven hir out of hir berth to the only place where s/he could find relief. Since hir memory had failed at Archernar shipyard, the Qin were hir only hope of regaining everything s/he had lost.

D'nar appeared in the doorway, muttering to herself as she looked down at a dataport. Her turquoise green flightsuit was unsealed down to her chest, revealing an expanse of charcoal gray fuzz. The Qin stopped short when she noticed Ash.

"You're too early," D'nar told hir.

"I can wait," Ash replied meekly. S/he didn't have anything else to do.

D'nar grimaced as she went to the tall counter that lined the back of the medical bay. She finished what she was doing on the dataport, then checked the samples in the diagnostic analyzer. Eventually she got around to reading the neurological scan done automatically on Ash every night while s/he slept in hir berth.

"You have a lot of recent activity," D'nar said thoughtfully.

"I had another flashback this morning. Is that good?"

D'nar picked up her bioscanner and flicked it on. "You Solians are so impatient. You've barely had the neurotransimulator patch for a decnight."

Ash felt that s/he was letting the biotech down. "It happened when the alarms went off."

"We got a few hits when we tangled with the Fleet." D'nar started to scan Ash's skull. "We've liberated Earth. Not that we'll be able to hang on to it for very long."

"Earth," Ash repeated. It was one of the words s/he remembered. Earth was a vague feeling, a place where s/he longed to be, full of hope and peace. But Ash had no memories of an actual place, and Jot had said s/he had never been to Earth.

D'nar lowered the nearest jumpseat and sat down with a sigh. She held the dataport up, ready to record. "Tell me about your flashback."

Dutifully, Ash started from the beginning. "I was lying down when I felt the bunk move and the lights flashed on. I jumped up quickly, but I didn't know where to go. The floor shook again and again. That's when I remembered something like that had happened before."

"Associational relinkage," D'nar said to herself. "Provoked by familiar sensory stimulation."

Ash rubbed hir palms against hir beige flightsuit. D'nar had said those words previously, and it was apparently a good thing. "I was standing in a room with a tall, arched ceiling and it was full of things. There was something soft and warm against my bare feet. I was naked and there were two Alphas talking. One grabbed me here." Ash gestured to hir crotch.

"Well, you were a pleasure slave, so that sounds about right." The big Qin sniffed and gestured for hir to go on.

"I can remember exactly how the Alphas looked. The woman wore a Fleet uniform, but the man had on some kind of drapery that was dark red. I think it was his ship we were on. The way he touched me makes me clench up . . ."

"You probably belonged to him. Or he was buying you."

Ash tried to fit that into the image. S/he had been owned by one of those Alphas.

"So you were on a ship that was attacked before. Is that all?"

"Well . . . no. After that, I remembered something else. I think it was a different place. I was in a narrow berth, smaller than my room here. I felt the ship shake, so I ran to the corner and curled up. I was really scared."

"That sounds like a neurostutter, remembering something that's happening as if it was in the past."

"Maybe," Ash agreed doubtfully. "After the flashback, I went and curled up in the corner for a while. It felt right. But then I wanted to come talk to you about it."

"It's all very interesting." D'nar stifled a yawn, tapping her dataport.

Ash put hir hand to the faintly buzzing patch at the back of hir neck. "I do remember something the first Alpha was saying. He said, 'You'll never see anything as strange again. A man and a woman in the same body.' Then the ship shook really hard, and both of them left in a rush."

D'nar waved one hand at Ash. "He was just talking about you being a herme."

"A herme?" Ash asked in confusion.

"You don't remember *that*?" D'nar leaned forward, her mouth opening in disbelief.

Ash felt uncomfortable. "I don't remember anything."

"Losing knowledge as basic as that . . . I'll have to take the neurotranssimulator down a few levels," she said thoughtfully.

D'nar shook her head and tapped rapidly on her dataport as she went to the counter. She slipped a biopatch into the unit to program it. Ash scratched slightly around the patch at the back of hir neck, wishing the irritating vibration would stop.

D'nar returned with the new patch. "Come on, I haven't got all day."

Ash had to bend hir head, offering up the back of hir neck. S/he suddenly remembered something similar . . . letting a curt Qin woman touch hir neck. Except then Rose was there protecting hir.

Ash felt relief as the biopatch popped off, but it was short-lived, as D'nar slapped the other one into place. S/he decided to not say anything about hir latest flashback. D'nar would probably think it was another neurostutter.

"Something the matter?" D'nar demanded when Ash raised hir head.

Ash said the first thing that came to mind. "What's a herme?"

D'nar turned, her delicate brows raised and her pale gray eyes fastened onto Ash's. "You're a herme. You have dual sex characteristics, male and female."

Ash went very still, feeling vulnerable somehow. S/he had felt different before; now it was worse.

"Give me your dataport," D'nar told hir. "I'll download some information for you."

Ash slipped hir dataport out of hir thigh pocket and handed it over to D'nar.

"You can compare your anatomy to the diagrams I'll give you," the biotech said. "I've done quite a bit of research on herme physiology since you came on board. There are different types, leaning either toward male or female. Many people who aren't hermes come close to hermatic specifications. But you're fairly unusual because you're fully developed as both a male and female."

Ash accepted the dataport and clutched it to hir chest. "I'm scared," s/he confessed.

"You should be." D'nar considered hir. "According to my bioscans of the other Solians, you suffered a lot more damage while you were a pleasure slave. Your captain believes you lost your memory because of that torture, although I haven't ruled out the use of chemical means."

Ash couldn't understand why s/he was in danger because s/he was both male and female. It didn't make sense, but then again, nothing else made sense either. "Thank you."

"Gratitude is unnecessary." D'nar waved over her shoulder. "Now get out of here so I can work."

Ash had to undo the brackets around the mirror in hir fresher so s/he could compare hir genitals to the diagrams in hir dataport. S/he hadn't paid much attention to what was between hir legs, but now that s/he looked, it was fascinating. According to the diagrams, s/he had a combination of male and female genitalia.

What with the stimulation of hir labia and experimentally probing hir two holes with hir fingers, s/he started to feel really good. There was nothing in D'nar's information that explained what was supposed to happen next. But it was not as though s/he had other plans, so there was no reason not to keep trying until s/he found out.

While Ash was squatting over the mirror rubbing hirself, the comm announced, *"G'kaan to Ash."*

S/he jumped up and tried to pull hir flightsuit on at the same time, forgetting that G'kaan couldn't see hir. "What? You want me?" s/he asked the ceiling.

"I'm going to the Relevance," G'kaan replied. *"Do you want to visit your crewmates?"*

Rose! It had been over a decnight since Ash had seen Rose. "I'd like that."

"Then meet me at the Pluck *in the docking bay."*

Ash sealed up hir flightsuit and ran out of the berth. S/he had carefully memorized the layout of the battleship so s/he wouldn't get lost. The pinnace bay was down seven decks, in the middle of the ship.

Captain G'kaan was waiting there along with M'ke, his old Qin advisor. M'ke was slightly bent and wizened, yet his watery eyes saw everything. Ash liked M'ke, because he was so calm. G'kaan was even darker skinned than D'nar, but his eyes were bright blue instead of gray. Unlike D'nar, there was a gentleness about him despite his massive bulk.

As soon as G'kaan saw Ash, he said, "Good, let's go."

Ash hurried inside the pinnace and carefully watched how M'ke locked himself into the grav seat. All s/he could think about was seeing Rose again. S/he wasn't sure why, but Rose was the most important person in hir life. Perhaps because Rose had saved hir time and time again.

As G'kaan went through the departure sequence, he glanced over his shoulder at Ash. "D'nar thought you should see some familiar people. It might help your progress."

Ash was surprised that the biotech had spoken to anyone about hir. "She said Solians were impatient."

G'kaan exchanged a look with M'ke, who raised his hand slightly in self-defense. The older man reminded him, "I told you, but you wanted the best."

G'kaan turned back to Ash. "Don't mind D'nar. She may not say the most appropriate things, but she'll be able to fix your memory if anyone can."

Ash didn't know what to say. "D'nar tells me the truth."

"She does do that," G'kaan agreed with a grin. "Prepare for departure."

As the pinnace lifted up and moved out of the bay, the first thing Ash saw was a planet hanging seemingly just out of reach. It was beautiful, with dazzling white swirls against a shiny deep blue. It took a few moments before s/he realized it was Earth. Hir breath fogged the portal as s/he leaned closer, not wanting to miss a thing. It looked perfect, but maybe that was another neurostutter, since she had never seen Earth before.

Then the dark gray, pointed hull of another spaceship swung into view. S/he remembered it from the trip s/he had made to the Qin battleship. That was the *Relevance*, Rose's patrolship.

Ash had a hard time catching her breath, as every nerve drew tight. S/he couldn't wait to see Rose.

The corridor by the airlock was so crowded, Kwort got pushed up against the controls. Rose was behind him, muttering directions, as if she intended to operate the airlock instead of letting him do his job. Chad was arguing with her about interfering, and she was quickly losing her temper. Jot and Nip were also there, practically climbing over one another to see through the portal. Only Shard's calm held back the chaos.

Kwort got the airlock open in spite of Rose, and there was an expectant moment before the lock on the pinnace swung up. Kwort hoped Ash was better. Maybe she would remember them now. He had worn one of his favorite, multicolored flightsuits in hir honor.

Ash stepped on board, a bit daunted by the crowd in the corridor. Rose spoke to hir but carefully didn't hug hir. Shard didn't either, because Ash didn't like being touched. Chad seemed uneasy, but then he had been uncomfortable around Ash since s/he had lost hir memory. Then Rose, Chad, and Shard headed down to the docking bay with G'kaan to take their aircar to Earth. G'kaan was going to teach them how to fly the little atmospheric vehicle.

Kwort made sure the airlock was sealed so they wouldn't lose contact with the pinnace while G'kaan was gone. Meanwhile Jot, in her enthusiasm, hugged Ash hello. "We just found out you were coming!" Jot exclaimed. "Clay's on duty, but he'll join us later. Nip, Kwort and I are off-duty."

Ash was staring right into Nip's face. Hir eyes seemed glassy. "I remember you! You were lying in a box and there was a little window I looked through . . ."

Jot clapped her hands to her mouth. "You're right! That was on Spacepost T-3. We put Nip in the biobed when his arm was almost cut off."

Nip smiled, swinging his arm up and down to reassure Ash. "It's working fine now. You remember that?"

Ash shrugged hesitantly.

Kwort joined them to shyly say hello to Ash. S/he recognized him from their escape from Archernar shipyard, but s/he didn't have any other memories of him. That hurt. S/he and Kwort had been best friends since he had accidentally blown up the *Conviction* and was stranded in Qin. Ash had given him a break when the Qin would have kicked him to death just for being a Delta. Ash's acceptance had encouraged the other Solians to take him on as part of their crew.

Now Ash was a shadow of hirself. There was none of hir competent self-sufficiency left. S/he looked unkempt and slouched as if s/he scurried unnoticed among the giant Qin. Hir hair draggled long over hir shoulders, making hir seem more feminine.

Ash glanced around. "Where's Rose?"

Kwort realized everything was happening too fast for hir. "Rose left with G'kaan. They're going down to Earth to look for someone Rose knew in the underground. We need to contact them so they can help us take over Earth."

"I thought Earth was liberated," Ash said.

"We've got control of the system, but the World Council is still in charge on Earth. They don't know what's happened yet. Rose says we have to throw them out of power, and the only way to do that is to get hold of the underground and surprise them with a coup."

Jot nodded seriously. "None of the abductees on the moonbase will admit they're with the underground."

Kwort agreed. "I bet a few of them are, but they think it's a trick. G'kaan wanted to give them the serneo-inhibitor. But Rose refused. She says it would be no better than what S'jen did to you."

"Me?" Ash asked in confusion.

"Yeah, when S'jen gave you the serneo-inhibitor."
Kwort kept forgetting how much Ash had forgotten. "It
happened right after we reached Qin. S'jen kidnapped
you and forced you to tell her everything about Rikev
Alpha. Because of the information you gave her, she was
able to intercept the *Conviction* and kill Rikev."

Ash looked completely lost.

Jot motioned for Kwort to slow down. "Rose will be
back in a while, Ash. You'll be able to see her again
then."

Kwort could tell Ash was disappointed, but s/he was
used to it.

"Let's go up to the lounge," Jot suggested to Ash. "I
have something for you."

In the lounge, there were several other off-duty crew
members, former pleasure slaves Kwort had helped res-
cue from Archernar shipyard. They knew that he had
been instrumental in their escape, and much to his em-
barrassment, they looked up to him almost as much as
they did to Rose. His role as senior bot tech on board
didn't hurt his image either, especially since he was training many of them. Some of the former slaves were wildly
uninhibited in their euphoria over freedom, and their
grateful, playful sexual advances almost made up for the
fact that he was probably the "most-wanted Delta" in the
Domain. That stunt Rose had pulled at the shipyard,
blowing up the battleship along with several other
spaceships, had sealed his fate as an outlaw. But he was
starting to accept that there were worse fates than working on a ship packed with willing, eager pleasure slaves.

Kwort nodded hello to the off-duty crew, but he
stayed with Jot and Ash. The others kept a respectful

distance, having seen Ash deteriorate in the slave barracks on the shipyard. Ash had nearly turned into a vegetable until Rose practically drowned hir in a last-ditch attempt to get a response from her. But that was better than what had happened to Dab, Whit, and Mote. The raiders who captured them along with the *Purpose* had reportedly been destroyed inside a spiral nebula.

Kwort's main concern was for Gandre Li and their crew. He had dragged them into Rose's escape from Archernar shipyard. What if they were caught? He had searched every beacon download for word about the courier *Solace*. He knew Nip felt just as guilty. Nip had talked about Trace constantly since his return. But despite Nip's self-proclaimed nonstop sexual escapades with Trace, she was in love with Gandre Li and had chosen to stay with her mistress.

Jot was showing Ash something on a dataport. Kwort sat down across from them, next to Nip. "What've you got there?"

"I've pulled some images for Ash." Jot turned back to Ash. "I've labeled each set with the name of the location along with the facts I found in the database. I also included anything your crewmates remember you saying about your past."

Kwort leaned over to see the familiar images of Spacepost T-3, exterior shots before and after S'jen's attack. The broken spindle sent a shot of adrenaline through his heart. He had spent a day with Horc on board that spacepost, and later he had suggested the Solians go there to salvage. They had been recaptured by the Fleet on that spacepost. Kwort would never go back again.

The image of the spacepost had such profound associations for Kwort that Ash's quizzical expression was strange. Kwort insisted, "You spent a year living on that spacepost, Ash, before S'jen attacked it."

Jot gave him a look. "Ash has lived lots of places. On Canopus Regional Headquarters, on Desmintary starbase in Archernar, even on the regents' planet in Spinca. I asked everyone, including you."

"Why?" Ash asked, but hir eyes were fastened on the monitor.

"I read the preliminary report from G'kaan's biotech. D'nar says you need familiar sensory stimulation to provoke associational relinkage."

With those big words coming out of her delicate mouth, Kwort stared at Jot. Nip seemed similarly amazed.

Jot keyed the dataport to show the interior of Spacepost T-3. "There are lots of images. I found hundreds in our database."

"Wait . . . I do remember this." Ash slowly ran hir finger down an interior shot of the central shaft of the spacepost. "It made me dizzy to look down. I remember . . ."

"That's right!" Jot encouraged hir. "Kwort said you must have lived at the top along with the senior officers because you belonged to the station's commander."

Kwort blinked. Yes, he had told Jot that. But he hadn't realized why Jot was pestering him with questions about the spacepost. If he had known it was this important, he would have taken more time with his answers.

"I didn't know you were doing this for Ash," Nip protested, echoing Kwort's thought.

"You were all busy training the new crew, so I had to do something when I was off-duty. I wanted to help Ash." Jot sat very close to hir, and for once Ash didn't seem to mind.

"Thank you," Ash told the young woman, clutching the dataport to hir chest.

Kwort was amazed at the change in Jot. It was almost as stark as Ash's transformation, but for Jot it was for the better. Her glossy black hair was neatly tied back, making her look older, and her childlike voice was lower and more measured. Her heart-shaped face was serious, as always. He remembered how Jot had fiercely protected Ash during their escape from Archernar shipyard. She hadn't shed a tear the entire time.

Now Jot was fondly gazing at Ash, a worry line between her almond eyes. "Are you sure they're taking good care of you over there, Ash?"

Ash shrugged slightly. "I'm okay. They're very busy."

"I can tell." Jot lightly brushed a few strands of hair away from Ash's face. "I can cut your hair for you, if you want."

Ash looked up at that. "It's different?"

"Yes, I can show you how you used to wear it," Jot offered.

Ash looked at Nip, hir eyes brighter than before. "Maybe that's why I don't recognize myself. Please, make it look like it used to."

Kwort watched in amazement as Jot fetched a brush, a laser, and a hand mirror. Jot kept herself immaculate, so she always had things like that on hand. He had never seen anyone, except for maybe Shard, spend more time primping her hair and skin. Ash was not usually one to fuss, but s/he readily put hirself in Jot's hands. It was strange, because Ash didn't seem to mind being adjusted and stroked by Jot. S/he usually startled away if someone touched hir.

Jot smoothed Ash's hair straight back from hir forehead. Hir hair was all one length, and it had gotten long during their captivity. Jot chatted about their old crew-mates, what they had been doing while Ash was gone, how Shard was causing a sensation among the newly freed slaves, and that Chad had paired up with one of the new bot techs. Jot even winked at Kwort and mentioned that their senior bot tech apparently was pursuing a "silent" partner. Kwort didn't realize that Jot had noticed his secret, raging lust for Clay, and he was glad to see that Nip didn't understand her innuendo. But if Jot knew, then Kwort would have to tell Clay himself before some-one else did. That was bound to be interesting. . . .

"You look much better like this," Jot gently told Ash. "Nip, hold the mirror up higher so s/he can see."

Nip held up the mirror and while he awkwardly tried to smooth his own wild brown curls. Kwort laughed at him. His bald ridges didn't need much grooming; a quick wash and dry was enough for him.

Jot leaned closer to Ash and passed the hand laser over the base of hir neck, carefully avoiding the biopatch on hir neck. "Hold still," she admonished, clasping Ash's shoulder to keep hir in place.

Ash's blondish brown hair was the same color as hir tanned skin. With hir hazel eyes and regular features, s/he was practically nondescript.

When s/he saw hirself, Ash's eyes grew wide. "I re-member!"

Jot stopped smoothing hir hair. "What is it, Ash?"

Ash turned to look up at Jot, running a shaking hand over hir own head. "You've brushed my hair before. I re-member how it felt . . ."

Jot glanced over at Nip. "Yes, I did. I took care of you in the slave barracks when you were slipping into catatonia."

"What's that?" Ash asked.

Jot sat down next to Ash. "You were withdrawing from everything. You wouldn't talk to us or do anything on your own."

"Oh." Ash went blank, struggling to think but coming up with nothing.

Kwort felt bad for Ash. It must be horrible to not know yourself, to not remember anything that had happened to you.

Ash looked so lost that Jot took hir hand. "You were starting to respond to us, Ash. You would have been okay, except that terrible Alpha got hold of you. He used you during his lust, and when you came back, your memory was gone."

"That was Rikev Alpha," Ash agreed.

"You remember him?" Kwort asked in surprise.

"No. Jot told me about him and Rose took me to see him."

Ash looked so sad that Kwort wanted to reassure hir. He pointed to Nip's mirror where s/he was reflected. The image seemed to waver between male and female depending on hir expression. "That's more like the Ash I know," Kwort said lightly.

Ash lifted hir head higher. "I like it."

With new admiration, Kwort watched Jot gather up her things. He wouldn't take Jot for granted again. She was finally growing up.

Kwort sat down next to Ash, putting his hand on hir shoulder, wanting to show hir how much he cared. It was a bold move for him, but s/he smiled hesitantly. Kwort felt much better. He knew that Rose would never let Ash stay this way. Rose could accomplish anything she set her mind to. If she thought the Qin would fix

Ash, then that was good enough for him. He would get his friend back, and they would all be okay in spite of the Domain. For once, he truly believed that.

He only wished Ash could stay here with them. He missed hir.

3

Gandre Li returned directly to the *Solace* from her meeting with the InSec commander of Spacepost M-6. The spacepost reminded her uncomfortably of Spacepost T-3 out in the Sirius sector. But this spacepost was in the Capetta sector, the closest to Canopus Regional Headquarters that her regular route took them.

"You're upset," Trace said as soon as Gandre Li walked into the day cabin.

Gandre Li shut the door and made sure the Alpha-grade baffler was on. It had proven to be a lifesaver when Rikev Alpha had repeatedly tried to plant surveillance on them. Not that anyone was on board to listen to them, but old habits died hard.

"You *are* upset," Trace insisted, her voice rising higher.

Gandre Li embraced her, burying her face in the Solian's shiny hair. "I'm jumping at shadows," she assured Trace. "We're taking on a new passenger, an Alpha analyst with the transportation department. He's going to be assessing the level of space traffic to see what effect the fuel shortage is having in Canopus."

Trace pulled back to look up at her. "*I could tell them

that. Ships are leaving the outer sectors in droves. I've never seen it so empty this close to Regional Headquarters, and there's at least *some* fuel here."

"Yes, it seems redundant to send someone out to count ships," Gandre Li agreed. "Especially when a creche child could tell them everyone's been forced to flee from the fuel shortages. So I'm thinking this analyst could really be an InSec operative assigned to observe us."

"Why? What happened? Did they ask you anything at InSec?" A scattering of freckles stood out on Trace's pale face.

"No. But our full fuel requisition was approved by the time I got back." Gandre Li nodded at Trace's stricken expression. "No questions asked. I didn't even have to refer them to the subcommander. I'm going to have another look at the approvals for this assignment to see if it's critical enough for permission to come down from above."

"Do you think they connected us to what happened at Archernar shipyard?" Trace plainly felt guilty about convincing Gandre Li to loan the stunguns to the slaves for their escape. They both knew that if they were discovered it would be catastrophic.

"Don't worry," Gandre Li assured Trace. As long as Trace was with her, she would make sure they survived. A decnight ago, it looked as if she had lost her lover for good. Instead Trace had chosen to stay with her rather than going to Sol with Nip. Gandre Li had seen no signs of regret from Trace, only fear that they would be punished for helping the Solians escape.

"Should we tell the others?" Trace asked.

"Yes, let's go now before they leave. The Alpha analyst will be joining us at the end of this shift."

Gandre Li took Trace's hand, giving it a squeeze, as

they went to tell the crew the bad news. They were in this together, as far as the captain was concerned. She just hoped her decision to help the Solians wouldn't be their undoing.

Herntoff Alpha stood in front of Commander Gralice, twisting his thin fingers together. He wanted to deny the commander's assertions, but he knew better than to contradict his superior. Gralice had been his supervisor for over a decade, so he should have known she would ignore the results of his self-examination.

Gralice was staring at him resolutely from behind her desk. Her tanned glow came from solar sailing while off-duty, while in comparison he looked sallow and sickly. Gralice finished by saying, "So the biotech knows you can't possibly have Peellene syndrome since you don't have the associated rise in hormone levels. And I don't want to hear your doubts again about our senior biotech's credentials. He may be a Beta, but he's one of the best in the region. You're back on duty as of now."

Herntoff shrugged his shoulders slightly, feeling the deep ache in his spinal column that was a harbinger of Peellene syndrome. He would have to monitor his own condition, as usual, instead of trusting to a subspecies to understand Alphan physiology.

Gralice slid a datarod across the reflective black desktop. Herntoff lifted his nose at the distinct fingermarks on the surface as he picked up the datarod. Its clear casing was also smudged. He held it distastefully between two fingers.

"That's your new assignment. You'll be a regional analyst again." Gralice snorted. "We get as much use out of your cover analyses as your real operations. This time you'll be monitoring ship movements in the outer region."

Herntoff knew she looked down on him. They all did, because they didn't understand him. "What is my target, Alpha-Commander?"

"Beta-Captain Gandre Li. Her courier, *Solace,* was docked at Archernar shipyard when the pleasure slaves were stolen. The day before, Cwart Deneb, one of the shipyard bot techs who was involved, was seen going into the *Solace* along with the captain's pleasure slave. The *Solace* was one of the last ships to debark before the patrolship was hijacked."

The connection was obvious, hence the need for him. He was to observe the captain and her slave to see who they contacted and what they knew about the destruction at Archernar shipyard.

"The two bot techs who were repairing the *Relevance* were found in a lifepod in Sirius," Gralice added. "Their testimony is on that rod. We haven't located Cwart Deneb. He could be in a lifepod somewhere with a malfunctioning beacon. Most likely he is still with the perpetrators."

Herntoff nodded once. "What is the turnaround, Alpha-Commander?"

"This should be an easy one for a man of your talents. The *Solace* will cycle back here in another eight decnights. You're to report your findings to me upon your arrival. There will be no intermediate contacts. The captain is a covert InSec courier, and she may track your movements. Additional background information and the specific areas of inquiry are on that datarod."

Herntoff slipped it into the pocket of his spotless green flightsuit. He couldn't help noticing that Gralice's flightsuit had frayed cuffs.

"You're to report to the *Solace* immediately," Gralice ordered.

Herntoff nodded and turned smartly on his heel. Behind him Gralice sighed in exasperation.

Herntoff smiled slightly as he left the commander's office. The last fourteen times he had reported to Gralice, he had spoken exactly twice at each meeting, asking—"What is my target?" and "What is the turnaround?" He didn't feel it was necessary to say anything more. When he had a request, he filed it officially. As his long term plan, he fully intended to stick to that formula for at least another fourteen interviews with Commander Gralice—meanwhile, he had a job to do.

"Greetings, Herntoff Alpha," Gandre Li said formally, as he stepped onto the *Solace*.

The Alpha merely nodded, busying himself with maneuvering a huge antigrav module through the airlock. Gandre Li reached out to help, but he irritably waved away her hands.

When Herntoff finally stood up next to his module, Gandre Li could see that he was not what she had expected. Herntoff was the thinnest Alpha she had ever seen. His face was sunken in, making his cheekbones and chin stick out sharply. Even the skin on his skull seemed uncomfortably tight. His green flightsuit was gathered into thick folds by his tightly cinched cartridge belt. Most people wore their belt on their hips, but Herntoff was neatly bisected in half by his.

"I'll call one of my crew to take your luggage to your room," Gandre Li said, bending her head to her comm link.

"No."

Gandre Li hesitated. "Your module is too big to go up the spiral steps or the tube. It will have to go in the cargo lift."

Alpha Herntoff stared at her. His fingers were twisting together at his waist.

Gandre Li gestured, trying to smile. "Fine, it's this way. You can follow me, Alpha."

They had to go past the cargo holds to get to the lift. Inside one of the holds, Takhan looked up from stacking the tubs of base food product used by the transposers. The Aborandeen was surprised to see an Alpha traipsing down the cargo corridor, but Gandre Li waved for her to continue on with her work.

Gandre Li opened the door of the cargo lift, then reached out to help maneuver the white module inside.

"No!" Herntoff lunged forward protectively.

Gandre Li jerked her hands back.

Herntoff didn't look at her as he shoved the heavy module into the cargo lift. Even with the grav stabalizers, it looked like it was too much for him to handle.

Gandre Li awkwardly stepped in and stood next to him, watching him from the corners of her eyes. Herntoff frantically glanced up at the ceiling and close walls of the lift. His agitation was contagious, and she found herself also looking up at the ceiling as if expecting it to fall in on them.

When they reached the lounge at the top of the ship, Gandre Li stood aside carefully. "You'll have this area for your personal use, Alpha."

Herntoff didn't pay any attention to the beautifully arched ceiling, with its center portal revealing the stars. Most people couldn't take their eyes off it.

Instead, Herntoff maneuvered his module directly

through the door Gandre Li indicated. He shoved the module into the largest passenger cabin, then hastily closed the door on it.

Gandre Li thought he was acting very suspiciously. What was he hiding in that thing? It was big enough to hold a dead body or two. Or a live one. . . .

Trying to look nonchalant, she went over to the spiral staircase. "The galley is downstairs. We took on supplies here in Capetta. I'm sure you'll be pleased with the variety of the cuisine."

Instead of looking at her, Herntoff was staring down at the table. It was her best one, big enough to seat ten people. When passengers wanted to have a formal dinner, she placed it under the overhead star portal.

Herntoff pulled at something in his hip pocket. A bit of filmy white came out, followed by a long streamer that expanded as it was released from confinement. He began rubbing the top of the table with it.

Gandre Li put her hand to her mouth as he methodically began to clean the table. He leaned over to look at the shiny surface from an angle.

"Do you have cleaning bots?" he asked.

"Yes. They finished in here earlier—"

"Bring them to me."

Gandre Li blinked. "All of them?"

Herntoff looked up at her, finally meeting her eyes.

After a moment, Gandre Li replied, "I'll be right back with the bots."

Gandre Li grabbed Takhan to help her gather up all the cabin-cleaning bots on the ship. They fit into two four-sided carrying units that were nearly waist-high.

"Why does he need them all?" Takhan asked.

"He seems to have a problem with the condition of the lounge." Gandre Li held up a quick hand. "I know, I thought it looked great."

"I monitored the cleaning bots last decnight," Takhan insisted. Her spiky blond hair seemed to bristle at the insult.

Gandre Li knew that Takhan was proud of her ability to get the most out of bots. She claimed it was in her genes, since Aborandeens were one of the ancient spacefaring families. To soothe her, Gandre Li said, "I think this Herntoff has a few unadjusted bots in his own system."

Takhan looked at her in surprise. When she saw Gandre Li's grin, she smiled back. Ever since Takhan had taken the risk of planting the stunguns for the Solians, Gandre Li had felt a bond growing between her and the Delta. It had been a generous act, out of character for the hostile and suspicious Takhan. Gandre Li couldn't help but be touched by it.

Gandre Li dragged the bots up to the lounge but stopped short when she saw that there were already small bots cruising on the tabletops and upholstery.

"You brought your own bots?" Gandre Li asked. Suddenly that big module didn't look so suspicious.

Herntoff came over to examine her bots. He checked the power readings and efficiency ratings on each of the floor and wall bots before finally choosing two of each. "These will remain here for the duration of my voyage with you."

"By your command, Alpha." Gandre Li bent down to pack up the other bots. When she placed the last bot in the frame, she added, "Let me know if you need anything else."

Herntoff turned away to adjust a wall bot running around a wall sconce.

Gandre Li carried the bot racks all the way down to her day cabin, where Trace was waiting. She was laughing even before the door closed behind her.

"What happened?" Trace demanded.

Gandre Li grabbed Trace into a hug. "That's *exactly* the kind of Alpha they send out to count ships!"

"What?"

"This guy is no Rikev Alpha. You could break him in half, and he's all twitchy. He even brought his own cleaning bots!"

Trace went over to sit on the sofa under the portal. "Does he have a pleasure slave?"

Gandre Li shook her head. "Unfortunately, no." There was no way of knowing when Herntoff's lust would hit, but he was going to be on board for a long time. It was likely he would try to use Trace.

Gandre Li hadn't discovered that Nip could have deactivated Trace's collar until after he was gone. She still wasn't sure why Trace didn't tell her. Apparently it was wrapped up in her guilty feelings about her relationship with Nip. Gandre Li wished Trace had gotten her collar deactivated so no one could use it against her. The next time she ran into the Solians, she was going to get them to shut down Trace's collar for good.

"I've got the injector ready," Trace said bravely.

The injector induced a high fever in Trace. Gandre Li frowned, because it was hard on her biosystems. "I hate for you to use it. Didn't you throw up again yesterday?"

"I think it's nerves," Trace admitted. "It's been happening since we left Archernar shipyard."

"I hope it's not something Nip gave you. Those pleasure slaves are used by a lot of people. They could pick up—" Gandre Li stopped when she saw Trace's expression. "I didn't mean anything by that."

Trace nodded, but she seemed sad. "I wonder what's happening on Ear—"

Gandre Li waved her hand to shush Trace. Even with the Alpha-grade baffler going, even though she believed that that nervous Alpha was no threat, she didn't want Trace talking about the Solians' plans.

Trace understood without a word. "I'm glad everything's okay with us now, Gandi."

Gandre Li put her arms around her precious girl. "I'll make sure it stays that way."

As they snuggled together, their touching sparked Trace's lust. Every few days since Nip had left, they had enjoyed some kind of sexual activity together. Gandre Li had been jealous at first over Trace's newfound sexual responsiveness. She used to be focused entirely on pleasing Gandre Li when her lust came once a decnight, and never pursued sex in between. But now Trace was insatiable. It was exciting and almost overwhelming for Gandre Li on the days when she was in lust. It couldn't be denied, Nip had awoken something in Trace.

Still, Trace had chosen to stay with her.

Gandre Li rolled Trace into her lap, freeing her hands to open Trace's flightsuit. She laughed along with the playful Solian. Trace's body had developed, too. She was more womanly, fuller in the bust and hips. There was something about her skin that was irresistible, and Gandre Li kissed her warm belly. Licking and biting, she held Trace's arms until she cried out in ticklish delight, wanting it to stop but wanting more. Loving Trace had never felt so good. . . .

* * *

The angle of the image was slanted, but the bot was positioned perfectly. Herntoff had to click through the various racked bots he had bugged to find one that he could use to watch the Bariss have sex with her slave. The Bariss wasn't even in lust. It was apparently entirely for the slave's benefit.

Herntoff had seen plenty of things in his time, but this was a new one.

When the remarkable sexual activities were over, the Beta-captain casually dropped one of the floor bots in the day cabin. Herntoff cycled through the various eyes he had implanted right under the captain's nose to watch her moving down the corridor, dropping another couple of bots in the galley before going downstairs. There was a sophisticated baffler in the captain's cabin, but his equipment was superior—he had developed it himself in his mobile tech lab. His specialty was biobots, but the quality of his work as an operative rested on his surveillance skills. These bugs were parasites, using the power of the cleaning bot so they were undetectable to sweeps. They tapped into the scanning systems on the cleaning bot, enabling him to see and hear everything within range. Only a hush field could interfere with his surveillance.

He switched back to the bot going through its cleaning cycle inside the captain's cabin to look at the Solian slave. The image was flattened and in gray tones because of the baffler, but he could tell the woman was inordinately satiated. Lying back on the sofa, she was practically suffused with sex.

It did nothing for him. His satisfaction was going to come with his success. These two had something to hide, like all the others. He would discover their secrets, and they would know who had brought them down.

4

Rose checked the scanners again to be sure they were focused on the immediate area around their parked aircar. She didn't want anyone sneaking up on them. It was dark outside and there was plenty of cover from the scrubby brush and grasses in the gullies lacing Oldtown Tijuana.

She was finally home. She had traveled from one star to the next, journeying through two interstellar empires to get back to Earth. Now it was payback time.

G'kaan had piloted them down in the *Relevance*'s armored aircar. It was the first time Rose had used the tiny spacecraft, which had its own docking bay inside her patrolship. The aircar was more notable for its ability to make atmospheric entry than for its speed, but still it was a nimble craft. So far, G'kaan only allowed her and Chad to watch how he piloted it.

The comm crackled, and Chad's hushed voice said, *"We're outside the arena. We're going in now."*

Rose pulled on the comm link around her neck "Check."

G'kaan glanced over. "Is something wrong?"

"I should be *with* them!" Rose retorted. It was killing her that Chad and Shard were walking through the streets of Tijuana right now. She knew exactly what they would see inside the arena. It was still too early for bloodsports, but the tiers would be crowded with revelers. Her gang stayed away from the hard drinkers in the pits, who drew as much blood from each other as the sanctioned bouts on the arena floor. She told Chad and Shard to search the tiered benches.

That's where they would find Bolt.

"It's not worth the risk," G'kaan patiently reminded her. "Word could get around that you're back."

Rose grumbled but she couldn't deny the simple truth. Even if she shaved her head or tried to pose as a guy, her friends would see right through her disguise. She knew Tijuana better than most, and everyone in the enclave knew her. If Bolt found out that she had returned, he would hightail it into the desert. She wasn't going to let him slip away that easily. Not after she had come this far.

None of the abducted Solians on the moonbase had been willing to admit they were members of the underground, so they had to make contact another way. It would be mass murder to dump the abducted Solians back on Earth. They would disappear quicker than you could say "pleasure slave." Rose needed the underground to help her break the back of the World Council.

The only underground member Rose knew was Bolt. If they could get hold of Bolt, he could contact the underground. She could also put her favorite plan into action. She intended to take tiny bits off Bolt until she found out what part he had played in her abduction.

Atmospheric interference made the comm crackle

again. *"Someone's told Shard that our target is at the* El Niño *bar."*

Rose bent over the three-dimensional image of Tijuana created from their close orbital scans. It was so clear she could see the trash piled up against the mudbrick and concrete walls.

"Okay, go out the front of the arena and walk three blocks," she ordered. "You'll see a wide street. Turn left and walk for another . . ." She silently counted the blocks. It was tricky figuring it out from above, but the map could be shifted to look down at an angle, which helped her recognize the buildings. "Go for eight blocks. It's in the cul-de-sac to your right. Got that?"

There was a long pause, then Chad replied, *"Check."*

Rose blinked up at G'kaan. "You trained him well."

G'kaan's expression was very Qin, revealing nothing. "Chad is quite capable. That's why you made him your second-in-command."

"Something like that." Rose would much rather have Ash as her second, but Ash was busy trying to remember hirself. Still, Rose had to admit that Chad was doing a good job. He even took her side and stopped by a pawnshop to buy a critical item on their way to the arena. Rose had filched a small globule of gold from their bot supply cache and pounded it into a lump to look like a tooth filling. Chad had caught on quickly when she mimed how he should act when he pawned it.

She had trusted Chad in particular with this job because he had begun passing on his Qin training to her and a few other Solians, such as Clay and Fen. They were working on hand-to-hand combat moves every day in an empty cargo bay on board the *Relevance*. Rose intended to be able to take out any alien who tried to stop her next time. She also wanted shin pockets like the ones the Qin biotechs had installed in Chad. Each leg held a miniature stunwand and a laser knife. Rose had bugged G'kaan until he agreed that she could come to the battleship *Endurance* for the surgery as soon as they had a break in the action.

But in spite of her new working relationship with Chad, Rose figured he would jump ship the next time he disagreed with her. He'd done it once before, so he probably would betray them again.

"We're outside El Niño," Chad reported back. *"We're going inside."*

"Check," Rose acknowledged. She gripped the armrests, leaning forward over the imager.

G'kaan pointed at the dense grouping of buildings. "Let's hope there's roof access. Otherwise, Shard will have to bring him through the streets this way." His finger sketched out the path directly north.

"Too far," Rose agreed. "Bolt could get suspicious."

Shard was her secret weapon. If anyone could lure Bolt, it would be her. Rose had drilled a few stock phrases of Spanish into Shard, and she sounded enticingly exotic with her accent. Of course, it wouldn't be conversation that would convince Bolt to follow her. Rose sometimes wished that Shard were a bit more responsible so she could be second-in-command, but Shard played around too much for the responsibility of being in charge.

The static became louder. When the channel opened, music filtered through. *"Shard has made contact with the target. I'm on my way up to scout the roof."*

"This is it." G'kaan reached for the controls to prepare the aircar for flight.

"Locked down," Rose confirmed, checking her seat. They would have to fly close over the rooftops to avoid detection by the radar tower at the airport. They had descended from space around the curve of the Earth, then skimmed the ocean waves to keep from alerting the authorities.

Static crackled. *"Roof access confirmed!"* Chad announced over the comm. *"The stairs come up through the shed near the front. I'll signal when Shard has the target."*

"Confirmed," Rose told Chad through the comm.

G'kaan frowned at the eagerness in her voice. She didn't care. She had been waiting to get hold of Bolt for a long time, ever since he had betrayed her along with two women from the underground.

"Now!" Chad quietly urged. *"They're heading to the roof."*

G'kaan instantly fired the antigrav engine. There was a hushed whir, like the wind. The moon was a sliver, so they didn't cast a shadow as G'kaan eased them over the closest buildings. Many had fallen in or were rebuilt with a jumble of boards and tin sheets. In some places the passageways between the lean-tos couldn't be seen from above. No one knew all the footpaths through the *barrio.*

Silently they drifted over the Tijuana enclave. G'kaan kept one eye on the map where their progress was marked by a red icon, and the other on the monitor that showed the view below them. It was disorienting to Rose to look up and see what was below, but she couldn't tear her eyes away.

"That's it," G'kaan said.

Rose was completely confused by the rooftops. "Are you sure?"

"There they are." With a touch, G'kaan refocused the monitor.

A shadowy image appeared. A man was standing near the shed on the roof. His back was to them, and his head was bent. As their angle changed, Rose saw someone kneeling in front of him. It was Shard.

The grav sled lowered. Bolt must have heard something, because at the last moment before they touched down, his head went up and turned. The white-blond hair and chiseled profile were exactly as Rose remembered.

G'kaan popped the door open and Rose was out like a flash. Chad had come up the stairs behind them and was wrestling with Bolt, holding both of his arms. Chad outmassed and outmuscled Bolt, but for a moment it looked close.

"I got him!" Chad exclaimed as G'kaan brandished a stunwand. To Rose, he added, "It's on the back of my belt."

Bolt was fighting him, but Chad had the edge and drove him to his knees. She reached around Chad and pulled a very large knife from its sheath. "Nice. . . ."

"Just what you asked for." Shard was out of breath from hanging on to Bolt until Chad could subdue him.

"You worthless bitch!" Bolt spat at Shard, trying to wrest out of Chad's arms. "Setting me up—"

Rose stuck the knife in his face. "Shut up!"

The knife had exactly the effect she wanted. Bolt's eyes fastened on the long silver blade with a dramatic hook at the end. It was honed to sharpness, but had a worn grip, as though someone had used it for a long time.

"Don't you remember me, Bolt?" Rose asked sweetly.

Bolt stared, disbelief and dread flashing through his face. "Rose! Where've you been, love? Haven't seen you—"

"Don't even try," Rose warned him, lowering the knife to his opened pants. His excitement had quickly waned, but he was still exposed.

His eyes grew larger. "Is this the way you treat an old friend, Rose?"

"I should cut it off," she threatened. "You sold me to the aliens! Do you know what it feels like to be raped every night?"

G'kaan appeared at her shoulder. "This isn't the place, Rose."

Her urge to start making him pay right then and there eased somewhat. In a safer place, she could take her time with him.

"Bring him inside!" she ordered, striding to the aircar.

Rose hung back as Chad flung Bolt onto the floor of the aircar. He quickly fastened wrist restraints on each of Bolt's arms. The patrolship had a whole locker of the remote-controlled restraints, and Rose was glad to finally put them to use.

G'kaan lifted the aircar off the roof and headed back to the safety of the northern gullies.

Bolt winced and flexed, as if ready to complain about his treatment, but one look at Rose made him close his mouth. He started to get to his feet, but Chad hit him with the shocker, sending a jolt from the wrist restraints across his body.

"*Chinga*—" Bolt exclaimed in a strangled voice. He lay on the floor of the aircar, clutching his chest. "Lay off me, will ya?"

Chad gave Bolt another hit for good measure. He

obviously didn't like Bolt, but maybe that was because he had cursed at their reigning sex queen.

Shard settled into one of the side benches as she watched Bolt writhe at her feet. Her red flightsuit was undone to her navel, and her cartridge belt rode low on her curving hips. "That was fun! Earth is my kind of place, Rose. These people know how to enjoy life."

"You did great, Shard."

Bolt couldn't understand Shard or Chad, because he didn't have a translator implant. Rose looked forward to giving him one herself. But for now, it helped that he could communicate only with her.

"Thanks, Chad." Rose took the sheath and fastened it to her own cartridge belt. Turning the knife in her hand, she approached Bolt. The aircar was swaying slightly as it moved.

Bolt spread his hands wide. The heavy restraints weighed them down a bit. "Hey there, Rose—"

He was forced to stop as the tip of the knife neared his throat.

"Don't you want to know what happened to Rowena?" Rose pressed the tip against the base of his neck. "Remember that woman from the underground? Well, I watched her die. And it's *your* fault."

"Why're you blaming me, Rose? I don't know anything about it."

"I'm going to kill you, and I'm going to love every second of it."

Bolt's eyes shifted, trying to see the others in the aircar, but Rose was too close to him. "No need to be hasty! You'll ruin the upholstery in your fine airplane."

Rose felt her lip twitch. She couldn't help it. His cocky attitude was so familiar. She had always been attracted to Bolt, with his casual style and over-the-top energy. She had had sex with him only once, the night he had introduced her to Rowena in the underground. It had been a fun ride, but definitely not worth getting abducted for.

She pushed Bolt back with the tip of the knife until he was sitting on his heels, his hands held up uselessly, unable to ward her off. He was as sexy as always, with those long-lashed eyes and that strong-boned face. She knew that if the aircar jolted too much, Bolt would suffer for it.

"I have to kill someone for betraying me," she told him. "It might as well be you."

"Please don't kill me, Rose. I never hurt you. We barely knew each other, but I had no bad blood for you."

She acted as if she were considering his plea. "Then give me the name of your civ boss, the one you do your dirty work for. I'll kill him first. Then you'll live a little longer."

"I don't work for the civs. You know that, Rose. That's not my style."

She expected him to deny it. Bolt was too smart to turn evidence against himself, especially when a knife was at his throat. She would get that out of him later. "Then there's only one other way. Take me to someone in the underground. And I don't mean an underling. I want someone high up. The highest up you know."

Bolt narrowed his eyes at her. "What do you want with the underground?"

Rose pressed the knife into his throat. A few drops of blood sprang out. If the aircar jolted now, he could get a nasty wound. "It's either that, or . . ."

"Yes!" Bolt exclaimed. "I'll do it."

"Who? Tell me."

Bolt was straining to hold himself away from the knife, his head tilted back. "Manuel, *Señor* Manuel. He owns the *La Baja* in Oldtown."

Rose finally eased away, looking into his eyes. "That's a gambling joint, isn't it?"

At his slight nod, Rose suddenly removed the knife from his throat. There was a ribbon of blood running down his chest. It felt too good to kill him outright. She had only just begun.

Turning to G'kaan, she said, "That's the place."

G'kaan gave her a weird look. "Now I see why you needed the knife."

Rose carefully wiped the blade on her thigh, leaving a streak of Bolt's blood. Then she resheathed it. "Laser-wands are fine. But never underestimate the power of ten inches of steel."

After she walked away, Bolt wiped the blood from his neck. So Rose was back. . . . She was trouble, he always knew it. That was no little nick she had given him. He was bleeding good and proper.

Rose's flunky, the big guy, was standing with his arms crossed and legs spread wide against the movement of the airplane. In one hand was a rectangular box. It must be the tech-device that made the wristbands shock him so hard he lost his breath.

The beauty was lying on the bench looking at him with greedy eyes, like she wanted to finish what she had started on the roof. It wasn't his fault. She had swept in and messed with his mind with that fine perfume of hers, her silky hair that was like mercury, and the way she brushed up against him in the bar. . . well, that was something he could think about later.

The huge alien in the pilot's seat was Bolt's real worry. A fancy airplane like this with an alien like that was bigger trouble than even Rose could stir up. That meant this was World Council stuff. He had never seen an alien before, but the towering black guy was impressive with his full head of glossy hair. His face was strangely formed, not quite right.

"Over there," Rose ordered. The big alien was driving, but Rose was clearly calling the shots.

The last time Bolt had seen Rose, she had cheekily waved as he left her in the Vault with Rowena and Juanita. It wasn't his fault the civs were onto him. The only way he could distract them was to give them a couple of useless underground members. He couldn't jeopardize the people who were actually accomplishing something. So when Rose showed up at the last minute, that solved all his problems. She knew everyone he did, plus she had access to the civ net because of her mother. It was perfect. The *policía* were apparently satisfied that Rose was the one making underground connections, because after she disappeared they had stopped snooping around his usual haunts.

Bolt had never expected Rose to show up again . . . he thought she was expendable.

The airplane bumped as it settled down at a sharp angle.

"Shard, you stay here with G'kaan." The beauty nodded and moved forward to sit next to the alien. "Chad, bring him along."

Bolt was pulled to his feet. He made sure his pants were closed up, then tossed the blond beauty a jaunty wink. She would finish up with him later, he was sure. She laughed and said something incomprehensible to the big alien, whose strange teardrop eyes bored into Bolt.

Chad jerked him along before Bolt could offer the proper silent challenge.

"Iraidor!" Bolt exclaimed, unable to help himself. "I can walk without you pulling on me."

Chad thumbed the box and Bolt winced as a low-level shock shot through his chest.

"Shut up," Rose advised him. "Let's go."

They scrambled up the side of the steep gully, one of many that broke up Oldtown. Chad hauled Bolt out by pulling on the back of his jacket. Bolt refrained from snapping at him again.

"Which way?" Rose demanded.

Bolt gestured and began to walk, weighing his chances of escape. If he could take them into the crowds near the plaza . . .

Rose grabbed hold of his arm. "Don't even think about it! Chad could kill you with the restraints before you took three steps." Her fingers tightened. "Actually, that might be the best way to execute you once I'm through."

She had a heavy-handed style, but it worked. Bolt led them through the narrow passageways, and across a tee-tering footbridge over a gully to the door of *La Baja*. It was an old gambling club with a crumbling plaster façade and a faded sign. From the way Rose looked around, Bolt would have bet she never ventured outside the enclave among the shelters and ruins of Oldtown. Rose had still lived with her mother the last time he saw her!

"Sure you want to see Manuel?" Bolt was on his own ground now instead of hers.

Her eyes were filled with contempt. "If you want to live out the night, Bolt, you'd better shape up."

Bolt shrugged. He was sure *Señor* Manuel could handle Rose and her hulking sidekick. He would get away in the melee that would ensue.

"In here," he told her, slipping through a side door of *La Baja*.

The old guy inside nodded when he recognized Bolt. It was one of Manuel's lifelong servants, more loyal than money could buy.

Bolt walked across the cracked concrete floors, looking into darkened rooms where rounded backs huddled over gaming tables. It was dark everywhere except for the spots of light that illuminated the cards or dice. Voices were low and urgent.

When he finally saw *Señor* Manuel, he pointed. "That's him."

"You two stay here," Rose ordered.

Bolt fidgeted, feeling Chad close behind him. Manuel wore an old-fashioned white shirt, which made him stand out from the crowd. For an older man, he was wiry and strong. Bolt had once seen Manuel take down a man twice his size.

Rose spoke to Manuel, and he looked sharply at Bolt. Then he nodded and gestured for them to follow. Bolt and Chad caught up at the back of the long room. There were stairs that spiraled up through the thick outer wall.

Manuel narrowed his eyes at Bolt. "What's this about?" he rasped in his smoke-ravaged voice.

Rose held up her hand. "You'll want this to be private."

Expressionless, Manuel led the way up the stairs. Bolt noticed that two of his men had detached themselves from the tables and followed.

Bolt had been in Manuel's office before on underground business. Usually he came up the outer steps. They had to file past a few more men on the mezzanine, who instantly went on the alert at the sight of Chad. Bolt grinned at the thought of Rose and her muscleman getting what they deserved.

When they were in his private office, Manuel pulled out a thin cigarette and expertly lit it. He waited for Rose to speak.

Rose checked out the room and circled back to stand in front of him. "Bolt, here, says you're with the underground."

Manuel blandly waved through the spiraling smoke. "He must have mistaken me for another man."

"No, you're the one I want," Rose assured him.

Manuel silently puffed, waiting for Rose to make the next move. Bolt was on his toes, expecting Rose to pull out her big knife to try to intimidate Manuel. His men would be on her before she could draw.

"There's something you don't know." Rose motioned over her shoulder with her thumb. "Bolt betrayed me. I was abducted along with Rowena and Juanita, and taken into space."

Manuel's dark, wrinkled face turned at the mention of Rowena. Bolt realized his own mouth was open. What was Rose up to?

"That's a rather fantastic story," Manuel said noncommittally.

"Then wait 'til you hear this," Rose told him. "They tried to make me a slave, but I busted out with a bunch of other people. I kicked my way around the Domain, destroying a couple of battleships until I got a spaceship big enough to blow my way back to Earth. Now we're here to make sure everyone knows the World Council is selling people to the aliens to use as pleasure slaves."

Manuel raised one brow. "Indeed? It sounds like you have everything you need. What could I do for you?"

"We need the underground to spread the word," Rose told him. "We don't have much time. We must have the element of surprise to take the civs."

"I begin to think that *you* are with the civs, out to get an innocent old man."

"I can prove it to you," Rose said with great satisfaction. "I'll take you up to the moonbase. You can see for yourself and talk to the abductees. I can make Bolt talk, and he'll tell you how he turned on me and Rowena."

Bolt wondered if he should make a run for it. This was not what he had expected.

Manuel paced over to Bolt. "This is the first you've heard of this," Manuel said flatly. "Except for Rowena, I see you recognize her name."

Bolt shifted his eyes. Rose was supposed to be on the end of Manuel's skewer, not him!

Manuel saw it all. He looked back at Rose. "I've always wanted to stand on the moon."

5

S'jen went through the empty rite of dedicating the day to her Qin ancestors, Clan of Huut. Empty, because she had spilled no blood from the Domain or its Fleet, so her own blood could not flow as a sacrifice to the ancestors. The ancestors were displeased that Admiral J'kart had ordered S'jen to turn back to Qin territory. Her battleship should have stayed in the Domain and made them pay for the devastation they had wrought in Qin. But J'kart had been implacable. He had chosen G'kaan to avenge the Qin. G'kaan, who disregarded the ancestors and laughed at their ancient beliefs! G'kaan, who was only half-Qin, had taken the offensive for their clans.

S'jen had chosen a small anteroom on Armada Central to perform her dedication. It was shift change, so it would be too late if she waited until they returned to the *Defiance*, her battleship in dock. She hadn't missed a day's dedication since her escape from the Fleet mining station, and now wasn't the time to start. She wouldn't have minded sharing the rite with her clanmate, E'ven, but he was guarding the door. Since she had returned to Po Alta, there were a number of devout worshippers who wanted to hear how the ancestors had supported her in defeating the Domain. They seemed to find her wherever she went, so E'ven had offered to make sure she wasn't interrupted.

S'jen unsealed her flightsuit to bare her chest. There were many scars, small ridges under her silvery fuzzed skin, left by past dedications. The rows of short parallel lines nearly reached her collarbone. The first few slashes low on her chest were from her youth, after her successful escape from the Fleet mining station and her safe arrival at Po Alta. Then there were a few successes during the decade and a half she rose in the ranks of the Armada, when she had been involved in the kill of a patrolship or a Domain ore freighter. But there had been only a few of those before she invaded the Domain and attacked Spacepost T-3. Now her chest was cleaved by her dedications, and all of the latter ones stood for significant kills.

She lifted her face, offering herself up. As always, she thought of her Huut ancestors—her father and mother, and their fathers and mothers, and her aunts and uncles and cousins—all killed by the Domain.

"On this day, I dedicate my life and my deeds," S'jen intoned. "In the name of my ancestors, Clan of Huut!"

At this point, if she had earned the right, she could draw the ritual knife across her chest, feeling the rush of communion with her ancestors.

This time, she looked down at her empty hand. The dedication felt meaningless when she had not won a victory for her ancestors. Instead of joining with them, there was the same awful silence that had enveloped her since she had brought her mighty battleship back to the safety of Qin. S'jen's only consolation had come when they reached the outer colonies of Qin. Then Admiral J'kart had given her a just reward. One by one, the *Defiance* had destroyed the vast mining stations built by the Domain to subjugate the Qin and steal their precious cesium fuel ore.

The mining station in Balanc had been last to go. Balanc was the innermost system that had been seized by the greedy Domain. The fourth planet had been the home of the Huut clan for over two dozen generations. Now its beautiful coastline was marred by charred pockmarks, the work of the Fleet battleship *Persuasion.* But the mining station where she had been imprisoned and seen her father die waited for her. Her ancestors had filled the *Defiance*, singing their fierce jubilation as S'jen's crew dragged the station with their attractor beam. Picking up speed, they shot the mining station toward the asteroid belt. S'jen had calculated the trajectory so the remaining three bulbous sections went into the belt at an angle to ensure maximum damage.

The station tore into the jagged boulders and moonlets, rupturing the first round sphere that had once contained the slave barracks. The hull peeled back in shattered fragments, as the station continued deeper into the asteroid belt. The decompression explosion ricocheted asteroids in every direction, setting off a chain reaction in the belt. Then the second sphere exploded, sending out fragments of milling equipment, dangerously radioactive from decades of processing the cesium ore. The final sphere contained the fuel cells. When that one blew, there was nothing to see but billowing flames and violently propelled asteroids.

S'jen had quickly pulled the *Defiance* away. The area around the asteroid belt would be unstable for years to come as the chain reaction worked its way around the ring and back again. Then they dropped a hazard warning for spaceships, and left Balanc. With the destruction of everything on the planet and the clans' evacuation, the liberation of her homeworld had not been the victory that S'jen intended.

She had not felt the ancestors since then. Clearly they were dissatisfied with her enforced inaction. Even her father's shade had gone silent, and it was too much to hope that he had moved on to the next dimension. She didn't want her father to exist in perpetual pain, but she couldn't wish for him to leave her alone in these crucial times. She relied on his constant burning presence in her life.

A muffled rap came from the door where E'ven guarded. S'jen quickly sealed her drab gray flightsuit and left the anteroom.

"Admiral J'kart has sent you orders," E'ven told her, holding out the comm link. "You're to return to the *Defiance* immediately."

At last! Perhaps her ancestors had heard her fervent pleas. The Domain would soon learn what she had done to their mining stations, and they wouldn't hesitate to retaliate against Qin.

S'jen slung the comm around her neck, reporting to the *Defiance* that she was returning as they made their way through busy Armada Central. She had been on the station all day trying to see Chief Commander T'ment or one of his senior subcommanders, hoping to convince them to send her battleship back into action.

E'ven knew better than to talk where so many could hear, but his eyes betrayed his own eagerness for them to return to duty. Her clansman had the same impatience to defy the Domain that she remembered in herself when she was his age.

S'jen turned into the Armada docking arm where the

Defiance waited. As she tried to enter, three civilian Qin stepped into her path.

"Greetings, S'jen of the Clan of Huut," said the eldest male. "We have traveled many light-years to see you."

S'jen was focused on the admiral's recall, but she couldn't get past their united front. "I've been called to duty and can't speak to you right now."

"It is as it was foretold," the younger male murmured. "The Crier never wavers in her duty."

The civilians wore flowing garments that exposed their arms and legs. Clearly they were used to being land-bound, since they didn't wear flightsuits. S'jen tried once more to get past them. "Let me by."

"We think only of you," the older man replied. "You, who championed our ancestors and saved the Qin."

S'jen frowned. "Then tell your Clan leader to support a Qin offensive in the council sessions. We must beat the Domain now while they are off-guard."

"It is as it was foretold!" the woman exclaimed. "The Crier has come!"

All three fell to their knees, holding up their hands, palms up in supplication.

E'ven was wary of them. "What's a 'crier'?"

The elder man was gazing reverently at her. "S'jen, Clan of Huut, is the Crier. The ancestors' champion who was foretold countless generations ago. Our acolytes have reported truthfully. The Crier has come!"

S'jen felt an immense irritation. She wasn't a reincarnation of the legendary Crier who had championed the ancestors twice when the Qin had been challenged with extinction. She was only a poor, damaged Qin with honest faith in her ancestors. Ancestors who were punishing her now for not doing her duty by vanquishing their enemies.

She pushed through the civilians, but they exclaimed after her, "We are your acolytes!" "Praise the Crier!" "We have come on pilgrimage!"

S'jen glanced back as E'ven also got through them. Everyone in the terminal had stopped at the commotion and were staring as the acolytes began chanting together, "Praise the Crier!"

By the time they reached the airlock to the *Defiance*, the voices were fainter. "What was that about?" E'ven finally asked.

"A bunch of desperate people looking for hope. They'd do better to talk to the Clan Council."

E'ven didn't reply, but he was looking at her more intently. S'jen didn't care, as long as there was good news waiting for her on board her ship.

When they reached the command deck, C'vid's expression said it all. "We're leaving Armada Central," S'jen spoke for her.

"Yes, as soon as Admiral J'kart reports on board. We're teamed with the battleship *Resolution*. The *Covenant* is staying here to guard Po Alta and Armada Central."

"Both the *Defiance* and the *Resolution*. . . ." Finally the tight band of tension around S'jen's head eased. Even the persistent ringing in her left ear, a souvenir from a mining overseer who had hit her with a bot, became fainter.

"We're going after the Fleet!" E'ven exclaimed.

The tips of S'jen's fangs showed. "Crew, prepare to depart!"

She would give her last drop of blood to meet the Fleet inside the Domain. With the help of the ancestors, she would teach them never to invade Qin again.

6

Heloga Alpha sat behind her desk with her head enshrouded in a golden veil. It was a lovely texture and one end was jauntily thrown over her shoulder, but it was impossible to conceal its true purpose. She detested the way everyone had stared at her broken, disintegrating skin. She had revealed her decaying face for only one day, but the frank looks of horror were too much for her frayed nerves. She was Regional Commander of Canopus, and they would respect her until she was dead and cold, or they would die first!

That included the regents' strategist, Winstav Alpha. Winstav had been sent to Canopus with his fellow strategist, Felenore, to investigate the Qin attack on Spacepost T-3. The situation had deteriorated rapidly since then. Now Heloga had more to fear from the strategists than she did from the marauding Qin hordes.

On one of her holomonitors, Heloga could see Winstav chatting with Oliv Alpha, her staff manager. Oliv shouldn't be talking to Winstav, but Heloga knew she had been weakened in her subordinates' eyes and now they flaunted breaking her rules. They didn't know she could see into every part of her administrative complex with its transparent walls. Lately her surveillance computer had been trained on Winstav. Right now he was leaning ingratiatingly over Oliv.

At first Heloga had disliked Felenore more because her appearance was disgusting. Her bug eyes and pitted, orange-tinted skin had repulsed Heloga. But Felenore was not nearly as dangerous as Winstav. To think that she had once considered the little Alpha attractive in a compact sort of way. Now she could only see his slimy manipulations.

"The difference between ordinary Alphas and regents," Winstav was saying innocuously enough, *"is that regents are ahead of the cusp while the rest of us must content ourselves with reacting. That is why the regents make the important decisions."*

"I know just what you mean," Oliv exclaimed. *"I always think ahead."*

Heloga distrusted Winstav's cultivation of Oliv and a few other key members of her staff. The strategist must have ulterior motives. Oliv was a particularly weak link in her chain of command. His interactions with Rikev Alpha had been the blackest mark on his dossier before Winstav had won him over.

"Good, then you've already positioned yourself for the inevitable." Winstav glanced upward, as they all tended to do when referring to Regional Commander Heloga.

It took Oliv a moment to understand. *"Oh, you mean the downward spiral . . ."*

Downward spiral! As if that brain-dead credit-grubber would even know which way was down!

"I'm sure you've notified your contacts in the inner

regions about the . . ." Winstav pointed down and turned his finger in little circles.

Heloga fumed at his condescending smile. She had plenty of life in her yet. They would find out for themselves what it meant to oppose her.

"Yes, yes, of course," Oliv agreed quickly.

"You want to be seen as ahead of the curve. Reporting as you're doing is good, but think what an image of . . ." His finger spiraled down. *". . . would do. The man who could get his hands on such an image would be seen as way ahead of others on the spot."*

Oliv looked apprehensively around to be sure no one could hear, as well he should at the idea of obtaining an image of Heloga Alpha!

"But how?" Oliv shook his head to himself. *"No one can get close to her."*

"You're a smart man, Oliv, nearly regent material, if you ask me."

With another knowing smirk, Winstav left Oliv nodding to himself and muttering. Now that idiot would start spouting off to everyone he knew in the Domain. Word must have gotten back to the regents on Spinca by now. At the very least, Winstav had alerted his superiors that Heloga's health was failing.

Heloga left Oliv behind and followed Winstav on his merry rounds. Next he spoke to Pring, a Gamma who had also worked with Rikev Alpha when he was briefly at Regional Headquarters. Heloga tagged that for further analysis. She was leaving no molecule unturned to find a way to bring the strategists down.

Then Winstav went into the interrogation room where the uninhibitor was set up. He was still interviewing Commander Yonith, Master of Fleet in Canopus.

Yonith had been de-ranked when their mining stations had been attacked and the Fleet officers were killed by the Qin.

Heloga's remote viewers couldn't follow inside the uninhibitor. The place was one massive scanner. Later she would get an official log of everything that happened during the interrogations.

Heloga's comm implant chimed. A text message from her Beta assistant, Waanip, said it was urgent that she speak with the regional commander.

Heloga sighed and keyed the holomonitors to disappear. She checked her veil in the adjustable mirror, wishing there were some way to make it look more elegant. Instead, she was afraid she resembled a heavily curtained window.

Waanip hurried into Heloga's office. "Senior Alpha Vernst, Master of Fleet, requested that I pass along a message."

"Get on with it," Heloga said impatiently. It wasn't like Waanip to mince words, but the veil seemed to have an off-putting effect on her and other people.

"Senior Alpha Vernst asks me to inform you that all four of the Fleet's mining stations in Qin territory have been destroyed." Waanip swallowed.

Heloga sat forward with a snap. "What! He asks *you* to tell me? Where is he?"

"Senior Alpha Vernst is working with Senior Alpha Gustance, Master of Industry, to determine a rationing plan for fueling the Fleet's ships. He begs your pardon but says he will give you his report by the end of this shift."

Heloga was so angry she was sputtering. "Get out!" she ordered.

Waanip turned and fled.

With an aggravated cry, Heloga pushed away from her desk and stood up. Pacing didn't help. Her fingers clenched repeatedly in their protective gloves.

Four mining stations destroyed! There were only two left in Canopus Region. It had been folly for Commander Yonith and Alpha Gustance to allow four of their six mining stations to be placed in hostile territory. Yet the buildup had taken two decades, and those stations had outproduced their most optimistic predictions for another two decades. Who expected that the Qin would suddenly fight back so efficiently?

This was the kind of mistake that caused regional commanders to be downranked—Heloga was not about to let that happen to her. "Waanip! Get back in here."

Heloga opened her own dataport and consulted the ship schedules. She had to throw the strategists off Canopus Regional Headquarters as soon as she could. The only way to do that was to fetch battleships—enough to take them straight into Qin, where they could deal with this menace once and for all!

Winstav thought the situation was falling apart nicely. He had managed to provoke quite a whispering campaign about Heloga's "downward spiral." No doubt she herself would hear about it soon, and that would unsettle her even more, causing her to make more mistakes and drag the Canopus region deeper into chaos.

Then he could save the day on the frontier of the Domain.

Winstav leaned in closer to Commander Yonith, and asked, "Had enough?"

The former commander of the Fleet in the Canopus

region was a sweating, twitching mass clamped into the uninhibitor. Her tan skin had a distinctly greenish cast, and her eyes were rimmed with busted blackish red veins.

"Please, stop," Yonith moaned.

She had once been a proud, arrogant woman. Winstav had interviewed her when he first arrived in Canopus to investigate the attack on Spacepost T-3. He had not imagined then that things would escalate into a situation he could use to his own advantage. No one knew better than Winstav Alpha how to lift his own line in a crisis.

Winstav glanced up and gestured curtly to the two uninhibitor techs. They knew the drill by now. One of them turned off the scanners and monitors as they left.

Winstav didn't remove the enveloping carapace that held Yonith so tightly. He stood where she couldn't see him, and whispered, "There's only one way to make it stop. . . ."

"Please, make it stop," she begged almost incoherently.

Yonith had resolutely told the truth under the uninhibitor, but even the truth as we know it is not completely accurate. The memory plays tricks that the subconscious can see through. Little by little her neurons were being torn apart under the stress of the questioning.

"I'm not going to hurt you anymore," Winstav murmured. "You're going to help me."

Yonith's breathing changed, indicating she was listening.

"The regents must have someone to blame for the Qin's ravages on Canopus. That will be you," Winstav assured her, "unless you can convince them another deserves the blame."

"Another?" she panted, trying but unable to turn her head.

"The one who is truly responsible, your superior . . . Heloga Alpha."

Yonith stiffened, every part of her resisting the suggestion to betray her commanding officer. She was Fleet, through and through.

Winstav knew it would be close. Yonith might stand by her regional commander and take the responsibility for sending the bulk of their mining facilities into Qin herself. But Winstav didn't think so—he had broken down her resistance through a masterful use of the uninhibitor.

"It's your choice," Winstav assured her. "No one will know about this conversation, but your assertions will be fully backed by my research. They will be true enough to not cause you harm."

Yonith was breathing faster, making strangled sounds deep in her throat.

"It's your line or hers . . . and she is dying as we speak." Yonith's eyes moved to his as he came forward, nodding. "Dying. Yes, I see you've heard the rumors. I tell you it's true."

Yonith started to relax under the carapace.

"Will you do it?" he whispered.

Yonith nodded. "Yes."

Winstav hid his elation as he quickly recited the half-dozen facts and figures Yonith would use to implicate Heloga Alpha. It was true that the regional commander was ultimately accountable for the inadequate strategic planning in the Canopus region, allowing the Qin to invade her territory. Winstav wanted to put a spin on things that would indicate a strong military mind was needed in Qin. Pirosha Alpha, a regional InSec commander in Spinca, had a superior record in the Fleet, and she would be grateful enough for Winstav's assistance to help him regain his rightful place in the Domain.

He barely finished drilling Yonith to be sure she had it correctly when one of the techs returned. "The regional commander orders that you to report to her immediately."

Winstav gestured to Yonith Alpha. "Take her down and back to the brig. I'm done with her. She won't have anything left for Spinca if we squeeze her too hard."

The tech nodded seriously, having seen Winstav at work.

Winstav left without a backward glance. He knew Yonith would do as she agreed. He had broken her. She would serve his purpose and die in the uninhibitor in Spinca.

By the time he had reached Heloga Alpha's office, Winstav had already moved on to his next plan of attack. He couldn't openly enlist Felenore in his maneuverings, but surely his fellow strategist could be of use somehow. The woman was nearly as smart as he was and she minded her own business. A very useful trait in a partner strategist.

But Winstav's goal was personal. He intended to return to power and glory in Rigel, the heart of the Domain where he belonged. Saving an entire region on the frontier would bring the praise he needed to rise again. His fall was not his own fault, and he had no doubt about a comeback given the right circumstances.

At Heloga's office, Waanip nodded to him, looking careworn. There was stubble on her balding head, and the skin under her narrow eyes was puffy. Her thin slash of a mouth trembled when she saw Winstav.

Winstav had thoroughly investigated Waanip, hoping to be able to subvert her. But Heloga knew how to treat her favorites. As long as Heloga was pleased with Waanip's performance, the Beta-assistant was enveloped in luxury. With Heloga's decline, there would soon be a new regional commander who would likely bring in her own loyal assistant. Clearly Waanip needed to be concerned about her future.

Winstav smiled encouragingly at her. "Everything seems to be running smoothly now. Maybe the situation will stop deteriorating and you won't have to give evidence to the regents."

Waanip flinched as if she had been jabbed in the stomach. Something must have happened. Winstav knew better than to try to pump the Beta, not with Heloga watching through the transparent walls. He knew his anti-Heloga campaign was working, and he intended to continue to hint to Waanip that she could end up in the uninhibitor like Yonith if she didn't cooperate.

Waanip's voice was high and strained. "You can go in now, Alpha Strategist."

Passing through the door, Winstav couldn't restrain a shudder at what lay within. Heloga's head was wrapped in gaudy gold tissue. She probably thought it was pretty, but it merely looked desperate.

He had seen the marks of her decline only once, right before Heloga adopted the veils. He had been shocked at the deep grooves on either side of her mouth. It was the first time he had personally seen someone who was dying. Heloga no longer seemed human, certainly not Alpha. Decent people killed themselves when the physical signs of decay appeared. But Heloga was playing into his hands by stubbornly hanging on to power.

"You must prepare to leave Regional Headquarters," Heloga ordered before Winstav reached her desk. "Two additional battleships are on their way here. They should be adequate for you to subdue the Qin."

Winstav didn't want this minor war to be resolved so quickly. He needed time to gain allies in Canopus, and for Pirosha to position herself as the best replacement for Heloga. Pirosha would undoubtedly emphasize in her initial reports his own part in stamping out the Qin, much to his advantage.

Yet he replied, "Indeed, I'm surprised it's taken you two decnights to come to this decision. The fuel ore shortages are shutting down shipping in the outer sectors of your region."

He could barely see the outline of her face under the veil—the dark pits of her eyes and the shadow of her nose. Her mouth faintly moved. "Commander Vernst reports that all four mining stations in Qin were destroyed."

"Are they unsalvageable?" At a bob from the gold veil, Winstav almost smiled. The regents would be furious when they found out. "Canopus only has two left," he reminded her. "That will never supply the fuel needs of the region."

"That is my concern." Heloga waved her hand dismissively.

Winstav wasn't about to let go of such an unexpected gain. "As strategists, Felenore and I must consider the ramifications. This must be reported to Spinca."

"*I* report everything to the regents," Heloga snapped. "The dangers on the frontier are well known. Ripolaz, regional commander of Velorum, wasn't held responsible when the Kund invaded the Domain."

"Protecting your own mining stations should have been a top priority," Winstav insisted.

"They were destroyed soon after you left them vulnerable in Qin."

"The Qin attacked your mining fleet, Regional Commander." Winstav retorted, parrying her attack. "Your defenses were inadequate and your intelligence was faulty."

Heloga stood up, leaning her hands on her desk. They were covered in burnished gold gloves. "Your job is to destroy the Qin, Alpha Strategist. Be ready to leave on my orders."

Winstav knew he had overstepped himself. He should save his strategy for his reports. "By your command, Regional Commander."

He bowed his way out of her office, not particularly unhappy with the way the interview had gone. The loss of the mining stations would hurt Heloga severely. Despite what she had said about Ripolaz, she could be downranked for that blunder.

All in all, things were getting very interesting in Canopus. If only he could delay their departure from Regional Headquarters for a little while longer.

7

━━ ⁓ ━━

Rose couldn't tell if the tour of her patrolship, *Relevance*, impressed Manuel or not. She had known plenty of men like Manuel growing up in Tijuana. These old guys were indestructible—leathery from the harsh sun, cagey in their conversation, giving nothing away.

G'kaan pointed out the portal of the airlock. "Tell him about the *Devotion*."

Rose was getting tired of interpreting for him. At least it was only one way. G'kaan had a translator implant, so he could understand what Manuel said.

"That's the patrolship we captured when we took the moonbase." Rose waited while Manuel took a long look. "It's older than my ship, but it has plenty of punch."

"Who commands that spaceship?" Manuel asked quietly.

"Some of G'kaan's crew. The Qin have more to spare than we do. We also captured a transport ship earlier today."

Manuel didn't react. "Do you believe you can hold off the Domain with these spaceships?"

G'kaan stiffened, but Rose ignored him. "We're doing all right so far."

Shard returned from her trip to the brig. "We put Bolt in a cell and Chad has gone back to the command deck." She shifted provocatively as she spoke, drawing all eyes to her, even G'kaan's. But Manuel was so tough he didn't give Shard a second glance. It was the first time Rose had ever seen a Solian who didn't react to Shard in drooling fascination.

"Go tell Kwort to meet us at the aircar," Rose said. It wouldn't hurt for Manuel to see another alien who was helping them. "We're going down to the moonbase."

"Sure, Rose," Shard replied seductively, but Manuel was like stone. She shrugged and laughed when her maneuvers proved useless. Shard had boundless confidence in herself.

Rose knew Manuel wasn't going to be an easy sell, that tough *cabrón!* At least the old guy had more character that Bolt, who had turned against his friends, or Rowena, who died without a struggle. Maybe the underground wasn't as weak as Rose had always thought.

The moonbase was echoing and nearly empty, with corridors and modular sections of rooms that went ever deeper and wider. Rose stuck to the basics with her tour, taking Manuel first to the control center with its massive scanners aimed down at Earth and into space. The moonbase was barely mapped out, with Qin combat teams still searching the levels. She showed Manuel the environmental systems, the destroyed laser array, and the docks where six small transports were waiting for their regular trips down to Earth to pick up new slaves.

"The underground can use these to bring your people

up here to staff the moonbase," Rose told him. "We also need a crew for the interstellar transport we captured."

"You'd give us this for nothing?" Manuel asked shrewdly.

Knowing he wouldn't respect a bad trade, Rose explained, "I expect us to work together. It'll take all of us to keep the Fleet out of Sol. I'd rather have Solians in control of Earth airspace than anyone else."

Manuel raised one brow, glancing at G'kaan and Kwort, the two aliens. But he didn't comment.

Next, Rose took him to the former command crew quarters where the abducted Solians were living. The Solians were busy translating the information from the Fleet database under the watchful eyes of M'ke and a few of the former pleasure slaves. They were making copies in over twenty major languages. The Solians had all been given translator implants, so they could understand Manuel's questions, but Rose still had to interpret their answers for Manuel until they found several Spanish-speaking abductees. Then Rose could get a break for a while.

The tour concluded with a look at the cube stacks where the moonbase and patrolship crews were kept in naked splendor. Kwort seemed uncomfortable with that. He had protested about stripping the crew before they were cubed. Because he was a Delta, he could empathize with them.

"This is how they cage Solians," Rose reminded Kwort as they entered the huge bay. "I was stuck in one of those cubes for weeks."

"It is a secure holding system," G'kaan agreed.

Manuel looked on them with great interest. "I've never heard of these transparent cells."

Rose had been impressed with his general level of knowledge about the moonbase activities, aliens, and the Domain. However, the underground didn't know everything.

The long-nosed Swark handlers were on the lowest row of cubes in front, huddled down at the back. Above them were a few of the flat-faced biotechs who had performed the inductions. They had a round hole for a mouth and smooth dip for a nose, and were beating on the glass wall that separated them. Rose rubbed her neck at the sight, remembering how they had given her the translator implant.

"These aliens all use Solians as pleasure slaves," Rose told Manuel. "But the Alphas are the worst. They're in charge of this whole operation. You want to see an Alpha?"

At Manuel's nod, she took him around to the back of the cube stack. There were several Alphas on the second tier. Rose hadn't seen the Alphas since they were confined in the cubes, shouting and swearing that they would destroy every slave who rebelled. She had thoroughly enjoyed it.

"Not so full of yourself now, are you?" she muttered, staring up at the Alphas.

"They hardly look like Alphas anymore," Kwort agreed glumly. He turned away as if to hide his face from them.

Rose wished she could keep a cubed Alpha on permanent display on board the *Relevance*. None of her crew would fear them then. They were naked as no other aliens were, without a trace of hair or thickened skin to hide themselves.

The female was the former commander of the moon-

base. Her face and arms were smeared with the greasy
slop that splashed down in the bowl embedded in the
glass. Her eyes were glazed, as if only a few days in the
cube had unbalanced her. So much for that so-called Alphan superiority.

"Better get used to it," Rose told them. "You'll be in
there for a long, long time." She would have preferred to
kill them all, but G'kaan had insisted that was a losing
strategy. He pointed out how the Fleet had retaliated
against the outer Qin colonies because of Admiral
J'kart's scorched-ship policy on the mining stations. But
Rose didn't think anyone who aided and abetted the
slave trade should be allowed to live.

"You captured all of these aliens?" Manuel asked, as if
he couldn't believe it.

"That one there," Rose pointed at the female, "was the
commander of the moonbase. Those two on either side
were her second and third commanders."

Several Solians appeared in the bay, watching them.
They were wearing the tan flightsuits usually worn by
the crew of the moonbase.

Rose gestured for them to come over. "These are a few
of the Solian pleasure slaves that were kept here on the
moonbase for use by the crew. They weren't raised on
Earth so they don't speak any language you'd recognize,
but if you get a translator implant, you could talk to them
yourself. They'll tell you plenty about what these Alphas
did to them. They'll tell you that we rescued them."

Manuel took a long look at the former slaves, whose
own glares at the Alphas displayed their fear and resentment.

"I put them in charge of the cubes," Rose told him. "It
seemed like the right thing to do."

Manuel nodded once, as if he had finally made up his mind. "I want a translator implant so I can speak to them and hear what they have to say."

Rose took Manuel into the long room with the tables where the inductions were done. G'kaan's biotech, D'nar, was downloading medical data on the Solians that had been accumulated for hundreds of years.

D'nar showed them how to implant a translator, using a tool that looked like a wide-barreled gun. She inserted a disc into Manuel's neck, and he barely flinched. Rose smiled at his display of native *machismo*. It was good to be with people from home!

G'kaan shook his head in warning, so Rose busied herself gathering a couple of tubes of translator discs and smashing the collar control in each one. They would be needing a lot more translators. She no longer wore a collar like the rest of her crew, but she had grabbed a case of the rings so they could use them as a cover. It would attract too much attention if they went into the Domain again without wearing collars.

Meanwhile G'kaan spoke directly to Manuel, who seemed to get used to the whispery effects of the translator transplant quickly. G'kaan intended to cement an alliance between the Qin and Earth's underground. Rose liked watching him work. He must have done this dozens of times while he was building his slave network in the Domain.

Rose chimed in every once in a while, but when Manuel spoke to some of the abductees and the former pleasure slaves, she figured it would be better to stay out of it. Manuel was on the road to being convinced, so she didn't need to push things.

Kwort headed down to the lower levels to check out what the combat teams had found while Rose turned to D'nar. "How's Ash's treatment going?"

D'nar was a pretty Qin with rich gray skin. But her tone was not inviting. "If you saw hir once in a while, s/he'd probably do better."

"Hey!" Rose exclaimed. "I've been busy saving the world."

D'nar shrugged. "You asked."

Rose felt uncomfortable thinking about Ash in hir current condition. She just wished Ash would get better and come home. She could really use hir help right now. "Are you saying you can't fix hir memory?"

"I've seen some progress. It will be hir own fault if s/he fails."

It was just like a Qin to be nasty no matter how hard she tried. Rose was starting to wonder how long this Qin-Solian alliance could possibly last. Only G'kaan seemed to really care what happened to Earth.

Manuel returned with a thoughtful G'kaan by his side. "I'll take you to Enzo and Margarita. They're the ones you need to see."

G'kaan piloted the aircar back down to Earth. Rose was clearly impatient, but G'kaan knew it was never easy to gain people's trust. He was astonished by how well their initial exchange was going. He thought that it was because Rose was one of them, and could bridge any gaps before they fully appeared.

G'kaan set the aircar down on the hilltop estate that Manuel had indicated. Kwort looked unhappy, and Rose had suggested they leave him on the moonbase. G'kaan hadn't had time to explain the moonbase's past to Rose, and he couldn't risk letting Kwort poke around and discover the truth. The combat teams had told the bot tech that some of the base personnel were still missing, so it was too unsafe to roam around.

Kwort brightened the imager so they could see the salt cedar trees and rock walls of the terraced hillside even in the dark.

"Is this right?" Rose asked Manuel. "This place must belong to a civ."

"Margarita es la única hija de Don Sebastian Rivera," Manuel said simply.

"Oh." Rose blinked a few times. "I guess it's too late now. There must be a cannon aimed at us."

"Who is it?" G'kaan had to ask.

"The Riveras own a lot of mountain land," Rose explained. "It's leased for growing crops. Don Rivera was the governor when I was a little girl."

"He lives here, with his daughter Margarita and her husband, Enzo," Manuel explained. "But Don Rivera is none of your concern."

"It could be a trap," Rose told G'kaan. She glanced at Kwort, clearly wishing she had brought Chad instead. Kwort's worried expression said the same thing. But as far as G'kaan was concerned, little ridged-headed Kwort was exactly what they needed right now.

"It's our turn to take a leap of faith," G'kaan told them both.

Manuel was watching closely. G'kaan thought that the seasoned man was glad to see their concern. As usual, when there was no advantage to be gained by speaking, Manuel waited. G'kaan was starting to get a feel for the reserved man.

G'kaan followed Manuel out of the aircar, along with

Rose and Kwort. As they climbed up to the house on the crest of the hill, a sharp racket rose. Soon they were surrounded by a pack of snarling black and brown animals. For creatures so small, they seemed particularly ferocious. G'kaan stood with his back to the others as Manuel ordered, "Stand still! The men will come."

Shadows appeared out of the night, and lanterns flared. G'kaan blinked, taking in the long weapons that were held ready for use. Manuel spoke to them in a rapid dialogue that his implant couldn't quite keep up with.

The dogs were called back and whined in the shadows cast by the lanterns, eagerly waiting for the signal to close in again. They walked the remainder of the way to the house, stepping up the slate steps to a wide porch. The porch surrounded the house and overlooked the lights of Tijuana. The colors reminded him of Rose, and she had never looked so right as in that house with its dark, wood-beamed ceiling and ivory plaster walls. The warm rosy floor of terra-cotta tiles echoed the color of her lips.

Inside, they were greeted by a mature man who was nearly as tall as G'kaan. The high-ceilinged room with its grand proportions suited him. His long crimson coat was crossed and tied at the waist, with black trousers and loose loafers for shoes. His dark hair was highlighted by a liberal sprinkling of silver strands.

Manuel introduced them to Enzo de Marco, who reached out his hand to each of them, clasping theirs in traditional politeness. He stared up at G'kaan for a few long moments. "You must be Qin. Yes, I've never met one of your kind, but your territory is one of our closest neighbors, isn't that so?"

G'kaan inclined his head, "You are correct. Qin and Sol have much in common, including a common enemy."

Manuel quickly interpreted G'kaan's words, adding, "They gave me a translator implant while I was on the moonbase."

Rose stepped forward, always ready to take center stage. "We've liberated Earth. Sol space is under our control, along with the moonbase."

"I've just returned with them," Manuel informed them. "I spoke to the people who were abducted and are on the moon. It's true, Enzo."

"And now we have to tell everyone on Earth what's been going on," Rose declared.

G'kaan wished he could join in. He exactly knew what to say to convince this urbane man, if only he could understand. Enzo's intelligent eyes took in each of them, seeing more than they realized. His expression softened indulgently as he listened to Rose, as if he understood her youthful bravado for what it was.

G'kaan held out the datarods holding copies of the bulk of the moon's database. "These datarods have the engineering specs for antigrav technology as well as plans for every Fleet installation in this system."

Manuel echoed him. "This is grav tech they give to us."

"Grav tech! How can that be?" Enzo took the rods directly from G'kaan. "For this, we'll need to fetch my wife, Margarita."

From behind him came a lovely contralto voice, saying, "Yes? You called me?"

G'kaan turned and saw a vision of womanhood. Her thick mane of hair and heart-shaped face reminded him of Qin beauties, but her flashing brown eyes and full lips were pure Solian. This was how Rose would look when she finished growing up.

Enzo didn't have to explain much to his mate. Margarita kept watching G'kaan especially, but maybe that was because he had a hard time taking his eyes off her.

Margarita took the datarods in her graceful hands but waved away Rose's dataport. "I'll use the interface. It's in my office."

As they followed Margarita and Enzo, Rose bumped into G'kaan. "Keep it in your flightsuit while we're working!" she murmured. "That's what I always tell my crew."

G'kaan gave her a horrified glare. "*What* are you talking about?"

"Tell me, are you in love with all women, or just the ones who stumble across your path?"

G'kaan almost snapped at her, but old Manuel had slowed to listen to them. Rose laughed at his expression. G'kaan wasn't sure why her needling bothered him. He had been devoted to S'jen for years without so much as glancing at anyone else. It was healthy for him to be noticing women now that he was without a mate and lust was approaching.

After the reprimand, G'kaan stayed back with Kwort, letting Enzo, Manuel, and Rose hover over Margarita. She sat at a complex terminal with a large monitor, technology that was obviously patterned on Domain equipment. Several stacks of modular components were fused to its frame. Margarita slid each datarod into the port, and a staggering array of documents were available, from the schematics of a grav impeller to personnel information for the crew on the moonbase.

Margarita took her time verifying the grav technology. G'kaan noticed that she copied and sent the information to several sources. "It's true," she finally admitted. "We can finally leave Earth."

G'kaan hoped the specs were now being copied and transferred across the planet. They had obviously gained communications technology from the Domain already. Once these enterprising people had the key to galactic travel, they would take the first step toward freedom. It was poetic justice that Qin had given it to them.

The information on the datarods gave them plenty to discuss. G'kaan's own crew were still analyzing everything, so he used his dataport to log what they said for cross-correlation. Kwort offered a few technical pointers, some that Rose translated and others that she ignored.

Margarita finally called out, *"Mira esto,* Enzo!"

Enzo avidly scanned the monitor. "It's a list of the civs from each major enclave who report to the World Council's Committee for Alien Affairs."

"So?" Rose asked.

"Rose, those people are in charge of meeting the quotas." Enzo patted his wife's shoulder. "They arrange the abductions. We can release this list in the broadcast along with the rest of the images and documents."

"Yes, like the World Council agreements with the Domain to fulfill certain quotas of 'exports,' " Margarita reminded him.

"At the same time, we can send back the abductees," Rose agreed. "They'll tell everyone in their enclave what happened to them."

Manuel was also considering their plan. "First we should alert the underground network around the world with our instructions. That will take at least a day. Then our people will be ready to take over once the news breaks."

Rose laughed out loud. "We'll chop off the head of the World Council, and leave the civs on this list to the mobs. Your people in the underground can move into the power vacuum."

Manuel nodded shortly, pointing to the monitor. "These are the Alien Affairs contacts for Tijuana."

"Let me see that!" Rose exclaimed. "I want to know who's to blame for my abduction."

"Exactly who we thought," Manuel said with a hint of pride, "Chevaz, Rico, and Saulzman."

As Rose looked, her face suddenly went pale. "Oh, no . . ."

G'kaan was instantly by her side. "What's wrong, Rose?"

"Silvia Rico," Rose said distantly.

She pulled away from them and went over to the window, keeping her back turned. G'kaan had never heard her sound like that. "Rose, what is it?"

"My mother," she said with her back turned. "Silvia Rico, Head of Foreign Relations."

Now it was Enzo and Manuel who were concerned. G'kaan could see their silent exchange—they thought it was a trap. But Margarita went over to Rose. "I've met your mother. She's done good things for Tijuana, as well."

Rose abruptly turned, her sardonic mask fixed in place. "That's my mother, always the do-gooder." She shook back her hair. "Guess I'm exactly the same."

"We could remove her name from the list," Margarita said gently.

Rose shook off her hand. "¿Estás loca? She's in charge, she'll pay like everyone else. Let the barrio deal with them."

There was an awkward silence. G'kaan couldn't insist that Rose spare herself because he knew that Enzo and Manuel were deeply suspicious. He also knew, having come from a tight-knit family, that Rose's decision was the hardest a person could make. Only if she had condemned her own child would it be any more difficult.

But Rose acted as if it were nothing.

G'kaan felt a shiver go down his spine.

Rose was glad to get back to her ship. The underground was busy doing their underground thing, and she was more than ready to leave Earth to them. But she had one more job to do before she could knock off for the night.

She snapped on the lights in the brig to their brightest. From the cell in the middle came a groan. "Wha' th' hell?"

Rose walked over to the wire mesh cell. It was about as big as an outhouse. "Comfy enough for you?"

Bolt raised his head up. "Oh. It's you."

Rose hated how blasé he sounded. She lifted the wide-barreled gun to her shoulder, getting out the shocker. Bolt still wore his wrist restraints. She could take him down with a twitch.

"I've got something special for you," she told him sweetly.

"What's that, love?" he asked, rubbing both hands through his shorn hair.

Rose deactivated the energy field that ran through the wires. She'd been stuck in a cell exactly like this one after a patrolship had picked up the Solians from Spacepost T-3. She had been forced to watch an enforcer drag Ash from the brig, and later watched Ash come back as a vegetable. Rose hadn't been able to do a thing about it.

She opened the door to the cell. Bolt started to stand up, but she ordered, "Sit down!"

He raised his hands slightly, then put them carefully on his knees. "You've got a screw loose, lady."

With one motion, Rose brought the gun to his neck. He leaned back until he was against the wire mesh, and she was kneeling on the bunk.

Her face was close to his, and she pressed the barrel of the gun in harder.

His lips were tight, but he didn't look away from her.

"This is going to hurt," she whispered.

Rose thumbed the trigger. Bolt screamed and thrust himself away from her, his hands clamping wildly at his neck. It took him a moment to realize he wasn't mortally injured. As his hands swiped and found no blood, he turned back to her, panting.

Rose cavalierly blew on the end of the gun. "Translator implant, you ninny. The first on a long list of revolting things I plan on doing to you."

She closed the door to the cell and activated the energy field that would keep him inside. Bolt hunched over on the bed eyeing her warily, his feigned superiority vanished. She thought he looked sexier that way, all vulnerable and hurt, his eyes shining from pain. He belonged to her now.

Rose snapped off the light and went in search of Stub for some much-needed sexual release.

8

Ash started with the medical charts D'nar gave hir, then spent a few days researching hir past as a pleasure slave. S/he was uncomfortably engrossed by the Qin's analysis of the Domain and their slave trade. Some of it seemed brand-new, and other times s/he felt like s/he was remembering things from hir own life. S/he especially felt that way when s/he looked at the holospecs of the *Purpose*, the old cargoship the Solians had hijacked. Jot and Kwort regularly sent over notes including things that hir friends remembered hir saying or doing, which also helped.

Hir mind was no longer responding to D'nar treatments. After the first flurry of flashbacks, s/he remembered nothing. The patch on hir neck buzzed just as irritably, without results.

"What's wrong?" Ash asked D'nar during hir daily skull scan.

"It's a waste of time." D'nar's dark gray face was inscrutable as she lifted off the neurocap and put it away. Today the biotech was wearing a glowing purple flightsuit. She was showing a lot of skin again, something the Qin didn't usually do.

Ash smoothed hir hair back as Jot had shown hir. "Why isn't it working anymore?"

"You don't want it to."

Ash wasn't sure s/he heard correctly. "What do you mean?"

"You don't want your memory back. There are only a few recorded instances of cases like yours," D'nar explained with professional detachment. "I'm analyzing my data to submit to Binirth Neuroinstitute. They may not accept it because the subject isn't Qin, but I figure it will get some attention anyway because the condition is so rare."

Ash felt like a specimen in a tray. As usual, s/he didn't know what to say.

"No matter what treatment I give you, it's not going to help until you're ready to remember." D'nar returned to the biounit to program a new patch for hir. "So don't blame me."

Ash suddenly didn't want D'nar to answer any more questions. "Do you have a datarod that can tell me more?"

D'nar glanced over at hir. "You have retrograde amnesia linked to severe emotional shock. Your language skills and short-term memory appear unaffected, but your identity and personal memories are gone. Your mind apparently decided you can't handle what happened so you forgot. Right now you're in what we call a fugue state. If you recover your memories, you'll probably forget everything that's happening now."

Ash didn't like the sound of that. Either s/he lost hir past or s/he lost hir present? "So I'm not really alive right now?"

"Oh, you're alive. But you're not truly aware of what's

happening." D'nar ripped off the old patch and slapped the new one onto hir neck.

Ash felt a spike of anger building inside of hir. "Is that why you're so mean to me?"

D'nar finally looked interested. "Confrontational behavior! That's not in your character profile. I'll have to add a footnote to my section on the development of new disposition patterns."

Ash headed for the door. Part of hir wanted to forget this terrible time of confusion and loss. Regardless, s/he was certain s/he was aware of what was happening.

Ash ended up standing uncertainly in the corridor outside the medical bay. If s/he really did want hir memory back, there was one person on board the *Endurance* who had known hir longer than anyone, even Rose. But s/he was afraid.

Then again, if s/he didn't snap out of it, s/he would stay like this for the rest of hir life. The walking braindead.

That made hir decision easier. S/he headed down to the brig.

Ash had to go through several checks and clearances before the Qin combatants finally let hir into the brig. "It's part of my neurotherapy," s/he tried to explain.

Hir request was sent straight to the top, and Captain G'kaan signed off on hir visit. His face on the monitor looked preoccupied. *"Ash can see Rikev if s/he wants. We've gotten everything we'll get out of him with the serneo-inhibitor."*

So the senior combatant on duty let Ash into the brig. The long room was brightly lit, including each of the empty cells. Rikev was in the middle one.

"Don't touch the wire," the combatant warned Ash before leaving. The door slid shut behind him.

Ash remembered standing here with Rose and G'kaan, looking at Rikev Alpha. Rose had expected the sight of Rikev to jolt hir out of the amnesia. If this worked, maybe one day s/he wouldn't remember doing this.

Rikev stood up, facing hir. His golden eyes were serene, and his glowing skin was a testament to his superior heritage. According to the Qin's data, Alphas claimed they were of purest humanoid stock without the numerous mutations that had occurred in other aliens. Yet the gene-twisting Alpha scientists continually made new and more intriguing humanoid hybrids. The data D'nar had given Ash on herme pleasure slaves questioned whether Ash had been genetically altered or was the result of a selective breeding program pursued in the creches. S/he must have been born and raised in a creche, but s/he couldn't remember it.

Ash told Rikev, "Rose says you're the reason I can't remember anything."

Rikev didn't move, standing with his arms straight down his sides and his head held high, as if s/he was hardly worth his notice. S/he wasn't sure he would answer. He hadn't spoken when s/he came with Rose and G'kaan.

But Rikev quietly replied, "You were broken before I used you."

Ash's eyes widened. "Then why did you pick me?"

"I knew it would be difficult to get a reaction from you."

"You didn't want me to react?"

"I like it when it's difficult." His full mouth curved. "I

had to use my cartridge belt on you, and even then you . . . accepted it."

Ash took a step back, hir heart beating faster. "I don't want to remember," s/he said automatically.

"That's when I penetrated you every way I could. You let me do anything to you."

With an oddly familiar sensation, Ash fell into a flashback. Rikev suddenly appeared in his brown Fleet uniform and heavy boots instead of the gray utility coverall given to him by the Qin. Next to hir was a long wall with streamers of green leaves snaking up to the high ceiling. Rikev's golden hand was approaching with the burning end of a laser wand. S/he watched it getting closer, and s/he could hear hirself saying, *"Accept it, accept it."* Hir eyes lifted to the brilliant blue spots of color hopping among the leaves as the laser burned into hir chest. Rikev ordered, *"Look at me. . . ."*

Ash screamed as hir hands scrabbled at hir breastbone. Then s/he was down on the floor, curled around hirself. It took a few moments before s/he realized s/he was back in the brig, surrounded by plain white walls.

Unsealing the neck of hir flightsuit, Ash looked down at the round puckered scar on hir chest where s/he could still feel the searing pain. "Did you burn me?"

Rikev looked amused. "No."

Ash pushed hirself up the wall, warily eyeing him. S/he felt dazed from the vivid flashback. "It must have been the first Rikev."

His eyes narrowed. "I see. You belonged to my clone."

Ash wasn't sure s/he should have told him that.

"How long was he your master?" Rikev pressed.

S/he felt compelled to answer. "Jot says it was over a year."

He seemed satisfied. "That's how you survived. You wanted what he did to you."

It couldn't be true. How could anyone want to be burned? But if hir flashback was correct, s/he had willed hirself to accept it with every bit of hir strength!

"No," Ash cried out, stumbling away from him.

"You need me to remember," Rikev called after hir.

Ash's hand was shaking so hard s/he could hardly press it to the palm pad. S/he burst through the door of the brig to get away from him. The combat team was looking at hir strangely. "Having fun?" one of them snorted.

"That's some therapy," the other agreed.

S/he could see the monitors showing Rikev's cell in the brig. Hir fit had apparently been very entertaining.

Ash put hir head down and scurried away.

The door chimed, and Trace checked to see who it was before letting Takhan into the day cabin. The past few days on the *Solace* had been long and boring for Trace. She was stuck inside the two rooms, trying to avoid the Alpha analyst on board. Their courier was leaving port again, and this was the first time Takhan had come to see her since the Alpha had boarded.

Tahkan pushed back the green hood of her flightsuit, letting her short blond curls spring free. "I wanted to let you know what we heard in the port. Qin battleships have invaded Sol."

Trace clasped her hands together, sinking down on the sofa. "They did it!"

"Like grabbing the wrong end of a laser welder, if you ask me." Takhan sniffed, jamming her hands into her pockets. Trace had seen bots the size of her fist come out of those copious pockets. "They say patrolships are warning ships away from the Procyon sector, and they're stationing patrols at every slip along that border of the Domain. People are talking about evacuation in case of a full-scale invasion. You can bet this is going to get the attention of the Fleet in a major way."

"But they liberated Earth," Trace insisted.

"For the time being," Takhan grudgingly agreed. "Let's just see what happens." A polite knock on the door interrupted her. "I told Jor to meet us here." As Takhan opened the door, she added, "They can't possibly hold it for long—"

Trace gulped back her retort when she realized it wasn't Jor. Herntoff Alpha was standing in the doorway.

Takhan went stiff and she carefully stared into a corner. Trace had never seen the Delta bot tech around an Alpha before, and it wasn't a reassuring sight. Herntoff was taller than the Aborandeen, but he was thin as a support beam. His cheeks were sunken in and his neck was too long and skinny. His wrists and hands poked out of the flightsuit, knobby and awkward. She had watched Herntoff move around the ship on their internal logs, but in person he seemed even more frail.

Herntoff ignored Takhan, staring at Trace. She stood up from the sofa and imitated Takhan, staring off to one side, trying to recover.

"Come with me," Herntoff ordered.

Trace glanced at Takhan, and her panic must have been clear. Takhan darted off, presumably to get Gandre Li.

Trace followed Herntoff up to the lounge and into his cabin, her hand clutching her collar the entire time. She should have asked Nip to deactivate her collar when she had the chance. She had never expected an Alpha to barge into her cabin and order her into his room. Protocol demanded that he speak to her master if he wanted to use her during his lust. She tried to calm down, assuring herself that he only wanted her to run an errand or something.

Herntoff slid his door shut behind him. "When did you last clean yourself?"

Trace had to answer because of her collar. "I just took a sonic shower."

His nose wrinkled slightly in distaste. He turned and rummaged in his large module. "Here, put this over your hair."

He held something out with two fingers. Trace took the piece of rustling cloth and turned it in her hands. There was an elastic band around the edges, forming a crude pleated cap. She pulled it onto her head and stuffed her shiny hair inside. Then she pushed it to the top of her forehead so it wouldn't slip into her eyes.

"Now, get undressed," he ordered.

Trace bit her lip hard. But she was a slave and had no choice. Her finger unsealed the bright orange flightsuit she had put on earlier that morning, hoping it would brighten her drab day. It fell open across her chest as she undid her cartridge belt. She held it in her hand a moment before dropping it on the floor. Usually, pleasure slaves didn't wear flightsuits—they wore skimpy tunics that were open on the sides, revealing everything at the slightest movement.

Herntoff turned away to dig into the big cargo module. He pulled out a large flat circle as Trace stepped out of her boots and flightsuit. She rolled the suit into a ball along with her cartridge belt and set it on top of her boots.

It wasn't like she was going to die. When this Alpha was done with her, she would get dressed and walk out of here. At least, she hoped she would. That was the problem with having absolutely no control over your life: anything could happen.

The door chimed, then chimed again. Herntoff didn't seem surprised. In fact, he watched her to see how she reacted. Trace's mind went blank in self-defense.

Herntoff opened the door. Gandre Li shifted to see around him, her face filled with alarm.

Trace crossed her arms tightly over her bare stomach, with only the sad cap on her head. She knew she looked scared.

"What are you doing with Trace?" Gandre Li demanded.

"You're interrupting my lust," Herntoff retorted.

Gandre Li kept looking at Trace. "She's *my* slave. Why didn't you tell me you wanted her?"

"Do you make a habit of defying Alphas?"

"Trace does *not* come with the price of a ticket," Gandre Li said firmly.

Herntoff pulled out his dataport and consulted it. "The merchant fleet database holds the *Solace*'s registry, of which states: Solian pleasure slave designated 'Trace' is assigned to service the crew and passengers of the *Solace*."

"What?" Gandre Li asked.

"Here it is, in the registry."

Trace shivered slightly. That was the description that automatically came with the category of "pleasure slave." She hadn't opened the registry of the *Solace* for years, not since she had checked to be sure Danal had been added correctly when he joined the crew. Who ever read a ship's registry?

Gandre Li looked like she was thinking the same thing. Herntoff started to close the door in her face.

Trace quickly shook her head so Gandre Li wouldn't try to stop him. They didn't need any trouble right now, not after helping the Solians escape from Archernar shipyard. Her lips twitched into a semblance of a smile, trying to assure her lover that it would be okay. But she desperately hoped that Gandre Li would think of something to save her.

When the door closed behind the captain and locked with a click, Trace thought she might get sick. With all the stress lately, her stomach was not too steady.

Herntoff looked at her for a long time as she stood there swaying, feeling as green as Kwort's complexion. Then Herntoff bent over the flattened cylinder he had pulled out of the module and, with a few quick twists, turned it into a table that floated waist-high. The flat top was shaped into three circles in a row, with holes cut out of the center of each circle.

Herntoff thrust each bony hand into a thin, stretchy glove. "Lie down on the table."

Trace shuffled over to him. She'd had only a few sexual experiences other than with Gandre Li, but none of the Alphas had used a table during their lust.

He lowered the table so she could climb on, perching on the edge of the center circle. The top of the table was covered in a firm padding. She shifted to place her legs on one end, and her buttocks slid into the hole in the center circle. She carefully lowered herself down so her head rested on the top of the upper circle while her shoulders were supported by the lower edge. It was surprisingly comfortable once she got into position.

Herntoff slipped straps around each of her wrists, fastening them through the hole. Then he spread her knees to either side of the bottom circle and strapped them into place.

Trace was fully exposed. If it had been Gandre Li leaning over her instead of this strange man, it might have been erotic. As it was, Trace tried desperately to think about something else, anything else.

Earth.

People on Earth didn't have to endure things like this. People on Earth were free. She remembered Nip's stories about Rose's life on Earth. Solians made their own choices there, and there was no rank. It was still hard for Trace to envision that, but lying on the table she could suddenly see how equality would make all the difference—

"Ouch!" Trace exclaimed at a sharp prick in her upper arm.

Herntoff inserted the syringe into a bioscanner. He was testing her for something. Since he seemed concerned about cleanliness, she hoped she had parasites. Big, hungry ones. Maybe he'd send her back to Gandre Li so she could be quarantined.

"I just got over Yynta virus," she offered helpfully.

He picked up a device and leaned into her face. His fingers pinched open her mouth so he could scrape the inside of her check. Then he gagged her with a knotted piece of cloth. She got the message and concentrated on breathing around the gag.

Herntoff proceeded to put her through the most intensive induction she had ever experienced. He probed and irrigated every crack, crevice, and hole in her body, from her ears to her toenails. She had gone through a few inductions as a girl, when she was being transferred from the creche to Gandre Li, but that had been a highly impersonal experience. Herntoff was different. He monitored every reaction, every wince, every twitch. His gloved fingers had an eager thoroughness that was maddening and more than unpleasant. Some of the things he did really hurt. Soon she was trembling, chilled and sweating at the same time.

Surely he didn't need to examine every microbe to have sex with her! She actually started to wish he would get on with it. Anything would be better than this total invasion.

Then Herntoff moved behind her, standing at the top of the table. Trace couldn't see him. It made her skin crawl. There was no telling what he would do next.

A slight hiss caught her ear. Straining, she tried to listen. Her eyes rolled back in her head, but the way the table was slanted, she couldn't see him.

Could he be . . . ?

Then clearly she heard Herntoff panting. He almost sounded like he was being strangled. Then with a long, rushing sigh, it stopped. He finally sounded normal again, a little out of breath, as footsteps moved around.

After a few moments, he plucked off her cap. With quick, practiced motions, he flicked off the straps tying her to the table and removed the gag from her mouth. "Get out," he ordered.

Trace rolled off the table, her knees buckling. She wobbled over and grabbed her clothes. The biotools Herntoff had used were piled on top of a case he had pulled from the module. The cap lay crumpled on the floor.

Herntoff was standing in the fresher, his back to her.

Trace didn't bother getting dressed. With her flight-suit and boots in her arms, she scurried out the door and down the spiral stairs to the crew deck. Without stopping, she ran back to the day cabin she shared with Gandre Li.

Gandre Li was inside, furiously working at her private terminal. When she saw that Trace had returned, she leapt up.

Trace shut the door and locked it, leaning against it. She realized this was going to be even harder than she thought. Gandre Li looked so upset and guilty as she quickly came toward her. "Trace, what happened?"

Trace could feel the throbbing from the tender bruises on her arms and inner thighs. "N-Nothing."

"But something must have happened. You've been gone for too long—"

Trace dropped her boots. "Don't! Don't ask me!"

She ran into the fresher, shoving the merry orange flightsuit into the recycler on the way. She needed a long sonic shower. She couldn't face Gandre Li right now.

Trace was sure that nothing like that ever happened on Earth.

9

——m——

Mote squirmed her way up the narrow access tube in the center of the umbilicals column. She had discovered she could hear the voices on the command deck of the raider if she stood on the top rung and opened the upper relay chamber. The umbilicals column carried the computer and data-relay conduits from the command deck of the *Vitality* down to engineering, so as a bot tech, she was expected to access this tube.

The three Solian pleasure slaves had been captured along with the *Purpose* when the raiders stole it, leaving Rose and the others stranded on Spacepost T-3. So far Mote and Whit had managed to convince the raiders that their free labor was worth more than their price on the black market as slaves, but Mote doubted that would last much longer.

"What's taking you so long?" Dab called from below. "Is it another cat? I swear they could get inside an energy conduit if they wanted to."

Mote urgently gestured to Dab, motioning her to be quiet. Then she whispered, "Come on up."

Mote had already shown Whit the listening post

under the command deck. She had discovered it during a routine bot diagnostic. Now was as good a time as any to clue in Dab. The more ears they had eavesdropping on the raiders, the better their chances of survival.

By the time Dab reached Mote, the voice overhead was finishing the timetable it would take to install a new shield generator. *"We'll have to use the port corridor. We can't afford to lose any more cargo space."* Mote knew it was Grex, the captain of the *Vitality*. The hardened raider had no soft spots that she could find despite all her wiles and charms.

"I'll get our new bot techs started right away on camouflaging it," Anny agreed. She was Poraccan like Grex, from a planet in the Volans sector. Poraccans were Deltas with black strands of hair, each as thick as an optic cable, hanging in a fat bundle to their waists. Mote could tell that Grex and Anny had known each other for a long time, but they didn't appear to be sex partners. Whit guessed that they were from the same family unit.

"The slaves always do a better job than our real techs," Grex muttered. Mote was glad to hear him admit that the Solians knew more than the Boscans, who were actually paid to do the job. She had worked hard enough with Kwort to learn the craft, but in this case it was native intelligence that gave the Solians an edge. Mote suspected that the tiny heads of the Boscans contained tiny, useless brains. She always wanted to laugh when she saw those miniature faces connected to such big, bumbling bodies.

"So why don't we dump the Boscans before we leave port?" Anny suggested. *"It doesn't rest well with me that they're taking a cut of our take for nothing."*

"No, the Solians have to go," Grex replied flatly.

Mote's fingers tightened on the rung. She had been looking for proof that Grex would abandon them.

"*But why?*" Anny retorted with a touch of passion. "*They've fixed almost every system on board* Vitality. *And they helped us sell that old freighter for a price good enough to get our butts out of hock. Not to mention we'd still be stuck in that spiral nebula in Perspokesor without them.*"

"*That was self-interest on their part,*" Grex dismissed. "*They had to clean out those silicates or we would have all suffered the same fate.*"

Dab jabbed Mote in the stomach, hissing, "See! We shouldn't have helped them."

Mote shook her head to silence Dab. If they hadn't helped the raiders repair the intake systems, Grex and Anny would be arguing about which of them would be better to *eat*. Mote would much rather be faced with a long walk into a strange port than be thrown back in the slave trade. She had hoped to win the raiders' loyalty by giving them the information they needed to legally claim salvage of the *Purpose*. Apparently it had worked for Anny. But after listening to them enough times, she knew Grex made the final decisions on board the *Vitality*.

"*I know they're qualified bot techs,*" Grex agreed evenly. "*But we're sunk if a patrolship discovers three uncollared Solians on board. They'll think we have a back door into Sol, and any semicompetent patrolship captain will turn our brains inside out to find out where it is.*"

"*We can get hold of collars, I'm sure,*" Anny insisted. "*And their disguises are working fine.*"

"*What if they slip? No, the risk isn't worth it.*"

"*What risk?*" another voice asked. Mote perked up

when she realized that Pet Delion had appeared on the command deck. The third command crew member was her secret hope, cultivated carefully during the decnights Mote had been on board the *Vitality*. He was a young humanoid, barely out of adolescence, but as brash and bold as they came, even though he wasn't always right. Mote liked his youthful enthusiasm during sex. Pet was a surprisingly considerate lover, and he never pushed her to do anything she didn't want to. Usually he was satisfied with straight intercourse with a minimum of foreplay, which suited Mote just fine. His three-day cycle had given her plenty of opportunities to make herself necessary to him.

Anny struck fast and deep. *"Grex wants to dump the Solians."*

"What for? They'll do anything to stay on board," Pet protested. *"If we give them a fraction of the cut the Boscans get, that'll mean more for the three of us."*

Grex's tone was ironic. *"You only want to keep your bed toy."*

Mote's eyes opened wide. She thought she'd been discreet. But apparently Grex knew all about her relationship with Pet Delion. Grex himself had persistently rejected her not-so-subtle offers when he was nearing lust. She couldn't understand it.

Pet Delion subsided, probably as surprised as she was that Grex had found out. But Anny valiantly kept up the fight. *"There's no safety in being a raider. I say it's worth it to buy a few collars and fake up a validation that we bought them to crew* Vitality. *Regardless, we can't leave them here in Shingadon. There's too much a chance they'll be picked up and questioned as uncollared slaves. Hopefully Manheim will have the collars."*

"He will." Grex was calm and firm. *"Then I'll take care of the slaves. Meanwhile, have them help with the shield generator."*

They dispersed to their duties as ordered. Grex would surely make the decision, no matter what Anny and Pet said.

Mote climbed down, and once they were standing at the bottom of the utilities column, Dab asked, "What are we going to do?"

"We're going to help Anny install the new shield generator."

"They paid for it with the salvage that was on board the *Purpose*," Dab retorted indignantly. "That was our hard work they sold for a shield generator."

"Consider it our trade so we can live on board *Vitality*. I'm sure you'll be glad to be protected by a stronger shield the next time we get into an argument with a patrolship."

"We won't be here long enough to enjoy it," Dab grumbled. "I'm not going to let them put a collar on me. I'll kill them all in their sleep first. Then we can steal this ship like Rose did."

Mote despaired of ever teaching Dab the art of self-preservation. "Leave all that to Whit and me. Unless you *want* to end up a pleasure slave again. . . ."

Dab warded her off, silenced as usual by Mote's threat. "Come on," Mote sighed.

After many hours of work, Mote was finishing the installation of the new shield generator with one of the mechanics who had been sent along with the unit. Since Mote's knowledge had been gained by experience rather than Fleet training, the mechanic didn't question her ability. As usual, she and Whit wore the Aborandeen-style flightsuit with a hood that covered their short-cut hair. They had added strategic padding to their flight-suits to give their shoulders and hips the rounded Abo-randeen curves. Dab, with her black skin and short stature, was posing as a Trallo, claiming to be Pet De-lion's kin. So far, nobody had questioned their disguises.

"So you're off next to Oberon II," the mechanic said to Mote as they finished linking the power connectors. Whit and Dab were down with the other mechanic mak-ing sure the feeds were installed correctly.

"Yeah," Mote agreed, though she had no clue where they were headed next. "You know what *that's* about. . . ." If he denied it, then she would shrug as if she refused to be the one to spread gossip.

"I won a bet that Grex would take the boss's job," the mechanic agreed with satisfaction. "Not many ships would run laser arrays with all the raider activity going on. Too many patrolships have been called away from their runs to guard against the Qin invasion."

Mote swallowed. So that's what the Boscans had been busy loading while the Solians were occupied with installing the shield generator. Since there was a need for a ship like *Vitality,* Mote figured those laser arrays weren't perfectly legal.

"The price is worth it," Mote bluffed with a smile.

"True, the *Regard* is one of the best in the business. Teaming with them makes sense for your crew."

Mote nodded sagely, realizing that the laser-array job was a test. Grex was hoping to team up with another es-tablished raider to increase their chances of fending off patrolships and other raiders. The last few battleships in Canopus had been recalled to the Regional Headquarters, presumably to be sent into Qin, but that left Canopus exposed. Shipping in the region was disrupted from the fuel shortages, except for the raiders who had always relied on their own covert black-market supply lines. The spacers in the rough ports they visited said it was freer, the way it was before Canopus officially became a region of the Domain. But the general alarm meant that the few patrolships left in the populated areas were quicker to go for the death strike when they did encounter a raider. Traveling in pairs would give them added protection.

Mote glanced up and saw Captain Grex standing at the other end of the blocked corridor listening to them. He was holding one of the ship's numerous cats in his arms. For a man who was considered ruthless by his peers, he was curiously kind to the small animals. Mote was trying to learn their secret appeal to the captain and often took one or two into the barracks when she was off-duty to pet and play with them.

"We're almost done, Captain," Mote said to cover her confusion.

Grex merely stood there as they finished the job. His burnt orange skin and smashed-in features made him appear to frown, but Mote knew that was a trick of his physiology.

Still, it was uncomfortable for her, though the mechanic didn't seem to realize anything was wrong. He powered up the shield generator and the systems were run through their final tests. Anny reported from the command deck that their shields had twice the energy capacity as before.

Mote decided it was a strategic time to retreat while Grex dealt with the mechanics.

As she passed, Grex said quietly, "I see right through you, Mote."

Mote met his eyes. "Then you know I won't do anything to hurt you."

Grex held her gaze silently until she turned away. Someday she would make him trust her.

Dab was helping Mote move a bench, but she was doing most of the heavy lifting as usual. Because her body was in better shape than ever since she had developed a more challenging exercise regime, she didn't mind helping when Captain Grex ordered them to create a workroom out of the narrow space that had been formed by closing off the corridor to hold the new shield generator. The workroom would help camouflage the new installation.

Dab wished she could live inside the skinny room. She didn't like the armored barracks with the eye in the ceiling. The three Solians were forced to stay in the raider's makeshift brig because the few berths on board were filled by the crew. It made Dab's skin crawl to know that any of the command crew could watch the Solians whenever they were lounging or sleeping. Their life on the tiny courier was barely a notch above slavery as far as she was concerned.

If Rose were here, she wouldn't put up with this—

Running footsteps caught up to them as Captain Grex and Anny arrived. Grex's scowl betrayed nothing, but Anny seemed flustered. "Move it," she demanded. "There's a port official at the airlock. You two get inside the workroom."

Mote activated the antigrav unit, lifting the unwieldy bench so Grex and Anny could pass underneath. Then she barked out orders to Dab, who did most of the work maneuvering the bench into place inside the workroom. Mote looked very different in her Aborandeen flightsuit, but she was still as worried and hyper as she had been on board the *Purpose*.

Mote closed the door, leaving it slightly open so she could look out. Dab went down to her knees so she could see, too.

Captain Grex and Anny reappeared at the end of the corridor with an Ubress. He carried a large dataport and was looking around eagerly, his crescent-shaped eyes and mouth carefully hiding his feelings. Dab particularly disliked Ubress because they demanded to be pleasured, forcing the slave to perform to command. They were relentless, exacting, and fussy.

"We don't need port certification," Anny was explaining. "Give us our debarkation time, and we'll call it quits."

"All major installations must receive a port certification. You were informed." The Ubress paused to check his dataport and gave them a string of official-sounding regulations along with the identity code of the installation company and their work order number. "I must also see the certification for your laser array. For a G-class courier, owned and operated by Deltas, this ship has a high profile."

"It's dangerous times for smaller ships," Grex replied gruffly. "Raiders everywhere you turn, running in packs now. An honest merchant can hardly survive."

"Hence the new shield generator." The Ubress seemed pleased with himself. "Your cargo manifests are also required. It will be interesting to see what an 'honest merchant' transports in these dangerous times."

Behind the door, Mote grabbed Dab's shoulder with one hand. "Ow!" Dab grunted.

"This is bad!" Mote hissed.

Dab knew that the ship had been loaded with components for laser arrays, and that they probably didn't have the proper registration for them. No Fleet official would let them out of sight with that much undocumented weaponry. The best they could hope for was that their cargo was impounded and they were released.

Grex was caught. He stiffly told Anny, "Show him the shield generator. I'll get the manifest and certification."

Anny managed a squashed smile as Grex abruptly left. "Nice of the Shingadon port to certify new installations."

"If you got a faulty system, you'd come complaining to our officials," the Ubress sniffed. "Saves us time in the long run."

Mote frantically shook Dab's shoulder. "That's a Gamma, isn't it?" At Dab's assent, she rushed on. "What do they like? Sexually, I mean."

Indignantly Dab stared at her. "Look it up yourself."

Urgently, Mote leaned over. "It's our only chance, Dab! Do you want to be servicing him and his friends tonight after we've been taken into custody by the port?"

Dab gulped. That was the *last* thing she wanted. "He's an Ubress. He'd respond to almost anything right now. He's in the pre-lust phase. I can tell by the swelling in his groin and how quivery he is."

Mote kissed the top of Dab's head in her enthusiasm.

Anny and the Ubress were nearing them when Mote opened the door. Dab pulled back, instinctively avoiding the Gamma.

"Anny, I'll show the port official our shield generator."

Mote's mouth opened slightly and the curved pink end of her tongue appeared suggestively.

Dab swallowed hard. She wasn't used to thinking of Mote in a sexual way, but even she couldn't deny that the girl certainly had a special sensual allure about her. Mote slinked forward, one deliberate step at a time, putting her body on display. Her shoulders dipped and her padded hips moved suggestively in and out. Since Mote was disguised as an Aborandeen, she looked even more mammalian and enticing.

Anny couldn't help seeing Mote roll out the welcome mat. Her eyes shifted quickly to the Ubress, whose crescent mouth had fallen open. Anny cleared her throat. "Fine, I'll leave this in your capable hands."

Mote leaned closer to the Ubress, murmuring, "Come this way. You can access it better from in here."

The Ubress pranced after her. Dab slipped out behind him. The door slammed closed, practically on her heels.

Dab blinked at the closed door. "Is Mote doing what I think she's doing?"

"Yes," Anny replied.

"With a port official?" Dab asked, as if she couldn't believe her eyes.

"It's a bribe." Anny glanced in admiration at the closed door. "Mote's making sure he won't rat on us. He gets what he wants, we get what we want. We have something on him, he has something on us. We're even."

Dab wanted to storm off to her semiprivate room but she was afraid to leave Mote with that slick Gamma. What if Mote needed her? She couldn't desert her just because Mote had bad taste.

Anny seemed similarly torn. She could call Grex

down from the command deck, but apparently she wanted to give Mote a chance to make this work.

"How long will it be?" Anny finally asked after a good chunk of time passed.

"What makes you think I know?" Dab demanded defensively.

"You're a pleasure slave, aren't you?

Dab let out a ragged breath. "Could be two hours or more." She was sure Mote hadn't known that when she went in there with the Ubress. She was probably on her knees right now, using her tongue on his body. Most Ubress liked being licked and penetrated by a flexible tongue, maybe because they had unusually small penises. Dab shuddered, trying not to remember her own sessions with Ubress.

Finally Captain Grex returned with the datarod. "What's going on here? Where's the port official?"

Dab and Anny silently pointed to the closed door of the workroom.

"What's he doing in there?" Grex realized Mote was gone. "She isn't . . ."

"She is." Anny let out a short laugh. "Better that he's in there instead of searching our cargo bays."

Grex clenched the datarod, and glared at Dab. "She better not be selling me out!"

Dab put her fists on her hips, facing him down. "Mote's saving your ass, Delta! Like she's done before."

Grex glanced at Anny, who crossed her arms and nodded in support of Dab. "Maybe . . ." he said reluctantly.

It was a full two hours before Mote appeared in the doorway. She looked weary, but her flightsuit was still on. Dab had been afraid the Ubress would realize she was not Aborandeen, but apparently he hadn't noticed. Mote flexed her jaw gingerly, and her face was shiny damp, but other than that she looked fine.

The port official bustled by without a word. It must have been daunting to see all of them waiting for him to emerge, but he didn't show it.

Grex signaled to Anny, who ran after the Ubress to let him through the airlock. She gave him the falsified manifest Grex had created while they waited. He glanced down at the real manifest on the datarod in his hand, knowing how close he had come to losing all those laser components.

"I take it he's satisfied by our certification?" Grex dryly asked Mote.

Mote pushed the hood of her flightsuit back, revealing the bright red fuzz of her hair. "No complaints."

Dab said apologetically, "Sorry I didn't tell you how long it would take."

Mote waved one hand. "All in a day's work." She was watching Grex as she said it.

Anny returned. "Well done, Mote! If we had lost this shipment, the *Regard* would never team with us."

"Any time," Mote assured her. "I'm sure Whit would help out if needed, too."

"You better ask *him* about that," Dab protested.

Mote shrugged and left for their room. Anny and Grex stared at each other as if silently communicating.

"If that's what you expect from me," Dab hastened to assure them, "you might as well toss me out right now. I'll do anything I can to help you with the ship, but I'm not pleasuring *anyone*."

Dab stalked off without looking back. She didn't care

if she ruined everything Mote had accomplished. If she got thrown back in the slave trade, she'd deal with it then. Not before. Not even to stay alive.

Whit helped Pet Delion set down the last pallet of laser array components in the muddy track next to *Vitality*. The courier had landed on Oberon II . . . a no-account ball of rock somewhere in the Pyxis sector.

Whit turned to look at the tops of the mountains around them, watching the pale green sky for any movement that could be an airship. It was a reflexive instinct. He knew Anny was at the scanners and would alert them if any vessel came near, but Whit couldn't stop searching the skies whenever the *Vitality* landed on a planet.

Pet Delion took a deep breath. "Like some kind of drug, isn't it?"

"For those who care about air," Whit agreed. Pet wasn't sure if that was an insult or not. The furry Trallo was much shorter than Whit, but he was cocky enough for a man twice his size. Whit liked to imagine the little guy having sex with tall, slender Mote.

Whit leaned against the pallet as Captain Grex walked toward the trio of smugglers who emerged from the two family yachts on the other side of the landing pad. Whit kept an eye on things, knowing he would have to be Grex's muscle if needed. The Boscans weren't bright enough to know when trouble was sitting on their face. The one thing they were good at was manual labor. They had unloaded the laser components from the cargo bays in record time. Whit was sure the bot techs feared for their jobs. The Boscans hadn't lost their small fleshy heads so far, but it was a dangerous situation for everyone on board the *Vitality*. Something had to give.

Whit had visited a handful of planets since joining up with the raiders. Wild places like this were why the Fleet would never completely control Domain space. There were too many hundreds of thousands of worlds, home to dirt-bound colonists who needed to make some kind of living. These poor planets formed a vast shadow domain that coexisted alongside the real one. It overlapped in places, but Whit was glad to see that Grex avoided the ports and starbases that belonged to the Fleet.

Pet Delion and the Boscans were lounging on the pallets soaking up the native sun, waiting for further orders. Grex had told Mote and Dab to wait inside the *Vitality*. He was reluctant to expose the Solians to more people than necessary. And ever since Mote had saved their cargo by pleasuring that port official, Grex had been even more uncomfortable around her—

Whit's eyes abruptly stopped in their sweep of the mountains. He suddenly focused on the bore of a fat laser cannon pointed at them. It was big enough to disable the *Vitality*.

Casually, he glanced away. Where there was one laser cannon, there would be more. Along with people watching their target.

Whit leaned closer to Pet. "Tell Anny there's a laser cannon in the woods." Pet's head lifted sharply, but Whit grabbed on to his arm. "Don't let on that we know."

Pet might hardly be a man, but he had already learned the need for deception. He laid back so his mouth would be close to the comm and quietly informed Anny of the situation.

"She'll let the captain know," Pet informed Whit, putting one hand over his face to shield his eyes from the sun.

Whit knew the crew of the *Vitality* had their own ways even though Grex wasn't wearing a comm link. Soon Grex casually turned from the negotiations to glance back at them. Whit positioned his body so he could point toward the laser cannon. It had a perfect shot down the *Vitality*'s intake ports.

"Should we be thinking about getting inside?" Pet Delion asked uncertainly.

"Not yet," Whit murmured.

"I was asking Anny, not you!" Pet retorted. His face fell a few moments later as Anny apparently told him the same thing.

After a tense wait, Grex broke away from the smugglers to return separately to their ships. Pet sat up as if shocked by a faulty bot. "Anny says we should get inside quickly."

"The Boscans won't listen to me," Whit reminded him.

Pet jumped up and called for the Boscans to follow him. Whit timed his retreat more slowly so he could meet Grex at the airlock. Pet and the Boscans went through at Grex's wave.

"Now what?" Whit asked quietly.

"We have to wait for them to verify the contents. The laser cannon are there in case we decide to take off without giving them what they paid for."

Whit uneasily stood next to Grex as several smugglers came over to the pallets. He could see only their eyes within the enveloping drapes, so he wasn't sure what type of humanoids they were. They began scanning and unpacking the components onto their antigrav sleds. They weren't taking any chances. From Grex's relaxed stance, Whit figured there was nothing to worry about on that score.

This was the best chance he would get to talk to Grex without being spied on by the rest of the crew. "The Boscans didn't see a thing," he told Grex. "It must be tough having only one crew member you can rely on."

Grex gave him a sidelong look. "You think highly of yourself."

"I think highly of the three of us. We have what you need."

"You slaves are nothing but trouble waiting to happen."

Whit shrugged. "Nobody's questioned us yet. And there are ways to enhance our cover." Mote had already mentioned her willingness to get biophysical alteration to give her the well-rounded curves that Aborandeens were famous for. She had tried eating more to put on flesh like Whit, but her genetically engineered body refused to become pudgy. Thankfully, they both had facial structures that resembled the square-edged Aborandeens. "You know Mote is worth her weight in credit chips. That port official might not have taken your bribe."

"What makes you think I was going to bribe him?" Grex watched the smugglers examine his cargo, giving brief piercing attention to the wooded hills.

"What else could you do?" Whit leaned in confidentially. "I also know you're thinking of leaving us somewhere outside of Procyon where three uncollared Solians won't attract as much attention. But I can guarantee that Dab won't keep her mouth shut about the *Vitality*. You know Mote and I can't control her."

"Dab *is* the only independent one among you."

Whit was surprised to hear grudging admiration in his voice. Grex probably didn't realize it himself. Whit agreed, "Dab would rather die than live a lie."

Grex's face seemed to relax as he thought about the spunky Solian.

Whit decided then and there to stop having sex with Dab. She wouldn't be happy about it, and he would miss his regular sex partner. But if Captain Grex could bring himself to desire Dab, that would be the best thing for all of them. Dab wouldn't have to know a thing about it. . . .

The smugglers were finishing their examination. Grex returned the go-ahead signal from the lead smuggler and ushered Whit into the airlock. "Let's get out of here."

Inside, Grex stared briefly ahead for a moment. Whit realized he was using a comm implant. The fact that Grex was finally revealing it to him must mean something.

The *Vitality* shuddered and lifted. Whit looked out the portal behind Grex. If the smugglers wanted to stop them, the laser cannon would open up now.

The yellowish mud dropped away, then the verdant hillsides. Soon they had cleared the upper peaks of the surrounding mountains and were aimed for the pale green sky. That was the best thing about couriers, in Whit's opinion. Like family yachts and shuttles, they could travel in space or down to a planet. Since he had been freed, Whit had seen more worlds than he had as a pleasure slave. He intended his travels to continue.

"You Solians will split one-tenth profit between the three of you," Grex told him quietly. "Don't say anything to the others until I drop off the Boscans."

Whit nodded, looking serious. "Good idea." This would be the first confidence he kept for Grex. Soon the captain would realize he could trust Whit with his life. Whit knew he could be a loyal crew member, because Rose had taught him how.

10

G'kaan held up both hands, trying to slow Rose down. As usual, her solution to every problem involved blowing something up. In this case it was the World Council building with the members of the council in it. "We need to consider every angle of this before we act. The World Council promotes trade of important technology and upholds fair laws around the planet. There will be chaos if we destroy it."

"We need to up-end everything to make change," Rose insisted.

Enzo and Margarita seemed equally as concerned. They had been living on the moonbase for the past few days and, with the benefit of their new translator implants, were helping to coordinate the preparations for the revolt. Enzo looked tired enough to drop, but Margarita burned with an unquenchable desire that reminded Rose of her own.

Rose had chafed at the delay while the abductees were quietly returned to their homes with instructions on how to proceed once the revolt began. G'kaan was counting on the abductees' help, but Earth was a huge and densely populated world. Qin colonies didn't have such a dense web of humanity. Even the central part of North America was filled with people despite the damage caused by the catastrophic eruption a century ago.

It had taken days to clandestinely return over a hundred abductees to different parts of the world. The abductees were eager to start spreading the word about the slave trade. They also carried the specs for grav technology and information about the Domain's operations in Sol. With such weighty data, G'kaan was a surprised that word of their arrival had not yet leaked. They were running out of time and would have to start soon.

Rose defiantly faced down her elders. "You don't act like leaders of a revolution!"

"Many people will die as a result of our actions," Margarita replied. "This isn't a decision to make lightly."

"Well, I saw lots of people die after they were abducted," Rose countered. "And the ones who didn't die were sexually tortured!"

"We're righting that wrong," G'kaan agreed. "But I think it would be wiser to bring the World Council onto our side. They could make the transition easier. It will be shocking enough for your people to find they're being culled as pleasure slaves."

"The council has a stranglehold on Earth." Rose glared at him. "We aren't Qin. Solians are emotional people, and the World Council does nothing but manipulate us. You've seen the crap they cram through the net!"

Enzo wearily passed his hand through his gray-speckled hair. "Rose is right, we must remove the power structure for this to work. The World Council has authority over the armed forces on every continent."

"It's not enough to take over the net and airwaves,"

Rose agreed. "We have to hit them hard or no one will believe us. Especially if the World Council is denying everything we say and backing up their lies with missiles."

G'kaan turned to Margarita and Enzo. "What do you think are the chances of convincing the World Council to join us?"

Margarita hesitated. She was truly the embodiment of native resistance. She had perfected the art over years, according to the stories she had told G'kaan. "While the Domain is held at bay, they would certainly make the appearance of joining us. The question is: What are the chances of Fleet returning to Sol?"

G'kaan gave her one look, and Margarita instantly understood their perilous position. He had tried to talk about it with Rose, but she couldn't seem to think beyond their immediate needs. He wasn't sure if Rose grasped that their stay in Sol would eventually be cut short by Fleet battleships coming back to take what they had lost.

"We must consider the future," Margartia murmured as her hand went into Enzo's. They were the ones who would be at risk on Earth when the Fleet returned, so it was their decision to make for their people.

"Who cares about tomorrow?" Rose countered. "We need to figure out what to do *now*."

Margarita gave Rose an indulgent smile. "The underground has been working to free Earth for generations."

"You didn't help me!" Rose put her hands on her hips.

Rose had her own biases and history that none of the rest of them shared, G'kaan reflected, but they all seemed to be in agreement on the basics.

"I'll use the *Relevance*," Rose declared. "But my missiles will take out more than the council complex."

"No, I'll do it," G'kaan assured her. "Lasers will make

a cleaner strike." The buildings that housed the World Council members and their offices covered a large section of an enclave at the end of the Zurich-see. Most of the people they would kill were innocent, and he didn't want to add to that number by being sloppy.

"Really?" When Rose realized they were agreeing with her, her anger suddenly disappeared. "Then what are we waiting for?"

G'kaan appreciated it when Enzo and Margarita insisted on personally viewing the attack on the World Council. Rose also wanted to watch, for her own reasons. G'kaan ferried them up to his battleship and led the way to the command deck.

He knew that their decision was final, but it was no victory for a warrior to kill thousands of civilian leaders without warning. He longed for some of S'jen's ruthlessness. She would press the fire sequence without a qualm.

Apparently Rose was the same way. She was grinning as G'kaan's experienced command crew took their positions. Margarita and Enzo stood to one side, where they could see the imager.

"Is the broadcast ready?" G'kaan asked. M'ke would be responsible for taking over Earth's communications and sending the information packets to the proper destinations according to language. The abductees had created packets in twenty-one major languages, figuring that would start a ripple-wave of translations.

"Affirmative," M'ke acknowledged. "The information will be sent simultaneously through the repeater satellites we've accessed."

G'kaan nodded to him and L'pash at ops, then seated himself at the helm. "Prepare to break high orbit."

L'pash looked at him in surprise. This wasn't part of the short liberation drill they had been practicing. During their last briefing session, L'pash had been as impatient as Rose was to complete their mission and get back to Qin. She was worried about going into lust while they occupied Sol, and was convinced that the Fleet would retaliate much faster than G'kaan's projections. But M'ke had agreed that they should remain in Sol for as long as possible to distract the Domain. Since L'pash had been overeager to abandon Sol, G'kaan had later called M'ke in alone to talk about their options for dealing with the World Council.

"Raise shields," G'kaan ordered.

"Shields raised." L'pash complied automatically, but her expression was sulky. She knew she had been left out of planning.

"I'm taking us down." G'kaan lightly touched the helm to bring the *Endurance* into a descent. Unlike smaller spaceships, a battleship couldn't maintain structural integrity within the troposphere. But they could enter the mesosphere, where atmosphere met space.

The deep arc of the blue and white globe soon blocked the blackness beyond. Helm response grew sluggish, and shields kicked into maximum coverage as the hull began to heat up from the friction. G'kaan needed to get closer for pinpoint precision.

L'pash concentrated on maintaining structural integrity, refraining from asking questions. She never showed weakness in front of the Solians, especially Rose. Rose usually seemed to forget that L'pash existed.

"Targeting scanners activated," G'kaan said grimly. His terminal blinked with information as they passed over the North American continent.

M'ke met his eyes briefly, understanding how hard this was for G'kaan. Margarita had her hands clasped under her chin as her lips moved silently, while Enzo's head was lowered respectfully. Rose leaned forward eagerly, as she always did during a battle.

The World Council complex was entering range. The mountains appeared in the imager. G'kaan made sure the lasers were on their lowest setting and narrowest aperture.

"Target locked on the World Council complex," G'kaan confirmed aloud.

His heart skipped a beat as his thumb hesitated over the firing sequencer. Children were in that complex where the council members and their staff lived . . . he couldn't—

But he must. An entire planet was at stake. It was the fault of his Qin ancestors that these Solians had been enslaved in the first place. G'kaan knew that he would have to accept the dishonor of killing innocent civilians in order to right the wrong Qin had done.

"Firing lasers." G'kaan pressed the sequencer automatically as he spoke. The red beams of concentrated energy slashed toward the folds of the mountains. A reflective blue lake burned ruddy with the light; then the explosion blocked out everything below.

Margarita let out a cry of profound regret, while her husband comforted her. G'kaan didn't want to look at Rose, afraid that he would see something that would remind him of S'jen.

"Broadcast," G'kaan ordered huskily.

"Downloading the packets," M'ke confirmed.

While G'kaan returned them to standard orbit, M'ke concentrated on his task. "Packets are replaying on all frequencies and information networks."

G'kaan couldn't help glancing at Rose this time. In those packets was information implicating her own mother. It wasn't only innocent people who would die today. Rose's mother would be killed along with the other guilty ones. Had she no remorse?

Rose met his eyes defiantly. She knew. And deep down she probably cared, but she wouldn't admit it, even to herself. The silence went on for a long time on the command deck until they approached Zurich-see once more.

"It's burning!" Margarita exclaimed, her hands at her mouth.

The imager magnified in rapid succession, locking on to the coordinates. Smoke and flames engulfed the sprawling enclave next to an impossibly blue lake. G'kaan grimly checked his terminal, but the settings were on minimum power. He wished he didn't have to see what he had done.

M'ke shook his head over his scanners. "Many of the building materials are combustible. Even missiles would have ignited it."

"All those people . . ." Margarita groaned.

Rose lifted her chin. "Good!"

G'kaan sat back, realizing there was nothing left for him to do. "Let the riots begin."

Rose was disappointed by how long it took to overpower the military centers that had once been controlled by the World Council. Too many missiles were fired at orbital satellites and neighboring enclaves. G'kaan's crew was kept busy putting down local military resistance all over the world.

Margarita and Enzo returned to the moonbase to run

the coup from there, coordinating their underground contacts and reestablishing contact with the abductees. The couple was upset when a third of the abductees didn't check in, but Rose figured they were busy rebelling.

It took two shifts for G'kaan to decide that it was safe enough for them to travel down to Earth. Rose wouldn't have missed it for anything, so she joined G'kaan and Chad in the armored pinnace called *Pluck*. Chad handled the scanners and soon pointed out that every large enclave was pocked by fires. Even some of the smaller ones were in turmoil. As they flew from one continent to the next, they saw the inferno everywhere except for the poorer areas where people were more widely scattered.

They hovered over an enclave on the Asian continent. Nearly a quarter of the buildings were lit up in flames.

"I've never destroyed an entire world before," G'kaan said morosely.

Rose thought that for a guy who had been fighting the Domain for most of his life, G'kaan was having a tough time dealing with their revolt. Guilt never did any good. She had sworn off it herself. Recently, any time she felt sorry for herself, she went to see Bolt in the brig. The sight of him languishing in the cell always brightened her up.

"The mobs seem to be destroying the airports and communications systems," Chad noted. "And breaking into warehouses and stores."

Rose was using her terminal to log different views for her crew to see. "It's like they're trying to cut themselves off from everyone else."

Chad shook his head. "I don't get it. Why aren't they working together?"

"They don't trust anyone," Rose told him. "I wouldn't."

From the helm at the front, G'kaan agreed, "It's typical for humanoids to fight amongst themselves in times of crisis."

"The problem here on Earth," Rose said, "is that a few people controlled everything and sold out the rest. That's the biggest reason I know for demolishing government."

"There has to be some sort of central coordination," Chad insisted. "As long as it upholds inalienable rights."

"Sure, the right to be left alone by aliens!" Rose figured Chad was parroting one of G'kaan's lessons. She could hear the Qin's inflections in every word.

"There are governments where everyone has an equal say in what happens to them. Like the Qin clans, and how we do it in our conclaves."

Rose laughed and pointed out the portal. "Did these people have a say in what we did to them?"

Chad shut up at that, while G'kaan looked uncomfortable. Just because G'kaan had trained him to be some kind of superspy, Chad acted like the Qin had all the answers.

Rose had considered giving Chad the transport ship they had captured so he could go back to Qin to fetch the hundreds of former slaves they had left on Prian. That would get rid of Chad, and it was about time they helped those poor Solians. Bringing them back to Earth would solve the problem. But G'kaan had already given the transport to one of his Qin corpsmen, and crewed it with a handful of Solian underground members trained in high-speed atmospheric aircraft. G'kaan claimed he had other plans for Chad.

From the Asian enclave, G'kaan flew up and over to North America. The band of enclaves that stretched across Canada were in good shape. The fields had already been harvested, and Chad noted that the grain silos that dotted the land were unharmed. Even the largest enclaves had little damage. Margarita and Enzo must be happy about that, since Canada was an underground stronghold. Rose remembered Jac, the older man abducted from Ontario, who had been in the cube stack with her. Where was he now in the slave trade?

G'kaan didn't spend much time with the middle of the continent, where a number of smaller enclaves were formed among concrete islands of ruins. Instead, he went directly to Tijuana along the western coast. There were minor enclaves surrounding Tijuana and a thick scattering of homesteads in the mountains. A lot more than Rose had realized, growing up secure in the heart of the city.

"Government buildings and airport destroyed," Chad ticked off. "The rail lines have also been pulled up. And lots of warehouse damage."

Rose set her lips. "People are hungry in the shelters and *barrios*."

G'kaan asked Chad to check on Manuel's bar. It was unharmed. The closest fire was burning itself out a few blocks away. The mud brick stopped it from spreading far. It looked as if Enzo and Margarita's hilltop house had also survived. They must have instructed their armed guards to protect their home.

Then G'kaan looked over his shoulder at Rose. "Now, how about your mother?"

"What about her?" Rose retorted.

"We should see if she's all right."

"Not interested."

Rose thought that would be the end of it, but G'kaan turned to face her. "You need to find out, Rose."

Chad was listening with interest. Rather than argue with G'kaan in front of him, Rose admitted, "She lives in the civ complex. We'll have to go higher up."

Her old apartment building wasn't burning, as she thought it would be. But other parts of the civ complex were on fire, including the massive council tower where the civs had their office suites and meeting rooms. Her mother had practically lived there, so Rose was pretty sure that was the end of the story. At least that was a clean death.

G'kaan set the pinnace down on the roof. G'kaan handed out primed stunguns and cautioned them to keep watch on all sides. Chad used one of his mini-laser-wands to burn open the locked door leading to the stair-well. Rose led Chad and G'kaan down two flights.

The regular lights in the hallway were off, leaving a pale glow from the round white emergency lights. The hall was dark and unusually quiet, with none of the familiar smells of cooking or sounds of music penetrating the walls that Rose remembered from her childhood.

Then they passed an open door. A ransacked room lay beyond. Rose hurried past it to her own apartment.

The door swung open at a touch. The huge window reflected the smoky orange glow hanging over Tijuana. For a moment, Rose couldn't see inside the shadowed room.

"Somebody's been here," Chad said, pushing past her.

G'kaan went over to the tumbled, slashed sofa, his feet crunching on broken glass and pottery shards on the tiles. "Move fast."

In a daze, Rose checked her own room. The sight of it woke her up. The red walls had been painted a bland tan and boxes were strewn across the floor. Her bed and furniture were gone, replaced by a large desk and a new couch. Rose realized that the stuff spilling from the boxes was her old clothes and belongings. She bent down and picked up her favorite poncho. The suede felt incredibly soft against her hand.

"Rose!" G'kaan called softly from the doorway. "There's nobody here. We have to go."

She dropped the poncho, wiping her hands on her flightsuit when she remembered the last time she had worn it. The night she had sex with Bolt. The night that he had introduced her to the underground.

Out in the main room, Chad was on his toes, waiting for them. "Let's get out of here—"

"Hold it right there!" A flood of bright light hit Rose's eyes, making her flinch. "Throw down your weapons!"

It was one of the security guards who protected the civ complex. "I live here!" Rose exclaimed, hoping Chad wouldn't stun the guard. "Rose Rico. You *must* remember me."

The light lowered slightly. "Little Rosa Rico? I thought you were dead."

Rose recognized Pilar, one of the more likable guards. The others had harassed her, but Pilar had been fair, at least. Chad held his ground, waiting to see what would happen, while G'kaan wisely stayed back in the shadows, hiding his Qin features.

Pilar aimed her light at the floor, "Where've you been, Rosa?"

Rose waved that off. "I'm looking for my mother. Where is she?"

"She was taken along with other civs. They broke in, killed Gonzales." Rose grimaced, having no love for that macho *renegado*. "The rest of the civs barricaded themselves inside their apartments. We're trying to keep everyone else out."

Rose's sympathy was with the peons. "Where did they take the civs?"

"To the arena." Pilar shuddered. "You better not go there."

Rose kept Pilar's attention on herself as they left so G'kaan could escape back up the stairs. Pilar wanted to lecture her about landing a craft on the roof. Rose shook her off figuring that some people would never get it. Everything was different now. The civs who had survived were going to have to come out sometime, and they were going to discover real fast that they didn't run everything anymore.

When Rose reached the pinnace, G'kaan looked at her questioningly. She retorted, "We're going to the arena."

"Are you sure about this?" he asked.

"You practically dragged me here. Now you have to see it through."

G'kaan shrugged and followed her directions to the bloodsports arena. Long before they reached the circular, tiered stadium, the streets were thronged with mostly dark-haired people. Inside the arena, the rows of seats were filled to overflowing, with the aisles and stairways perilously full.

In the center of the arena, makeshift gallows had been erected. People hung from the ropes, their feet twisting. More civs were being dragged out to be strung up. The audience in the arena cheered at this early, impromptu display of blood, even if it wasn't a sport.

Rose narrowed in the scanner to see if she could identify her mother's features in one of the hanging corpses. There were plenty of women strung up, with their long, dark hair blowing in the gusts of wind, but no matter how hard she tried, she couldn't recognize her mother among them. Not that she had any doubt that Silvia was dangling there dead right at this moment.

"She got what she deserved," Rose muttered.

G'kaan frowned at her. "You better not cut off all your feelings, Rose. You don't want to end up like S'jen, do you?"

Rose shrugged angrily. "What do you want from me? Tears because my dear mother, who abandoned me, is gone? It was *her* fault I was abducted!"

"Are you sure about that?" G'kaan asked quietly.

Rose jerked her chin, refusing to look at him. "As sure as I am about anything."

Chad looked up from his terminal in horror. "Well I think this is awful. I bet some of those people are innocent."

"No civ is innocent," Rose said flatly. "They had it coming."

After taking logs of the arena, G'kaan silently pulled away. Rose was glad he didn't encourage Chad. She knew the truth. Nothing would change until they wiped everything clean. Earth would be a better place without her mother.

11

C'vid glanced up from her routine scans of the gravity pocket to see Admiral J'kart absorbed in the latest dispatches from the defense net. The Qin Armada had deployed nearly a hundred warships in a dense web around their territory, excluding the four ravaged colonies that had already suffered the worst. The battleship *Defiance* was posted in the innermost layer of that web, prepared to be dispatched to half the surrounding gravity pockets in the event of a Fleet invasion.

S'jen was at the helm, her face stony with resentment. Her hands were clasped in her lap, because their ship was motionless not far from the pivotal grav slip. The waiting game didn't suit S'jen. C'vid was worried about her. Nobody else, other than B'hom, ever worried about S'jen. People who didn't know her thought she was invulnerable, but C'vid knew how much S'jen had been hurt.

C'vid sighed and turned back to the comm. At least their battleship had been sent to support the defense net instead of being left behind at Po Alta—

A light flashed among the gravity indicators as a

surge of gravitons was detected by the scanners. "Captain, there's a ship coming through the slip!" C'vid announced. The warship on the other side had already checked in this shift, so this could be the beginning of a Fleet offensive.

S'jen was accessing her terminal, using the navigational scanners. "Battle alert! Weapons charged."

Everyone on the command deck was suddenly wide awake. The admiral tapped into C'vid's scanner to see the data for himself.

As the gravity burst stabilized prior to entry, C'vid added, "It's the right size for a warship."

In the imager, a three-dimensional icon of the *Resolve* appeared in their pocket. C'vid could see through the semitransparent imager to B'hom grinning across from her.

The transceiver beeped. "They're hailing us." C'vid hardly waited for S'jen's acknowledgment to open the channel, routing it to the imager.

The new captain of the *Resolve* appeared. A'ston had frosted tan fuzz, and looked very much like J'kart. C'vid was used to seeing G'kaan as the captain of the *Resolve*, so it was a bit disorienting. The *Fury*, their old beloved warship, was stationed on the outer edge of the defense net, also under a new captain.

"You can stand down, Captain S'jen," Captain A'ston said. *"This is no alert. But we do have news from the Domain."*

S'jen nodded stiffly. "Admiral J'kart is on the command deck. You can proceed."

"Admiral, our long-range scouts have picked up rumors that are gaining credibility in Canopus." A'ston's fangs were showing in her enthusiasm. *"They're saying a*

Qin battleship has invaded Sol! Procyon is filled with patrol-ships that are sealing the borders of the Domain."

"G'kaan!" Admiral J'kart shook his fist in satisfaction. "He has struck a blow worthy of Qin's highest honors!"

A'ston fiercely agreed. *"The Domain is in panic."*

S'jen was blank-faced. "Anything else?"

"Isn't that enough?" A'ston retorted. *"I leave it to you, Admiral, to pass the news to Armada Central."*

C'vid closed the channel, terminating Captain A'ston almost too abruptly. She did it because she could tell that S'jen was upset by the news.

Admiral J'kart, on the other hand, was more pleased than C'vid had ever seen. "Sol!" he exclaimed in great satisfaction. "That should distract the Fleet from Qin quite nicely."

"You knew about this, Admiral?" S'jen asked.

"G'kaan's orders were to strike the Domain, his target unspecified. Sol was his own plan." J'kart nodded to himself as if thinking about G'kaan's genius in choosing such a pivotal objective. C'vid had to admit that it was brilliant.

"Surely the Armada should send another battleship to reinforce the *Endurance*," S'jen said reasonably. "It is better to meet the Fleet there than in our own territory."

Admiral J'kart briefly considered it. "No, that would leave half our defense net without battleship backup. The protection of Qin is our priority."

"Taking the battle into the Domain would be in defense of Qin," S'jen countered.

"The Fleet might have enough battleships to send them to both Sol and Qin." Admiral J'kart held up his hand to stop her rebuttal. "It is enough that we have sent one of our four battleships into action. Your job, Captain, is to rendezvous with the courier to relay this news. I'll prepare my analysis to be returned to Armada Central."

S'jen's chin lowered but she held her tongue. C'vid felt her own heart ache. S'jen should be out there! She had more than earned it after proving she was right about the Domain. But here she was, relegated to the safety of the rear lines while G'kaan struck a telling blow for Qin.

J'kart left the command deck with a stern glance all around. He liked to keep a tight rein on his ship. And that was the biggest problem for S'jen. In a very real way, she was no longer truly the captain of her own ship. It had not been obvious when J'kart and S'jen had agreed on strategy and tactics during their mission to liberate the outer Qin colonies. But ever since they had returned to Armada Central, the friction made it obvious that they were not united in their goals.

S'jen input the coordinates to rendezvous with the courier, then fired the converter. The *Endurance* leapt to its highest speed under her hands. To C'vid's eyes, S'jen seemed to sag ever so slightly.

It was near the end of their shift when the courier finally answered their hails. C'vid could barely read the ship on their long-range scanners.

J'kart briefly returned to the command deck to hand over a datarod that C'vid had downloaded and transmitted to the courier. She made a copy of it for herself, as she did with all of J'kart's transmissions since they had left Armada Central. She and B'hom had been protecting S'jen, unbeknownst to her, by monitoring communications. So far there had been no official displeasure over S'jen's incessant requests to become combat-active.

S'jen flatly acknowledged J'kart's order to return to their previous location near the gravity slip. Before he left the command deck, S'jen had turned the *Endurance* and was heading back at the same rapid pace. C'vid got the feeling that for S'jen, any movement was better than none.

There was only one other ship on the scanners—a small family yacht. C'vid realized that the yacht was changing course to match the *Endurance*'s trajectory. They were on an intercept course.

"You see that little ship?" C'vid checked the ship's insignia. "It's the *Faith* out of the Tanaris colony."

"What are they doing way out here?" B'hom asked.

S'jen's large eyes took in everything on her navigational scanners. "Hail them."

C'vid opened a general channel and hailed the small yacht. A confirmation signal passed through the channel. "They've acknowledged."

"On imager," S'jen ordered.

Three Qin crowded into view, peering uncomfortably close. The one in front wore blue and yellow robes that left his arms bare. "*S'jen, Clan of Huut!*" he cried out. "*We have come in pilgrimage!*"

S'jen sat back abruptly. C'vid realized these must be the fanatics E'ven had described on Armada Central. Her hand moved to close the channel.

"*We are your humble acolytes!*" the Qin exclaimed, bobbing his head in his enthusiasm.

"I don't have acolytes," S'jen retorted. "Go home."

"*Praise the Crier!*" the younger woman cried out, as if she couldn't contain herself any longer. The other two echoed her as if that was the proper thing to do. "*Praise the Crier!*"

"This is a war zone," S'jen declared. "You have no business being here."

The ancestors must be represented to claim this victory as their own," the man intoned.

C'vid had heard S'jen say similar things time after time. There was nobody more religious than S'jen. Yet she seemed furious that these people of faith had sought her out.

"Cut the channel," S'jen told C'vid.

C'vid hesitated, then did as she asked. "They sound sure of themselves."

"I'm not the Crier," S'jen said flatly, loud enough for everyone on the command deck to hear.

C'vid concentrated on the scanners. The *Faith* continued following the *Endurance.* The yacht was falling behind now, but it would catch up at the gravity slip.

"Tell E'ven to meet me in the combat bay," S'jen ordered.

"Aye, Captain," C'vid agreed. She notified E'ven, who was ready to jump at S'jen's slightest command.

C'vid watched S'jen leave the deck, then hurried through her lockdown of the comm. When her replacement arrived, C'vid informed her about their tagalong yacht and S'jen's desire not to be bothered by them.

As they left, B'hom turned toward the galley, as usual after their shift. C'vid shook her head. "I want to see something first. I'll be right back."

B'hom didn't press her, and C'vid was glad she didn't have to explain. He was the most agreeable and easygoing man she had ever met, quite the opposite of S'jen. But B'hom was just as devoted to S'jen as she was.

C'vid went down to the combat bay where the combatants worked out. S'jen was with E'ven in one corner.

They were doing the intricate balance and countermoves of *kantara* that S'jen had taught E'ven. They went up on their toes, their arms and stiffened palms moving faster than she could see.

S'jen was turning E'ven into a dangerous weapon like herself, honed to sharpness. In the beginning, C'vid had been bothered by it. E'ven was barely out of adolescence. He should be with his own clan falling in love for the first time and discovering his own path. Instead, he followed S'jen. Just as C'vid and B'hom had followed S'jen since she rescued them from the mining station.

They were all S'jen's acolytes. They certainly weren't her friends. S'jen didn't confide her thoughts or feelings to anyone. She was singular that way, unlike anyone else. Her most vibrant quality was her desire for revenge and her single-minded focus. It had never made sense until now.

S'jen was the Crier.

That's why S'jen's religion was everything to her. That's why her purpose shone so brightly. There was no one else like S'jen, and that's why C'vid and B'hom had stuck to her so faithfully when everyone else thought she was a madwoman. That's why E'ven only needed to meet S'jen to know he had to follow her.

S'jen *was* the Crier.

C'vid had somehow known it the entire time. . . . S'jen had saved Qin in the name of the ancestors, and she would do it again. And again.

But first they had to change their current situation. Right now, their only chance of seeing battle was if the Domain had enough battleships to send them to both Sol and Qin. For S'jen's sake, even though it would put her own people at risk, C'vid fervently hoped they did.

* * *

Winstav Alpha managed to delay their departure for Qin. The *Subjugation*, another battleship, had arrived at Canopus Regional Headquarters. Winstav wasn't quite ready to go subdue the Qin. He intended to lead the Fleet's retaliation force into Qin, but Pirosha Alpha had responded to his message with a request for more time to solidify support for her candidacy as the new regional commander of Canopus. Heloga would undoubtedly use his delay to her advantage in her reports to the regents on Spinca. Even Felenore was starting to question his reluctance to depart.

Despite having a veritable network of spies in Heloga's administration and a dozen paid professionals to gather information, Winstav ironically got just the data he needed when he went to the slave compound to choose a new pleasure slave for his lust.

The Delta handlers jostled among themselves to serve Winstav, who was a frequent patron of the compound. Winstav was not above cultivating Deltas and was known for tipping big. He favored a Poid who had recently revealed information about the inner workings of the slave compound, including the fact that Heloga had visited only once in the last few decades. She had come fairly recently, to view a selection of dominant males who were immediately put down by the regional commander's enforcers. Heloga had selected one slave, who was never seen again.

As they waited in the viewing room for the select assortment of slaves, the Delta handler offered, "Have you heard about Sol, Alpha Strategist?"

Winstav considered it, but Sol hadn't been mentioned in any of his reports. "What about it?"

The Delta's blue face was stupidly eager. "They say, though I wouldn't know if it's true, that a Qin battleship has invaded Sol. They've taken our pleasure slaves!"

"Where did you hear this?" Winstav demanded.

"The regular shipment of raw pleasure slaves didn't arrive yesterday. According to the bosses, they got word from the last transport that a Qin battleship was seen in Procyon, heading toward Sol. Not that I would know, Alpha."

It was too good to be true. Winstav stared at the blue Poid, wondering if the slave trade did offer the fastest way for rumors to travel. Certainly nothing was more regular than the subsidized slave shipments that rotated between Fleet bases and space stations.

The regents would be hit where it really hurt if this rumor was true. The loss of four mining stations was worse, but it was mind-boggling to think of Qin occupying Sol. He felt his own impending lust building up pressure inside. This news made him feel anxious that he might not be able to satisfy his need because of the Qin. Surely the regents would feel the same way, even though most of their pleasure slaves were bred in creches.

A line of choice slaves were marched into the viewing room and stepped onto the blocks. Winstav strolled around the room as the slaves struck poses, showing themselves off to best advantage. They had nothing in common, but were the best of the available slaves on Canopus. His love of variety and impulse was why he never possessed his own slave. He would be bored by the second lust. In fact, he preferred to resist lust rather than use a slave he had already exploited.

As he deliberated between a genetically altered female and an alien-hybrid fresh out of the creche, Winstav knew he would have to follow up on this Sol rumor soon. But first, he would indulge himself thoroughly.

It took a full day for Winstav to confirm the reports about Sol. According to Heloga's staff, two patrolships were missing and the flow of native pleasure slaves had completely stopped. No ship that entered Sol had come out again. Winstav was impressed with the Poid's accuracy, and decided to make him a well-paid informant, dismissing most of his other investigators, who had turned up nothing.

He informed Felenore that his analysis had led him to believe the Qin would strike a significant target, with Sol as the most likely candidate. She believed him when he claimed that as the reason he had delayed their departure. She was currently living on the battleship *Subjugation*, preparing to leave for Qin. The *Subjugation* was a newer class than the old battered ship, *Persuasion*, that they had used to travel to Qin last time. She agreed that Winstav shouldn't wait for her to return to Canopus Prime to confront Heloga about the news that a Qin battleship had invaded Sol.

As soon as Winstav arrived at Heloga's office, Waanip shook her head. "The Senior Alpha is seeing no one."

"I'll wait."

Waanip held out one hand to stop him from sitting down. "It won't do any good. She's not seeing anyone."

Winstav stood over the absurdly flat-faced woman, remembering how his last pleasure slave had resembled an Alpha more than most Betas, including Waanip. That was the beauty of a gene-job. "I have urgent news for Heloga Alpha."

"Leave it with me on a datarod and I'll make sure she gets it," Waanip demurred.

Winstav almost reminded Waanip that she would need friends when the new regional commander took over, and that it would be better not to alienate him. She must know that people loved to see the mighty fall, especially when it included some of the mighty's minions. But the knowledge that Heloga was probably listening as hard as she could from the other side of that wall was enough to make Waanip stick to her boss.

"Every second you delay will be counted in my report to the regents," he threatened instead. "My news is critical to the safety of the Domain."

Waanip hesitated, but his plea was difficult to ignore. Winstav recognized the slight inattention that indicated that she was using her comm implant to speak to Heloga. After a few moments, the Beta-assistant finally nodded. "Heloga Alpha will speak to you through the comm."

She turned the monitor of her terminal around so it faced Winstav. At first he thought Heloga was at home, but when her carefully shrouded form appeared he recognized the view through the windows behind her. Heloga was in her office, on the opposite side of the nearby door. It could be construed as an insult that she wouldn't allow him inside to speak to her. Winstav hadn't seen Heloga in person for over a decnight, not since he had acquired a molecular imaging camera in the shape of a Regent's Star, the honor that he often wore on his breast. The real Regent's Star had been given to him after his most notable triumph, a strategic attack that had driven the Kund from the Velorum region. The Kund had eventually returned to the Domain with a vengeance, invading the neighboring region, but that didn't negate his initial success.

This new Regent's Star was capable of recording even the most obscured images. Winstav was sure that someone in his supply line had leaked his intentions to Heloga. Likely that was the real reason she had been avoiding him.

"What do you want?" Heloga was a diffuse silver blur because of the closely tied veil over her head.

"What do you intend to do about the Qin invasion of Sol?"

It was interesting to note that Waanip was surprised, indicating that Heloga could also still be in the dark. A few moments passed in silence, then Heloga ordered, *"Wait."* The monitor showed swirls of gray and pink.

Winstav sat down, quite satisfied. Heloga was checking his information. His spy network must be doing better than he thought if he had gotten the news before her.

When Heloga returned to the monitor, he pretended not to notice. *"Winstav,"* she ordered, *"you and Felenore will take the* Subjugation *and the* Persuasion *to Sol along with four patrolships. You will secure that system before proceeding on to Qin."*

Winstav had no problem with slapping Heloga down in front of Waanip. "May I remind you that strategists don't take orders from regional commanders. We are here at the regents' command."

Heloga gestured theatrically with one gloved hand. *"Obviously, you must liberate Sol and destroy the battleship before invading Qin!"*

"*Obviously* our first duty is to protect Canopus," Winstav retorted. "Felenore will take the battle squadron to Sol. I will wait here to take command of the *Allegiance* when it arrives." *Allegiance* was the newest battleship in Canopus, deployed in the wealthy inner sectors close to Spinca, that attracted so many raiders. The battleship should reach Prime within another decnight.

"You refuse to do your duty?" Heloga sneered through her veil.

"Perhaps you need a more adequate briefing, Heloga Alpha," Winstav drawled. "I'm sure once Commander Vernst considers it thoroughly, he will realize this Sol attack could be a feint by Qin to draw our battleships away from Regional Headquarters. No, the *Allegiance* must remain here until we see which way the Qin will jump."

Winstav knew he had gotten the better of her. The thought of a Qin battleship orbiting Canopus Prime was apparently too much.

After too long a pause, Heloga replied tightly, *"It's on your head. I will inform the regents."*

Heloga cut the comm. Winstav let a bit of a grin pull at his lips as he looked at the door that lay between him and Heloga. She was probably glaring at him, throwing angry insults at him, along with the responsibility to stop the Qin in their tracks.

There was only one more thing he needed—an image of Heloga's ruin of a face. That would add the final crowning touch to his ongoing, ruthless dissection of Heloga's command ability.

Now might be his chance. Heloga was still in the building, and it was getting late. She usually departed before everyone else.

Winstav left the office, murmuring into his wrist comm in the hall, "C-V execute."

A few moments later, a voice replied, *"Acknowledged."*

Winstav's steps were measured, giving his accomplice

in InSec plenty of time to deactivate two eyes in the surveillance network that covered the public areas of the building. Heloga undoubtedly tapped into the network at will, and she must have her own eyes inside the private offices. There was no other way she could know everything she did. However, somehow she had missed the fact that Sol had been invaded. Clearly she was slipping in her downward spiral.

Winstav casually nodded and bid good-bye to a few of the staff waiting at the lift tube. They stepped into the tube one by one, but Winstav passed through the door to the stairs leading to the roof. It was commonly known that one of the perks Heloga had given the strategists was the use of her rooftop landing pad. For security reasons, the tube wasn't open to the roof. Winstav's aircar waited up there to take him back to his assigned quarters, a rather palatial establishment that he rarely used with the exception of sleeping. Usually his evening hours were filled with meeting contacts and nurturing potential allies in every level of Canopus society.

Winstav waited on the landing halfway up the stairwell, avoiding the eye over the door to the roof. Heloga would be watching that one to see if he went to his aircar.

Winstav pulled out his dataport and prepared an order to transfer command of the *Allegiance*. Heloga had already given them command of the other two battleships. This would be his excuse to see her, though he hardly needed one after their last conversation.

Winstav didn't have to wait long. The door below was opened by Heloga's Beta-commander in charge of her personal security. Winstav nodded pleasantly to him, secure in his right to be in the stairwell.

Heloga followed on the Beta's heels and didn't look up until it was too late.

Winstav stepped to the front of the landing, angling the camera in his Regent's Star at Heloga. The micro device recorded ten images through rotating spectroscopic scanners. It should penetrate the filmy veil.

"What do you want?" Heloga demanded.

"I need you to sign this transfer of command for the *Allegiance*," Winstav requested.

"The battleship hasn't arrived yet." Heloga sailed past him up the stairs.

Winstav followed her onto the roof. The sunlight would make the images even sharper. He prepared to trigger another ten shots. "Your refusal could cost you everything, Regional Commander."

At that, Heloga finally turned to look at him. Despite the veil, he could see her rage through her jerky motions. She grabbed the dataport and entered her authorization with shaking hands. Then she threw the dataport at his feet and hurried inside her aircar.

Winstav was astonished at her loss of composure. The aircar lifted with frantic haste as he bent down and retrieved the dataport. Heloga had authorized the transfer of command to him alone.

Now he had everything he had desired, including his own battleship. Felenore would be perfectly happy confronting the Qin in Sol with her two battleships, while he would stay at Canopus Prime to oversee the demise of the regional commander. Then, together, they would demolish Qin.

12

G'kaan and Rose were on their way to the docking bay on board the *Relevance*. It had been less than a decnight since the revolt on Earth, and Rose was busy going from one place to another, inciting Solians to throw off the yoke of the Domain forever. G'kaan had been impressed with her short, impassioned speeches that hit heavily on the degradation and violence that Solians faced as slaves. She truly cared about their fate, and that's what made them listen to her.

"Let's stop by the brig for a second," Rose insisted, ducking through the door.

G'kaan knew they were going to be late for their next rally, but he hadn't seen Bolt since they had captured him. He couldn't understand why the cocky Solian had betrayed his underground associates at a mere threat by Rose. Though Rose had found no proof, G'kaan thought it was entirely possible that Bolt had informed on Rose, causing her abduction.

Bolt was reclining back on the bunk in the small cage. The other cells were empty in the compact brig. His bare feet were propped up on the wall at the back, his arms akimbo and hands behind his head. His mouth was puckered in a quiet whistle.

Rose stared at him silently, but Bolt pretended not to notice. "He looks too comfortable," she said to G'kaan. "Maybe I should strip him naked like they do to slaves."

Bolt lifted one brow, his mouth curling up. "Want another look at the goods, do ya, Rose?"

From the way Rose glared down at Bolt, G'kaan suddenly realized they had been sex partners. Surely Rose had never been intimate with this scum! It was only the Solian sensuality that made it appear that way. "Rose, how can you be sure this man betrayed you and deserves to be locked up?"

Rose stalked closer. "I'm sure."

Bolt stood up, his mocking eyes trying to be earnest. "Rose, you know I wouldn't hurt a fly. I put more miles on my boots for the underground than anyone else. Ask Manuel!"

"*Manuel* never trusted you," she retorted.

G'kaan cleared his throat. "You should have picked up the serneo-inhibitor, Rose, while you were getting your shin implants yesterday. We could test him, and if he's not guilty, send him home."

"You got drugs for me?" Bolt asked. "I'm up for it."

Rose was looking at G'kaan. "It's on my list of things to do. I've been a little busy, if you haven't noticed."

G'kaan wanted the matter settled. He would prefer Bolt back on Earth instead of here, where he could taunt Rose. If he was guilty, then he could be properly punished. "I can bring D'nar over to do it for you."

Bolt grinned behind the mesh. "The more the merrier! Is she a strapping big girl like you?"

G'kaan was starting to see where Rose got her attitude. Every Solian he had met on Earth had boundless confidence in themselves.

Rose leaned closer to the mesh. "Admit your guilt and you may survive. . . ."

There was no mistaking her deadly tone, or the knife and stun gun on her hips. Rose turned to leave.

They reached the door before Bolt called out, "You'll find I'm innocent, Rose."

Rose ignored him, shutting the door to the brig. "Let's get going."

G'kaan noticed that Rose moved right on without another thought for Bolt. She had done the same thing when she shrugged off her mother's disappearance and probable death, never looking back as they flew away from the arena.

When they reached the docking bay, Nip and Jot were waiting near the aircar. All of the Solians took regular turns on the rally circuit with Rose. Mainly they talked about the life of a pleasure slave in the Domain, comparing it to the freedoms detailed by the Declaration of Human Rights the underground had created under their new name—Free Sol. Unfortunately, even the set of basic beliefs conflicted with those of some cultures: Don't physically hurt others, let every adult make their own personal choices, rule by majority vote, right to property and possessions, etc., etc. The concepts were clear enough, but Rose was the one who made it come alive. Mainly she was hacking her way through the discrimination that still existed within the various enclaves by leaning on Sol's lowly status within the Domain.

Rose took the helm of the aircar to practice piloting, while G'kaan monitored everything through his terminal. She methodically went through the checklist, notifying the command deck of departure, then engaging autopilot to take the aircar out of the bay of the *Relevance*.

As they headed down to Earth, G'kaan had trouble concentrating on the helm. He wished that Rose didn't remind him so much of S'jen. They were both decisive, bold, and convinced they were right. But Rose didn't have S'jen's religious fanaticism, for one thing. Rose also cared deeply about her crew, and her intimacy with each one of them was startling to see. G'kaan was used to the typical Qin reserve toward each other, even those of their own clan. Where S'jen was cold and hard, Rose was vibrant and passionate. Her eyes were a marvel of telling glances and expressive reactions. . . .

Suddenly G'kaan realized what was happening. He was entering *enfullem*, the preliminary stages of Qin lust, which came approximately once every four standard years. *Enfullem* lasted a handful of days prior to lust, allowing the Qin to imprint on their intended mate. During the last lust, S'jen had refused to join with G'kaan as she had done in the previous two times. G'kaan had been in agony for days until the intense biological yearnings finally eased. He had not realized until it was too late that S'jen would deny her lust, and he had been unable and unwilling to find another partner in the final stages of *enfullem*.

As the aircar set down in the airport of the enclave, G'kaan knew he should return immediately to the *Endurance* to be with L'pash. Jealousy had caused some rough patches recently with his senior ops corpsmen, but clearly they were meant to be together during this lust. L'pash had done everything right. Everyone on board the battleship knew they would mate.

Then why was he fantasizing about Rose's lush lips instead of the dramatic blaze on L'pash's nose?

Trying to force his thoughts into the proper groove, G'kaan joined the Solians at the hatch, where they were greeted by the agitated leaders of a large southern European enclave. Rose ordered around the native Solians in the same impatient, blunt way she commanded her crew. It seemed to have a mesmerizing effect on the older Solians. Or perhaps that was from the knowledge that their people had been made slaves in exchange for the weapons and bot technology given to the World Council. G'kaan hoped they would never return to their former ignorance. It was the least Qin could do for them.

No matter how much he regretted the deaths that had accompanied their strike on the World Council, the attack certainly worked as Rose intended. Margarita and Enzo were coordinating a coalition of underground and resistance movements under the Free Sol banner, so they could effectively oppose the Domain when the Fleet returned. It bothered him that Rose had not listened to his latest warning that they would have to abandon Earth. She was so resistant to the idea of another Fleet invasion that it was difficult to talk to her about it. He still hadn't explained the origin of the slave trade. Every day it was getting more impossible to do so. He was afraid the news would shake their alliance with Free Sol as well as with Rose. She was so dedicated to liberating her people that she couldn't imagine failure.

Just like S'jen. . . . At least Rose didn't believe she was infallible, as S'jen did. That was one of the worst character flaws in his former mate that Rose didn't have. Rose readily admitted making mistakes and usually learned from them. She admitted she was flesh and blood, unlike iron-cold S'jen. He really admired that about Rose—

G'kaan caught himself and refocused on thoughts of L'pash. L'pash was his future.

Rose thought there was too much talking that needed to be done during a revolt. She had assumed her days would be filled with action, but mostly they were spent giving boring speeches in large assembly halls like the one they were currently in. She had to repeat herself over and over again for the interpreters who translated everything she said. She always remembered to urge people to build their own spaceships with grav impellers. Solians wouldn't be free until Earth was no longer isolated.

There were only enough translator implants for the leaders of Free Sol around the world. Some of these people had moved up to the moonbase to join Enzo and Margarita in coordinating control of the enclaves. Rose had agreed to give her speeches after they realized that personal testimony went a long way toward convincing the enclaves of the danger from the Domain.

With each trip down to Earth, Rose brought different Solians with her. Shard and Nip were liked everywhere, so Rose often asked them to accompany her. Jot was primarily of Asian descent, so she enjoyed visiting the Eastern enclaves. Clay was surprisingly effective despite, or perhaps, because his physical alteration made him unable to speak. Stub was too lazy to be a good ambassador, but at least the redhead was friendly and relaxed.

The surprise was Fen, their new ops officer. She had been one of the slaves on Archernar shipyard, and had quickly proven herself on the command deck as well as at the rallies. Her dark skin resulted from a genetic mishmash of generations of interbreeding in the creches. Only a few of the twenty Solians on board the *Relevance* could claim predominant ancestry from one part of Earth. Clay was one of the lucky ones—his ancestors were from India. His berth was now filled with tasseled tapestries and statues of many-armed gods.

When the rally was over, Jot noticed a quaint stone building near the assembly hall. Their hosts instantly offered to give them a tour of the ancient cathedral. Rose wasn't very impressed by the dark, dingy place after the imposing space stations she'd seen, but Jot and Nip were entranced, as all the former slaves were by everything on Earth. One of the highlights had been a celebratory barbecue on Margarita's hilltop estate that had included Ash. Kwort had raved over the Mexican food, claiming it was the best thing he had ever tasted. They had also gone to the ocean so they could run on the sands and splash in their native water. Every time the Solians came down for a rally, they begged for more sightseeing than Rose could stand.

When they returned to their aircar, Rose said, "Let me try a departure." G'kaan left the controls to her, and offered a few suggestions now and then as she went through the liftoff sequence and activated the antigrav jets. The aircar was much more responsive than the patrolship, but it flew by autopilot as well.

G'kaan examined the scanner readings. "A ship's approaching Earth."

Rose checked the navigational scanner. "Is that the *Devotion*?" R'yeb's patrolship was supposed to be several hours out on a perimeter patrol, checking the remote comms they had planted.

"There's no message on the open channels," G'kaan

replied, clearly worried. "Your patrolship is moving to intercept."

"Chad," she warned through clenched teeth. "If you mess up my ship . . ."

"Where's the *Endurance*?" Nip asked from the seats behind them.

"Not on scanners," G'kaan replied. "They should be on a perimeter sweep opposite the *Devotion*."

Rose triggered the ID beacon on the patrolship. The return appeared on both their terminals. "It's the *Tranquillity*, one of the patrolships assigned to Sol."

"They must have coasted in with their converter shut down," G'kaan explained. "I've been expecting something like this. The senior Alpha in Procyon must be frantic to find out what's happening in here."

"So they'll take a peek and run away again?" Rose asked hopefully.

"They'll tell the Fleet exactly what our status is." G'kaan magnified the scanners. "Their current course takes them into weapons range of the moonbase."

Rose grimaced at the thought of the Free Solians left unprotected on the moonbase. Including Enzo and Margarita. Obviously their defense plan had some glaring holes in it.

She quickly composed a message to alert the moonbase, a warren of tunnels that riddled the dusty ball. Apparently at one time there had been a lot of aliens living on Earth's moon, managing a brisk trade in pleasure slaves. G'kaan still had a number of combat teams searching the base, trying to create a map of the place. With enough time, the Solians could retreat far enough below ground where the patrolship's missiles couldn't penetrate.

"The *Relevance* is picking up speed," G'kaan announced. "Chad's interposing your ship between the *Tranquillity* and the moonbase."

"No, Chad," Rose warned.

From behind her, Jot asked, "Isn't that what you would do? The moonbase has to be protected."

"Yeah, but I'd do it better."

A tense silence fell on them as G'kaan hurriedly scanned for his battleship. The proximity of Earth blocked half the surrounding space. He took the helm from Rose and moved into a better position to scan behind the planet. Rose kept their forward scanners aimed on the patrolships.

"The *Relevance* is coming to a halt," Rose finally said.

G'kaan checked them. "Good, Chad doesn't need to go out to meet them."

"Why not?" Rose demanded. "He could draw them away from the moon."

"I can't find the battleship anywhere, so it must be stealthed," G'kaan explained. "That means they know the patrolship is here. There are a few points they could be using for their approach."

"What are you talking about?" Rose demanded.

"Chad knows the *Endurance* will close with the patrolship under stealth."

"I think you're kidding yourself," Rose told him. "Chad isn't that smart."

G'kaan smiled and shook his head at her. Rose didn't know what to make of it. She grew more impatient as the strange patrolship continued its sweep, circling Earth at the same rate as the moon. Chad shifted the *Relevance* to keep it in front of the moonbase. Rose couldn't understand why he didn't try to close with *Tranquillity* to drive it off. She would have. Maybe Chad was negotiating with them, or trying to pose as a real Fleet captain. Something had to be going on—

"There's the *Endurance*!" G'kaan called out, pointing to the imager.

The Qin battleship appeared close to one side of the patrolship. As soon as the patrolship realized the Qin had arrived, they tried to retreat. But the *Endurance* was already on top of them.

The battleship seized the patrolship in their attractor field. Their engines failed, and the patrolship went still. Without firing a shot, the Qin had captured another Fleet ship.

"The *Endurance* came in from the sun!" Rose exclaimed. "That's why they couldn't see it coming."

G'kaan grinned at Rose, the tips of his fangs showing. She thought he looked cute like that. "If Chad had moved to meet them, the Fleet ship would have altered course and could have seen the battleship."

"All right," Rose admitted. "Chad did good. You must have told him that's what your battleship would do."

"I've run hundreds of simulations with Chad," G'kaan agreed. "He'll make a great captain."

Rose remembered the transport she wanted to give to Chad, but G'kaan had refused to let him go back to Qin. "Then let Chad command the *Tranquillity*."

G'kaan slowly nodded. "That's a good idea. We can train qualified Free Solians to be Chad's crew."

Nip laughed out loud behind Rose. "He'll love it! Maybe some of our crew will go along to get him started."

"Would you?" Rose quickly countered, looking over her shoulder.

"Not likely," Nip drawled. Jot quickly agreed, "I'm staying with you."

Rose felt better. She'd be glad for Chad to take a few of the Solians she had rescued from Archernar shipyard, as long as he didn't take Fen or any of her old *Purpose* crew. She had already lost too many people she cared about. Now, finally, she would get rid of Chad and put him to good use!

G'kaan put the aircar into parking orbit to await the return of the *Relevance*. "I'm going to tell Chad it was your idea."

"Don't bother." Rose didn't need any credit for giving the big guy a leg up. She was just glad to get him off her own ship. Even though he'd been helpful since his return, he still argued too much.

She wondered if it was her imagination that G'kaan kept looking at her in a weird way.

The combat teams from *Endurance* were in charge of taking the Fleet prisoners from *Tranquillity* and placing them inside the empty cube stack on the moonbase. Ash went to the battleship's docking bay when the combat teams returned from the base, having dropped off their prisoners. S/he heard some of the weary combatants talking about the battle on board the patrolship. None of them had died, but two were seriously injured. Several combat teams had stayed on board to secure the captured patrolship.

Ash almost followed the combat teams down to the familiar medical bay. S/he liked to see new things, but s/he was afraid s/he would forget everything once hir memory returned. Why bother living if nothing was real?

Instead, Ash headed up to the galley. There were a dozen corpsmen who had been with G'kaan on his warship when Rose had rescued hir from S'jen. Ash kept seeking out these crew members, hoping one of them could jog hir memory. The sooner s/he returned to hirself, the sooner this awful dual existence would end.

The galley was unusually full, and it seemed like the crew were acting strange even from hir limited knowledge of Qin. They were gathering in groups, speaking intently with one another, their voices raising in passion that Ash had never seen in the emotionless crew. They were eating a lot, too, practically gorging. S/he even noticed crew members who had slipped away from duty to grab a few bites.

Ash fetched a cold drink and searched the crowded galley. A few of the tired combat teams entered ahead of hir, raising quite a din as they started to recount the fight the Fleet had put up on the patrolship. The excited noise rose in the galley.

Then Ash saw L'pash in the far corner. Ash slipped through the crowd, ducking gesturing arms. The Qin were much bigger than hir, with those sharp, white fangs and long arms. It was almost a little frightening to see them lose their dignified reserve.

L'pash glared at hir, and Ash faltered as s/he sat down. "Do you mind?" s/he asked hesitantly.

"What do I care?" L'pash snapped. "Apparently you have the run of the ship."

Ash wasn't sure what that meant, but this was the first time that s/he had caught L'pash alone. "Can I ask you a question?"

"It depends," L'pash said suspiciously.

"Do you remember me from the *Resolve*?"

"Of course I do. You're the one with the brain problem, not me."

Ash bit hir lip. S/he couldn't argue with the truth. "Do you remember anything that happened with me?"

"I never paid attention."

"But you did see me sometimes," Ash persisted. "What was I doing?"

L'pash gave hir an incredulous look. "You were always with Rose."

"I know that," Ash said helplessly. "I need to know more so I can get better."

"Maybe if you went back to Rose, you'd get better. Maybe then she wouldn't spend so much time with G'kaan."

"When is Captain G'kaan returning?" Ash had tried to see him yesterday, but he had stayed on the moonbase while the battleship performed its perimeter sweep.

Ash was sorry s/he had asked when L'pash bared her fangs. "He should be back *now*." L'pash pushed away from the table and left, clearly upset. Ash sat there nervously, and was wondering what to do when D'nar appeared in the door of the galley.

"Ash!" the biotech called out. She squeezed through the crowd, her charcoal face lit up with glee.

Ash was taken aback when D'nar landed on the seat next to hir, letting out a small whoop as another crew member dodged out of the way.

"What are you doing here, Ash?" the biotech asked. "You're like a round peg in a square hole."

Ash raised hir glass by way of explanation.

"This is *enfullem*." D'nar swept her hand at the gathered Qin. "This is for Qin, not you."

"What's happening?" Ash asked.

"We're in the pre-stage. Lust should hit in another few days. Then you won't see anyone for a while. We'll all be holed away with our mates."

Lust . . . Ash had seen the Solians having sex in their lounge, but the Qin never did that. "There's a special time for lust?"

D'nar rolled her eyes. "I'll give you a datarod tomorrow, Ash. But you'd better get back to your berth now."

With that warning, Ash reluctantly left the galley. But s/he couldn't spend endless days alone in hir berth staring at the curved walls. S/he would never recover that way.

Ash had to face a harsh reality. S/he wasn't getting better. S/he needed the stimulus of familiar people and s/he needed the desire to get well.

There was one person on board who could help hir break through the wall in hir mind. The one person Ash had known longer than any Qin or even any Solian. Rikev Alpha could help hir recover hir memory, if s/he was brave enough to try it.

When Rikev Alpha saw Ash in the doorway of the brig, he was pleased. Ash was confused and lost, and s/he had come to him for guidance. Soon enough, he would be able to make hir do whatever he wanted.

"You're here for more memories," he told her.

"Yes." Ash edged inside the door of the brig as if reluctant to come closer.

Rikev refrained from speaking, knowing that could frighten hir away. Ash was so skittish that s/he had to be played expertly. Rikev knew he could handle a pleasure slave like hir because s/he was exactly what he preferred. Naturally, his clone favored the same type of slave he did.

Rikev had few regrets about his capture by the Qin. It

was true that the datarods of evidence proving that three Qin posing as Polinars were responsible for the sabotages in the Archernar sector had been destroyed. But he could easily reconstruct that information from the various stations he had visited. His only difficulty had been resisting the Qin's serneo-inhibitor. His superbly conditioned mind withstood the paltry assault, so the Qin were unaware that he knew they were responsible for the sabotage in the Domain.

Indeed, now that the Qin had taken over Sol, Archernar was of relative importance. Rikev had acquired a wealth of information about their strategy and tactics from the combat teams who guarded him. From their dwindling numbers and haphazard visual checks, Rikev could tell that the combat teams were being stretched thin. Apparently they were still searching the abandoned tunnels of the moonbase, as well as occupying captured Fleet vessels. Likely there wasn't even a combatant on duty right now outside the brig. They had become complacent with him.

"There are things I know about you," Rikev told Ash.

Ash went closer to his cell. "Like what?"

"According to your collar you were picked up from the derelict Spacepost T-3. But there was no other information about your prior masters or training. However, I can tell you have the reflexes of a well-trained slave, perhaps from Rigel itself."

Ash reached up, but s/he wasn't wearing a collar. Rikev wasn't sure how the Qin had managed to remove the collars from the Solians.

"Did you hide on the spacepost after the Qin attack?" His intent was to get hir to keep talking rather than gaining information from him.

"I don't remember."

"But you do know something," he insisted.

"Yes, Jot said we went to Qin first, then came back to salvage from the spacepost."

More confirmation that the Qin were controlling the Solians. Rikev didn't want to frighten Ash into leaving. He needed to make hir trust him. "Do you remember the spacepost?"

"Flashes," Ash admitted. "I remember a wall with plants . . . and you were there."

He didn't bother to point out that it had been his clone. For his purposes, it would be best that s/he confused the two. S/he had been Rikev's slave. Surely obedience was trained into hir very bones by now. "Tell me more."

Ash came forward a few steps, separated by the electromagnetic mesh. He could smell hir confusion and desire to please. S/he was truly submissive.

"I remember kneeling next to the wall with the plants," Ash replied. "The little blue things hopping around were called *ciladas*. I can see it all alive and moving, but sometimes I remember it with the plants dead, their trailers floating and black. And the room is messed up . . ."

S/he shook hir head, breaking off.

Rikev leaned close to the mesh. "You see me and hear my voice, and it brings some of it back. But it's not enough."

Ash nodded, not taking hir eyes off his.

"Sight and sound will never be enough," he told her. "You need more to trigger your memory."

His hands lifted to touch hir, stopped by the mesh. Ash was breathing faster, unable to move.

"You must feel like my slave, then you will remember everything."

"No!" Ash exclaimed, backing up a step.

"You know it will work. You're afraid because you want it."

"No!" Ash denied. "Nobody could want that."

"What if you liked the things I did to you?" Rikev pressed. "You're afraid to find out who you are. But it's still inside you, and you'll be the same whether you have your memory or not."

Ash rushed away, putting hir hands to hir head, trying to flee from the truth. Rikev returned to waiting patiently, as always.

13

Gandre Li was on her way to make a commercial pickup on the Pasachoff starport when Trace stopped her at the airlock. Trace had been roaming the ship freely ever since Herntoff Alpha had used her for his lust. The second time had happened a few days ago, but Trace still refused to tell her anything about it.

"I'm going into the starport," Trace said. "I've always wanted to see Pasachoff Major up close."

"You're not serious," Gandre Li protested. "It's too dangerous—"

"Staying in your cabin doesn't keep me safe," Trace interrupted. "I might as well live a little. I've been everywhere, but I haven't seen anything. I'm going crazy stuck on this ship all the time!"

Gandre Li was really worried about Trace. She had lost a lot of weight this quarter. And she spent too much time sleeping or lying in bed staring at nothing. Now her expression was resolute and she was wearing a dark blue flightsuit with a black scarf hiding her bright bronze hair. At first glance, no one would notice she was Solian.

Herntoff Alpha was away counting ships, and the

crew was on leave, so Gandre Li decided to speak plainly. "Are you doing this because of Herntoff?"

"These Alphas use me anyway," Trace countered. "Why can't I have some fun?"

Gandre Li was nearly frantic trying to convince Trace to confide in her. They had barely spoken since Herntoff had first used Trace. "Why won't you talk to me about it? I only want to help you—"

"Stop asking me!" Trace exclaimed. "*Nothing* happened!"

Gandre Li didn't believe it. Trace was breathing hard with her fists clenched at her sides. That neurotic Alpha must have hurt her badly. But it wouldn't do to upset her lover any more. With difficulty, Gandre Li swallowed her questions.

"Whatever you want, Trace. It's your choice." Gandre Li entered the authorization code for the airlock.

They both entered the small space, too full of words neither of them could say. When they stepped out, Gandre Li checked the seal on the airlock. It felt strange leaving the *Solace* empty. Usually Trace was on board watching over everything.

The short airlock passage opened onto a wide corridor that ran along the back of the starport. It was busy with Deltas pushing grav sleds and passengers hurrying where they needed to go. Gandre Li gestured upward for Trace to look at the weblike bracings of the dozens of levels of docking ports.

"I've seen this through the eyes," Trace murmured, "and on the schematics, but it feels so much bigger in person. Listen to all that!"

Gandre Li led her through the interior corridors to the planet side of the starport. Humanoids filled the corridors of the busy starport, each intent on their own business. Trace stared at everything and everyone with frank curiosity. As usual, Gandre Li got a lot of attention because she looked like an Alpha and she was glad to see that nobody noticed Trace in her nondescript disguise.

When they reached the interior, Trace's mouth opened as soon as she saw the vast windowed wall with Pasachoff Major hanging in splendor beyond. The gas giant was striped yellow, orange, and red from the toxic gases that whirled in layers in the dense atmosphere.

"Ohh . . ." Trace breathed, her hands pressing against the clear plasteel. "It's so bright."

"Practically a second sun," Gandre Li agreed.

"Look, there are ships." Trace pointed to the lights twinkling off various yachts and intrasolar spacecraft.

"There's more than a dozen settlements and colonies around Pasachoff Major." Gandre Li put her arm around Trace's waist. "There's a live volcano on Secondus Moon. Maybe on our next visit we can take time to see it."

Trace grinned at the idea. "A real volcano with flowing lava? Gandi, can we really go?"

Gandre Li agreed, pointing out the various settlements on the moons shooting by in their orbits, waiting as long as she dared before telling Trace, "We'll come back and pick a restaurant, but right now I have to get moving or I'll be late for my appointment."

"I'll wait here for you," Trace offered, unable to look away from the window.

Gandre Li tugged gently on her arm. "Oh, no! You're staying with me." When Trace walked sideways to keep the windows in sight, Gandre Li assured her, "You'll be able to see outside from where we're going."

Trace reluctantly came along. Instead of a grav tube, Gandre Li took the lift on the inner edge of the starport, taking a roundabout route to the offices of the Pangalactic Trading Company. Trace's eyes were shining in enjoyment, watching everything.

Gandre Li regretted that she hadn't taken Trace on more outings like this. Maybe then she wouldn't have been bored enough to get involved with Nip. What else did the poor girl have to do? She was so naïve that this walk through a second-rate starport was a huge event in her life. Besides, Trace was right—staying locked up on the *Solace* hadn't kept her safe.

Gandre Li refused to leave Trace in the waiting room, taking the Solian right into the senior director's office to negotiate a contract for courier services between Pyxis and Capetta, with pickups at various points between. Trace switched from staring out the window of the prestigious office to frankly watching the Beta-director. Gandre Li did most of her commercial work with Betas who owned and operated their own businesses. This Beta-director ignored Trace, who was clearly lower in rank, in his preoccupation with the delivery schedule for his messages.

Gandre Li pocketed an authorized copy of the contract after the Beta agreed to deliver the datarods to the *Solace* before the end of the shift. As they left, Gandre Li was satisfied at having a job that didn't involve InSec.

On their way down to the restaurant level, Trace was enthusiastic about the various choices. Gandre Li wistfully commented, "You're so easy to please, Trace. I'm sorry I haven't done it more often."

Trace looked like her old self, beaming in delight. "I like watching you work. It makes me feel like I'm a part of it."

"What are you talking about?" Gandre Li protested. "I couldn't run the ship without you."

Suddenly, the Solien's expression darkened. "Yeah, who would pleasure the Alpha passengers?"

Gandre Li didn't know what to say to that. Trace knew very well how important her contributions were to the *Solace*. Trace concentrated on looking out the window as the lift started down to the restaurant level. They were alone, so hesitantly, Gandre Li asked, "Do you regret not going with Nip? You'd be in Sol right now with the others."

Trace stiffened, but didn't answer.

"You don't have to lie to me," Gandre Li insisted. "I know you wanted to go."

"Part of me did," Trace finally admitted. "Gandi, I don't know what's wrong with me. Everything feels different."

Gandre Li wished she could comfort her. "I can always take you to Sol after we drop off Herntoff. If it would make you happy, I'll do it."

"No, I would miss you worse than anything." Trace wrapped her own arms around Gandre Li. "I'm not happy right now, but I do want to be with you. Just be patient with me, okay, Gandi?"

"Always, Trace." What else could she say?

Trace woke up in the middle of the night knowing that something was very wrong with her. She hadn't been feeling well for ages, but the bioscanner had found nothing significant except for some stomach and throat inflammation. Ever since Herntoff had started using her for his lust, she had been feeling worse.

After struggling with her fear for a while, she rolled over and shook Gandre Li. "Gandi, I think I'm really sick."

Gandre Li murmured, "Hmm? What's wrong, Trace?"

"I think Herntoff did something to me."

That brought her wide awake. "What did he do?"

Trace felt horrible. "I didn't want to tell you because it's so humiliating. He ties me to a table and . . . examines me."

Gandre Li's raised brows said it all.

"He takes tissue samples." Trace finally sat up, unable to lie still thinking about it. "He uses these strange medical devices on me. It's like an induction only worse." She showed Gandre Li the bruises on her arms and inner thighs. "What's he doing to me?"

"Don't worry, Trace." Gandre Li got up and pulled on a fresh white flightsuit. "I'll get the bioscanner and we'll figure this out. You wait for me here."

Trace felt a lot better now that she had finally told the truth. Gandre Li left as Trace stood up and nervously paced around. It didn't seem to matter what position she was in; there was always a cramp, as if something was festering inside of her.

As she wandered into the day cabin, she saw the cleaning bot. The battered black dome was familiar after living for years on the *Solace*. It was one of many that scurried around the ship. But lately the bots gave her the creeps. They seemed to follow her everywhere.

Even though Trace knew it was silly, she picked up the bot and tossed it out of the day cabin. Now she *knew* she was sick.

Gandre Li returned with the bioscanner and a medical kit. "Lie down on the sofa."

Trace reclined back on the sofa in her thin sleep shift.

"Your legs have gotten so skinny." Gandre Li passed the scanner down her body, covering every quadrant. "You need to eat more."

"I've been eating like mad lately," Trace complained. "I feel bloated and full."

The scanner beeped and Gandre Li consulted it. "Basic metabolic rate has increased. That could mean thyroid problems. And compared to your last exam, your blood plasma has increased but your red blood cell count is down. It says that's anemia."

"So something *is* wrong." Trace was glad to know she wasn't imagining things.

"There's also discolorations on your genitals," Gandre Li said grimly.

"What does that mean?" Trace asked with rising alarm.

"Several possibilities are listed."

Trace pushed up on her elbows. "Tell me."

"The most likely diagnosis is a tumor in your lower abdomen."

Her hands clutched at the pulling feeling in her lower stomach. "I knew it!"

"The diagnostic is prompting a direct scan." Gandre Li read it, then gently told Trace, "Lie back down and pull up your shift. I'm going to have to put the scanner on you."

Trace pulled her shift up to under her breasts. She could hardly think, and was grateful that Gandre Li was here taking care of her.

Gandre Li lightly passed the end of the scanner across her skin. Then she did it a few more times, going lower each time.

"Okay, pull your shift back down. You're shivering." Gandre Li went over to the terminal and plugged in the bioscanner.

Trace let it drop down to her knees. She went over as

an image appeared on the monitor along with a dozen lines of text.

It showed a dark blob in the middle. It looked huge!

"That's the tumor?" Trace asked breathlessly. "How big is it?"

Gandre Li staggered slightly, sitting down abruptly. "It's not a tumor, Trace."

Trace dropped to her knees, holding on to Gandi. "What is it!"

"You're pregnant."

Trace abruptly sat down on the floor. Gandre Li turned to her in concern, but Trace wailed, "I can't be!"

"You are, according to the bioscanner." Gandre Li traced her finger on the monitor. "See, there's the head. And there's the body curved, and the feet."

"It's impossible . . . I was sterilized in the creche." Trace remembered it well. She had felt a certain envy for the few girls who were chosen to become breeders because they got to stay in the creche while everyone else left.

"It says here that one out of every thousand Solians is fertile after the sterilization procedure." Now Gandre Li looked grim. "But Solian-Alphan hybrids don't usually survive unless the mother receives hormone treatments."

"But . . . it can't be Herntoff. He's never . . ."

"Has he inserted anything in you?" Gandre Li asked.

Trace squirmed. "Yes."

"Then that must have done it."

Trace was breathing faster. "What do I do?"

"He must have intended to impregnate you." Gandre Li was reading the bioscanner. "And he's giving you the hormones to keep—"

When Gandre Li broke off, Trace knew it was bad. "Gandi, you have to tell me."

"It's not Herntoff." Gandre Li was having a hard time speaking. "According to the scan, you've entered your second trimester."

Trace shook her head. "What does that mean?"

"You're more than one-third of the way through your pregnancy. Herntoff only came on board ten days ago."

Trace's hands closed over her stomach, this time protectively. "You mean it must be—"

"Nip," Gandre Li sighed. "I knew he was going to give you something."

Trace couldn't say anything for a few moments. "I guess Nip's one in a thousand, too."

"Well, I guess it's better that it's Nip and not Herntoff."

"What are we going to do, Gandi?"

Gandre Li lifted both hands. "I have no idea."

Trace's eyes were wide. "We have to do something!"

Gandre Li realized she was not being very comforting. She knelt down next to her lover to give her a hug. "It'll be okay, Trace. There's nothing we need to do right now." She would have to make sure Trace got the proper nutritional supplements. According to the bioscan, her systems were severely depleted of necessary vitamins and minerals.

Trace clung to her as if she were being pulled out an airlock. "But Herntoff will find out!"

Gandre Li tightened her hold. If anyone discovered that Trace was pregnant, the Solian would be taken away and placed in a breeding creche. "I'll figure out a way to get him off this ship. I'll dump the contract tomorrow if I have to. Once he's gone, we can deal with this."

"I can't have a baby!"

"Why not? Billions of women do." She wiped the tears from Trace's cheeks. "Really, Trace. I was nine when my mother had my brother. I saw what happened with her, and everything was fine."

"She was okay?" Trace asked.

Gandre Li remembered that Trace never had a family. She was raised in a creche, one of hundreds of children who were trained to be pleasure slaves. Alphas were also raised in creches, as were many Betas who copied the upper ranks in the Domain. Gandre Li happened to have been born on a rustic planet. She had received a contraceptive implant and never really thought about it again.

"We'll find a doctor who's not on the Domain net," Gandre Li assured her. "There are plenty of planets we can get to. When I grew up in the Gyan region, it was the frontier like Canopus is now. Plenty of women had babies in our outpost."

Trace sniffed. "How can we raise a child on this ship?"

Gandre Li heard her unspoken fear. She couldn't even protect Trace; how could they protect a baby? "We'll do whatever it takes."

Trace was shaking with nerves, so Gandre Li put her to bed. Before she lowered the lights, she saved the scanner image of the curled-up fetus before joining Trace.

The next day, Gandre Li couldn't help looking at the image when Trace wasn't in the room. She kept smiling to herself as she traced the nose and the tiny fingers. Trace's baby . . . it was a miracle.

14

Whit was in the access tube under the command deck of the raider, where he could hear Grex and Pet Delion, when Dab found him. The Solians had been assigned to monitor the systems during their coming engagement with the raider *Regard*, but they'd been told nothing specific.

"You're as bad as Mote!" Dab exclaimed.

"They're in place for the ambush," Whit whispered. "The *Regard* has just confirmed a target. Don't you want to know what's happening?"

"They'll tell us what we need to know," Dab retorted.

Whit kept his place, aware that most of Dab's irritation came from the abrupt end to their sex games. He couldn't explain that he hoped Grex would take his place because Dab would reject the captain out of hand. Instead, Whit stayed away from Dab as much as possible while making cautious advances to Anny. Anny knew what she was about better than anyone else on the ship, including Grex. The little woman with the squashed face had a man in every starport, and was just the mistress Whit had been looking for.

"There!" Whit murmured. "The target's approaching. It's a courier."

"Fleet?" Dab asked, interested in spite of herself.

"No, it's with the merchant space guild. They would abort if it was Fleet—"

Whit broke off at something Pet Delion said. The name sounded familiar. He strained to hear more. From above him, Grex's deep voice echoed down, *"Once the* Regard *reaches the coordinates, we'll cut in front of the* Solace."

"The *Solace* . . ." Whit repeated.

"What about the *Solace*?" Dab demanded, louder than before.

"Shhh!" Whit hushed her.

"What's going on?"

"I think the target is the *Solace*."

"Gandre Li's ship?" Dab blinked up at him. "No! We have to stop them."

Whit started down the rungs, knowing she was serious. "There's nothing we can do about it, Dab. Don't get any wild ideas."

"I'm not going to stand here and watch them raid the *Solace*! We owe Gandre Li our lives."

"These raiders don't owe her anything," Whit reminded her.

Dab tucked her chin into her chest in her stubborn way. "We're part of the crew now. I'll tell Grex he can't raid the *Solace*."

"We're in no position to demand anything." Captain Grex had only recently yielded after the Boscans suddenly walked out for a "better berth." It had been a stroke of luck for all of them. They were now wearing collars with a fictional past embedded in them. Dab had nearly ruined everything by refusing the collar, and only when Mote showed her that it could be removed with a click and twist, and that it no longer could shock her, did Dab reluctantly agree.

"Do you want to end up like Shard and the others, back in the slave trade?" Whit asked, using their last-resort argument with Dab.

"Rose wouldn't let Grex attack the *Solace*," Dab said flatly.

Whit grabbed Dab before she could leave. Only their long and true relationship kept Dab from belting him. Her arms were nearly as developed as his own, though she was as short as Anny. Dab exercised much more than he did.

"Let. Go." Her lips barely moved.

Whit released her flightsuit, realizing he couldn't stop her by force. "It's our lives at stake, Dab. You have to think about me and Mote."

"As long as I'm free, I'm going to do what's right." Dab marched right up to the command deck as if it was her privilege to tell the captain what to do.

Whit trailed after her, knowing that Dab would never be able to understand the nuances of their situation. She thought in absolutes.

Whit entered the command deck of the old G-class courier after Dab. It was as spacious as all command decks were, with curving walls and an arched ceiling. But over the decades extra terminals had been cobbled on, including the biggest one, next to the helm, which controlled the laser array. It gave the raider a cluttered, haphazard look that even the old *Purpose* couldn't match.

Grex was at the helm, with Pet Delion at the comm.

Anny was stationed on the lower decks near the new shield generator, monitoring the installation under battle conditions.

"Get back to your posts," Grex ordered over his shoulder. Pet looked up, startled by their arrival.

"Dab," Whit urgently called from the doorway. "Do what he says."

Dab went right up to Grex. "You can't attack the *Solace*. The captain saved our lives."

Grex stiffened. "How did you know our target was the *Solace*?"

"You can hear the command deck from access tube sixty-three." Dab pointed directly down.

"Indeed . . ." Grex looked sharply at the terminals, no doubt remembering there was an access tube beneath them. Whit winced at Dab's bluntness. He was glad that Mote wasn't here. She was going to have a fit when she found out!

"You've been spying on us!" Pet Delion exclaimed indignantly. His boyish youth seemed to fall away when he was angry. Now he glared from Dab to Whit.

"So it appears," Grex agreed.

"I'm not interested in listening to you," Dab said with perfect sincerity. "I want you to stop attacking that courier."

Whit looked at the imager where she pointed. The tapered cone of a P-class courier was approaching, with the parabolic comm dish visible on the underside. The icon indicator identified it as "*Solace*."

"Maybe you're the one spying on us," Grex said carefully, looking at Whit.

Whit shrugged, knowing it was useless to lie with Dab around. "We'll stop."

"I'll put a lock on that access tube," Grex retorted pointedly.

Dab urged, "Captain, please don't attack Gandre Li's ship. It's wrong."

"What about the *Regard*?" Grex asked her. "A successful raid on this courier will seal our agreement."

"You're right, we do have a responsibility to Captain Handicant," Dab agreed. "But I can't be a part of this crew if I'm expected to attack my friends."

Whit held his breath as Grex stared at Dab. "How many friends do you have?" the captain finally asked.

"Not as many as I'd like," she said honestly. "And some I'll probably never see again."

Pet looked puzzled; his anger was already ebbing. Whit wondered if Anny would see their spying in the same light. She liked to be in control, so he would have to be especially ingratiating with her after she found out. He would be glad to make nice as long as Grex didn't toss them out an airlock.

"So if *I* was your friend," Grex asked Dab, "would you be as staunch in your defense of me?"

"Of course! You *are* our friend. You gave us a job so we could stay out of the slave trade. I'll never forget what I owe you for that."

Grex actually smiled. Whit felt himself relaxing, realizing that Dab had just wormed her way even deeper into the captain's affections. It was contrary to every expectation that a raider captain would value honesty and integrity.

"Then I agree to your request," Grex told Dab.

She broke into a real smile, something Whit hadn't seen in a long time. He knew better than most how endearing Dab could be when she was happy. There was something irresistible about a strong woman letting down her guard and inviting a man in.

Now, in front of all of them, Dab knelt down next to Grex, taking both his hands in hers. "I will be true to you, Captain."

"I believe you will," Grex murmured.

Whit quietly started to withdraw, feeling that he was intruding. Pet didn't have the same reticence and he was frankly grinning at his captain. But at the sound of a double beep, Pet turned back to his terminal, exclaiming, "The *Regard* is in pursuit. The *Solace* is heading toward the target coordinates."

Dab stood by Grex's side as he quickly input a number of commands. Whit thought the captain was preparing to attack in spite of what he'd agreed, but Dab seemed to have no doubts.

"The courier is approaching our target coordinates," Pet Delion said anxiously.

Grex glanced up at Dab. "Since Handicant is not one of our proven friends, I'll have to do this carefully."

It seemed that Grex was excusing himself. Dab actually nodded permission, much to Whit's amazement. How did a third-rate pleasure slave who'd spent a decade servicing Deltas get such faith in herself?

"The *Solace* is at the target coordinates . . . now!" Pet announced.

"Firing converter." Grex powered up the *Vitality*.

In the imager, the *Solace* jogged sharply to port as the *Vitality* appeared from the scant covering of debris. The *Regard* had planted the shifting, twinkling flats of hull plating to serve as their cover.

But before the *Vitality* could overtake the surprised courier, their engines died. Whit could feel it through his feet as they were jolted forward. Even the inertial dampers couldn't compensate for such an abrupt change in momentum. Whit knew Kwort would recommend checking the gyros on the converter stabilizers to make sure they were still in synch after such a sudden reversal.

The *Solace* shot by with the *Regard* trailing uselessly after them.

"They're getting away," Pet reported. His tone was part outrage at seeing their prize escape, and part curiosity at their captain's behavior. He kept glancing at Dab as if she looked different somehow.

"Thank you," Dab said quietly. "I don't suppose we could talk to the *Solace*?"

"Not with the *Regard* so close," Grex agreed. "We can't let Handicant know what we did."

The internal comm buzzed. *"What happened, Grex?"* Anny called.

Grex stood up. "I'll go explain it to her. Pet, when Handicant returns, tell him we've had a gyro failure and that I'm on it with my bot techs."

Pet nodded, his eyes round. "He's going to be mad."

"I never liked his attitude anyway," Grex tossed off. "If he has a problem with it, we'll find another raider to team with."

Dab followed Grex from the command deck, with Whit trailing after them shaking his head. Mote would never believe this. The captain actually had a tender expression on his face. It was ironic that Dab might be the one who secured a permanent place for them on board *Vitality*.

Gandre Li knew it had been close. If the second raider had maintained acceleration, her ship would have been cut off. Scans indicated that both raiders were equipped with modified laser arrays.

She glanced at Trace, who was on the edge of her jumpseat as the other raider turned and gave up the chase. Jor and Danal stayed long enough to power down emergency systems activated during the battle alert. All three of her crew had been in bed, and they would surely have a hard time returning to sleep after that scare. But it was better than the alternative. The crew quietly left the command deck when they were safely on course within the Indus system.

"Luck," Gandre Li finally admitted to Trace. "Pure, dumb luck saved us."

Trace nodded, still shaking too much to answer. She had arrived on the command deck moments after Gandre Li sounded the battle alert.

"We're going to take advantage of this," Gandre Li added.

Trace came over to her. "What do you mean?"

Gandre Li put her arm around Trace's waist, patting her rounded belly below her cartridge belt. "I'm going to use this ambush to solve our little problem. We're heading insystem now. We'll be at Starbase S-6 early tomorrow."

"What are you going to do, Gandi?"

"I'm going to take an exemption and refuse to complete Herntoff's contract. First I'll report this attack to Fleet authorities. According to guild rules, we're allowed to break our contract if raider activity becomes a serious threat to our ship."

"We'll also have to dump the Pangalactic contract," Trace worried.

"So what?" Gandre Li replied stoutly. "What's important is that I'll be able to leave Herntoff here without repercussions since it's a Fleet post. We can skip our InSec rounds in Procyon, too, and head straight into Sirius."

Trace her belly. "I hope this works. I don't want to go through another one of Herntoff's inductions. What if he finds out?"

"I won't let that happen." Gandre Li cast an experienced eye on Trace, noting how pale she was under her freckles. The poor girl needed to be examined by a professional to make sure her pregnancy was progressing normally. "Once we're in Sirius, we'll swing by Ganymede. That's just the place to find a biotech who won't gossip."

"Gandi, I've been thinking, it would be a lot easier if we asked the biotech to . . . stop it right here." Trace rushed on as if to ignore her protests. "It's too risky! For all of us. If we're found out, it would mean the end of everything we've worked for."

"I'm working for *us*." Gandre Li tightened her hold.

"But you know I'm right," Trace warned. "The crew may leave when they find out."

"They aren't going anywhere. If everything else we've done hasn't scared them off, this isn't going to." Gandre Li patted her belly again, smiling fondly as she imagined the new life growing inside her beloved Trace. It was going to be their baby, their family. Gandre Li hadn't realized how much she wanted to replace the family she had lost until she'd found out that Trace was pregnant. Now it was all she could think about. All her worries and responsibilities still loomed as large, but she felt a power to handle things that she hadn't before. She had to protect Trace's innocent child.

"You go rest," Gandre Li assured Trace. "I'll take care of everything."

Trace gave her a hug, and on her way out paused in the doorway. "I love you, Gandi."

"I love you, too."

As Trace left, a cleaning bot started back down the doorjamb, scrubbing off the dirt and smudges.

Herntoff sat stiffly at his monitors. Through the surveillance bugs on the cleaning bots, he had collected an enormous amount of data, which he sorted and catalogued every day. Much of it would have been deemed useless by a less patient operative. But Herntoff was operating at a high level now that he was in the thick of an investigation.

Herntoff knew he was feeling better because he was no longer exhibiting the spinal inflammation and painful symptoms of Peellene syndrome. The disease was not known to go into remission, so it appeared he had never been infected. Herntoff didn't plan to inform his superior, Commander Gralice, that he had been mistaken in his diagnosis. It would not have been the first time he had to endure her smirk.

Meanwhile, Herntoff was well on his way to implicating Gandre Li and her crew. The most incriminating information involved discussions of the Qin invasion of Sol. The pleasure slave had openly expressed a wish that the Qin would prevail in Sol, and none of the crew had protested her treasonous talk.

He wasn't going to let a mere Bariss stop him from completing his job by invoking a technicality in his contract. Surely he could convince InSec to countermand her requested exemption, but that would mean breaking his cover.

He had never broken cover to ask for help, and he

didn't intend to start now. Clearly the weak link in this operation was the pleasure slave. Why did she need a biotech?

Herntoff went down the spiral stairs to the captain's quarters and buzzed at the door. After a few long moments it slid open, revealing the slave. She wore a flight-suit, as usual, but it was too big for her and hung in baggy folds from her loose cartridge belt.

"Come with me," Herntoff ordered.

Her eyes opened wide. She seemed confused, knowing his lust wouldn't occur for another two days.

Herntoff started walking, refusing to allow the slave to hesitate. The captain was still on the command deck, while the rest of the crew had retreated to their joint room after the battle alert and were now having sex in the large bed. Herntoff had watched for a few minutes, noting that only two of them were actually in lust while the third interacted passively. The Gamma and the Aborandeen had apparently been driven into lust by a bio-physical reaction that sometimes occurred after extreme danger. It was an ancient genetic survival trait, embedded in the cellular mandate to pass on the body's genetic code. Herntoff knew that often obscure information like that could be the key in his investigations to unlocking the truth.

Herntoff went into his room and locked the door behind her. "Get undressed."

"But . . ." She doubled over as the shock hit her from the collar.

Herntoff got out the round exam table and unfolded it. She would have to obey eventually, and he didn't intend to argue with a pleasure slave.

Soon, she was strapped down to the table. Herntoff

felt a stirring in his loins at the familiar ritual. Perhaps the danger from the raider attack was adding to his own response.

He had armed himself with one of the *Solace*'s bioscanners, because it had the slave's baseline readings stored in the memory. His own scans of this slave had indicated that her metabolic rates were outside the norm for Solians. But that was not unusual. Many of the Solians he used were not in good health. The stress and physical strain of being a pleasure slave broke down the fragile Solians very quickly. Even the most well trained slaves were quickly used up.

According to the *Solace*'s bioscanner, Trace's baseline readings were usually well within norms. There was a recent change. The data in the scanner dated back to last quarter.

Herntoff used his own terminal to correlate Trace's medical history with the extensive tests he had performed on her during his last two lusts. Usually he only gathered data on slaves for his personal enjoyment, and it wasn't incorporated into his investigations.

Her eyes followed him, wide with fear. That was because of her secret. She knew he would discover it.

It was so thrilling that Herntoff teetered on the edge of lust. He even stood behind her head, rubbing his genitals through his flightsuit, stimulating himself to rise.

The monitor beeped, indicating that the bioanalysis was complete. He was fully prepared to ignore it, but lust wouldn't come. After a few moments, his excitement petered into nothing.

He went to look at the screen. The Solian was pregnant.

In one swift glance, he took it all in. The development of the fetus, the physical condition of the host, the changes in her body. There was a tiny, growing person inside of her . . . her belly would swell as her internal organs shifted to accommodate the enlarging mass . . . labor would eventually come to clench her body into expelling the new creature . . .

Herntoff spasmed and climaxed, not even aware that he was fully in the throes of lust. It was an experience he had fantasized about regularly, although never with such complete satisfaction. He groaned in abandon, writhing over the terminal.

He didn't even care that the slave could see him. She was more than a pleasure slave now.

When he began to come back to himself, he was afraid it was a cruel mistake. Since his lust was fixated on bodily functions, he had often longed to work in a breeding creche. But his talents lay elsewhere.

As Herntoff absently cleansed himself, he confirmed the results of his analysis. The Solian was indeed pregnant. In fact, in another two decnights, she would be halfway through term.

Herntoff went over and examined her minutely, feeling her belly with both hands, running a deep scan, and examining her internally. He was careful not to do anything that could dislodge the fetus. In fact, he absently patted her on the leg to calm her as he inserted the speculum.

She cried and shook her head back and forth, but she didn't say anything coherent. Otherwise Herntoff would have gagged her.

He had never seen a pregnant woman before, so he could excuse himself for not realizing her condition in spite of his medical expertise. It simply proved the point he had made many times that bioscanners were not what they should be. However, pregnancy was uncommon outside of creches. Slaves were sterilized, so it was extremely rare to find one that had remained fertile, much less one that was actually pregnant.

As he stood over her, staring down at her naked body and rounded belly, he knew he couldn't let her go. If he told InSec, they would take custody of her immediately. Only a licensed creche could breed Solians. Of course there were black-market breeders, and abominations regularly appeared in the slave trade that came from their experiments. Usually unlicensed creches inbred too much, producing mentally and physically deficient specimens.

Herntoff knew what to do. He loosened the straps. "Get dressed."

He rifled through his module to get a lock. When she was back in her flightsuit, her cheeks shiny from tears, he ordered, "Come."

He took her to the berth next to his large suite. It was meant to house slaves or lesser-ranked assistants who traveled onboard the *Solace*. "Get inside."

As she stepped inside, she said, "I need to tell Gandre Li—"

Herntoff shut the door in her face then attached the lock. Its magnetic seal clamped on to the metal of the door and the wall, creating an unbreakable bond. Herntoff entered his code and retina scan for confirmation. Now no one else would be able to get inside. The only other door in the small berth opened into his suite.

He knew he would have another four or five decnights to enjoy this priceless specimen. He might even be able to delay their journey, claiming he needed to visit space stations not listed on their schedule. He decided to research ways of forcing the slave to go into premature labor so he could watch the development to its conclusion.

When they eventually returned to Spacepost M-6, in Capetta, he would turn Gandre Li over to Commander Gralice. Harboring a pregnant slave would be enough to condemn the Beta-captain, but his own investigation would lead to far larger consequences in light of the Qin invasion of Sol. A personal benefit would be Gralice's chagrin when she realized that his medical knowledge had uncovered the truth. Perhaps she wouldn't be so quick to doubt him in the future.

It would be another successful mission with a bonus beyond his wildest dreams. Smiling to himself, Herntoff went up to the command deck to inform the captain.

Gandre Li was feeling hopeful. Now that she had figured out a way to dump Herntoff, Gandre Li felt she could handle anything else that happened. The raider ambush had unnerved her more than she wanted to admit to Trace, but soon everything would be fine.

To her surprise, Herntoff Alpha appeared on the command deck.

"Welcome to the command deck." Gandre Li tried to be self-possessed. "Did you get my message about the raiders? You'll probably have to talk to the base authorities yourself."

She smiled at him, wondering if she should break the bad news to him now. He wouldn't like having his contract broken.

"You will complete our contract," Herntoff said flatly.

Gandre Li thought for a moment that she had spoken out loud. "What was that?"

"I know your Solian is pregnant."

Her mouth opened in shock. "Trace?"

Herntoff nodded shortly.

Gandre Li's gut twisted in panic. She wanted to deny it, but he undoubtedly knew. "Where's Trace?"

"The slave will remain in my custody until our contract is completed. When I leave, you'll get her back."

It was too fast for Gandre Li. "I don't understand. You want to keep Trace?"

"Yes, until our contract is completed."

"You're *not* going to tell the authorities?"

Herntoff looked at her as if that was obvious. But his nervous twitching had a new urgency. That's when Gandre Li realized that he was getting off on the fact that Trace was pregnant. In some twisted way, it almost made sense, because Trace said he examined her during his lust. Gandre Li had never heard of anything like that before.

"The slave will stay with me for the remainder of my contract," Herntoff said flatly.

"You're not going to keep her locked up!" Gandre Li felt panic rising.

"Yes, nothing will be allowed to interfere in her condition."

"But I have to take her to see a biotech—"

"Your only concern is to complete our contract and continue on to lower Pyxis and Procyon." Herntoff turned and left the command deck.

Gandre Li sat down abruptly. How did he find out? What could she do! She could hardly think. This silly ship-counter could cause her to lose Trace for good.

When she got her legs under her again, she ran down to her quarters. They were empty.

Gandre Li sat down on the edge of their bed. The covers were curled back as if Trace had been napping there a moment ago. She touched the cool sheets. "My Trace . . ."

15

"Another biotech to see you, Regional Commander," the majordomo announced.

Heloga was almost beyond hope. Too many biotechs had come to her with grand plans for rejuvenating her disintegrating skin, but none had come close to stopping the ravages. A few were responsible for worsening the damage. She had rewarded the ones who made a sincere effort, knowing they would spread the word about her needs, and she killed the incompetents, knowing that would cut down on the nuisance factor. Her once-adored Fanrique was an early casualty of her worsening condition.

She almost denied this biotech entrance, but she couldn't totally abandon the hope for a cure. "Very well," she sighed.

Heloga went into the small reception room and seated herself. She adjusted the veil she wore even in the privacy of her own home. All the mirrors had been removed or covered so she couldn't accidentally catch a glimpse of herself in this altered state.

A Beta clumped into the room carrying a large, flattened box. He was ungainly, with a particularly long neck, and the biggest hands and feet she had ever seen on a humanoid.

Her majordomo deferentially introduced him, "Dyrone Beta of Canopus Prime," before leaving them alone. Dyrone waited for Heloga to speak first. Heloga knew the Beta-commander of her personal enforcers would already be watching through the security cameras, as per her standing instructions.

"What kind of biotech are you, Beta?"

"Me? I'm no tech, Regional Commander. I'm the second costumer for the Southern Quadrant Dance Troupe on Canopus Prime," he proudly declared.

"What makes you think I need a costumer!" Heloga triggered her comm implant to order the majordomo to remove this bumbling man.

"I can certainly do better than that veil," he sniffed. His raised nose and long neck added to his disdain.

Heloga hesitated. If she could cover herself better, she wouldn't have to isolate herself anymore. She had avoided people ever since Winstav began his campaign to get an image of her ravaged face. She was sure that he had succeeded when he intercepted her on the stairs at the administrative complex. If Winstav sent an image of her to Spinca in her current state, she could be summarily relieved of duty and sent to a retirement colony.

"You're wasting my time," Heloga warned him.

"Yes, Regional Commander." Dyrone set the black box down on the polished floor so it stood on its narrow end. "This unit is a molecular imaging field. They're fairly common in the entertainment field to create visual effects." Dyrone squatted down and pointed out various dials and screens, spewing in rapid tech-speak about depth of field and cohesion properties.

She interrupted him. "What does it do?"

"It forms a field over your skin, a few molecules thick. We use it to turn a chorus line different colors, like purple or green. Or you can program it to create the appearance of certain types of humanoids." He grinned at her in false modesty. "I've programmed a few other twists into the MIF."

"What makes you think I want to be purple!"

Dyrone opened his mouth and laughed, showing his back teeth if she cared to look. Repulsed, it was all she could do not to order him out. But there was something about his explanation that intrigued her.

"Turn the regional commander purple!" Dyrone chortled. "Not likely. No, I've programmed the MIF with images of *you*, Heloga Alpha. I can simulate the way you look."

Heloga touched the veil over her face. "Are you serious?"

Dyrone held up a silver disc. It was micro-flat, and as wide around as her palm. "Put this directly against your skin, Regional Commander. You'll have to take off your outer garment, but you can leave on the support unitard."

Indignant, Heloga straightened up. "What makes you think I'm wearing a support unitard?"

"Anyone with half an eye to see could tell you that, Regional Commander." He leaned forward with the disc. "Guaranteed satisfaction is my rule."

Heloga decided to kill him if his fancy machine was unsatisfactory. He somehow managed to insult her with every word.

She retreated behind a screen in the corner of the room, away from the security eyes. She had tested the screen herself to be sure that nothing could penetrate its electromagnetic core. Some of the "biotechs" who had conned their way past her majordomo had turned out to be informants or spies for various enemies she had gathered over the decades. She was still interrogating one who had come last decnight. She was sure he had been sent by Oliv Alpha, her own staff manager.

Tearing off the veil and enveloping wrap, Heloga winced at her image in the mirror on the back of the screen. Her face was corrugated and shrunken, with her lips shriveled into a grimace. Her ears, which had once been celebrated in poetry and sonnets comparing the whorls to delicate shells, were like leathery flaps. Her body had also sagged and collapsed, distorting her once-perfect form.

Trying to avoid looking at herself, she placed the disc on her upper chest, underneath the gray unitard. "Nothing's changed!" she exclaimed in anger.

"I'll turn on the MIF." There was a click and a slight whirring sound.

Heloga turned back to the mirror and gasped. A white sheen enveloped her. The unitard disappeared except for the seams, where it looked like her skin had developed a ridge underneath.

But her face! It was *restored!*

Her fingers touched her skin, feeling the nastiness of a bumpy, flaking surface, but her eyes saw nothing but smooth satin.

"What do you think?" Dyrone called. "Amazing, isn't it?"

"C-can anything penetrate this field?" she called, not forgetting her danger in spite of her shock. "Like a molecular imaging camera?"

"Impenetrable!" Dyrone sang out with great pride. "That's why we have to program holes in the field over your ears, eyes, nose, and mouth."

Heloga put her finger in her mouth. She couldn't feel the field at all, yet it was undeniably there.

"Do you mind?" Dyrone appeared behind the screen. She would have commed her enforcers at once, except she was still too engrossed in her newly reformed appearance.

He put down the box and knelt next to it. His neck bent in a smooth arch. "The skin texture is too shiny, exactly as I thought. I only had images from the 'net, which give it a glossy quality."

Dyrone made a few adjustments, and she lost the plastic sheen that she hadn't even noticed at first. "Astonishing . . ."

"Let me resynch your mouth. Maybe the tissue damage is interfering in the movement."

Heloga clenched her fists at his arrogant frankness about her condition. But her mouth was moving better, expressing her displeasure for her. "How does it work?"

"The field adjusts to your movements. I've enhanced the sensitivity of your mouth and eyes so that it will pick up everything you do."

Heloga tried it. "It seems to work."

"Now for the tone. I've got a slightly pinkish white on you now. You want some color or it looks too flat."

Heloga realized that that was why there seemed to be very bad lighting in the room. "Ivory. My skin is a creamy white."

"Ah, the color of mother's milk!"

Heloga almost choked at his crude reference. She would definitely have him killed—

Suddenly her complexion was perfect. She never imagined it would be possible to return to her former beauty. She had a healthy glow, and there was depth to the shadows around her nose and the hollows of her cheeks.

Tears flowed down. She could feel them, and she appeared to be exquisitely happy, but she couldn't see the drops.

Dyrone chattered on. "It's got a precise depth of field, so it'll cover sweat but not bulky clothing. It has no trouble with fat bulges or smoothing out any imperfections. That unitard has got to go! You need more support here." His hands closed in on her waist, pushing it together and up. "And in the bust and arms. I've got just the item for you."

At that moment, Heloga would have shared lust with the man, she was so ecstatic. She didn't care if he touched her anywhere, as long as she could look like this again.

"How long will it last?"

"The MIF unit has to stay near you, at least in the same room. And its power source needs recharging every decnight or so."

Heloga clutched his arm, her fingers digging into him. Even her hands had returned to their exquisite elegance! He had given her the illusion of a manicure with gold-tipped nails.

She would never let him go. She would coddle, spoil, and subsume him to be sure she could remain like this. It was more than vanity, it was her life.

The public test run of the MIF was Heloga's first step toward subduing her enemies. Heloga ordered her Beta-commander to outfit Dyrone as one of her enforcers. Then she appointed one of her own enforcers to watch over Dyrone, who wore the MIF in a backpack that usually held a mobile stungun recharger.

The Beta was big enough to be an enforcer, but he slouched and shuffled his feet. He would learn soon enough, and her own abrupt reemergence into the public eye would distract everyone until Dyrone settled into his role. To appease the costumer when he realized he couldn't return to his old life in the theater, she had allowed him to choose three Solians for his own private use. Dyrone had insisted that he needed to be able to exchange them for new slaves any time he wished. From her own recent experience, Heloga had an idea what someone could do with three pleasure slaves at one time. She approved the request without comment.

All she cared about was stepping into the sunshine without that awful veil. The MIF prevented her from feeling the sun's warmth or Prime's artificial breeze, but that was fine. Sometimes she still felt naked, and had a moment of panic wondering if everyone could see how she really looked. She kept glancing in the palm mirror she carried to assure herself that she was indeed beautiful again. Dyrone had supplied her with a superior unitard, which was almost as revolutionary as the MIF, enabling her to wear a tailored gold bodysuit. Dyrone had draped a long, sheer white scarf around her shoulders that floated to the ground behind her, adding the perfect touch.

When Heloga appeared at the northern groundport with her entourage of enforcers and personal assistants, it caused a riot. They cut through the teeming travelers, who quickly made way for her magnificence. It brought the groundport to a halt, disrupting travel throughout Canopus Prime. She could have taken her own aircar from her rooftop pad directly to the starport, but that wasn't conspicuous enough to suit her.

Heloga loved every moment. She spoke condescendingly to her staff, letting them deal with the port officials. Instantly she had clearance for the starport that orbited Canopus Prime. The best transport available was cleared of passengers for her personal use.

It was a short hop to the orbital starport. Heloga's entourage was met at the airlock by the senior Alpha-commander, who followed her like a devoted cleaning bot. She pointed out various unattractive features of the starport for him to repair, realizing she hadn't been off Prime for over two standard years. That would change in the future. In particular, this starport was the gateway to her regional headquarters, and it should reflect the tone of her rule.

Hundreds of people appeared in the corridors to watch Heloga stroll by. She was herself again, with everyone hanging on her slightest word. Her only worry was making sure she didn't lose Dyrone in the crowd. He stumbled after her, frankly staring at the wonders of the starport.

Heloga refused an offer of refreshment from the Alpha-commander. There was something she had to do immediately. She went straight through the weblike port to the docks at the rear. The regular courier to Spinca was preparing to depart.

Taking only Dyrone, her Beta-commander, and an assistant, Heloga entered the courier. The Beta-captain of the courier met her at the airlock, his flightsuit undone at the neck. "What an unexpected pleasure, Regional

Commander!" he exclaimed, sounding very much the opposite.

"Get me the regents pouch," Heloga ordered.

The Beta-captain blanched, but quickly turned and headed to the secure vault. Heloga followed to be sure the Beta didn't try anything funny. When he pulled the pouch out of the vault, she went through each datarod. One by one, she inserted the rods into a dataport held by her assistant. Heloga had programmed it to search for images of herself.

Out of twelve datarods, one contained images of her. They had been taken on the roof of the admin building near her aircar. The film of the veil was hardly visible, and the wrinkled mass of her face was clear. It could have been any ancient Alpha living out its last days in a retirement colony, but the dataport said the image correlated to her features.

There was text with the images. Probably coded messages from Winstav to his contacts on Spinca. Heloga smiled as she pocketed the datarod. "That will be all."

"But—" The Beta-captain almost protested the unorthodox seizure of the datarod from his official pouch.

Heloga waited to see if he was that stupid. He smiled faintly and let it go. The Beta-captain was clearly afraid for his life, which pleased Heloga. No one but a regional commander would be able to get away with violating the contents of the regents pouch.

She was courteously shown off the courier. Heloga waited with her entourage outside the airlock until the courier departed on schedule. She had timed it to be sure no one could sneak another incriminating datarod on board.

No doubt Winstav would make arrangements for the

next courier. Meanwhile she would appear in many places and allow her image to be logged by everyone. That should obliterate any doubtful evidence he had obtained.

Heloga pulled a blank datarod from her other pocket, carefully checking that it wasn't the one from the regents pouch. She needed that one to find out who Winstav was talking to in Spinca. She dropped the blank datarod on the titanium flooring and crushed it with her boot heel. It spangled into crystals and white power.

There was quite the crowd watching her. Heloga knew her meaning would get back to Winstav.

When Winstav reached the lower lobby of the coliseum, everyone was talking about Heloga Alpha. Winstav had come to the coliseum because one of his informants had notified him that Heloga had suddenly appeared. News of her trip up to the starport earlier that day had spread throughout Canopus Prime, and he was sure that the datarod she had crushed had contained the image he took of Heloga. At least the identity of his contacts was safe.

Now the regional commander was in her box for the grav-disc championship after disappearing from the public eye for decnights. All of the comments Winstav overheard were complimentary toward Heloga, as if she was firmly in control and observing every casual conversation.

After buying a ticket for a public box, Winstav entered the bottom levels. Each box had several deep tiers and movable chairs for two dozen people. Taking a seat close to the clear plasteel, he strained to see Heloga on the opposite side of the rink. The game was well under way and the players balanced on their grav discs, zipping after the antigrav sphere.

But the real show was in the regional commander's private box. Everyone in the arena was focused on that instead of the players, despite the relative importance of the game. Heloga sat in the center of her box, allowing admirers in small groups of two or three to approach and greet her before being ushered back out. Certain high-ranking Alphas in her command structure were permitted to stay for somewhat longer than mere society Alphas.

Winstav knew it had to be a trick. He had seen her condition. He had taken the latest images himself. That woman wasn't Heloga. It must be a body double. Maybe even her clone.

But if anyone else doubted, they didn't dare say it out loud.

Winstav left the public box and circled the arena, heading upward. Literally everyone was talking about Heloga as he approached the private boxes. Her enforcers were letting only people on Heloga's "approved" list through their perimeter defense. Winstav was waved through immediately. Two personal assistants were walking among the high-ranking Alphas who were waiting outside Heloga's box for an audience.

Several Alphas left the box, having seen the regional commander. "Perfectly stunning, as always!" one woman exclaimed. "It's terrible what lies some people will tell."

Her eye turned toward Winstav. Part of his plan to gain influence in Canopus was to spread the news of Heloga's downward spiral. With something as certain as death, it hadn't seemed necessary to conceal he was leading the pack of concerned citizens.

As befitting his direct association with the regents, Winstav was soon allowed to enter Heloga's private box. A few enforcers were stationed inside the door. They let him through at the Beta-assistant's signal.

Heloga was seated on the only chair in the box with her back to the doorway, as if she were watching the game. Winstav closely examined her skull, gleaming like a white pearl. As he came down the steps, her elegant profile appeared.

Winstav couldn't believe his eyes. When he had last seen Heloga without her veil, deep grooves cut into the flesh on either side of her mouth. Her lips had been wrinkled and cracks radiated from the corners of her eyes. The deterioration had continued rapidly according to the spectral images he had recently taken of her.

But now Heloga's face was flawless.

"I expected to see you sooner, Winstav Alpha." Heloga gave him smirk. "Your informants must be slipping."

Winstav instantly knew this was no body double. "Regional Commander, it is a pleasure to see you out again."

"Yes, I have just recovered from a bout of severe dehydration due to a faulty environmental rheostat in my personal rooms. Perhaps you noticed it affected my skin slightly." Heloga lifted her face, and smiled. "But the problem has been repaired."

Winstav was sure that some poor building tech had paid with his life for that cover story. Mechanical failure!

"I'm glad you're recovered," he said belatedly. It wouldn't do to act as if he had lost his wits. "Perhaps we could meet tomorrow and go over the plans I worked out with Felenore for our counterattack on Qin. She should arrive in Sol soon, and after that we will be free to stamp out the menace for good."

Heloga inclined her head graciously. "Then you should get under way to assist in the attack on Qin."

Winstav couldn't mistake the unmasked hatred in her eyes. "I look forward to that, Regional Commander."

There was nothing else Winstav could do but reassess every one of his plans.

16

———m———

Lust was fast approaching. G'kaan could feel it creeping over the *Endurance* like a mist. He ferried the last two combat teams from the moonbase up to the battleship. Their duties on the moonbase had been severely cut back since *enfullem* had started, and now no Qin would leave the *Endurance* until after lust was concluded.

G'kaan headed for the command deck as the combat teams disappeared in search of their mates. He would have to find L'pash soon. The corridors and commons were crowded with crew, including the diminutive Creh. Noise rang out from the normally restrained Qin, who smiled and frowned with a strange abandon. G'kaan knew that he was considered to be an emotional man, and he wondered if this was how he usually appeared to other Qin.

M'ke greeted him as G'kaan entered the command deck. "So you've brought back the last of the combatants?"

"Every crew member is accounted for." It would be torturous to be left isolated on the moonbase without a partner. "How's our perimeter?"

"The remote comms are relaying perfectly. We'll know the moment any ship comes into range."

After the *Tranquillity* had penetrated their defense screen, G'kaan had placed every one of their remote comms on the perimeter, linking them to each other to create a latticed bubble around Earth. That gave them three hours to respond even if a ship coasted through. That was enough time for the crew to throw off lust and go to battle stations. G'kaan was relying on the distance from Sol to Regional Headquarters to slow the response time, but that might not be enough. If the Fleet showed up in the next few days, it would be horrific to have to fight their way out while staving off lust. Yet they couldn't withdraw completely and abandon their allies.

"You've got everything you need?" G'kaan asked M'ke. By regulation, every ship in the Armada had at least one elder who could maintain control of the ship while everyone else was in lust. M'ke and E'stal, the third comm tech, would split the shifts between them.

"You've done all you can." M'ke pulled on his whitened whiskers, a fond smile on his lips. He hadn't gone into lust for over a decade and was beyond such emotional turmoil. "Go join L'pash."

"I have to return Rose's aircar. I'll be back soon." He had gotten in the habit of using the more nimble aircar as he taught Rose how to fly. She had the manual dexterity needed to control the smaller vessel and was becoming a good pilot. G'kaan had informed the leaders of Free Sol that no one was likely to visit Earth or the moonbase for a few days. G'kaan had managed to explain their lust as an "important clan observance."

As G'kaan left the command deck, two Creh ran past

him, chasing one another. Voices spilled from the galley as *enfellum* reached a fevered, happy pitch.

G'kaan hurried toward the airlock. He had the same nervous energy and impassioned need to do . . . something. He kept remembering the last lust, when he had searched for S'jen, playfully at first, thinking she was trying to inflame him, then more frantically as it became apparent that she wouldn't allow herself to be found. He never did discover where she had secreted herself during that lust, but he had finally retreated to his cabin on board the *Resolve* and had gutted it out alone. That experience was likely affecting him now.

L'pash caught G'kaan at the airlock. "I was wondering where you were," G'kaan said lamely. The last time he saw L'pash was this morning. She had been very angry that their ships were staying in orbit during lust. She had yelled after him that he would regret it when G'kaan finally stalked away.

"I've been waiting for you." Her tone was accusatory. She looked different with her mane of hair tousled, unlike her usual, smoothed-back style. It reminded him of Rose for a moment, but he wouldn't allow himself to think about Rose while he was with L'pash.

"I had to transport the combat teams back," he explained. "We couldn't leave them on the moonbase."

"Well you're here now." Her hand touched her own chest where her flightsuit was opened. Her sleeves were also rolled up, exposing silvery gray down on her arms. L'pash reached out to him, but he shifted away.

"I have to return the aircar." G'kaan looked over his shoulder at the airlock.

"Leave it there."

G'kaan felt himself heating up, responding to L'pash.

Maybe he could leave the aircar at the airlock. . . . Then two other crew members loped by, so intent on getting somewhere that they bumped into him, knocking him farther away from L'pash. "The Solians might need their aircar."

Frustration flashed in her eyes and the white hour-glass blaze on her nose stood out. "You've hardly been with me for *enfullem*!"

"We've been together every night, L'pash." His tone was harsher than necessary, and he knew it. "I'm doing the best I can. We've invaded Domain space. I have more important things to worry about—"

"*Nothing* is more important," she flatly denied, convinced by tradition that it was the truth. "Without lust, there would be no new generations of Qin to venerate the ancestors."

G'kaan had a different perspective on religion, and last year's disastrous lust hadn't helped matters. But he didn't have time to explain it to L'pash now. "I'll be right back."

"I'll go with you." L'pash took another step closer.

"Rose will have to fly us back." He couldn't imagine L'pash and Rose together right now in the same small aircar.

"Rose!" L'pash almost screamed in frustration.

G'kaan decided she was too emotional to go along. L'pash might kill Rose if the girl made fun of their lust. And Rose was bound to laugh at them.

G'kaan pulled away from his intended mate and stepped into the airlock. As he punched the code, he assured her, "You wait here. I'll be right back."

"You won't come back." Her eyes were huge and glassy.

"Don't be melodramatic. I have to come back. It's lust."

L'pash crossed her arms tightly over her stomach.

As the hatch closed, G'kaan forced himself to look at her from inside the airlock, feeling guilty about leaving her during this heightened emotional time. But he couldn't strand the Solians for three days without their aircar.

"I'll hurry," G'kaan promised as he closed the airlock.

First G'kaan had to locate the *Relevance* among the three patrolships in orbit around Earth. R'yeb had returned in her patrolship, *Devotion*, from their continuous perimeter sweeps. She had taken an elder Creh on board as part of her crew to watch over her ship during lust.

G'kaan passed close by the *Tranquillity*, the Fleet patrolship that was now captained by Chad. His crew consisted of native Solians and former pleasure slaves rescued from Archernar shipyard. Chad was smart; he understood, unlike Rose, that eventually they would be overpowered by the Fleet. Their resources were severely limited, while the Fleet could send several squadrons of battleships into Sol if they had to.

With such weighty matters on his mind, it was no wonder he was not preoccupied by *enfullem*.

G'kaan received permission to dock from Jot. *"I'll notify the captain that you're boarding,"* Jot told him with a shy smile. *The young girl had become very professional at the comm*, G'kaan thought. *And she owes it all to Rose.*

As one of the new Solian crew members opened the hatch to let him enter the *Relevance*, G'kaan was surprised that Rose wasn't waiting for him. He didn't see anyone else, but echoing through the corridors were raised voices and rapid chatter, much like on the *Endurance*. Here there were also high peals of laughter ringing out. Qin never laughed. It made him smile.

He started down the corridor after the male Solian, noticing how cold and rigid the straight lines of the Fleet ship were compared with the softened curves of the *Endurance*. He had to get back to L'pash quickly.

"Hey there, G'kaan, old boy!" Stub called out as he came down the spiral steps. "Rose said to send you up."

"Where is she?" As Stub came down, G'kaan noticed he wore a blue rag draped around his hips and nothing else. It was more exposed skin in a starship than G'kaan had ever seen before. He didn't know where to look, so he kept his eyes fastened on Stub's.

"They're in the lounge above. I'm getting another pitcher of bubbles and I'll be right up." Stub winked at him as he went by. "Have a jolly Qin-lust!"

G'kaan's brows raised. "What do you know about that?"

"Hey, it's your *bacchanal!* Rose thought we should join in. I mean, who figured the Qin would throw a three-day orgy? It goes to show there's always something new around the next star."

G'kaan thought it was a good thing L'pash hadn't come. Apparently the Solians were mimicking their lust. Shaking his head, he went up the stairs to the lounge. Having fun should be the lowest priority for Rose, but she had apparently put it first, probably to boost morale. It might not have been wise, but it was right.

The lounge on the *Relevance* was full. Rose and the others had packed it with the gifts and cultural tokens of appreciation they'd been showered with on Earth. Now it was a veritable museum of Solian culture. The walls had disappeared under tapestries, paintings, and decorative hangings. There was nothing left of the Fleet modular furniture. Only ottomans, piles of cushions, and ingenious folding stools served as resting places for the Solians, while tables and shelves were crammed with intricate statuettes and devices in a bewildering variety of shapes.

The clash of bright colors was subdued in the shadows. Strategic pools of light illuminated groups of off-duty crew who were playing and talking. He couldn't get over these Solians with their games and sense of fun. G'kaan had never met other humanoids like them.

"There you are!" Rose called from a nest of cushions. Stub returned and handed around the pitcher. He leaned back against Rose's legs in familiar intimacy.

G'kaan remained by the spiral stairs. Kwort called out a greeting from the other end of the lounge, where he reclined with Clay and some of the new bot techs. The Delta looked inordinately satisfied among the Solians.

Then the music swelled as Shard started to dance in the center of the lounge. The song had a heavy driving beat. The boneless motions of her arms, and the graceful dips and twirls entranced him. And Shard was Rose's second-in-command now that Chad captained his own ship!

Rose appeared by his side. "I figured you'd be enjoying your orgy by now."

"It's not an orgy, Rose."

"Don't tell anyone." Rose grinned in delight. "That's what I've been saying. They're celebrating the 'Qin-lust' down on Earth, too. I think it'll be a worldwide holiday along with Liberation Day. Why don't you come sit down and enjoy it for a while?"

G'kaan felt like he was falling into her incredible eyes. He forced himself to look down, but all he could see were her taunting bare toes. "Let's go downstairs."

Rose gave in and followed him down the spiral stairs to the main corridor. "You haven't said anything about my new poncho. Shard made it for me." Rose held her arms wide so they came out of the fabric that draped around her body. Her legs were exposed from the top of her shapely thighs. The poncho swung tantalizingly free and open. He could put his hand on her hip and slide it underneath—

"No." G'kaan clenched his fists. He had to think about L'pash, not Rose! "You have to take me back to my ship."

"Not now," Rose protested. "I have a couple hours until I go back on duty. Why don't you wait a while?"

"I can't. L'pash is waiting for me."

Rose took his arm and led him through an open door. It was a miniature replica of the lounge above. A couple was lying entangled together on a low, wide bench. Their naked limbs looked smooth in the dim light. The man on top moved his hips, his buttocks clenching rhythmically in unmistakable lust.

"In here," Rose said, taking G'kaan into a adjoining room.

The floor and furniture were hidden under layers of gorgeous native fabrics, layered among soft fur pelts. Candles glowed in wall niches, unable to rival the light from the large slanted window that revealed the wide arc of Earth. The blue and white planet never looked so brilliant as seen from a darkened room.

He stumbled on the thick, soft floor coverings. "What is this place?"

"It's supposed to be the captain's cabin, but I took a berth so it could be used as our playspace. The main lounge is for recreation, and this is for more sexual stuff. But today's the lust so there's no holds barred. There are no boundaries, except no sex on duty, that's always been my rule."

"Rose, I . . ."

She lifted her face to him, her full lips opening. "What do you want, G'kaan?"

Rose knew what he wanted, but he struggled to say, "I have to go back to my ship. *Enfullem* is almost over."

"I'd say something's about to begin," she laughed.

"Lust." G'kaan swayed on the unsteady flooring.

"That's a *Solian* specialty," she reminded him.

It had been a spur-of-the-moment thing to bring G'kaan into their playspace. Rose could see Nip intertwined with Grit in the room beyond, spurring her on. G'kaan had been so intense the past few days, staring at her with his startling blue eyes as if he could possess her by sight. He had a new way of speaking to her, low and confidential, that seemed to pull her closer.

Actually, she felt as giddy as a young girl with a crush, and decided she should indulge herself after the horror of Earth's revolt. She hadn't expected that much murder and gore from the liberation, but she knew it wasn't done. And she refused to think about her mother. She had woken up again this morning with Silvia's face hanging over her. For some reason, she remembered how her mother used to sing in the mornings as she got ready for classes, and how her smile once was the best thing in the world. As she got older and struck out in her own direction, she had forgotten that during their never-ending battles.

So Rose was feeling punchy, and when it seemed like G'kaan was going to leave her high and dry after whipping her into a frenzy, she had impulsively declared a three-day orgy in honor of the Qin. The Solians had followed along as usual.

Then G'kaan came to her like an unexpected gift. She figured the playspace reeked with enough sexual pheromones to knock an enforcer squad on their butts. Would G'kaan finally, at long last, show his desire for her? Or would duty drag him back to that dreary Qin bitch who dogged his every step?

"Rose, I've done a terrible thing," G'kaan admitted roughly.

"That sounds promising."

"I imprinted on you during *enfullem*."

She smiled. "Is that all?"

His eyes widened, almost as if he had expected her to be shocked. He probably hoped she would reject him so he could go back to the battleship where he belonged.

"You're not getting off that easy." Rose took his hand in hers. He was so restrained and completely covered up by his flightsuit, but his hand was hot. Instead of jerking away, as she half-expected, he returned her grip firmly

G'kaan pulled her against him. He was so much taller that Rose had to tilt her head back to look up at him. "Will you join with me in lust, Rose?"

"Such a formal request! Sure, why not?"

"It lasts for three days."

A laugh was building, but she didn't dare. "I think I can handle a three-day commitment. We're not going anywhere."

G'kaan kissed her, and every thought fled. She had never been so thoroughly kissed in her life.

When they finally drew apart, breathing heavily, Rose declared, "If that's a sample of what's to come, I may have to call in reinforcements!"

G'kaan grinned at her, but he refused to be turned from his goal. He marched over to slide the door shut. Rose noticed that he locked it. She didn't mind privacy with G'kaan. After that kiss, she was willing to go along with his ride for a while. Sooner or later, she'd get her turn.

With gentle hands, first brushing her cheek with his fingers, he undid the clasp that held her ponytail in place. She shook out her hair, and his hands buried in the strands, clenching tighter for a second, holding her firmly.

"Nice," she murmured happily.

His hands dropped to her poncho. "Off," he ordered, snaking it over her head. With that tossed aside, she was bare from tip to top.

Rose stood with one hand on her hip, giving him her best Shard imitation. "Now your turn. . . ."

It was much harder to unseal and unpeel G'kaan from his uniform. His belt was heavy with cartridges and clever Qin devices. She decided to snoop through the belt at her heart's content during their post-sex cuddles.

Even without his boots on, G'kaan was a tower of strength, perfectly proportioned, and apparently so far gone in lust that he didn't have any modesty. Rose ran her hands up and down his body in frank admiration, loving the way his strong muscles were covered with a fine silky down. He was very different from hairless, boyish Stub. G'kaan was like a black, velvet-gloved fist.

"Hold up your hands, palms toward me," he told her.

Rose put up her hands as if she were surrendering, lifting her face to his.

"Think of your soul, the part of you that connects you to everyone else."

Rose shook her head. "You've lost me."

"Think of your intentions when you came back here to liberate Earth. Your motivations and your best desires."

"Okay, I can do that."

G'kaan put his palms to hers. "Just think. And feel."

Rose wished he would go back to kissing her again. But he was standing close, looking so frankly into her eyes that she had to try it his way. She settled into her stance, his feet outside of hers, their bodies almost touching. He was steady, and she balanced against him.

As she gazed up at him, she thought about why she came home. Because it wasn't fair how they treated Solians. That's why she risked their lives breaking out of Archernar shipyard. She had figured out inside the cargo hold of the *Purpose* that she could fight back by taking one step at a time.

She smiled at G'kaan because he had helped her save Earth. She couldn't have done it without him. From that first time, when he heard her plea and helped her save Ash from S'jen, G'kaan had been a rock. Even when he broke their Armada contract, she hadn't blamed him.

His face was exultant as well, maybe thinking of their victories together. Rose felt a hum throughout her body. She wanted to touch him, to lean against him, but their hands held them apart. Her palms burned and trembled as she longed to clenched his fingers, to deepen the contact between them.

"Yes!" she cried out.

He caught her up to him, holding her so tight she couldn't breathe. "Now!"

It took hours for their first long rush of coupling to come to an end. But eventually the sexual rubbing and stroking tapered off enough for Rose to start thinking about all those rich, fatty foods the crew had dialed up on the transposers for their celebration. She was almost too worn out to be tempted, and that said a lot.

"I always thought you Qin were uptight." She lolled on the cushioned floor. "I guess you save it up for this one big shot."

"Lust comes in waves." G'kaan was lying on his back, perfectly relaxed. "Otherwise we'd die from the physical strain."

Rose's stomach growled. "Or starvation. I'm going to get us something to eat."

She got up and took a step, but he thrust his hand out. "Don't leave!"

There was an urgency that made her stop. "What's wrong?"

"It breaks the lust if we part now."

Rose thought that was a little much. "What if I have to pee?"

G'kaan eyed the fresher that opened off the room. "Don't be surprised if I want to follow you in there."

"The more the merrier!" Rose laughed. "Okay, I'll call for a delivery."

She went to the door and unlocked it. It was probably the first time it had been locked since the Solians came on board. Jot was sleeping on the bed in the larger room. She had probably partied hard after coming off duty. But according to G'kaan, it would break the magic spell if Rose went to the galley herself.

"Jot! Hey, Jot!" Rose called.

The girl looked pretty when she woke up, with her sleepy, relaxed expression. She didn't ask any questions when Rose requested a large number of provisions. Then again, Jot lived to serve. One trip to the galley would probably satisfy her more than an orgasm.

Rose flopped down against G'kaan to wait for good things to come. "What do your people do if the baby needs changing during lust?"

He tucked her into his shoulder. "The elders take care of the children. There's a pretty legend that the young and the old have to perform a fertility ritual during lust, praising the wind and the sun and the land. It gives them something important to do while everyone else is off . . ."

"Making more babies," Rose finished.

His arm tightened around her shoulders possessively. She felt a pang of regret and figured she better clue him in. He might want to go back to the *Endurance* and hunt up L'pash if he was hoping for offspring.

"No babies for me," Rose said flatly. "When they abducted me, I was sterilized, like all the other pleasure slaves. None of us can have kids."

He sat up. "They did that to you!"

Rose hadn't thought about it much since she had found out. Babies were one of many things she had left behind when they abducted her. She had never been very maternal, and there was no use crying over it now. But that reminded her of another reason to use the serneo-inhibitor on Bolt so she could take it out on him. Ironic that her own mother had been involved in that loss. . . .

Rose didn't want to think about any of that. Just like she didn't want to think about poor Ash alone over on that battleship. She should have gone to get Ash for their orgy, but she usually did everything she could to put Ash out of her mind. She hated the way Ash was now. It was as if s/he was dead but hir body lived on. Rose needed Ash even more since she had found out about her mother, but her one staunch support was no longer there. And like her mother, there was nothing she could do about it.

Jot returned in time to cut off her dire thoughts, bringing a full tray of food and word that Grit was covering for Rose on the helm. Rose sealed the door shut again at G'kaan's request.

Rose picked through their choices, and seized on a flask of hot fudge and a tub of tiny marshmallows. "It'll be sticky, but I promise to lick off every drop," she told G'kaan, holding the flask poised over his belly, ready to pour. "But then you have to lick it off my face."

G'kaan gave her an odd look from his prone position. "You know I can't do any more until the next wave hits."

But Rose saw his reaction to her teasing movements as she crouched over him, displaying herself. "I think you have a little more Solian in you than that. You know, we can have sex anytime we want."

And as it turned out, G'kaan did have more Solian in him than he thought.

17

L'pash stayed at the airlock, her eyes fixed on the aircar that remained stubbornly fastened to the *Relevance*. She kept praying to her dear, dead mother to make it return. Sometimes she pounded on the clear plasteel with her fists, driving her rage toward the patrolship. G'kaan must feel her pain . . . he must know how he was torturing her!

She left the airlock over and over again, searching through the ship as if she had lost something precious. Everyone else holed away to engage in lust. She knew Qin didn't die from unconsummated lust; it only felt that way. There were great legends of heroes who had stayed at the helm of their ship or fought off wild beasts during lust. Once an entire compound on Binirth refused lust because of rising floodwaters. They saved their livestock and every clan member while the compound was buried under tons of mud.

L'pash had always thought those old stories were romantic, but there was no romance in this.

The corridors of the battleship were empty and it was quieter than ever before. As she lay on the floor, her back to the airlock, her periodic sobs were the only sounds that broke the long silence.

"I thought I'd find you here."

L'pash wearily looked up at M'ke as he stiffly knelt down next to her. The frosting of white around his nose and mouth reminded L'pash of her own father back on Omnium. Even without the hourglass blaze, M'ke was a lot like him.

"G'kaan isn't coming back, is he?" she asked. "He told me to wait for him here. How could he do this to me?"

M'ke tightened his lips. "G'kaan thought he was returning. That's what he told me."

"Then *why* isn't he here? Everyone knew he would mate with me. Didn't you know?"

"That was my impression."

"Everything was fine until *enfullem* started. He allowed himself to imprint on that . . . that . . . pleasure slave!"

M'ke couldn't defend him.

"He's no better than S'jen," L'pash said bitterly. "And I felt so bad for him last time. I thought S'jen was a monster for making him go through lust alone without one word of warning or excuse. I thought it proved she was mad."

"Not mad," M'ke said. "As we found out recently, S'jen refused lust because she's infertile."

"At least that makes some kind of sense! What reason does G'kaan have? I sympathized with him." Her hands clenched into fists at the thought of his treachery. "How could he choose *her* over me?" L'pash couldn't even say Rose's name. She would scream if she tried.

M'ke sighed. "I owe it to you to be honest, L'pash. You know about his dual heritage, that his mother was Solian."

L'pash nodded. She had treasured every difference because it made G'kaan unique. Even his blue eyes were exotic and alluring.

"But you aren't aware of how it's tormented G'kaan from his earliest days. His Solian nature has manifested itself in many ways that he has trained himself, through great struggles, to conceal."

L'pash frowned at that. "Every child has to learn how to behave. It doesn't excuse him now."

"No, I offer no excuse. Merely a partial explanation. Since we've come to Sol, G'kaan has been surrounded by people who embrace the aspects of himself that Qin rejected. That's why he's taken every opportunity to be among Solians and go to Earth."

"Are you saying that he's becoming more Solian than Qin?"

M'ke frowned. "G'kaan has a dual path. I'm sure he will continue to follow both, but I doubt that Qin will completely dominate his life again. This lust proves he won't let go of his Solian self."

L'pash shuddered at that. G'kaan was Solian, like Rose and her uninhibited, boisterous crew. L'pash had hoped it was a phase and would end with their current mission. When the Fleet finally smashed into Sol, they would have to scatter. Then the *Endurance* could return to Qin where they belonged.

Now, according to M'ke, G'kaan was different. Surely his choice to abandon her showed he was turning away from all that was sacred. If he had a child with Rose, it would be almost completely Solian.

"Would Clan Vinn claim a Solian child as their own?" L'pash sneered.

"I doubt Rose would return to live among the Vinn as

G'kaan's mother did. That would be the only way her child could be of our clan. The circumstances are very different."

"Does G'kaan know this?"

"Clearly he hasn't thought it out, but he must know that Rose is unlikely to become clan Vinn."

"Yet he choose her anyway," L'pash said hopelessly.

"I'm very sorry," M'ke gently replied.

After a while, the old man helped her off the floor. L'pash couldn't stop herself from looking out the portal, but the *Relevance* was out of sight in orbit. G'kaan wasn't coming back.

M'ke insisted on taking her to the galley so she could eat something after her long, depressing vigil. The rest of the crew were tucked in their berths and the private spaces they had carefully created during *enfullem*, including stashes of food and liquids. L'pash had eaten copiously during *enfullem* as usual, and had put on weight in anticipation of lust.

She picked listlessly at some fruit preserves as M'ke returned to the command deck to watch for signs of the Fleet. Even though she knew G'kaan wasn't coming back for her, she still felt the deep lustful urge to mate. It twisted her stomach, tightened her throat, making it hard to breathe. She pushed away the plate and rested her cheek against the cool tabletop, willing the torment to stop.

"Are you okay?"

Every muscle in her body clenched at the Solian voice. It was Ash, coming forward in concern. "You look sick."

L'pash snarled, showing her fangs to their fullest extent.

Ash retreated almost to the door, then stood there irresolute. S/he was slender, halfway between the height of the Qin and the Creh. But hir face was pale and fleshy, the color of an old bot shammy. Hir mouth was slightly open and hir shoulders hunched forward, as if life was too much for hir.

L'pash didn't have any patience with Ash's loss of memory. That was pure weakness. But at least she wasn't the only one in pain. "Oh, come in and eat if that's what you want."

After much hesitation, Ash finally got a bowl of something as bland as hirself. S/he came slowly over to L'pash's table, giving her plenty of time to protest. L'pash ignored hir, awash in her own misery.

When Ash sat down opposite her, L'pash discovered that the Solian's eyes were blue. Not bright blue like G'kaan's, not so steady or sure. Ash's eyes were bluish gray, pale and washed out like the rest of hir. Under L'pash's intense glare, Ash blinked a few times, as if not knowing where to look.

Blue eyes . . . L'pash couldn't sit still any longer. The lustful urge had eased around M'ke because he was an older man. But now her desire to mate was overwhelming. If she could be with anybody on the ship, she would do it gratefully. But Armada regulations demanded an even number of crew, not counting the elders, so everyone had paired off long ago in preparation for lust. Triads were sometimes formed, but it was far too late for her to attempt that now. Negotiations took place during *enfullem*. And it would have been galling to approach a couple after her none-so-subtle pride over G'kaan's status and bravery.

Ash ate hir food neatly and rapidly, sneaking brief

looks at L'pash. Ash evidently lived like a small creature on a busy boulevard, darting between the moving feet and taking what s/he could find, expecting to die at any moment.

L'pash wondered if she could bring herself to mate with Ash. It seemed like it would be impossible to her that a Qin and a Solian could mate although G'kaan himself was proof that it could happen.

L'pash sat forward intently. "Tell me, Ash, can you function as a male?"

Ash drew back, clearly confused. "I don't understand."

"Sexually, can you perform like a male?" L'pash pressed.

"Yes. According to D'nar, I can."

L'pash raised her brows at the mention of the biotech. Certainly D'nar would know if there was a medical problem. "You don't know yourself?"

Ash shrugged slightly. "I don't remember. . . ."

"You mean you haven't had sex since you lost your mind?"

"No."

L'pash was surprised. From what she had seen, Solians were constantly in rut. What if Ash was the only Solian in the galaxy who couldn't have sex? The temptation to scream was building again.

"What about me?" L'pash demanded harshly. "Will you join in lust with me?"

"With you?" Ash countered, hir voice going higher.

"Yes! What's wrong with me?"

"But . . . D'nar said lust isn't for me."

"That's because she didn't think anyone would *want* to have lust with you."

Ash pulled back as far as s/he could. "I didn't know you . . . would like to be . . . intimate with me. I thought you liked G'kaan—"

"Don't say that!" L'pash stood up, leaning over Ash. "I can't stand it, I must go into lust. You're the only one!"

L'pash turned away. If she was rejected by this Solian, she would fall on her dedication knife and end it right now. She'd had only three lusts before, and this fourth one was to have been the culmination of years of devoted companionship with G'kaan. Before, L'pash had always mated with one of her Bos clanmates. It was comfortable and safe to be with a fellow Bos. But this time G'kaan had made it clear to everyone that he would choose her. They had spent every night of *enfullem* together, touching one another and sleeping together. They had discussed what they would do if L'pash conceived. She had been torn over the possibility of having a baby from this lust. She didn't want to leave G'kaan or her post on the *Endurance*. She had always been glad before when she wasn't blessed so she could use her intelligence and ability to serve in the Armada. But with G'kaan, it felt different. She wanted to have children with him, and after they were grown, she intended to return to duty in the Armada. But those dreams were shattered now.

Ash came up behind her. "Okay."

L'pash felt the tension in her belly easing. Ash's pheromones must be compatible to affect her this way. But when she looked at Ash, L'pash felt appalled at herself for being so weak, and angry at G'kaan for betraying her into this.

Ash stood before her like a good pleasure slave. Surely she could take this offering in her time of need.

Breathing heavily, L'pash knew she couldn't go to her

berth. She had prepared it as a love nest for G'kaan, draping the walls and ceiling in blue-toned swaths of cloth. Everything in that room had been placed with an eye toward pleasing G'kaan and sealing their relationship.

"Take me to your berth," L'pash ordered.

Ash didn't know what to think. S/he had responded to L'pash because of her desperation. Ash certainly knew what it felt like to need something so badly it hurt. S/he couldn't understand why the Qin lust was so overwhelming for everyone, but L'pash was in pain and needed to have sex.

Without a word, Ash led the towering Qin woman down to hir berth. When the door was closed, it was like being inside an egg. It felt bigger than the berths on board the *Relevance,* because the walls pushed out in the middle and the ceiling was arched. Plus the shelves and cupboards were inside the walls rather than hanging on the outside.

"I don't like the color," L'pash said flatly.

"It's like the sky on Earth." Ash had gone down with Rose to the barbecue at Enzo and Margarita's house, and it had been one of the highlights of hir short life. So she had gotten a blanket the same color.

"Change it," L'pash ordered.

Ash hastily opened the unit next to the door and entered a number at random. The walls and ceiling changed to dark green. "How's that?"

L'pash eyed the blue blanket on the bunk, but didn't object again. They were silent for some awkward moments. "You're used to this, aren't you? In your life as a pleasure slave."

Ash swallowed. "Yes, but . . ."

"You don't remember. Right."

It was not a good beginning. Ash was more nervous than ever. L'pash didn't even seem to like hir. But s/he was very lonely.

"Take off your flightsuit," L'pash said.

Ash automatically obeyed, unbuckling hir cartridge belt. Hir thumb unsealed the front of hir flightsuit down to hir crotch. S/he didn't hesitate as s/he shrugged out of it and stepped out of hir boots, though s/he wasn't sure if s/he really wanted to do this.

L'pash raked her eyes over Ash. She seemed tense and eager, yet curiously detached as she assessed Ash's body.

Without warning, Ash was caught in a nightmarish flashback. A Coomen Beta-captain was avidly examining hir naked body. S/he knew he was a Coomen from his concave face, and s/he knew he was dangerous from the way he spoke. Ash felt a burning pain in hir chest and arms—shock restraints on hir wrists! S/he dropped to hir knees, bending over, trying to relax the clenched muscles in hir chest. But s/he could see the Coomen running his hand over hir smooth chest and down to hir genitals, his palm scraping mercilessly with every touch. But s/he couldn't pull away as he commented, "Very strange . . . but you'll do."

Anything, s/he chanted to hirself, *I can stand anything.* S/he thought of Rose and felt a moment's strength from the image of her friend's angry eyes—

"What's *wrong* with you?" L'pash demanded.

Ash gasped on the floor, disoriented. S/he struggled to speak, hearing the anger in L'pash's voice. "A flashback . . ." s/he managed to say.

Ash finally staggered to hir feet, still seeing brightly

colored spots in hir vision from the shock restraints. The memory felt real. Now she had another piece of her past, albeit a nasty one. S/he wondered when s/he was going to have a flashback of something nice. Maybe all of it had been awful. Maybe there was a good reason she had forgotten.

"D'nar has been stimulating my memory," Ash tried to explain. "I can't control it."

"You mean you collapse at any moment like you're having a heart attack?" L'pash flung up her hands. "I might as well throw myself out an airlock and be done with it."

"I'm okay now," s/he told L'pash, feeling sorry for her.

For a moment, Ash thought it was all over, but L'pash unsealed her flightsuit as well. She turned away from Ash, showing the strong muscles of her back and the rounded curve of her buttocks. Her naked legs were long and powerful. When L'pash faced hir again, her ashy skin looked incredibly soft, as if s/he could sink into it. . . .

Ash felt a stirring in hir loins that sent a different sort of jolt through hir body. L'pash came closer. "Lift up your hands."

Ash mirrored what L'pash did, gently resting their palms together. L'pash moved in until she stood a breath apart from Ash. The Qin was so tall that Ash lifted hir chin hesitantly, afraid of such closeness.

"Look into my eyes and think of your soul," L'pash told her.

L'pash's eyes were large and tear-drop-shaped, with enormous pupils.

"My soul?" Ash asked.

"Solians do have souls, don't you?" L'pash asked, exasperated. She showed a hint of fang.

Ash didn't remember what a soul was. S/he almost reminded L'pash that s/he didn't have anything of hir own. But there was only a fragile thread holding their hot hands together. And as tenuous as their contact was, for Ash it was the most intense thing that had ever happened to hir.

S/he gazed up at L'pash's face, mesmerized by the white hourglass blaze on her nose. Ash figured since s/he was nothing, an empty container, s/he would think about L'pash instead. S/he had listened to the crew and combat teams every day as they talked in front of hir, as if s/he didn't exist. They often spoke about L'pash. She was part of the leadership triad along with G'kaan and M'ke, and as Senior Ops was in charge of making sure the ship was running smoothly. The crew thought she was demanding but sincere, yet they belittled her small assumptions of authority because she was G'kaan's intended mate.

The combat teams were different. They merely tolerated the command crew and the Creh bot techs, and had their own personal code because of the danger they entered during their missions off the ship. Ash had heard them compliment L'pash, especially her boldness in risking her life by going under cover with G'kaan and M'ke. That was the part of L'pash that Ash liked best, the stories about them building the underground slave network in the Domain.

But Ash couldn't concentrate while s/he was staring up at L'pash. S/he was too aware of her naked body, the way her breath moved her chest, the flare of her hips so close, and those marvelous full breasts barely within sight. Ash suddenly wanted to devour L'pash's breasts, and could hardly keep hirself from reaching out and stroking her smoky skin. . . .

"Yes," L'pash said encouragingly.

Ash wondered if hir soul was in hir genitals, since s/he was raging hard. S/he longed to crush against L'pash, to cling and bury hirself in that warm, enveloping body.

L'pash cried out, her eyes going wide. "Now!"

Ash dived in with abandon.

It went on for a long time, a lot longer than the sex Ash had seen on board the *Relevance*. S/he had intense spasms of pleasure many times over, but L'pash always wanted more. Insatiably, she carried Ash along. Ash explored her strapping body in every way. And in a real sense, Ash got to explore hir own body as well. S/he was different from everyone else, that was sure, but s/he could feel pleasure just the same.

In the end, L'pash pushed Ash off the bunk. "Get away," she said languidly.

Ash didn't mind. L'pash had been relentlessly fierce, taking her pleasure exactly as she wanted. Ash also tried some things s/he had seen among the Solians, like kissing her genitals and rhythmically smacking her buttocks. L'pash had been eagerly receptive.

Ash wondered why s/he had never had sex with hir Solian friends. Jot had said that almost all of the Solians, including Shard, had tried, but s/he had resisted. Ash thought Shard was even sexier than L'pash, and that was saying a lot. Once again, hir past didn't make any sense from this perspective.

Ash laughed to hirself as s/he lay on the blue blanket

that had fallen to the floor. S/he was going to tell L'pash how funny it was sometimes having no past, but the Qin's expression was grim.

"Is something wrong?" Ash asked, leaning up against the bunk.

"I'm leaving," L'pash said flatly. She sprang up and went to grab her flightsuit, pulling it over her legs with annoyed jerks.

The Qin gave hir disgusted looks until Ash felt embarrassed about being naked. S/he pulled the blanket over hir body, sitting up on the edge of the bunk.

"Didn't you have fun?" Ash had to ask.

"Fun!" L'pash glared at hir. "I can't believe myself. Lust is about perpetuating the clan. It's a sacred ritual!"

Ash sank back further.

"I'm going back to my berth—don't come anywhere near me," she ordered. "I want to break this charade before the next wave of lust hits. And you better hope I don't get pregnant!"

Ash couldn't speak.

L'pash paused at the door, her eyes narrowing at Ash. "Don't tell anyone what we did, do you understand me? Nobody!"

"I won't," Ash whispered.

18

E'ven roamed the corridors of the battleship *Defiance*. The crew was celebrating *enfullem* with lust bearing down on them, while E'ven was still searching for his mate.

Actually, he knew his mate would be one of several older women who were vying right now for the best of the younger studs. E'ven knew he was the consolation prize for the loser, and that didn't exactly satisfy his needs. That's why his body insisted on searching the huge battleship over and over again, as if his real mate were somewhere in hiding.

The Creh had all paired off and were raising a din in their lounge. The combat teams were also paired off, as were most of the command crew. It was the end result of the intricate social maneuvering that had started as soon as the new crew had boarded the *Defiance*.

E'ven had missed all the preliminaries. This was only his second lust, so he wasn't exactly sure of himself. He had shared his first lust with a girl in the farm-slave gang on Balanc. His relationship with F'bec had happened gradually. She was in his age group and he often paired up with her to work. Or he crouched next to her while they ate. But it wasn't until their lust together that he realized how much he cared for F'bec.

The Domain overseers didn't try to stop the Qin from going into lust because the slaves had damaged the farming station and themselves too much in rioting when their biological response was denied. None of them had been able to get away privately, so they hung their bedding around their bunks and hid within makeshift tents. He remembered how different lust had been when he was younger and still living in the ruins of Clan Huut. He and the other children had helped the elders perform the fertility rituals. There was always a new crop of babies later.

E'ven hit the bulkhead with his fists. Soon after his first lust, F'bec had been removed along with the other pregnant women. It was unusual for a girl in her first lust to conceive, but F'bec had. E'ven never heard about her again. He had checked the lists when Balanc was liberated, but her name was not included. It was another burning hole inside of him because of the Domain. It was only one of the reasons he stayed on duty as much as he could or worked out with S'jen until he fell into his berth exhausted.

Because now S'jen was his life.

The warning lights flashed along the top curve of the corridor. *"Docking sequence engaged."*

E'ven recognized N'col's voice. She was the third comm officer, one of the women who had grudgingly sat next to him in the galley a few times during *enfullem*. This was her tenth, and probably final, lust, and she was clearly hoping to partner with a crew member who had not spent the last year in the irradiated environment of a cesium mining station. It didn't matter that the ship's biotech had pronounced him intact . . . unlike S'jen.

He shook himself out of the typical *enfullem* befuddlement and headed down to the junction of the main airlocks. The *Defiance* was locked down in preparation for lust and there hadn't been any dockings for decnights. He wanted to see what was going on.

The sounds led him starboard. The biotech was waiting impatiently at the airlock with a grav board. C'vid was standing at the controls, opening the hatch. When she turned, the white frosting around her eyes made her distaste starkly clear. E'ven was getting used to being ignored by the bulk of the crew. They knew he was on board the flagship of the Armada only because he was Huut. But C'vid was closer to S'jen than anyone else, and she had always been friendly with him.

"I thought the Armada was locked down," E'ven said.

"Apparently a crew member on the *Faith* suffered an injury," C'vid said dryly. "They need our medical services."

The biotech rolled his eyes as if it was a big nuisance, but E'ven felt his hairs standing on end at the thought of those "acolytes" coming on board. They bothered S'jen. "Let them go back to Tanaris."

"He'll be dead by then," the biotech drawled. "Severe bleeding does that to a body."

E'ven snapped his mouth shut, knowing he couldn't win a battle of words. S'jen had not been happy when the yacht insisted on drifting outside the perimeter lines of the *Defiance*. However, short of closing down the shipping lanes, there was nothing she could do to get rid of the *Faith*. That coupled with their complete inactivity made S'jen seethe. E'ven spent quite a few days taking the bruises that came with his clanmate's *kantara* lessons.

"Airlock cycling open," C'vid announced, entering the release code.

E'ven backed up as the seal popped, and the hatch slid smoothly aside. The first acolyte to enter wore a lavender and yellow robe with dark patches spreading through the loose weave. She was holding up her companion who had a makeshift bandage pressed to his chest. The white cloth was stained reddish black.

The biotech moved in as they spilled from the airlock. "Put him on the grav board," the biotech absently ordered. "How long has he been bleeding like this?"

"We don't know. S'amis found him," the female in the stained robes explained as they laid him down. "There was a lot of blood on the floor."

The biotech whipped the makeshift bandage from the acolyte's broad chest, then clamped a bot healer on to him. The edges curved to fit around his torso, and his shaking slowly stilled. The biotech examined the monitor while the other three acolytes made sure he didn't fall off the grav board.

The biotech lifted his hands in horror. "This came from a dedication ritual?" The woman nodded unhappily as they started down the corridor, towing the unconscious acolyte along with them.

The younger woman stayed, looking up at E'ven with frank curiosity. Her skin was so pale she was almost white, with her fluffy hair hanging far down her back. "You're E'ven, the Crier's clanmate."

E'ven frowned. "How did you know?"

"I've seen a holo of you two." Her head cocked. "You don't look like her."

E'ven smoothed a hand over his dark forehead. He had gotten used to being snubbed by everyone.

"I'm acolyte S'amis," she introduced herself with a smile. The tip of her fangs flashed for an instant.

C'vid stepped up. "The *Faith* can remain docked until the biotech has completed his exam. You must stay on this level, and only use the corridor between the airlock and the medical bay."

"Certainly," S'amis agreed, still looking at E'ven. "But we are free to have visitors, aren't we?"

"Yes." C'vid glanced at E'ven, who couldn't take his eyes off the girl. S'amis's expression was alive with feeling and intent. Her bare arms were alluring, and he could glimpse her body as the pale blue and pink drapery clung and shifted with every movement. Very different from a flightsuit . . .

S'amis shifted closer to E'ven. "Am I truly in the sacred presence of the Crier's mate?"

It took E'ven a moment to realize what S'amis was asking. "Uh . . . no!"

C'vid was also taken aback, but her mouth snapped shut against her retort.

S'amis seemed pleased. "That's much better. You can rebuild Clan Huut faster if you each bear children. Have you chosen your honored mate yet, E'ven?"

E'ven felt like he might die at her bluntness. He coughed, turning away from them.

But S'amis put her hand on his shoulder. "It would be the achievement of my life to serve Huut by mating with you, E'ven. I would go to Endunara and help Clan Huut prosper. I would bear you strong children—"

E'ven shook her off and walked away. Behind him,

C'vid politely ushered S'amis back into the airlock to the yacht. S'amis called out, "Come see me, E'ven."

E'ven waited at the junction for C'vid. He was angry that the crew thought he was inferior, and irritated that S'amis wanted him only because he was S'jen's clanmate. He didn't know what he was going to say until he blurted out, "C'vid, *can* S'jen go into lust?"

C'vid raised her brows. "You know why S'jen denies her lust. Everyone knows, thanks to the Clan Council investigation after she destroyed Spacepost T-3."

E'ven clenched his teeth. S'jen had never said anything to him, but he would bet she hated having her sterility publicized. "I thought that made lust impossible for her. But that girl seems to think that S'jen could mate."

"Yes, S'jen joined with G'kaan twice before she realized the damage that had been done to her reproductive organs. Now she chooses not to."

"*Chooses?*" E'ven repeated, unable to believe anyone could deny what he was feeling.

"S'jen has extraordinary willpower."

"But why?" E'ven shook his head at his own stupidity. "Why shouldn't S'jen enjoy lust even if she can't have a baby?"

"You're asking the wrong person," C'vid reminded him.

E'ven slowly nodded, realizing that she wouldn't break S'jen's confidence, even if she knew. Which he sincerely doubted. S'jen wasn't the type to complain.

As S'jen's clanmate, he was closer to her than anyone else. Didn't that give him the right and the obligation to speak to S'jen? After all, lust was a clan matter.

* * *

S'jen had completed the lockdown and went over the procedures with Admiral J'kart and the other elder on board. Each one was assigned a shift on the command deck monitoring the comm and scanners. S'jen intended to take the third shift herself during lust. If there was a battle alert, which S'jen ardently hoped for, the *Defiance* would be notified by the warship on the other side of the grav slip. That would give the rest of her command crew plenty of time to shake off lust to meet the Fleet. S'jen knew it would be a tactical advantage for the Fleet to attack during the Qin's vulnerable time. She was almost expecting it.

S'jen was returning to her quarters right before lust commenced, when she saw someone kneeling outside her door. It was one of those crazed fanatics who refused to wear a flightsuit in space. The woman's scanty drapes barely covered the naked curves of her body as she swayed, chanting the day's dedication.

S'jen went to the nearby comm and signaled the combat commander. "Get a combat team to the captain's cabin on the double. We have an intruder from the *Faith*."

The young woman held up both palms to S'jen, rapt at having her appear. "Praise the Crier!"

"Get back to your ship," S'jen ordered. She would have to seal the airlock against them. The man who had cut himself too vigorously during his daily dedication would be staying in their biobed during lust. He had nearly died from the blood loss caused by his injuries.

"I am your humble acolyte," the girl pleaded, her eyes large and dark against her pale skin. "I shall pray to the ancestors as you enter the holy rite of lust."

S'jen avoided her imploring hands as she stepped into her day cabin. The door slid shut behind her, blocking out the fanatic's benediction, "Praise the Crier!"

S'jen stood by the door in case the combat teams buzzed her. She couldn't bear to hear the woman's blasphemy as they removed her.

When the door slid aside, E'ven was standing there alone. "What happened? The combat team took S'amis away."

"It's nothing." S'jen considered him for a moment. Except for their *kantara* sessions, she had been avoiding him during *enfullem,* knowing that she could inadvertently imprint on him. "I wanted to speak to you, E'ven, about clan business."

"Good, so do I." He came in farther, letting the door slide shut behind him.

S'jen didn't know how to soften it. "I received word today from Endunara that as part of the settlement plan for Huut, all offspring from intermatings will be considered Clan Woot. There's no estimate, of course, but as many as half of our seventy-two refugees could be intermating with Woot."

"Why would they do that? Our women should bring new children to Huut."

"That's the terms of the settlement. You know the Huut refugees refused to relocate to Prian in spite of Endunara's proximity to the front. Since Prian is on the furthest edge of Qin, few clans are making the attempt. But it's the only colony planet that has land to give to a clan."

E'ven clenched one hand. "Huut should hold on until we can return to Balanc."

"I agree, E'ven. But that could take years. Our people

have already suffered two decades of Domain occupation and have little fight left in them."

"So Huut will be swallowed whole by Woot!"

"Yes," S'jen agreed. She hated that the Domain had cheated her at the last moment. When she thought her clan had finally been saved, one battleship had come in behind their defenses and destroyed her homeworld. Other Qin colonies feared the same fate, which was why the *Defiance* was placed far back like a spider in a web, ready to intercept the Fleet wherever they penetrated Qin territory.

E'ven paced, his hands working against each other. He had filled out quite a lot, and stood tall and strong, reminding S'jen of the young men she had known in Huut. E'ven was darker than her immediate family in Pentakost, but so much about him seemed familiar, especially his headstrong ways.

"Then I might as well deny lust, like you!" E'ven finally exclaimed.

Her breath caught at the terrible thought. "Lust is a sacred right. Whether or not your children are Huut, they will be your descendants. You must do your duty to yourself and Qin."

"Would you like S'amis to be my mate?" E'ven pointed to the door. "She pledged to help us rebuild Huut and bear my babies, all because I'm the Crier's clansmate!"

"No. . . ." What if other acolytes were invading Endunara to mate with Huut because they had some crazy idea that she was the Crier? S'jen thought that would be almost as bad as the extinction of Huut.

"I can't accept that fate," E'ven pressed. "To mate with a woman who worships you through me."

"Never," S'jen said in a hushed voice. "Surely there are others on board . . . J'staal or M'rika—"

"They have mates." E'ven's eyes were hard and flat, suddenly much older than his mere nineteen years. "I'll be lucky to get N'col, if she can't do better. And you know she'll never bear another child."

S'jen was shocked. N'col was nearly of her mother's generation, and E'ven was almost young enough to be S'jen's own child!

"I was too embarrassed to tell you," E'ven admitted. "I'm low man on the ship, with no clan to back me. And I'm at the maximum safe levels for cesium exposure. Even having *you* for a relative doesn't make up for that."

It was true that most children were born into the woman's clan, but some men managed to tempt mates into their own clan. Only the most prosperous clans increased that way, and Huut was on the verge of extinction. E'ven was an apprentice in training; he would need another decade to get enough experience to staff the center consoles. Until then, he could barely support himself on corpsmen compensation. Why had she never thought of all that?

E'ven faced her squarely. "Since it means nothing, I'll deny lust. At least I'll be in the best company."

S'jen herself had been an outcast for so long that it didn't matter anymore. But it mattered with E'ven. How could this fine young man, her own clanmate, be judged inferior by her own crew? How dare they!

"I measure Qin by a different standard," she declared. "When I see you, who has courage to burn and an unquenchable need to destroy our enemies, I say yes! This young man is the epitome of what a Qin should be."

E'ven reached out for her hands, clasping them. "I try to be worthy of you and our ancestors."

"That effort is everything. If only every Qin felt as we do. We would have a fighting force that could roll the Domain away from Qin forever. But so many give into their pains, like the poor remnants of our Huut. If only they could stand tall like you, resisting defeat, then Huut would survive in spite of these obstacles to grow powerful once again!"

E'ven pressed her hands. "Even if we lose Huut, then we will still be Qin's protectors."

S'jen felt the warmth of his palms, and her body responded in spite of her intentions. "I've imprinted on you," she gasped. Her hands pulled as if to reject the lure of lust.

But E'ven held on, not to be denied. "You wouldn't refuse our ancestors this rite?"

S'jen had been determined to forgo lust because it would be a useless, empty gesture by a woman who was not truly a woman. But now . . . she couldn't deny her own response. It went deeper than her body. It was a vibrant connection to the past, to her father and mother, and to the future, to the ancestors who would come after them.

It was ordained. "E'ven . . . will you join with me in lust?"

His fingers tightened on hers, and a shining light appeared in his eyes. "Yes, S'jen! Oh, yes!"

C'vid had just finished another gratifying lust with B'hom. This was their fifth together since S'jen had rescued them from the Fleet mining station. C'vid had lost a lust along with everyone else on Balanc when the Domain invaded their system. She'd had two halcyon lusts before the invasion, but never conceived. After the Fleet enslaved her, she had flown the badly shielded ore transports that had ruined both her and B'hom. That, and the loss of their clans, was probably why S'jen had become the focus of their lives.

C'vid went into the galley, and noticed that S'jen and E'ven were there. They were picking at the remnants of a huge meal, leaning back in their chairs. C'vid expected to be the first one out of lust, but E'ven was clearly satiated. She wondered who he had mated with . . . and stopped short when it dawned on her.

S'jen and E'ven! S'jen was too relaxed, too languid to have denied lust. C'vid remembered what had happened last time. S'jen was tight for decnights afterward. But now she was chewing with a dreamy abstraction that was very different from her usual incisiveness.

And E'ven . . . he was as proud as a newly minted admiral with a squadron of battleships. He kept glancing at S'jen with possessive certainty. He looked more mature, and not all of it was due to S'jen's strict diet and exercise regime. She must have overlooked how much of a man E'ven was becoming.

"Well, well . . . you two seem to have enjoyed yourself," C'vid said approvingly.

S'jen gave her a rare, beautiful smile. "We did."

Her expression when she looked at E'ven was indescribable, but it had something in it that C'vid had never seen before . . . contentment. S'jen had never been content with G'kaan. In fact, she had always pushed away G'kaan's affection. She needed someone more subtle, and E'ven struck the right note of quiet adoration. And why not? He was devoted to S'jen.

Who could be better for her than her own clanmate?

"I'm glad," C'vid said quietly. She had never mentioned lust to S'jen, not after her captain had returned to the *Fury*, where G'kaan had come looking for her again and again. Now S'jen seemed curiously approachable.

"Go get B'hom and join us," S'jen told her. "We're going to be here awhile."

C'vid felt her own smile. "We'll be right back!"

C'vid hurried to her berth, hoping she could fetch B'hom before S'jen returned to her usual steely self. He also deserved to see S'jen happy for once in her life.

19

Rose dived for the pilot's seat, so G'kaan settled into the comm terminal of the small aircar. "Prepare for departure," she announced gleefully.

G'kaan spared her an amused glance as he hurried through the final checks from the copilot's seat. G'kaan was glad to let her get as much practice as she could before—

He broke off at the terrible thought, even though it was undeniable. Rose needed to be able to fly the aircar herself because at some point, soon, she would be on her own. It was remarkable that the Fleet hadn't invaded Sol during their lust, but G'kaan had timed their invasion well. They would hold Sol for as long as they could, but eventually he would have to return to defend Qin. Somehow, from the eager way Rose discussed possible targets in the Canopus region between bouts of all-consuming sex, G'kaan didn't think Rose would be retreating to Qin with him.

But the Solians acted as carefree as children, never thinking of the dark times to come. From the command deck of the *Relevance*, Stub confirmed, *"Departure sequence engaged."*

"I can see that," Rose retorted.

"Don't get ahead of yourself there, Rose."

"Not much room for fun." Rose tossed her head at Stub, knowing he could see her in the imager on the command deck. "It's just a short hop to the *Endurance*."

"You could find fun inside a converter casing!" Stub laughed. *"I know you better than that, Rose."*

She powered up the aircar as G'kaan monitored the compact systems. Stub didn't seem to have missed his usual sex partner for the past several days. G'kaan, on the other hand, felt rather jealous of their banter. Every time he had asked Rose about Stub, she made some kind of joke. Apparently Rose didn't take Stub very seriously.

"Stabilizers on," Rose announced with a wink at G'kaan.

He nodded back, his own smile faint, knowing that he had delayed his stay on board the *Relevance* too long. With the remarkable new ability that Rose had taught him, G'kaan could have sex any time he wanted. He had proven that to himself many times over.

G'kaan flicked the control that disengaged the seal. The tiny ship shifted then pulled away smoothly from the patrolship. Leaving and entering dock were the two most dangerous procedures because it relied on the manual skill of the pilot. Rose did everything with bold confidence, even when she was wrong.

"Debarking complete," Rose informed the command crew of the patrolship.

"Gotcha. Fortitude *out,"* Stub signed off.

Usually the aircar was parked in the *Relevance*'s docking bay, but G'kaan had been in a hurry when he arrived. That reminded him of L'pash. She would be furious, and he deserved the full force of her anger. But at least she knew he wouldn't return. She told him so herself at the airlock. She must have made other arrangements with her cousins.

They were silent during the short ride. G'kaan thought back over what had happened, while Rose, most likely, focused completely on the helm. She wasn't one for introspection. G'kaan knew it would take time for him to assess everything. Even in lust, the most sacred Qin act, he had discovered a strong Solian core inside himself.

His only regret was not telling Rose the truth about the moonbase. The longer he put it off, the more difficult it became. Besides, that was ancient history and didn't have any real bearing on their present mission. It could also interfere in their newly formed Qin-Solian alliance. Yet G'kaan felt guilty because, in a way, he was using Sol once again as a bargaining chip with the Domain. The Qin would give up Sol, leaving behind the threat that they would take it back if the Fleet invaded Qin.

"There's your ship," Rose pointed.

The *Endurance* gleamed sliver in the sunlight, with reflected lines of light accenting the rounded cone. It moved silently, cutting cleanly through the darkness. That was *his* battleship. As strange as he felt after his unexpected lust with Rose, he knew he belonged on the *Endurance*.

When they docked at the airlock on his battleship, G'kaan turned to Rose to say good-bye. But she stood up. "I want to see Ash before I go back."

G'kaan almost stopped her. What if L'pash saw

Rose? But that was his own problem, not Rose's. He couldn't let anything interfere with Ash's therapy.

As he walked through the corridors with Rose, he nodded to various crew members who were still in their post-lust euphoria. But their eyes were doubtful and wary. They apparently knew he'd been away during lust, and they were probably thinking about all the rumored perversions practiced by Solians. G'kaan had seen enough to know many of the stories were true. Earlier today, Shard and Nip had come into their private room and started having sex on a nearby pile of cushions. Only Rose's enjoyment kept him from protesting, and soon the uninhibited sex had sucked him in and driven his lust to heights that astonished him. Watching them merge together as he felt himself melt into Rose . . .

His crew would be shocked if they knew the truth.

Rose was snickering as she followed him onto the lift. "They act like you sprouted another head or something. Is it really so weird to have sex with a Solian?"

"It's not amusing," he told her. "My crew must trust me."

Rose's eyes were alight and interested, and her hands ran up the sides of his flightsuit. "I had no idea you were such a rebel, G'kaan!"

In spite of his worries, G'kaan felt his body respond to her expert touch and the recklessness of being in a public place. His hands went to the generous curve of her hips, pulling her closer. "My mother was a Solian. From what M'ke says, she lit up my clan like laser fire. He says there's no one as playful or passionate as—"

The door of the lift slid aside. G'kaan looked up into L'pash's outraged face.

"Oh!" L'pash exclaimed, hands on her hips. "You're barbaric!"

Rose's arms tightened around him, not letting him go. "I wouldn't have put it that way myself, but come to think of it, he is kind of . . ."

L'pash's eyes shifted contemptuously from Rose to G'kaan. "At least I know what decency and honor is!"

G'kaan disengaged himself from Rose and joined L'pash in the corridor. "I'm very sorry, L'pash. I'm ashamed to say I didn't know my own intentions during *enfullem*."

"You *owed* it to me," L'pash insisted. "You kept me from finding a mate for lust."

"But you said you knew, L'pash. I thought you would make other arrangements."

"I don't mind sharing," Rose put in.

G'kaan winced, as L'pash barely restrained herself from striking Rose. He remembering his own aborted lust four years ago when S'jen disappeared. It had been painful, physically and emotionally. He had suffered a great deal afterward. L'pash had been there for him, supporting him when he needed a good friend.

"Everyone on board expected me to be your mate." Her upper lip lifted in a slight sneer. "You can hardly be sanctimonious now! You're no better than S'jen. In fact you're worse. You *knew* what you were doing to me."

Her voice rose and a crew member paused at the end of the corridor, looking their way. "L'pash . . ." he warned.

"It's a little too late to deal with this quietly, *Captain*. We should have discussed it before lust."

Rose raised both hands. "I'm outta here. I don't like a lot of drama with my sex. I'm going to see Ash."

She started to leave, but L'pash glared at the back of the Solian woman. "Good riddance! Why don't you take that mental defective with you?"

Rose turned on her. "What did you say?"

"Qin ships are for Qin," L'pash retorted. "Not Solian nutbags."

"Stop it!" G'kaan ordered. Two other crew members joined the first, frankly watching the fight.

"I'll gladly take Ash away from here!" Rose shouted.

"Maybe you can finish messing her mind up," L'pash retorted snidely.

"You *puta*—"

G'kaan had to grab hold of Rose's arms as she lunged at L'pash. Rose struggled, but she was short and comparatively slender. "Stop it, both of you!" he ordered again.

L'pash crossed her arms, defiantly snarling down at Rose, "Let her go! If she touches me I'll kill her."

"You wanna prove that? You don't know who you're talking to—"

G'kaan gave up and bodily carried Rose back into the lift. He hit the door button, holding Rose back with one arm. As the door slid shut between them, he forced himself to look into L'pash's hurt, furious eyes. Her anger was much stronger, fueled by her jealousy because he had chosen Rose over her. At least S'jen hadn't mated with another man after leading him on for years.

He wasn't sure he could ever fix things between him and L'pash.

"Let me go!" Rose exclaimed as the lift headed down again.

"Rose, you have to see it from her side. L'pash didn't have a mate for lust!" He felt awful. Somehow he had put the consequences out of his mind. Lust was good at wiping out things like responsibility. Impulse and desire reigned free. He had convinced himself that she had joined with her cousins, but there hadn't been enough time. He remembered his last lust, resisting the lure of breaking in on friends because it would be disruptive to include someone they hadn't imprinted on, even if they wanted to welcome him with open arms.

"I guess I'd be steamed if I knew I wouldn't get sex for another four years," Rose finally admitted.

"You've got to go back to the *Relevance*," G'kaan told her.

"But what about Ash?"

"Not now, Rose. My crew is still emotional because of lust. Nothing like that would have happened with L'pash if she was in her normal state of mind."

"I want to make sure Ash is okay. L'pash sounds like she's got something against hir."

"L'pash doesn't go near hir," G'kaan assured her. "You can come back in a couple of days."

The lift stopped on the deck where they had started. G'kaan tried not to rush Rose off his ship, but he sighed with relief when they reached the airlock without seeing anyone else.

Rose shook off his hand. "You know, I thought it was funny when I could watch you mixing it up with your women. But it's not so great *being* one of them."

She stalked through the airlock, leaving him high and dry. He had been thinking of stealing one last kiss, and getting in one last squeeze. But Rose never followed anyone else's plans.

The airlock clanged shut and sealed with a puff of air. He waited for her ship to depart. This was the airlock where he had left L'pash. He wondered how long she had waited here, and he knew he wouldn't be able to talk to her about it. L'pash would never forgive him.

The aircar broke away, dropping with a smooth dip from the side of the *Endurance*. In the back of his mind he reminded himself to warn Rose about the dangers of downward departures in front of the intake tubes, while the rest of him wished he could have gotten one more kiss before she left.

Rose put the aircar into flight, glad to leave the battleship. She had often wished the Qin would loosen up. But even when they were uninhibited, they were dreary. She actually felt sorry for them, living it up for only a weekend every few years. G'kaan would probably turn back into his old stuck-up, awkward self. Too bad. He was a lot of fun once he let go.

"Moonbase to aircar," the comm announced.

"Rose here," she replied, keying the imager on.

Chad appeared in front of her. His brown flightsuit was open at the neck, and his sleeves were rolled up, showing his muscled forearms. *"You alone, Rose?"*

"Yeah, I just dropped off G'kaan."

"Then why don't you come down and pick up me and Kwort?" Chad gave a slight whistle through his teeth, one of Clay's signals for danger. They hadn't shared their secret language to the Qin. For Chad to be using it on an open channel surely meant something serious.

Rose narrowed her eyes. "I'll be right there," she agreed.

Rose had a lot of practice landing in the docking bays on the moonbase. She had ferried more than her share of Free Solians up and down from the moon. She settled the aircar into the bay, passing through the electromagnetic forcefield similar to the technology in their flightsuits. Chad and Kwort were waiting at the end of the docking cradle. Kwort was wearing one of his technicolor flightsuits, and that helped guide her in.

Once she joined them, she asked, "Shouldn't you be drilling your crew, Chad?"

"I'll put the *Tranquillity* against your ship anytime," Chad retorted. "At least most of my crew have had some kind of flight training on Earth."

Rose waved one hand. "A minor point against space experience. Why'd you drag me down here?" She glanced meaningfully at Chad's aircar, nestled in the adjoining cradle.

"Well, while you were playing Ravish the Maiden with G'kaan, I took the chance to check out the moonbase."

Her eyes opened wide. "You think the Qin are hiding something from us?"

Kwort nodded along with Chad. "We found the proof, Captain."

Rose stood in a huge bay, with an arched ceiling big enough to hold the arena back home in Tijuana.

"There it is." Chad shoved his big hands into the pockets of his flightsuit.

Antigrav platforms lined every wall. In the center was a stupendous square machine pierced by a gigantic spike. It looked as if it was tilted up on one corner with the spike projecting from the top of the square into the upper corner of the bay.

"What is it?" she asked, tilting her head. It looked familiar somehow.

"An orbital laser cannon," Kwort said in awe. "That's the support platform in the middle. . . ."

The odd angles and rows of hatches suddenly made sense. Rose had often seen the laser cannon above Earth, orbiting exactly opposite the moonbase. This cannon was lying on its side, whereas the one in orbit floated with deadly intent, its muzzle aimed into space. The spaceships plotted a course around it carefully, even though it was remote-controlled by the moonbase. Nobody wanted any accidents with a cannon that could disintegrate them at close range.

"The Qin must have found this," Rose agreed. It had taken some time on the grav sled to get through the winding and seemingly never-ending tunnels and bays, but the bay was in one of the uppermost sections of the base. "They couldn't have missed something this big."

"The bay is listed on the maps they gave us, but it doesn't say it's occupied."

"Why didn't they tell us? It would increase our firepower by fifty percent."

"Yeah, if it worked," Kwort put in. "But it's broken."

Chad shrugged at Rose, and she could tell he felt the same way. Broken or not, this cannon was a resource that should have been shared.

Rose had doubted Chad's loyalty, but looking at him now, she knew she never would again. G'kaan had been Chad's mentor and had supported him more than her. But Chad and Rose were Solians. They would always be on the same side.

"Are you sure it can't be fixed?"

Chad joined Kwort at the diagnostic terminal. "Stand here."

Kwort activated the terminal as Rose braced herself. The antigrav units lifted the console along with platform they stood on. With smooth acceleration, it rose up the spaceframe of the laser cannon. Rose could see the exterior shell of polytanium welded into segments. They formed pathways for the utilities grid underneath. She hadn't realized how big the laser cannon was, but it was nearly as long as her own patrolship. Much of that space was taken up with the plasma generators and solar fuel cells.

"See this," Kwort explained, pointing to the screen on the diagnostic terminal. "The primary and secondary emitters are fused. It was brought in here for repairs."

"Then it could be fixed," she insisted.

"Their bot techs gave up a long time ago." Kwort shrugged. "The thermal feedback blew out the energy conduits right down to the main trunk. The channels are ruined. They'd have to be completely ripped apart and rebuilt, which it looks like they started to do."

"Maybe we interrupted them," Rose suggested.

"We think they gave up a long time ago." Chad maneuvered the diagnostic unit down and to one side. "See that dust buildup?"

Rose leaned against the baffling force that kept them from falling off the edge. A pile of ashy dust covered the horizontal surfaces. "I thought this place was sealed."

"Even with the best sealants, fines like that eventually get in. But it must have taken decades for the dust to get piled that high."

Rose nodded in agreement. At least the Qin weren't guilty of holding back a source of defensive fire. "Why do you think G'kaan didn't tell us about this?"

Chad shook his head. "I've got all my off-duty crew searching the base right now. When I found this baby, I brought Kwort down. He's been poking around to see if he could get it going again. Tell her what you found."

"It was in the firing logs," Kwort explained. He operated the diagnostic unit, taking them lower and out to one side of the platform. A round indentation marked the subprocessing node. Kwort tapped in some commands, and the screen came alive.

"The scanners continually record cannon operations. I've activated the logs for the last engagement for this cannon."

Rose looked over Kwort's head, squeezing in closer to Chad. She was reminded of G'kaan, in how tall and solidly built Chad was.

On the screen, the spectrally enhanced view of star-spangled space shifted. The stars turned into streaks of white light. As Rose tilted her head, the edge of Earth came into view. The blue haze of atmosphere gleamed for a moment, but the image was shifting too fast for it to focus. The view came to rest facing the atmosphere directly below.

"The cannon's pointing at Earth," Rose realized. "Can the other one do that?"

"I checked after I saw this. It can," Kwort agreed. "But the Creh techs locked it down in its outward position before the Solians came up."

"We'll have to do something about that," Chad said flatly. "All it would take is someone getting control of the cannon, and everyone on Earth is in danger."

As the log continued to play, the edge of a continent came into view under swirling patches of clouds, leaving behind the glinting sea. The stark brownish green edge was enhanced, and Rose could see the fine line of white along some of the curved bays.

"Hey, there's Tijuana!" she exclaimed, pointing at the bottom of the screen. From flying in, she had learned to pick out the slender finger of land on the coast where her enclave rested.

Kwort was busy explaining, "From the angle of the shadows, this laser cannon was once positioned nearly halfway between the current cannon and the moonbase. I think they were each responsible for covering one-third of the defensive perimeter, which would give them better coverage."

"But it's facing inward," Rose protested.

"Watch . . ." Chad warned.

As the cannon passed over the continent, the scanners enhanced the image again and again, bringing a smaller section into focus. Rose could see the jagged peaks of the mountains that ran in a thick column down the western half of the continent. The ones at the southernmost edge reached Tijuana. But here the rocky tops were covered in blinding white snow.

"The cannon is being remotely engaged by the moonbase," Kwort warned her, pointing to the symbols that ran along the bottom of the log.

Even Rose recognized the fire sequence from her own patrolship. "It's—"

A fat stream of deep purple erupted from the cannon. From the scanner's close angle to the muzzle of the cannon, most of the screen was blocked by the incandescent stream, burning so furiously it was almost invisible as it swallowed all light.

Rose gulped as the beam squarely punched into the mountains. A plume of boiling dirt rose into the air, billowing up around the plasma beam. But the thick column of plasma seared on, making her flinch away from the recording.

Then everything disappeared in a huge explosion.

Rose gasped. "What was that?"

"I checked the coordinates," Chad said quietly. "They targeted a magma chamber not far beneath the surface. It was rising, bowing up the land, and when the plasma broke the tensile surface a supereruption occurred." Chad shrugged as if he didn't need to explain.

The scanners pulled back to view the growing mushroom cloud that blocked out half of North America. "The northern volcano . . ."

"You knew about this?"

The cloud was rapidly receding as they cannon continued in its orbit. "It was the greatest disaster ever. It happened sometime in the twenty-first century, I don't know exactly when. It took out the most powerful country on Earth, and that's when the World Council began to gain influence—" Her head snapped up. "The Domain did this!"

"Yes, it's tactically smart to take out the leading defense force when you're subjugating a planet. The Fleet's done that plenty of times, according to G'kaan. But Solians have been slaves for thousands of years. These logs are only about nine decades old."

"Maybe we were close to figuring out about the slave trade."

"Whatever the reason," Kwort put in, "I think this cannon was brand-new when it jammed. The levels were at maximum in order to punch deep enough through the crust to hit the magma. The valves on the feedback channels froze open and that's probably what fused the emitter channels. It apparently was only test-fired at minimum levels, so nobody realized there was a flaw in the valves."

She looked down at the now black screen. "Do you have a copy of this?"

"Yes, in my dataport. And Kwort also has a copy." Chad's expression darkened. "I've instructed my search teams to signal me if they pick up any other discrepancies between the map the Qin gave us and the base itself. But the combat teams should be down again soon, and they'll chase us out again."

"Not this time." Rose wasn't sure why the Qin would hide something like this from the Solians. Earth was their homeworld and they had the right to know everything about the Domain occupation. She thought G'kaan agreed with that. "I'll tell G'kaan that I've given complete control of the moonbase to Free Sol. He can't argue with that. Let's go tell Enzo what we found, and maybe they can spare other searchers."

"That's another thing," Chad added. "Why did the Fleet need to build a base this huge? They've only been using a small corner of it. The rest is fast running into ruin."

"When you know the answer to that, let me know." Rose smacked her hands together. "Meanwhile take us down. I'll go back to the *Relevance* and run interference with the Qin. They'll probably redeploy to their defensive positions soon anyway."

Kwort settled the diagnostic unit onto the floor of the bay, as Chad replied, "I don't think so. G'kaan told me he's planning to wait in orbit for whatever comes."

"That won't give us much warning, even with the remote comms."

"It makes sense to concentrate his forces. Especially if the Fleet sends in more than one battleship." Chad gave her a sideways look. "Thank goodness we have the Qin on our side. Good job with G'kaan, by the way. Sealed with a kiss. . . ."

Rose snorted. "Oh, please!"

"I've seen you do it before," he reminded her.

As obnoxious as Chad was, he had been trained by G'kaan, so he was the best person to assess the Qin's behavior.

Rose made a decision. "When I'm done on the *Relevance*, I'll come back and help you here. You can tell me what you think G'kaan is up to."

20

"It will be okay," Gandre Li assured herself, as she'd been doing since Herntoff had taken Trace prisoner. For a decnight, Herntoff had refused her pleas to see Trace. Gandre Li couldn't sleep, she couldn't concentrate, all she could think about was Trace. She didn't know how to be alone anymore. Trace had been by her side constantly since InSec had given the young Solian to her. Gandre Li tried to be patient, but she couldn't wait any longer.

"Careful, the hatch will drop when it's unlatched," Takhan warned. She held the antigrav sled steady for her captain. All three of the crew had been helping Gandre Li try to reach Trace, but so far they'd had no luck.

Gandre Li keyed open the hatch, holding it with one hand. It swung down, as Takhan had warned. She positioned herself directly underneath the access tube.

"Lift me higher, Takhan." Gandre Li held on to the lip of the hatch as the sled silently rose. She had to bend and crawl into the access tube on her belly. Like most Bariss, she was bigger than other humanoids and it was a tight fit.

She pressed the comm strapped around her wrist. "Danal, Jor, is there any sign of Herntoff?"

"Negative," Danal replied in his precise way. He was inside Spacepost P-19, keeping an eye on the various entrances into the upper landing disc.

"The docking arm is clear," Jor also acknowledged from his position in front of the airlock.

"I'm going in," Gandre Li announced.

On the deck above was the lounge and the passenger cabins. The upper and lower safety hatches inside the cabins had been sealed as per guild regulations. It was intended to prevent crew members from unauthorized entry into passenger quarters. Takhan had tried to open the lock on the door with her bots, but was baffled by the unusual seal.

Gandre Li crawled rapidly forward on her knees and elbows. She was so familiar with her ship that she didn't need the bulkhead crossings to know when the cabins were overhead. She went another body length to avoid the bunk, then lay down and rolled on her back so she could access the upper safety hatch. That would bring her through the floor into the small adjoining cabin where Trace was being held captive.

Pressing the two outer taps, she pushed against the hatch to pop it open. It jumped out of her fingers and clattered to one side.

Gandre Li was through the hatch almost as fast. But it took a few moments to see by the light on her wrist comm. The cabin was empty.

"Too late!" She clenched her hands into fists so tight her bones cracked. She should have come through the access tube the first night Herntoff took Trace. He must have noticed their tampering with the lock.

Gandre Li went to the door between the two cabins. On the other side was the grand suite that Alphas and Betas used while they were on board. The two cabins at the front end of the lounge were much smaller.

Trace was in there, and Gandre Li already knew she couldn't get through Herntoff's lock. So she had to enter via the access tube. Breaking the seal on the cabin of a paying customer was a serious infraction. She could be heavily fined and might even lose guild membership if Herntoff successfully pressed charges. Yet she could always countercharge that Herntoff had held her slave hostage. The guild members were all Betas, so they would sympathize with her, having been the brunt of Alphan privilege themselves.

At this point, Gandre Li was past caring about a guild inquisition. She was deep into desperate measures. She had to see Trace.

Back down into the access tube, she pulled the hatch over her head and pressed it into place. From inside the cabin, a fine red line would show around the hatch as a warning to the occupant that it had been opened.

Gandre Li took a deep breath and crawled forward. She was going to break guild regulations. When she reached the hatch that she had targeted, she rolled over and grasped the tabs. She hoped the *Solace*'s record was strong enough to withstand a few squawks from a Fleet bean-counter.

She pressed the tabs and pushed, but nothing happened. Wiggling forward, she got her foot underneath the hatch. With a grunt, she released the tabs and kicked. It felt solid under her boot, as if she were kicking one of the bulkheads.

She kicked a few more times, throwing her body

into it. The smooth metal didn't show a dent, but it felt like she had pulled something in her hip. The hatch didn't budge. Hoping it was a faulty hatch, she tried three others to get inside the cabin. Eventually, she had to give up in despair, raw from the pounding. She lay there breathing heavily, thwarted by Herntoff once again. He must have locked the hatches from inside somehow.

Trace could be dead, for all she knew.

Gandre Li crawled backward, dragging herself through the tubes. When she reached the open access hatch, Takhan raised the pallet to the ceiling so the captain could slide out.

"She's in Herntoff's cabin," Gandre Li told her mechanic. "He's sealed his hatches somehow."

Takhan's eyes opened wide. "He likes magnetic locks, doesn't he?"

Gandre Li shrugged, hoping there weren't worse things in that giant module for Trace. Supposedly Herntoff only examined her during his lust. Now that Trace was pregnant, that could have changed.

Gandre Li still hadn't told the crew about Trace's baby. It would be better for them if they didn't know. So she was back to lying to her own crew.

"I could try the lock again," Takhan offered.

Gandre Li put her hand on the woman's shoulder. Takhan was young but she had experienced more than most people. She had lost her Aborandeen family, though she knew which region their ship was traveling in. Gandre Li didn't even have that. Her mother and brother had disappeared a decade and a half ago, "relocated" by the Life Sciences Institute. Despite several trips back to Verger in the Gyan region, Gandre Li had found no trace of them. They could have reached her through the guild registry, but she never heard a word.

That was why she had created a family with Trace. "Thanks anyway, Takhan. I have another idea."

Gandre Li didn't confide her next plan to anyone. Takhan was the bot expert, but Gandre Li had grown up playing with the maintenance bots on her mother's science outpost, taking them apart and putting them back together again. While her hands were busy deactivating a wall-cleaning bot and opening the casing to get into its guts, she remembered how her mother had smiled as she refused to move on board the first old intrasolar transport Gandre Li had acquired. Her mother was a homebody, loving those jungles on Verger. Her brother, Bineet, had still been in school when Gandre Li decided to risk making a life for herself outside the system. He had been about the same age as Trace was when InSec had given her to Gandre Li. Maybe that's why she had felt protective of the girl for a long time, never pressuring her into having sex.

Gandre Li tried to concentrate on the "brains" of the bot. She intended to program it to make patterns on the wall when it cleaned, spelling out a message to Trace. That would require some elaborate reprogramming of the drive sequence.

When she first noticed the minibot inside the casing, she thought it was one of Takhan's efficiency regulators. But it wasn't stamped with the ship's seal as all bots were supposed to be. Takhan was not the type to forget something like that.

The minibot was smaller than her fingernail, and it was nestled against the phase-interface nodes of the scanner array. The faded maroon casing belled out at one end. Gandre Li squinted. It looked almost like . . . no, it *was* a tiny amplifier!

The minibot was a bug, and an ingenious one at that. It was linked directly to the scanner array of the cleaning bot. It could tap the software interface at the nodes, reading whatever the bot's antennae scanners picked up and relaying the data. Because it was a parasite, it had no scanner emissions to be picked up by their sweeps. With the wall bot deactivated, the bug couldn't use its scanners. But there might be others—

Gandre Li quickly glanced around. There was a floor bot behind her, humming slightly as it rolled slowly away from her across the floor.

She stretched, flexing her neck casually, even though she knew nobody could be watching her. The bot-bug must have been left over from Rikev's reign of terror.

She had transported plenty of InSec types, and she was sure Herntoff was not the kind of Alpha who would be interested in planting surveillance on a courier crew. Then again, anything was possible, especially after Archernar shipyard. She glanced at the small window in her terminal that showed Herntoff Alpha sitting in the lounge. He'd been there ever since he returned from his counting session today on the spacepost. They were scheduled to depart at the beginning of the next shift, after their supplies were loaded.

Feeling spooked, Gandre Li grabbed the floor bot as she left the day cabin, making sure its antennae couldn't see the unassembled wall bot on her desk. She dumped it off in the corridor and headed to the medical bay.

The crew were on leave until their departure from Spacepost P-19. The sector had been almost shut down by the Qin invasion of Sol. But the patrolships were pulling out to surround Sol, letting shipping resume in Procyon again. Gandre Li had seen several patrolships on their way into the sector, explaining why there were so many raiders now in Pyxis, the neighboring sector they left behind. It was actually safer here even though they were closer to the Qin invasion.

She picked up the bioscanner from its cradle and ran an autodiagnostic of its condition. Working perfectly.

Back in her day cabin, she checked to make sure there were no other cleaning bots in her rooms. She was going to have to ask Takhan to take every one of them apart to fish out the minibots. Any Alpha who had the same equipment as Rikev might be able to use them. From beginning to end, Rikev Alpha had been too much for her. Only his timely death had saved them.

She programmed the bioscanner to perform a genetic analysis, then tightened the focus of the aperture. Using the laser light to target the tiny minibot, she activated the scanner. She had to hold her arm very still to avoid reading the surrounding components.

The scanner beeped when intake was complete. She set it in the cradle of her terminal and accessed the data from there. Some might call her paranoid, but she always got a genetic sample of her paying customers. The codes were kept in secure files stored in the subprocessor in her day cabin, off the ship's net. She had discovered a long time ago that it was impossible to secure anything in the main database of her ship.

The results from the scan indicated that DNA from two individuals other than her own had been detected on the minibot. She had contaminated it herself when she opened the cleaning bot. She bet the other one was

Takhan, and she was right. Proof that Takhan did a thorough maintenance job, forcing her genetic scraps inside the casing of the cleaning bot. Gandre Li had been responsible for enough cleaning bots to know that they needed the most care because they were designed to pick up debris. Takhan hadn't found these bugs because routine maintenance didn't involve opening the casing unless significant repairs were needed. And at that point the bot was usually discarded for a newer model.

The other scrap of genetic material was a partial strand, but it was enough to preliminarily identify it as an Alpha. Gandre Li ran it against her database of previous passengers, and as she expected, a match sprang up.

It was Herntoff Alpha.

She checked again to be sure, thinking it couldn't be Herntoff. But then again . . . He was twitchy and insignificant, but InSec didn't pick their operatives because they were superior Alphas. As long as they got the job done, that's what mattered to InSec. They must know after decades of transporting their operatives that Gandre Li could identify any ordinary undercover agent. Herntoff was unusual even for InSec. He had completely fooled her.

If Herntoff was watching them through the cleaning bots, then he knew everything. Not only about Trace's pregnancy, but about the help they had given to Rose and the Solians who had liberated Earth.

Gandre Li checked on Herntoff in the monitor. He was still sitting in the lounge. He didn't know yet that the wall bot had been deactivated. She tucked the heavy bioscanner into her large thigh pocket along with a few of her bot tools.

Then she closed the cleaning bot and activated it

again. She set it on the wall with a pat, and returned to her duty files. Lately it was increasingly difficult to get fuel, so she had to fill out the various requisition forms and authoriziation releases. So she might as well get on with it.

She tried to act normal, keeping the window on Hertnoff open on her monitor. He got up at one point and went into his cabin. Even with the angle of her cameras, she could barely see an empty slice of the room in the brief time the door was open.

She concentrated on her shipwork knowing that Herntoff could be reviewing the logs of the surveillance bots, especially the one in her room. There would be an unexplained gap of several minutes, and she knew her behavior was critical right now.

Her heart was beating too fast. She had been lulled into underestimating Herntoff by his neurotic behavior. It had seemed like a wonderful gift to get his contract, exactly what they needed after the courier delay charges caused by taking Rikev to Sirius. But Rikev may have told InSec about her. And since *Solace* was one of the last ships to leave Archernar shipyard before Rose's spectacular escape, a red flag must have been raised in some InSec commander's office.

If Herntoff was an InSec operative and his mission was to investigate her, she was a goner along with every member of her crew, including Trace.

Gandre Li trembled when Herntoff appeared again in the lounge. He had only been inside for a few minutes and he looked exactly the same as usual.

She needed confirmation. Because if it was true, she was going to have to take drastic action.

She nonchalantly grabbed her large cup to get some

elixir. She often went to the galley to get a cold one. This time she took a roundabout route to stop by the command deck. Even though the *Solace* was in dock, the command deck was bright and active with autoprograms watching over the environmental controls and operating systems.

Holding the cup next to her terminal, she checked the status of the ship. Unobtrusively, she swept the small cleaning bot from the surface into the cup. There was a big floor bot on the other side, but it couldn't see her. The small bot was upside down in the cup, so its scanners were also blocked.

She ducked into the fresher and checked carefully for bots. The little room was already scrubbed cleaned, probably by the bot in her cup.

She deactivated it, then peeled open the carapace with one of the picks she had secreted in her pocket. There, next to the scanner array, was another dull red minibot. She aimed the laser sighter of the bioscanner on the minibot, trying to keep her hand from trembling. The process was quick, but it felt incredibly slow. She had to get the bot activated and back into circulation.

Finally the bioscanner beeped and correlated the results. It was faster this time, because there was only one sample on the minibot and it was a match from her first run. Herntoff Alpha.

Somehow Gandre Li got the cleaning bot back together and activated in record time; then she deposited it on the terminals. Mechanically she fetched the elixir and went back to her day cabin. The floor bot tried to follow her inside. Normally she would gently jostle it in, and she shuddered as she forced herself to do exactly that. It settled into its routine, the seemingly chaotic pattern that ensured the floor was thoroughly cleaned.

She sat down at her terminal and activated the monitor, complete with the window that kept an eye on Herntoff. She couldn't change her routine in the slightest, or he would know she had broken his cover.

As she pretended to do her shipwork, her fingers faltered. Her life was over. With sophisticated minibots like that, she couldn't hope that Herntoff hadn't included lip-synchronization software to track what they were saying. They thought they were alone when they had talked about Rose and the Qin invasion of Sol. Not to mention their veiled references to Archernar shipyard. Along with Trace's pregnancy, it was more than enough. She would be taken into custody by InSec when they returned to Capetta, and would be questioned again under the uninhibitor. Depending on her answers, her crew would be next. Who knew what would happen to Trace and her baby!

Funny how things could change so quickly. For a long time, Gandre Li had been gradually moving away from the Domain and her InSec life. Even though it was suicide, even though it would be nearly impossible to make the alterations necessary to reidentify the *Solace*, even though they faced destruction by scores of raiders off the Fleet-beaten track . . . she had no choice.

And there was no time to waste. Herntoff was obviously a professional. She would give herself away sooner rather than later. She also couldn't allow her crew to get involved because things could go hideously wrong. So it had to happen now, before they left Spacepost P-19, which made it even riskier.

According to the chrono, Herntoff would head down

to the galley for a meal soon. He usually piled a tray with twice as much food as he needed and took it up to his cabin. Gandre Li had checked the transposer, which disgorged lots of bland, healthy food that Trace must hate. Herntoff was remarkably rigid in his routines, so she had no doubt when he got up and moved to the spiral stairs that he was on his way down.

Gandre Li dived for the cupboard that held her stunguns. They were fully charged, as usual. Rose had used them last.

She darted through the door and around the side corridor, priming the gun. She would have a good shot of Herntoff as he turned the corner. Raising the gun with both hands, she sighted down the corridor . . . and knew she was about to step over the edge of the abyss.

Before she could think twice about it, Herntoff appeared. He saw her and flinched back. Her finger tightened on the gun and the energy jolted into him. She felt the gun buzz in her hands as he went down.

Gandre Li had stunned other people before, including a crew member who'd gone berserk. But this felt like it happened much quicker than her previous experiences.

Herntoff was suddenly a much bigger problem lying on the immaculate floor of her ship.

Gandre Li hastily assembled her gear. She bound Herntoff to the antigrav board and took him up to the lounge in the cargo lift. He would be unconscious for a while, but to be safe she shoved the primed stungun into her cartridge belt, and grabbed wrist and ankle restraints on the way up.

Outside Herntoff's cabin, she adjusted the grav board until it stood straight up. Prying open one of his eyes, she tried to get the lock to accept a scan of his retina. Unfortunately "pupils fixed and dilated" was not a mode the lock accepted.

She steered Herntoff into one of the opposite cabins, then locked the wrist and ankle restraints on him. For good measure, she left him bound to the antigrav board. If he was an InSec operative, even he might be able to get out of that. She knew the only way to stop him would be to kill him.

By the time her crew returned, she was halfway through the bulkhead. They trooped upstairs at the grating sound of the laser cutter and stared at her as if she had gone mad.

"Maybe this is how Rose feels," Gandre Li told them with a grin. "It's not bad! A nice rush of adrenaline can really give you a boost."

"What are you doing, Captain?" Jor held out his hands, looking from her face to the tip of the laser cutter.

"You think I'm a danger to myself and others?" she countered, lifting the cutter a bit. "Maybe you should go to your quarters until I call you. Or better yet, get your stuff and get out!"

Jor glanced at Takhan, then shook his head. "You're not throwing us off the ship that easily."

Takhan nodded, her head cocked. "You should be using the higher frequencies for that bulkhead."

"Thanks." Obviously hints weren't enough. "Listen, I'm trying to get you guys off the hook if you're questioned later. So why don't you be a good crew and obey your captain for once?"

"We're already in it up to our eyeballs," Takhan said flatly. Danal nodded along with Jor, who added, "If you think we're going to stand here and watch you break into our passenger's cabin, you're wrong."

"You're going to stop me?" Gandre Li retorted indignantly.

"No, we're going to help you." Takhan took the laser cutter away from her. "Sheesh! It's a wonder you haven't cut off a finger holding it that way. Now stand back."

Gandre Li knew they had as much right as she did to throw their lives away. All she cared about was Trace.

Takhan neatly and rapidly cut a large chunk of bulkhead out of the ship. Her expression was fierce, like the others, wondering what they would find on the other side.

Jor helped Takhan lift the cut piece away, and Gandre Li was the first one inside. The round examining table that Trace had described was set up in the main room. The module was open and she saw some equipment on the table that looked like a scanner receiver, but she didn't stop in her search for Trace. The Solian wasn't in the sleeping nook, so she checked the last place left, the fresher.

The door was locked from the outside, but Takhan cut it open with a couple of passes with her laser cutter. So much for subtly. When the door opened, a blast of warm air greeted her.

"Trace!" Gandre Li cried out.

The Solian was naked, crouching down on some blankets in the corner. Her head raised in confusion, revealing that she had become disoriented from being locked in the small space for so many days. Remnants of food on a tray showed that at least she had been fed.

Gandre Li helped Trace stand up, feeling how frail she was. With Trace naked, the bulge of her belly was very pronounced, more than Gandre Li remembered. Trace tried to see but her eyes blinked in the brighter light.

"I felt it," Trace murmured.

Gandre Li wasn't sure if she knew the others were in the room. "That's fine, Trace. Let's put this around you." She wrapped a large towel around Trace's shoulders. Not that there was any reason to hide the baby from the crew now. They would have to know everything to decide if they wanted to abandon the Domain along with her and Trace.

As if hearing her unspoken thought, Trace smiled mistily up at Gandre Li. "I can feel the baby move, Gandi. It's the most incredible thing. . . ."

Trace's head dropped onto her shoulder. Gandre Li picked her up to carry her downstairs. "Don't go in the starboard cabins," she warned the crew. "Herntoff is in there."

They couldn't help looking that direction. But Jor asked, "Baby? Is she delirious? Trace *can't* be pregnant."

Gandre Li met their eyes, and that was enough for them to know the truth. "I have lots to tell you. But first we've got to get Trace back where she belongs."

21

Winstav was amazed when Heloga appeared at the Arts Complex on Canopus Prime wearing a translucent lavender mist. Her dazzling ensemble rivaled the fashions he had seen on Rigel not too long ago. His own sheer body stocking was just as stylish, but he subverted fashion to the ability to melt into a crowd by including the standard evening cape.

Heloga's personal style was back as well. She strolled through the ornate, golden lobby of the amphitheater as if she owned the place. It was a reminder that she had power over every person and every budget in the region.

Winstav had been following Heloga everywhere, trying to discover the secret of her revival. He had seen her decaying face with his own eyes, and her impending death had been clear. Yet somehow she had completely recovered her youthful gleam. He had scanned and imaged her from every angle and under every condition, but she was restored to perfection.

As if to forestall reports of her demise, Heloga had appeared everywhere, including openings, parties, fashion shows, concerts, games, and social events. Her image appeared in association with anything of note that happened. She had also done several official interviews currently being publicized throughout Canopus, assuring the populace that the Qin would be dealt with severely.

As full as her social calendar was, Heloga's work performance also snapped back to its former heights as she summoned delinquent subordinates into her office for a personal reaming. She sent two of her own staff, including Oliv Alpha, to the Alpha Institute on Spinca for evaluation. Oliv, once a useful informant, wouldn't even speak to Winstav prior to his departure. No one doubted that Heloga was completely in command of herself, Canopus Prime, and the region.

Heloga wafted through the adoring and respectful crowd who were attending the dance performance at the Arts Complex amphitheater in the northern quadrant of Prime. As her entourage of assistants and enforcers passed by, Heloga paused next to Winstav. Her smile deepened. "I expected to see you here, Winstav. You're always found in the best places."

"As are you, Regional Commander." At one time he would have called her Heloga, but it paid to be cautious now that her star was in the ascendant.

"Enjoy it while it lasts," Heloga warned.

His smiled. "Of course, there won't be any concerts where I'm going."

"Yes . . . you've lingered here too long, delaying the destruction of Qin. I will be forced to lodge a protest with the regents if you don't take the *Allegiance* to join the battleship squadron immediately."

It was a direct attack in a public place, not what Winstav had expected. Heloga was haughty, hardly deigning to look at him, while her voice was loud enough for people in the area to overhear.

He couldn't allow her to rattle him. "Your Fleet commander agreed that it would be prudent to retain the *Allegiance* in case the Qin attacked Regional Headquarters."

"The border has been sealed off by my patrolships. The Qin battleship is in Sol, and you should be there assisting Felenore."

Winstav had reached that conclusion himself as far as overall strategy was concerned. But he had remained at Regional Headquarters to complete Heloga's downfall while building a solid following that he could offer to the incoming regional commander. According to his latest information from Spinca, Pirosha was currently the most likely candidate to advance in rank and assume Heloga's place.

But now everything had changed.

Heloga's smile was exactly the same. "The battleship squadron should be entering Sol by now. You will proceed directly to the Qin border to rendezvous with Felenore for the final sweep. I want the job done by the end of the quarter. I've assigned four additional patrolships to assist you."

He was looking closely at Heloga's mouth, or he would have missed it. There was a slight lag between the sound of her last few words and the way her lips moved.

"That's very generous, Regional Commander," Winstav forced himself to reply. His grace period was over. He would have to deal with the Qin before he could finish Heloga off. He knew her days were numbered, but that wasn't enough.

"I expect the *Allegiance* to depart by tomorrow."

Winstav gallantly started to reply, "But, Regional Commander, how could I miss your party—"

Ignoring him, Heloga gathered her entourage and sailed away without giving him the chance to finish. The enforcers closed in around her, keeping everyone at a distance except for those Heloga greeted. Winstav trailed along behind.

He was certain Heloga's rejuvenation was artificial. That small hesitation when she was speaking was intriguing. But it was not enough.

Kristolas Alpha, the manager of the Arts Complex, fawned over Heloga as he welcomed her. The tall Alpha with the creamy complexion even put one hand protectively at her back as he ushered her into the best balcony in the theater. Winstav remembered Kristolas from Heloga's public display of jealousy over Olhanna. Now Kristolas was overly attentive, perhaps caught up like everyone else on Prime in a desperate effort to get back into the good graces of their mistress.

Heloga was back on top, and there was nothing Winstav could do about it. He might as well board *Allegiance* tonight and concentrate on vanquishing the Qin.

Winstav glumly sat in a nearby balcony, watching Heloga more than the performance. He wasn't alone in his fascination. Heloga preened and shifted her perfect body under the misty covering, obviously pleased that she was the center of attention. Kristolas and several other favored male Alphas were seated around Heloga, and they took turns whispering to her while plying her with savory morsels throughout the show. Her personal enforcers lined the back of the box, their eyes wary as they faced the audience, who were staring at Heloga rather than the stage.

In fact, there was only one person in the theater who watched the performance. One of Heloga's enforcers wasn't scanning the audience defensively. Instead, the Beta with the long neck was straining to see the dancers. He seemed to mutter to himself, sometimes shaking his head, other times nodding eagerly, his brow furrowing. His behavior was incomprehensible. Clearly he was so enthralled by the activity on the stage that he wasn't doing his duty. Heloga glanced back at her enforcers a few times throughout the evening, but her expression was more self-satisfied than irritated by the Beta's behavior.

Winstav consulted his database implant. As he thought, the Beta with the long neck was new. There was no information on his previous residence prior to joining Heloga's household. Winstav ran a search for the name that was listed, but found no identity matches for that kind of Beta. His database implant was more extensive than most since he had worked in so many regions, so he tended to think that it was no coincidence. The Beta was not who he appeared to be.

Heloga had acquired that lovely complexion around the same time the Beta appeared. Indeed, Winstav's Poid informant in the slave compound had remarked that Heloga had a new favorite who was allowed to go through pleasure slaves as if they were water.

When the show ended, the Beta resumed his duties. His post was at Heloga's heels. The other enforcers actively helped Heloga through the crowds, blocking off aisles and corridors to make way for her. But the long-necked Beta merely moved his head back and forth, keeping watch.

As they passed, Winstav noticed that he was wearing

a large flat knapsack on his back. It looked like a charger for stunwands, with a slot for the wands to fit into. It wasn't an unusual piece of equipment for personal enforcers to carry, but it was the first time he had noticed it among Heloga's security team. Maybe Heloga was making a point, but then again, maybe it was something else.

Winstav waited at the back of his balcony until the theater emptied out. The cleaning bots were moving among the seats as he slipped into Heloga's balcony. Her chair was larger and better cushioned than the others. Pulling his dataport from his cloak, he scanned it hoping to find unusual energy emissions or a chemical residue. There was nothing but bits of her genetic material with every chromosome exactly in its proper place. This wasn't the first time he had scanned the area after Heloga left with nothing unusual turning up.

But Winstav was a perfectionist. As he examined the chair, he noticed something peculiar. The fabric was dark red to match the maroon and gold decor of the theater. High on the back, a smear of white stood out against the plush material.

He aimed his scanner at the spot. It turned out to be thousands of flakes of skin cells. Nothing strange about that except . . . there was so much. As if Heloga had rubbed the skin off the back of her head as she turned from one admirer to the other.

He touched it with his finger. Dry powder the same color as Heloga's skin. She was absurdly proud of her ivory complexion, but Winstav preferred more robust features, like his own cinnamon tone.

With all the clues to the puzzle finally in hand, it was easy to put them together. It would take a bit of direct action, but he had already proven himself capable of that. Winstav knew that he wasn't beaten. The end result would be his return to the heartland of the Domain where he belonged.

Heloga surrounded herself with mirrors, especially in her private suite, where she could gaze at herself and practice different expressions to her heart's delight. She had ordered Dyrone to eliminate the less attractive grimaces, so now she always looked her best. Whenever she was working, Dyrone retired to a small side office to create new fashions for her and to style her makeup and manicure. Now it was a snap to prepare for an event. It gave her a lot more time to focus on her unruly staff, and she expertly whipped them into place.

The worst time was in the morning and before she went to sleep, when she had to turn off the MIF and face herself. She always wore the new supporting undergarment, and she tried not to see her bony skull and the wrinkled mass of shriveled skin stretching over her face.

Heloga shook off the memory, lifting her head so her cheekbones caught the light. There were several media crews filming her first private party of the quarter, and she owed it to the millions of people in Canopus to look her best. She was their savior, the regional commander who could exterminate the Qin and bring prosperity to the region once again.

So she was throwing a magnificent gathering for the most powerful Alphas on Prime. It was in the grand Varliqui Ballroom with its towering cylindrical atrium. A spiral ramp ran around the inner walls, rising from the floor to the ceiling. Every surface was reflective—walls, ramp, tables, benches, even dishes. . . . Heloga wanted to revel in herself.

In the center, an island was raised far above the floor of the ballroom. The outer edges of the island were lined by benches where they could sit and look down on the Alphas milling below. People also filled the spiral ramp that rose to the very top of the atrium.

Heloga stationed herself on the island with Dyrone posted at the doorway. Then she could freely roam around the circular space without worrying about losing him and the MIF in the crowd. Dyrone had outdone himself tonight by creating a fiery garment that appeared to burn and glow like live coals. Everyone gasped in amazement when they saw it.

Only two dozen of Heloga's favorites were allowed to join her on the central island. After the Renewal Festival when Kristolas and Olhanna had made a fool of her, only those who proved their deference would be allowed close.

Ironically, now that she had established these new procedures, Kristolas had once again gained access to her inner circle. He was most attentive from the moment she reappeared on the scene. Heloga never forgave Kristolas for abandoning her, and she blamed him for the stress that caused the severity of her physical decline. She would never be intimate with him again, but she liked to have him at her feet for everyone to see.

Kristolas returned with a glass of stimulance. He had only been gone a moment to fulfill her wish and hadn't dawdled among the elite and socially influential guests.

"As you requested, Regional Commander." He placed the glass in her hand, stroking her fingers briefly with his own.

"Such prompt service." Heloga was glad that she had prepared for this moment by asking Dyrone to program gloves into her gown tonight so she could cover her skin. She knew Kristolas wanted to touch her. His return to her side was a wonderful fringe benefit of her reemergence.

"You know I'd do anything for you," Kristolas assured her.

Heloga led him to the center of the island, where a round, raised platform was encircled by mirrored steps. She went to the top, where they were lifted above everyone else on the island. This was the first time she had brought him up, though she had favored a few others.

Elevated above the rest, Heloga and Kristolas were reflected in the mirrored ballroom. The upper half of the atrium was devoted to antigrav dancing, and her guests swam and twirled far above their heads. The colors and faces were reflected a million times, as light shattered like a prism against the mirrors. But it was her own image, bathed in flickers of fire, that filled her sight.

She took a deep breath, feeling vibrantly alive. Nobody was more admired or worshipped throughout the region. She had her once-beloved Kristolas back by her side, his adoring eyes focused only on her. Her nemesis, Winstav, was going into battle, where she hoped he would die while demolishing the Qin for her. Everyone in Canopus was in her tight grip, and she could squeeze them dry in her service.

Heloga took a deep breath, turning to Kristolas. She wanted him to kiss her, to crown this moment with the sensual thrill he always gave her. Nobody was more dominant than Kristolas, and that was the only reason he had regained her good graces. His absolute deference was pleasing because only she could see his possessive, lustful glances. His quiet presumption that she still belonged to him was breathtakingly arrogant, making her yearn to throw herself at his feet and grovel in his love once more.

Kristolas leaned forward, his hands pulling her waist closer. He always knew the right moment to take her. The lure of his touch almost made her forget . . .

She jerked away, stepping back to the edge of the platform. The music, voices, and laughter were at their highest pitch.

"I've told you how sorry I am," Kristolas pleaded behind her. "I've always played with our limits. I thought that was one of the reasons you loved me. If I made a mistake and went too far, surely you can forgive me."

Heloga raised one hand to stop him. "Go." She wished she could admit she was over the petty demands of jealousy or pique. She longed to give herself to him. But it was impossible. All she had left was the illusion of life.

Kristolas silently left the platform, undoubtedly planning his next subtle attack. But it didn't matter. Nothing he could do would get past her guard, no matter how highly he keyed her passion. If he touched her, he would feel her cracked, drawn lips and sagging, wrinkled skin.

Heloga lifted her head, remembering that she was the center of attention. Even the dancers watched her as they twirled overhead. She still had this. . . .

There was a high-pitched ringing sound, as if a large bell had been struck. As Heloga glanced around, a gasp arose. Guests looked up at her in surprise, their mouths opening.

Heloga looked down at herself. Her body, along with

the flame garment, seemed to flicker, going white for a moment, stuttering as if the MIF matrix couldn't hold.

Heloga ran to the edge of the platform where Dyrone was posted. But he was lying facedown on the mirrored floor. Another enforcer was kneeling next to him, making frantic movements to strip the backpack off so he could roll Dyrone over. The MIF had a gaping black hole in the center and smoke trickled out. The enforcer responsible for Dyrone's safety looked up frantically, indicating it was not good. The other enforcers rushed toward the platform to protect Heloga.

The gasp rose to an outcry. In front of everyone, Heloga's vision of perfection disappeared. She stood on the mirrored platform wearing only her beige unitard and gloves. Her sagging, puckered flesh bulged under the heavy support material.

But it was her face that caused the most horror. Her mottled, shrunken skin with rheumy eyes and a sneering hole for a mouth. The camera crews got everything, complete with close-ups. All of Canopus would know what she truly was.

Heloga spat defiantly at them, "Who are *you* to look at *me*? I rule this region!"

In spite of their sick fascination, her guests began backing away. Even her enforcers retreated. Soon a hushed stampede started for the doors, fleeing the vacuum pit she had become.

Only one person didn't move. Winstav was standing on the spiral ramp across from her. He smiled, a spot of deadly stillness as everyone else fled.

22

When Ash arrived in the brig, the combat team on duty were in the weapons locker. They were testing the components on the recharging racks that held the lasers and stunwands. Meekly, Ash stuck hir head in the door and gestured wordlessly toward the brig. One of the big Qin women snorted and turned away, while the other nodded more courteously before turning back to her work.

The affects of lust had worn off, and the Qin were back to their usual taciturn selves. Ash had enjoyed their giddy reactions during lust . . . except for what had happened with L'pash. But s/he didn't talk to anyone about that. Even D'nar barely spoke to hir anymore.

Ash edged into the brig, letting the door slide shut behind hir. Rose had come to the *Endurance* a few days ago, but had left without seeing hir. That was the first time since s/he had arrived on the battleship that Rose hadn't seen hir. After that, Ash insisted that D'nar double the neural treatments. S/he didn't even care about the maddening itch from the patch against hir neck.

And every day, Ash visited Rikev. The combatants were tired of seeing hir by now, but s/he was having lots of minor flashbacks. S/he often remembered a face or heard a voice. Or s/he could recall being in different rooms. Yet these isolated memories weren't linked to anything else. Who was that woman with the bright red hair? Where was that place with the crystal walls? Why did s/he feel weightless in that storeroom?

"You're back for more," Rikev said quietly.

Ash went closer to his cell, careful not to touch the wire mesh. S/he had brushed against it once, and it gave an unpleasant jolt. "I need to know more about Archernar shipyard. That's where I lost my memory."

Irritation flashed across Rikev's face. It was odd for him to express emotion. "Talking won't help. You know what must be done."

Ash glanced down at his hands as they clenched. "I can't let you out."

Rikev turned and went to the back of his cell. Ash came forward a step. Something was different. Rikev's most distinctive trait was his self-control no matter what happened. But now he seemed frustrated.

Ash had to ask, "Is something wrong?"

His back was to hir, but his head turned so s/he could see his profile. "Can't you tell?"

"No . . ."

His hands clenched again. "I need you."

There was raw desire in his voice. That was when s/he realized. "You're in lust."

After a moment, he replied, "Yes."

It was frightening. Rikev had been telling hir for days that s/he could regain hir memory if he touched hir. It was true that seeing Rikev and hearing his voice had done wonders for opening up tiny chinks in hir mind. D'nar agreed that interacting with Rikev was helping hir recovery. Yet this self-guided therapy was excruciatingly slow.

"Rose says you nearly killed me last time." Ash couldn't forget the marks all over hir body, the size of hir little finger, with sharp corners dug into hir flesh. Rikev claimed he had used his cartridge belt on hir to make hir react. He said he liked to watch hir writhe and cry out. S/he had never had a flashback of that.

Rikev slowly turned at the back of the cell. His face was shadowed. "They'll kill me if I hurt you. I only want sex."

Ash didn't know what to do. Sharing lust with L'pash had brought back no memories. Even though s/he had enjoyed it at first, the humiliating rejection had been the worst experience in Ash's short memory. But sex with Rikev was sure to bring back more of hir former life. It might even break through the wall s/he had built in hir mind.

Rikev came closer to the mesh, seeing hir silent struggle. "You know I'm right."

Ash agreed, but s/he was really scared. He had hurt hir badly on Archernar shipyard. Because of that, Rose wanted him dead. And Rikev's clone had been hir abusive master for over a year . . . but that was why it might work.

S/he could either take the risk or keep on living this way, alone on a shipful of people who didn't like hir. Separated from hir friends because s/he had lost hir memory. And missing Rose desperately.

"I don't want to live like this," Ash finally admitted. "But I'm afraid of you."

A crease appeared between his eyes, Rikev's only sign of annoyance. "The combat team must be watching us.

You'll get what you need and I'll get what I need, if they don't stop us too soon."

Ash knew the combat team wasn't watching right now, which actually made hir feel better. S/he didn't want anyone to see hir having sex with Rikev. But he acted like his fear of the Qin's reprisals would keep him in line. S/he knew the door was already locked with hir print.

"Are you going to hurt me while we do it?" s/he asked.

His voice was strained. "A little hair pulling, maybe a few smacks."

Ash put hir hand to hir cheek. "Not my face."

"I'll stick to your ass," Rikev agreed dryly. "Can we get on with it before my lust passes?"

Ash looked into his eyes, seeing how impenetrable they were. S/he knew the comm on the terminal would carry all sounds, so if s/he screamed it would catch the attention of the combat team in the weapons locker.

S/he went back to the door and opened the control panel. S/he was going to throw hirself into the sun hoping to emerge whole again.

Rikev didn't react as Ash turned off the current in the mesh of his cell. The faint bluish haze disappeared from the crisscrossing wires. The door was still locked and would have to be opened from outside.

It had been a long tedious journey to get to this point; nearly six decnights stuck in this stinking, Qin brig. The combatants had slipped plenty of information during the initial days when he had regular sessions under their serneo-inhibitor. But they were sufficiently security-conscious to give him no opportunities to escape during his interrogations. Now that they were done with him, the door to his cell hadn't been opened in dec-nights. There had been no other changes in the schedule except for during their absurd lust, which left them exposed for several days. But the Fleet hadn't appeared, much to his disdain.

So Rikev had concentrated on the only person who could be pressured—Ash. It had been difficult to reveal enough of his ruthless arrogance to awaken memories in hir, while acting as if his situation was hopeless in order to appear harmless. S/he was not stupid, which made his task harder, but he had nothing else to concentrate on in this Qin hellhole.

Ash returned to stand outside the door. Hir expression was resolute but fearful, as it should be. Rikev had not expected hir to give in this soon.

"They're right outside," Ash reminded him.

"Of course." Hir timidity was a strong prod to his lust. Yet Rikev, as always, had himself firmly under control. Lust was a minor consideration after his time in isolation and he had become adept at refusing it.

"I won't harm you," he added, seeing hir hesitate.

Hir hand went to the security latch. The tiny click as the door swung open signaled his freedom.

Rikev leapt into action, knowing that surprise was his best weapon. He grabbed Ash, with one hand on hir arm and the other on hir throat. S/he let out a strangled cry as he flung her face-first into the back of his cell. Hir head hit the bulkhead with a muffled thud.

Ash went limp in his hands. Quickly he carried hir to the main door of the brig. He pressed her flaccid hand against the pad and the door slid open.

Rikev held Ash as a shield, ready to be fired on. But

nobody was at the terminal. A red flashing light indicated a cell door was open.

Rikev paused as voices trickled calmly out of a nearby doorway. It sounded as if they were doing routine maintenance.

That changed his strategy. He hauled Ash back to his cell and flung hir down on the bunk. As he pulled the blanket up and around hir head, rolling hir over on hir side, he realized s/he was still alive. He briefly considered killing hir to keep hir silent, but there was too great a risk of being recaptured. That would surely be his death if he killed Ash. So he clanged the door shut, locking Ash in.

Returning to the main entrance, he noted that the red light was no longer flashing. A Fleet ship would have another marker indicating that the cell had been opened, but he didn't understand the configuration on the monitor.

Rikev closed the brig door behind him, hurrying past the terminal and down the corridor. He had seen the outside of the battleship from the lifepod before he was captured. One thing he noted was that the docking bay was on the curved underside of the ship. That was his first target.

Rikev waited in the access tube that contained the umbilicals for the two pinnaces while they were docked. Voices in the bay above him indicated that the Qin were responsible about their small-ship maintenance. There were several people walking around the pinnace currently on deck.

Rikev knew he would have to move soon. At any moment, Ash could wake up and call for help. He hadn't heard a general intruder alert, but it was certainly coming. Sitting this close to escape, he regretted not killing Ash and shutting hir up permanently. The Qin wouldn't have noticed he was gone until the stench of decay overpowered the heavy musk that saturated their ship.

Everything Rikev needed had been easy to find. He wore a new cartridge belt around his waist and had spare cartridges filling his pockets. They looked similar to Fleet issue, which was reassuring. He had also acquired a vacuum pack with a jet harness and replacement tubes.

First he needed to get a good look outside the docking bay. The one portal he had passed had revealed only stars. Stealing the pinnace was out of the question, since only the command crew could unlock it from the cradle. A manual override would take too long. If there wasn't a planet nearby, he could crawl out in his flightsuit and cling to the outer surface of the ship until another option presented itself. But the command crew would know from his passage through the forcefield barrier that he had left their ship.

The voices in the docking bay rose higher, and someone called out. Rikev eased up the ladder to see. The three Qin were tramping toward the airlock leaving the bay. Perhaps it was a shift change or a meal call. Whatever caused it, this was his chance.

He waited until they passed through the door and secured it behind them. His own access tube had a blast door that would automatically fall if the pressure dropped in the bay. The key to his escape was whether the space doors were open or closed. With one pinnace gone, it was likely they were open.

Rikev climbed up to the floor of the bay. Then he

hurried along the edge of the large space, hoping to avoid the security cameras that undoubtedly watched the pinnace sitting in the middle. There were several large bot diagnostic units pulled up around the ship near the open maintenance hatches.

As he expected, the space doors were retracted with only the azure forcefield against the vacuum. He could see a slice of black starry space long before he reached the front of the bay. Below, the curve of a blue and white planet appeared.

Rikev slung the jet harness on his back and was buckling the front as he reached the space doors. He could see enough of the planet to note the blue waters and smallish chunks of land. Sol, a world teaming with pleasure slaves. Not a terrible place to be stranded, but unfortunately an atmospheric entry was impossible without a vehicle.

Then he saw the chalky white moon. It was enormous, as big as Canopus Prime. But this moon clearly didn't have an atmosphere. It was pocked with thousands of layers of meteor craters.

The Fleet base was on Earth's moon. There would be weapons inside that he could use to prevent the Qin from recapturing him. The battleship had already passed the moon.

Rikev activated his flightsuit, checking to be sure the blue haze surrounded himself. He avoided looking at the gray Qin flightsuit he wore. His senses had been starved on board this barbarian ship.

He gave a short test blast on the jet harness, feeling it jerk him upward, lifting him off his feet. Everything was go.

Rikev knew the first few moments would be the most

critical. He backed up to take a running start. With powerful strides, he charged forward. He made sure his angle was correct, hoping to get as much momentum going as possible, as he dived into the forcefield as if it were a pool of water.

Then he was out in space.

The battleship receded behind him. Rikev gave a short blast on his jet harness, feeling the pressure as he was pushed faster. He didn't dare use a continuous blast, because the battleship's scanners would detect it. The last thing he needed was for a pinnace to home in and grapple him before he could reach the moon. He expected an alarm would sound from his passage through the forcefield, but it would take them a few moments to figure out what had happened. To throw them off the scent, he set his course to one side of the moon. He could always adjust with his jets as he closed in.

The battleship blithely continued on its way. Apparently it would take more than a few moments for them to realize what was happening. That meant he would have time to reach the moonbase. A small spaceship, even an intrasolar one, would be ideal. Once he had control of a ship, he could hide in the system to await the return of the Fleet. Soon he would be on his way back to Regional Headquarters with firsthand information about the Qin invasion that would undoubtedly bring him the rank he deserved.

Rikev was sure he would succeed as the pockmarked moon rapidly neared.

When they heard the alarms, Rose and Chad hurried up to the control center of the moonbase. It wasn't the best timing, as they had just accessed the moonbase's original control room. It had taken days of searching to find and then unseal it. Everything inside had rounded corners with no hard edges, completely different from the modern control center that resembled the command deck on Rose's patrolship.

"Is the Fleet coming?" Rose exclaimed as they entered.

Free Solians filled the control center, training each other on the advanced systems. Enzo was looking over the shoulder of an older woman seated at the scanner. "We've had an unauthorized departure. The manual override was triggered on one of our transports. It bolted out of Bay Four a few minutes ago. We've checked but no one's missing."

Rose frowned as she stepped over to the comm. "Get me G'kaan on the *Endurance*."

It took a few moments before the G'kaan's ebony face appeared in the imager. *"Rose! Rikev Alpha has escaped. I was notifying your ship, I didn't realize you were on the moonbase."*

"One of the base transports has been stolen," she told him. "It must have been Rikev."

G'kaan looked off to one side, gesturing with one hand. Rose knew he was checking with M'ke at scanners. *"We don't have anything from this end. We'll pull out of orbit when we reach the moon to scan the area."*

"Acknowledged," Enzo agreed.

Rose thought she heard L'pash's voice. G'kaan hesitated, but finally turned back to the imager. *"Rose, we need you on the* Endurance. *It's Ash. S/he's been hurt by Rikev. S/he's the one who let him out of the brig."*

"Ash!" Rose couldn't believe it. She couldn't quite hear what L'pash was saying, but the jealous woman sounded practically hysterical. "I'll be right there."

* * *

Chad took one look at Rose and insisted on piloting the aircar up to the *Endurance*. She was still too angry about what they had discovered in the old control room on the moonbase. She should have expected something like this when she found out that G'kaan was reluctant to hand over the base to Free Sol. But Enzo had handled the negotiations, and won ownership by agreeing that the moonbase couldn't fall back into Fleet hands. So the Qin combat teams were busy planting explosive charges on the laser cannon and in the key levels of the base that would demolish it. Rose had no patience for talk of the Fleet's return, but it had kept the combat teams occupied while the Solians continued their search of the lower levels, unbeknownst to the Qin.

G'kaan was waiting when Rose came through the airlock. In spite of their sexual bond, Rose was enraged by the leap of interest in his eyes. G'kaan had lied to her, and she had the proof.

"Rose, we didn't realize what Rikev was doing with Ash. S/he asked to see him as part of hir therapy—"

"Where's Ash?" Rose demanded, cutting off his attempt to placate her.

"In the medical bay." G'kaan strode next to her and Chad. "S/he isn't badly hurt. A concussion, but D'nar says s/he'll fully recover."

"No thanks to you. I should have seen hir the last time I was here."

Rose ignored him as she stalked through the battleship. She glared at every Qin who passed by, and in the lift, she ground her teeth together to keep from screaming at G'kaan. Chad's mouth was twitching and his hands kept flexing, but somehow he also kept silent. Chad had been the one who insisted that they needed the Qin in order to repel the Fleet from Sol, so they had to maintain their alliance no matter what terrible things they had done in the past.

When they finally reached the bay, D'nar was programming a healing hot by the door. Ash was lying in the biobed looking thinner and paler than usual. The bloody patch on hir forehead looked horrible.

Rose sternly stuffed her rage down. "Ash, are you okay?"

"Rose?" Ash blinked up. "Rose, I didn't mean to—"

"Hush, it's not your fault," Rose told hir firmly. "I shouldn't have left you here."

Ash relaxed back slightly. "Why didn't you come see me? I wanted to talk to you. I had to do something to break through this fog. . . ."

Rose shushed her again, patting hir on the shoulder. She looked up at D'nar. "Can s/he get up? I want to take hir back to the *Relevance*."

D'nar sniffed, concentrating on the bot. "We can do a better job of healing hir here. You should leave hir in my care."

"That's what you said *last* time. Now s/he's worse than before." Rose scowled at G'kaan as he came up to the biobed. "Ash is coming with us. Chad, get a grav board and we'll carry hir."

Ash struggled to sit up. "I can walk."

G'kaan tried to stop hir. "No, you can't let hir, Rose. S/he's not well."

"*I'm* taking care of Ash from now on."

D'nar lifted her hands in resignation and retreated to

the other side of the medical bay. "Then don't blame me! Concussions can be nasty, and s/he hasn't got much of a mind left to risk."

Chad returned with a grav board, but Ash was sitting up now, bracing hirself against Rose. Rose expertly ripped the patch from the back of Ash's neck. "You don't need that anymore."

"Thanks," Ash whispered, rubbing her neck.

"That was hurting you, wasn't it?" Rose demanded. "What else have they done to you, Ash?"

Ash's head drooped. "Mostly they ignore me. Except for L'pash . . ."

"L'pash!" Rose bent down to see Ash's face. She had an awful feeling. "What did she do?"

"I . . ." Ash seemed afraid. "L'pash was in lust, so she asked me . . . I thought everything was okay. But then she got mad at me."

"L'pash had sex with you!?" Rose exclaimed indignantly.

"I'm sorry," Ash almost sobbed.

"It's not your fault, Ash." Rose's focused her outrage on G'kaan, who probably thought she was just angry about her friend. He didn't realize she knew about the atrocities committed by Qin. "L'pash took advantage of Ash in hir condition!"

G'kaan looked sick. "I didn't know! Ash, why didn't you tell me?"

"L'pash said I couldn't tell anyone."

Rose leaned closer to Ash. "Did she hurt you, Ash?"

"How can you ask that!" G'kaan demanded. "L'pash would never—"

"No?" Rose was so angry she couldn't hold it in any

longer. "We know the truth, G'kaan! Chad and I found the old control room for the moonbase. It's the original hardware, thousands of years old."

Chad was also glowering at Chad. "It's not on the maps. Your combat teams hid it from us, didn't they?"

G'kaan hesitated. "I was going to tell you about that."

"When?" Rose demanded.

Ash urgently tugged on the arm of her flightsuit. "What is it, Rose?"

"The Qin were the first ones who abducted Solians." Rose was still watching G'kaan. "According to the archives in the old control room, they've been stealing human beings from Earth for thousands of years. They were the first to trade Solians to the Domain. That's how the Alphas found out about us."

Rose was vindicated by G'kaan's expression. He didn't want to admit it but he couldn't deny it. Even D'nar's mouth tightened into a defensive line. Apparently it was common knowledge among the Qin that they had long ago enslaved the Solians.

"Qin didn't use Solians for pleasure slaves," G'kaan insisted, as if that made it all right. "The Solians who lived with my ancestors were like part of the family, trusted servants—"

"You sold us to the Alphas so they could rape us!" Rose exclaimed.

"How could you lie to us?" Chad agreed. He seemed to feel more betrayed than Rose. She'd had sex with G'kaan, but she never really trusted him.

"I knew you'd take it badly," G'kaan tried to explain. "The Qin Council emancipated our Solian slaves nearly a century ago. We aren't like that anymore."

Rose shuddered when she remembered the images

they had viewed of the short Creh performing inductions on frightened, screaming Solians. It had been so similar to her own induction that she couldn't stand it. They were *Qin*. Allies and friends . . . her own lover.

"Your people are nothing but slave traders," Rose sneered. "I bet the Domain stole your business once it expanded this far, didn't they? That's when they blew up the volcano to wipe out the most powerful country on Earth, to make it easier to set up their pipeline of native slaves."

"Rose, how to you think *I* feel?" G'kaan demanded. "My own mother was descended from slaves who served Clan Vinn. But it was Solians like her ancestors who convinced Qin that it was wrong to enslave any humanoid. I'm on your side—"

"Yeah, *right*." Rose helped Ash off the table. Ash was steadier now, though s/he was also looking warily at G'kaan. "We're out of here."

Rose and Chad walked Ash back to the airlock as G'kaan trailed after them. Rose wanted to turn and scream at him to vent her fury. But the most important thing was getting Ash back to their own medical bay for treatment. Rose needed to find out if s/he had been abused by L'pash.

Chad helped Ash through the airlock. The poor herme was nearly in tears at the thought of going home. Rose kicked herself for leaving Ash with the Qin for so long. No matter how much medical knowledge they had, Ash needed to be with hir loved ones to recover.

"Rose, I'm sorry . . . I should have told you." G'kaan held his hands out, his eyes pleading with her. "But I could never figure out how. I knew you would hate us for it."

Rose held one finger up. "If L'pash hurt Ash, I'm coming back to kill her."

"Rose!" G'kaan exclaimed, exasperated yet still contrite.

She shut the airlock behind her, cutting him off. The last thing she needed was his apologies. He should have told her the truth.

Hours later, Rose left Ash under the care of Shard in their tiny medical bay. The bioscanner said hir concussion had not caused any brain swelling, and s/he was responding well to the bot healers that Kwort had programmed for hir. Shard managed to draw out the details of Ash's sexual encounter with L'pash, and it appeared nothing coercive or abusive had happened except that L'pash had rejected Ash seconds after the first rush of lust was over.

Rose knew that must have hurt hir, but it wasn't quite enough to justify killing L'pash. She had been really looking forward to storming back over and confronting the sulky Qin with the help of her hunting knife.

So after Ash was stabilized and comfortably tucked in under Shard's tender eyes, Rose was free to release her long-bottled anger. Yelling at G'kaan hadn't been nearly satisfying enough.

She went down to the brig. Most of her time had been spent with Chad and Kwort on the moonbase, so she had seen Bolt only once since lust. Kwort said most of the base was ancient, and it had been cobbled together sections at a time, creating a mutilayered maze. Now that she knew what to look for, it was more similar to Qin construction than Fleet. In the past, entire clans of Creh and Qin had lived on the moonbase. Rose hated to think of how she had ignored the little Creh. They were the henchmen who did the dirty work for the clans.

Bolt looked up when she appeared. His feet were propped against the mesh and his hands were behind his head as he reclined back. Rose was tempted to turn on the current of the cell, but it wasn't needed to keep Bolt inside.

"What's doing, Rose?" Bolt called out cheerfully. "Whipped the galaxy yet?"

"Working on it." Her hands went to her hips as she surveyed him. Keeping him caged wouldn't break him. It would take outright torture to do that.

"When you have a moment to spare, doll, could you hurry up with the lie-detector test?" Bolt gestured with one hand at the cell. "It's time for me to be moving on, don't you think? Got a revolution to help. Freedom for all, and that sort of thing."

Rose didn't want to admit that she couldn't ask G'kaan for the serneo-inhibitor now. "It was your fault I was abducted."

Bolt tilted his head. "In a way, it's true. I'm the one who introduced you to Rowena and Juanita. I took you to them that night. If I had refused, you'd still be playing girl-games back in Tijuana and Earth wouldn't be liberated right now."

"You're a smooth one, aren't you?" Obviously her crew had been talking to him.

"Just telling the truth. Looks to me like I did you and the rest of the world a favor by showing you the underground."

Rose narrowed her eyes. Maybe the torture could begin now. . . .

Bolt sat up. "Truth is, the people you can't trust are

aliens. Those are the ones you should watch out for, not me. I'm just like you, Rose, another Solian caught up in the Domain, facing the slave trade."

Rose fumed. She shouldn't have given him so much time to think. Bolt was too good at twisting things, at becoming what people wanted him to be. For that reason, Manuel didn't trust him. However, none of Enzo's people had found any evidence that Bolt was directly responsible for her abduction.

Bolt stood up, coming close to the mesh. His blue eyes reminded her of G'kaan. "Us humans have to stick together, Rose. You can trust me."

"Mierda!" she exclaimed.

"You know what I think, Rose? You're afraid to have me tested because you don't want to find out the truth. You want to go on thinking I did you wrong, like everyone else in your life has done you wrong, including your 'dear' *mama . . .*"

Her stomach clenched inside of her at the thought of her mother. She had tried so hard to forget Silvia, her perfect face and hair disheveled by the shoving mob as they dragged her into the arena and hanged her for selling human beings as pleasure slaves . . . including her own daughter.

Rose leaned closer to the mesh, her voice dangerously low. "I don't trust *anyone.*"

She left without hearing what Bolt had to say. She didn't care how many people had to suffer; she wasn't going to be duped again. Not by Bolt, not by G'kaan. Not by anybody.

23

Gandre Li glanced at Trace, who was standing next to the helm on the command deck. "We should know soon—"

"There it is!" Jor transferred the data from the *Solace*'s gravity detectors to audio.

The booming reverberation was loud and prolonged, indicating that a battleship was passing through a gravity slip. It was immediately followed by another one equally as loud and long. Gandre Li tightened her lips as four smaller bursts announced the smaller ships going through the slip.

"There were two grav bursts before the battleships," Jor added quietly.

"That's Fleet," Gandre Li agreed. Only they could amass that much firepower, and it was aimed directly at Sol. Unfortunately, her tiny rogue courier was caught in between. "They're losing ground. I make it fourteen hours behind us now."

"We're running very hot," Danal quietly agreed from ops. For the past few shifts, lights had been flashing with increasing regularity on his terminal.

The *Solace* was speeding full-bore ahead with a patrolship right on their tail ... followed half a day behind by six other patrolships and *two* battleships.

They couldn't get caught, not with Herntoff Alpha trussed up in the spare cabin. It hadn't taken long to examine Herntoff's things and discover that he was indeed an InSec operative. When Gandre Li saw the flawless observations he'd made on each of them, how he had examined and even predicted their behavior, Gandre Li was amazed that she had caught him by surprise. The one thing he couldn't have guessed was that she would chuck her entire life out the airlock because of a slave. Anyone who saw the luxurious interior of the *Solace* would assume she had too much to risk. Herntoff hadn't grasped the importance of her relationship with Trace.

Once they discovered the danger they were in, Takhan had argued for killing Herntoff at once and dumping his body in deep space outside a pocket. The Aborandeen claimed it would be self-defense. But Gandre Li couldn't do it. She might be an outlaw, but she wasn't a killer.

Now she was afraid she would have no choice. The *Solace* had started out deep in the Procyon sector, and Gandre Li had plotted an unusual course in an attempt to avoid Fleet patrolships. It added three more days to what should have been a four-day journey.

But they had run into a patrolship anyway, posted on the border of the Domain. Gandre Li had used her InSec credentials to inform them of a data transfer, bringing the *Solace* close to the patrolship. Then she dashed through the gravity slip the patrolship was guarding. The patrolship was positioned at a bad angle, and by the time it maneuvered through the slip, it was barely out of missile range behind them.

That was yesterday. Since the *Solace* was a fast ship, well maintained by Takhan, they had gained precious seconds on the patrolship. There was only one more slip directly ahead that would take them to the outer perimeter of the Sol system. Gandre Li had plotted a course for the Centauri-Sol slip because that would put Jupiter not far away. It would take hours to reach Jupiter, but from there it was only a slip to Saturn, which was currently fifteen degrees away from Earth. Rose would be there along with her Qin friends. One patrolship and one battleship would hardly make a dent in that battle squadron fourteen hours behind them, but the Fleet would surely be distracted long enough for her lowly courier to make an escape.

As long as they didn't run into another patrolship ahead, they might make it.

Two quiet beeps alerted them. "Entering long-distance scanner range of the gravity slip," Jor announced. There was a few tense moments as they held their breath and waited to find out if there was another patrolship lying ahead. Good tactics would dictate it in order to cut off any ships that got through the perimeter.

Trace slipped her arm around Gandre Li's shoulder without a word. Gandre Li hugged her around the waist, feeling the large swell of her belly. There hadn't been one moment of regret for what she had given up. Having Trace beside her again, knowing she and her baby were protected, made it worthwhile.

"Scanners aren't detecting anything," Jor finally said, looking up with relief. "There's no patrolship."

"At least, not outside the lee," Gandre Li added quietly.

Jor nodded, but both he and Danal were breathing

easier, knowing they had passed another hurdle. "We'll have to see what we find on the other side," she added.

Mote was fast losing patience with Dab. "You have to ease up, Dab. You can't push the captain so hard."

The three of them were standing in their narrow workroom. Whit was by the door, leaning against the table, while Mote was sitting next to him dangling her feet.

Dab was standing at the back, her arms crossed, flexing her muscles into generous curves. "I say what I think. Grex knows that."

Dab was tough and immovable, as usual. Mote wasn't sure why she kept trying to ram some sense into her. Dab had managed, through no effort of her own, to fall into a torrid sexual relationship with Captain Grex. From what Whit had described, Dab had convinced Grex to abort their attack on the *Solace*, thereby destroying their budding partnership with the *Regard*. A couple of days later, Mote stumbled into Dab as she was emerging from the captain's day cabin. The short, dark woman was practically glowing. Every time Mote asked her about it, Dab simply claimed it was "private."

"Fine, you obviously know how to handle the captain better than I do," Mote retorted. "But we wouldn't be stuck behind the Fleet's perimeter line if you hadn't argued him into leaving the Domain and going to Sol."

"But Rose could be in there with the Qin," Dab insisted. "And now that we're stuck behind the Fleet line anyway, we might as well check out Sol. Don't you *want* to find the others?"

"More than you'll ever know," Mote said flatly. "But that doesn't mean I'll jeopardize my place on this ship to do it. Leave that for Grex to decide. He can't get caught in the middle of an interstellar war."

Dab flung up her hands and turned to Whit. "You don't agree with her, do you?"

Whit's legs were stretched out and crossed at the ankles, and he looked more relaxed than either of them. "Dab should say whatever she wants to Grex. That's what he likes about her."

Mote blinked at Whit, her mouth agape. Whit had been her ally since they were hijacked, siding with her in trying to restrain Dab. It was not what she expected.

Whit shrugged at her expression. "I've been speaking my mind for the past decnight, and the captain seems to like it—"

The door slid open behind Whit, and Grex appeared. Mote thought he overheard what they'd been saying, but Grex quickly focused on Dab. "Your friends are approaching."

"Rose?" Dab exclaimed, rushing forward.

"No, the courier, the *Solace*."

"Gandre Li!" Mote exclaimed. "What are they doing outside the Domain?"

"Something must be wrong," Dab decided.

Grex nodded, approving her quickness. "There's a patrolship right behind them. The courier is running at full speed, barely out of weapons range."

Dab pushed past Mote and Whit, joining Grex at the door. "Let's go."

Mote jumped off the edge of the worktable to follow. She did manage to give Whit a wry half-shrug. He was right. Dab didn't need any help managing Grex.

It was a short walk, and by the time they got there, Anny and Pet Delion were at the comm and ops. Pet

Delion's normally cheerful expression was frighteningly serious, while Anny's compressed face revealed nothing.

Grex took the helm with Dab standing next to him. Whit and Mote stayed back to one side where they could see the imager. It showed a close-range schematic of two icons approaching the gravity slip.

Mote could tell at once by the position of the *Vitality*'s indicator that they were hidden within the lee of the grav slip. It was labeled Centauri-Sol, so that meant they were in the pocket one slip away from Sol.

"The yellow one in front is the *Solace*," Grex told Dab. "The patrolship behind is usually assigned to the Sirius sector. It must have been pulled here for duty after the Qin invaded Sol."

Dab looked down at him. "We have to help the *Solace*."

"It's not as easy as it looks," Grex told her. "We picked up eight grav bursts."

"Eight?" Mote blurted out incredulously.

Anny took the opportunity to say, "It must be six patrolships and two battleships. They're barely fourteen hours away. We should get out of here."

"They must be going to Sol," Grex agreed.

"Then that settles it," Dab insisted. "We have to destroy that patrolship and go with Gandre Li to warn Rose."

Anny let out a snort. "You don't even know if your friends are in Sol. The last we heard, a Qin battleship is in there."

"Rose must be there," Dab said stubbornly. "Besides, the Qin are our friends."

Mote bit her lip, but she had learned her lesson where Dab was concerned. She was on her own.

Anny ignored Dab, telling Grex, "You know if we're smart, we'll wait until these two ships pass through the slip, then pull back a few hours to avoid being seen by the battle squadron. Once those ships have gone through, we can get away from here."

"We sure can't stay in the lee when eight ships pass through," Pet Delion agreed. "The latches on the laser array could separate under the stress."

"No, we have to help Gandre Li," Dab countered.

"How do you know the *Solace* needs our help?" Anny asked. "They could be working with the battle squadron."

"That looks like a chase to me," Dab insisted.

Grex nodded thoughtfully. "Anny's right, we need more information. Since the patrolship is directly behind the *Solace* from our position, can we open a close-range channel without the Fleet ship reading it?"

Anny hesitated, as if knowing Dab was gaining ground, but she had too much respect for Grex not to answer. "Yes, a tight beam should do the trick. Their converter emissions should drown out any lateral leakage."

"Then hail the *Solace*."

Anny stiffened, but she did as he ordered. A few moments passed in tense silence. "They're not answering."

Dab said, "Tell them we're friends of Rose."

"I'm getting another hail," Jor announced. "This one has a text message attached."

"What does it say?" Gandre Li asked. The comm hail had been completely unexpected. The channel was so tight Jor barely had time to locate the signal coming from dead ahead of them. It must be a ship in the lee.

Jor's eyes opened wide in astonishment. "Captain, it says: 'We're friends of Rose.' "

"Rose!" Gandre Li exclaimed. "Not again."

Jor was nodding as if he couldn't believe it either. "That's confirmed. They have an open channel waiting. Do you want to accept?"

Gandre Li groaned. "Don't we have enough trouble right now?"

"Oh, talk to them, Gandi!" Trace gently shook Gandre Li's shoulders. "Maybe they can help us."

"That'll be a first," she grumbled. "I'm always the one saving their butts."

But one look at Trace's pleading face, and Gandre Li knew she had to do it. "All right, but I want you out of sight, Trace." No use exposing her if this was a trick of some kind.

Trace retreated to her jumpseat, sitting on the edge in anticipation. Danal and Jor exchanged looks as Gandre Li nodded. "Open the channel," she ordered.

Gandre Li expected to see the face that popped up far too often in her nightmares. Rose had come to symbolize fear and danger in her dreams. But the man who appeared was a humanoid she didn't recognize. From the long, thick bundles of hair hanging from the top of his head, he must be a Delta. His facial features were smashed together in the center, masking his expression.

"*Captain Gandre Li?*" he asked politely.

"Yes?" This was absurd, they were running for their lives!

"*One of my crew is concerned about you. Since she's a friend of Rose, she feels she has a debt to pay if you require assistance.*"

From the other side of the command deck, Trace quietly exclaimed, "Yes!"

"Who is this friend of Rose?" Gandre Li countered suspiciously.

A Solian stepped into the frame, standing next to the Delta. Her skin was nearly black and her hair was clipped close to her head. *"I'm Dab. I was a bot tech for Rose on the* Purpose—*"*

"Dab!" Trace shouted out, running to Gandre Li's side. "Nip told me about you. She looks just like he said."

"You know Nip?" Dab exclaimed, leaning closer. *"Did he get off the spacepost? Last time I saw him, he was in a biobed."*

Gandre Li realized it was too late to hide Trace. The Delta seemed similarly resigned to letting the Solians handle the conversation.

"We picked Nip up in a lifepod," Trace explained. "He's fine. He's back with Rose now. She stole a patrolship from Archernar shipyard, and they're inside Sol with the Qin. They liberated Earth."

"I knew it!" Dab clenched her fists. *"We have to warn her about that battle squadron behind you."*

"That would be easier," Trace pointed out, "if we didn't have this patrolship on our tail. We picked it up trying to get out of the Domain."

"You're in trouble with the Fleet?" Dab asked.

"I think that's an understatement. Gandre Li saved me from a really twisted Alpha, but we're dead meat if they catch us."

"I think we can take care of that," Dab said. *"I'll be right back."*

The imager returned to the real-time view of the patrolship too close behind them. Its deadly pointed snout

and dark, armored hull made it look even more dangerous.

Gandre Li put her arm around Trace, feeling the bulge
of her belly bump into her. "I hope you're right about
this, Trace."

Mote watched the argument without saying a word.
Whit was equally enthralled. Dab didn't even notice
they were there.

"Gandre Li is running to protect Trace from a stinking
Alpha," Dab insisted. "I think they deserve our help."

"No! It's too risky," Anny shouted again, refusing to
listen to Dab anymore. Mote had to hand it to Dab, she
stopped fighting with Anny when she realized she
couldn't influence her the way she could Grex.

Grex looked from Dab to Anny, as if weighing their
arguments. Mote was sure that Anny, his longtime second-
in-command, would win out in the end. They were too
much alike, perhaps because they came from the same
people. But she knew it would was more difficult for
Grex to stand by and do nothing now that they had let
the *Solace* know they were here.

Anny pushed just once more. "Sometimes you have to
sacrifice what you want in order to survive, Grex. You
know that as well as I do."

The captain's head lifted and his eyes abruptly
blazed. "Not me. Never me, Anny."

Anny winced. "You know I had no choice, Grex."

Mote held her breath. This was the secret between
them, the mystery behind their odd relationship. Grex
looked at Anny as if she had betrayed him. Mote had
seen indications of it before. Whit thought they were sib-
lings, but Mote refused to believe it. Clearly they weren't

lovers, but perhaps in the past they had been . . . and Anny had chosen the easy way out of a difficulty at Grex's expense.

Grex turned to Dab. "We'll help the *Solace*. But there's got to be something in this for us."

Dab started to grin. "Ask Gandre Li if she likes her bargain. She helped us out and now the favor's returned when she needs it most."

Grex laughed shortly, giving Dab's arm a squeeze. Anny was staring down at the comm, refusing to look at them. Pet Delion was more scared than anything. Mote also had to wonder if this would cause real problems between the crew. But that was something to worry about only if they survived their engagement with the patrolship.

As the slip rapidly approached, Gandre Li ordered Trace back to her jumpseat so she could put the grav lock on. When she slowed the ship to the gravitational constant, the patrolship leaped closer exponentially.

The patrolship fired its missiles right on cue. Gandre Li had already activated their stern defense systems, prepared for this one moment when the patrolship had a chance to hit them. The antiexplosives scattered behind them, catching most of the missiles. The two that detonated near the *Solace* rocked the ship.

If Dab was lying and that was a patrolship hiding in the lee, there was no way the *Solace* could avoid a deadly barrage of fire.

But her courier glided into the gravity slip and was instantly transported nearly four light-years away. Gandre Li couldn't see or hear anything but the distortions within the gravity field.

When their ship appeared in the gravity pocket, Gandre Li was disoriented at first. It felt like ages, but it probably was no longer than usual. Only this time it was vitally important.

"Is there anything on scanners?" she cried out.

"Seeking . . ." Jor muttered. "No, nothing! There's no ship within range."

Gandre Li shook the fuzziness from her head, confirming Jor's data. She got the converter fired and the *Solace* was off like a shot. They needed distance in case the patrolship came through after them instead of the raider. "Now we'll have to see what the Solians can do."

As Mote was waiting for the attack down in engineering, she almost wished she had sided with Anny. It was sheer stupidity to take on a patrolship at such close range.

But she was prepared to do damage control with Whit and Dab. They had distributed bot sealers in every compartment, and the automatic hatches would lower if there was a loss of pressure. Even the cats heard the alert signal and retreated to secured areas.

"Are you set?" Mote asked through the wrist comm.

"Check," Whit said crisply.

"Check," Dab echoed, seemingly oblivious of the fact that she, the lowest-ranked bot tech, apparently had more say in what happened on board than their second-in-command.

Mote had been impressed by the way Dab had insisted on riding with the converter, the most dangerous position. Whit was down by the lasers, while Mote was posted halfway between the two shield generators. They were already whining at high speed, preparing to instantly form a bubble of protective energy around the ship as soon as they left the lee. If they could keep these three critical systems going, everything else could wait until the battle was over.

Hopefully it would be over quickly. A short, victorious engagement was what they needed.

The warning lights went off, indicating that their attack was imminent. Mote locked down the gravity on her jumpseat, wishing she didn't have to be alone. But there was a monitor within sight, so she could see the rounded snub of the *Solace* go through the slip, making the raider rock around her. Behind the *Solace* was the pointed wedge of the patrolship, bearing down on them. The flat monitor wasn't as lifelike as the three-dimensional imager on the command deck, but it was scary enough.

The data scrolled along the bottom indicating the patrolship was rapidly closing. Mote counted her frantic heartbeats as the deadly ship slowed for entry into the grav slip.

Suddenly the *Vitality* appeared on the screen. It was directly in front of the patrolship.

Mote jerked back, instinctively trying to get away from the awful sight. Laser beams appeared on the screen. She could feel the surge from their generators as the beams sustained then struck again.

The patrolship was driven off course while *Vitality* streaked over it, firing lasers at point-blank range. Mote couldn't be sure what was happening through the flashes of the patrolship's stressed shields. But it was too fast for the Fleet ship to return fire with their missiles. Clearly this kind of direct assault was effective, but it was discouraged among raiders because it called too much attention to a sector. Battleships usually responded whenever there was wholesale slaughter of a Fleet ship.

The patrolship skewed wildly away, but its hull began to disintegrate along the top curve. Those poor people didn't have a chance. Mote cried out as the patrolship blew up.

It was a good thing she was locked down, because *Vitality* shook so hard that Mote's head slammed back against the padded headrest. Alarms went off around her, but the shuddering went on and on. For a moment, she thought they were too close. They had blown up their own ship. . . .

The shaking eased and *Vitality* appeared on the screen, shooting out of a sparkling shower of debris into starry space once more.

On the command deck of the *Subjugation* with the *Persuasion* in close formation, Felenore calmly watched the imager from the admiral's chair. It had taken two long decnights to reach Sol from Canopus Regional Headquarters, but soon they would arrive at Earth.

"There's another grav burst, Captain," the comm officer reported.

Captain Ronstoph looked up at Felenore. "That's two of them, Alpha Strategist. Looks like it could be raiders traveling ahead of us. They've entered the Sol system."

"Much as I expected." The rats were fleeing the oncoming juggernaut. It had been happening since they left Canopus Prime. But a few odd ships in the mix wouldn't make any difference. They would likely catch the first slip out to avoid Sol.

Leaving the Qin for Felenore.

24

G'kaan used his navigational scanners in conjunction with M'ke's multiemission scanners in their search for Rikev Alpha. Rikev had taken one of the transports used for Earth-to-moon transfers, so he was spaceworthy even if he didn't have a grav impeller to leave the system. G'kaan was certain that Rikev was somewhere near Earth keeping an eye on them, while M'ke thought he had pulled back to hide among the moons of Jupiter to wait for the Fleet to arrive. Saturn and Jupiter were in ideal conjunction for an intrasolar slip to Earth. But G'kaan couldn't risk uncovering Earth to go search Jupiter. If Rikev was that far away, he wouldn't be able to detect their comm transmissions and wouldn't gain more useful information to tell Fleet.

"Full spectral scans of the Earth's moon are complete," M'ke reported. "Aside from the coordinates already noted, I've found nothing."

"Understood," G'kaan replied. The coordinates were being visually checked by several combat teams using one of the pinnaces. So far, the *Pluck* had found a dozen debris sites from early exploration and core sampling done on the moon. There were also a few old automated mining stations that were now abandoned, so the combat teams were having to search every level.

Rose was of the opinion that Rikev went down to Earth to hide, so Free Sol issued an alert along with an image of Rikev through their new comm network. Enzo and Margarita had insisted that the world network be Earth-based so the new coalition of regional governments that formed Free Sol could remain in touch once Fleet returned. There was no doubt that the Free Sol movement would coordinate the resistance against the Domain once they were reoccupied.

G'kaan wished they could protect Earth from that fate, but militarily it was unfeasible. The Fleet would undoubtedly send in a sizable force to retake the system. He had succeeded in diverting attention away from Qin for a handful of decnights, while preventing the abduction of a few thousand Solians. Most important, the population of Earth had been alerted to their fate, and were prepared to fight the Domain using their own technology. A number of manufacturers had been established in concealed locations—mainly old missile silos and underground bunkers—and the underground was busy building grav impellers and advanced weapons systems.

"Captain, the *Pluck* is reporting back," M'ke announced. "There's no sign of the transport or the Alpha."

L'pash let out an exasperated sound. It wasn't like her, but L'pash had been acting peculiarly ever since lust. G'kaan could hardly blame her when it was his own fault for abandoning her.

"That's unfortunate," G'kaan forced himself to say lightly. "It would have been clever for Rikev to hide in the shadow of a crater with his systems powered down."

"He doesn't need to be clever," L'pash sniffed. "He's got the *Solians* helping him."

The three other crew members at the auxiliary stations shifted uneasily at L'pash's snide comment.

G'kaan clenched his jaw, restraining his retort. L'pash wasn't aware that her lust with Ash was no longer a secret. He had ordered D'nar to not speak about it, but the biotech was too blunt. She never thought before she spoke. Despite her intelligence and best intentions, G'kaan knew it was only a matter of time before the entire crew knew.

Then things would really get ugly with L'pash.

M'ke soothingly interjected, "All of us are culpable in this matter. Regardless, we obtained everything we could from the Alpha. His escape will not cause our mission to fail."

L'pash muttered something incomprehensible, but she peered down at her terminal. G'kaan gave M'ke a grateful glance. Naturally, he had told his advisor everything that had happened. M'ke couldn't give him sound advice if he didn't thoroughly understand the situation. M'ke believed that L'pash would request a transfer to another ship once they returned to Armada Central, and her offended Bos clansmen, his well-trained ops officers, would probably leave with her.

M'ke didn't hesitate to blame G'kaan for disrupting his crew. It showed a serious lack of judgment for the captain to deceive one of his command corpsmen, even if it was done under the duress of lust. Armada Central would have no official reason to look into his actions, but that was beside the point. They had invaded enemy territory—this was no time for him to cause dissension among his crew!

"Prepare the docking bay for the *Pluck*," G'kaan said to her.

L'pash refused to look at him. "Aye, Captain."

Her voice was biting cold, as if she could hardly force herself to acknowledge a routine order. The command deck had become a tense, grim place to be, replacing the calm efficiency G'kaan had carefully honed among his corpsmen.

G'kaan knew he had to continue to act normally. "Once the *Pluck* returns, we'll begin a near orbital search pattern. Send word to R'yeb that—"

"Captain!" M'ke interrupted. "Our remote comm is picking up two incoming ships. They appear to be on a least time course from the Saturn-Jupiter slip."

"Classification?" G'kaan asked.

"From the size of the grav burst it looks like a patrolship and something smaller, perhaps a courier. It will take approximately two hours to confirm."

"Are any of the other comms picking up incoming signals?" There were six comms spread out in a perimeter line three hours away from Earth orbit, thereby extending their scanner range to nearly six hours from Earth, almost all the way to Jupiter as it swung through its massive orbit around Sol.

"Negative."

"Has the *Pluck* docked?" he asked L'pash. Usually she would report it, but she was neglecting that lately.

"They're locking down now, Captain."

G'kaan knew what he had to do. Those ships were small enough to be captured and added to the Free Solian Flotilla. "Initiate Flytrap!"

* * *

Rose practically bounced in her seat. "Ready for ambush?"

"All systems report go," Stub informed her with a sunny smile.

"So now we wait," Rose told both him and Fen at the comm.

The last time they had sprung the ambush Rose had dubbed "Flytrap," they had caught another slave transport complete with clear cubes to hold its crew. The Free Solians had quickly staffed their new ship with technically qualified people who were eager to help the resistance.

Now they had two interstellar transports, including the first one that had just returned from Qin with the Solians left on Prian. The two hundred pleasure slaves Rose had liberated along with the *Purpose* were upset about their long stay on Prian. Most were nearly starving to death. It convinced Rose that Solians were on their own. The former slaves were taken in by various Earth enclaves, but the ones who were toughened by the experience had been inspired to become crew members in the Free Sol Flotilla.

Since Chad's crew on the *Tranquillity* had the least amount of battle experience, his ship stayed with the two transports near Earth to defend the moonbase. Both Rose's patrolship *Relevance* and R'yeb's *Devotion* were in position along with G'kaan's battleship about an hour away from Earth. The planet was a shiny *peso*-sized half-moon from their position.

The patrolships were assigned the smaller of the two targets, while the battleship would handle the larger ship. Neither of their emissions matched Fleet specs.

Rose thought it was bizarre. Why would independents come this deep into Sol? Word must have spread that the system was a black hole for every ship that entered. G'kaan thought it could be a trick, but Rose figured they should take a free handout when it was offered.

Fen pursed her lips, cocking her head to listen to the comm plug in her ear. "There's something coming through on an open audio channel . . . it's so far away I can't get a lock. . . ."

Rose had taken Fen as her comm officer because she was the sharpest of the former pleasure slaves. The tall, dark-skinned woman had caught Rose's eye in the slave barracks on Archernar shipyard because she always managed to get the best of everything. Her curly black hair was tied up in tufts with muticolored ribbons that hung down her back. From her ears hung brightly colored balls that matched the ropes of ceramic beads around her neck.

"I'm boosting the feed to try to clear the signal," Fen informed her.

The two ships were still several hours away, at the edge of their ship's scanner and comm range. "Let me hear it," Rose ordered.

Fen nodded, operating her terminal. Over the speakers came a static-filled buzzing. But there were words underneath. ". . . *calling Cap . . . of Qin . . .*" Static buzzed harshly, then cleared somewhat. ". . . *andre Li of . . . courier So . . .*"

"What was that?" Rose demanded. "Did she say Gandre Li?"

"It sounded like it," Stub agreed, his face splitting in a grin. "What would they be doing here?"

The voice continued in a patient drone with static drowning out every other phrase.

"I'm getting a hail from the *Endurance*," Fen announced.

"Respond," Rose ordered.

G'kaan appeared in the imager. *"Rose, It's a courier claiming to be the* Solace.*"*

He couldn't retreat behind a formal Qin mask anymore. But she couldn't forgive him for lying to her. She should have found out about the history of the slave trade from him, not from a database he had tried to hide on the moonbase.

"I'll believe it's Gandre Li when I see her," Rose retorted.

"I'll tie you in and hail them through the remote comm. That should give us a visual."

While G'kaan's crew obeyed his orders, Rose glanced over at Fen. That was a capability they didn't know about. Luckily, Rose had been able to guilt G'kaan into giving her one of his remote comms so they could use the technology themselves. They were encouraged by Kwort's efforts to duplicate the precious device. Fen nodded back, already considering the implications of being able to hail a ship at extreme distances.

Rose's interaction with Fen reminded her of Ash and how they used to be such a good team together. The herme was much happier now that s/he was home, but hir memory was just as blank as before. Rose was spending her spare time with Ash, and encouraged hir to start retraining on the comm with Fen. Rose wasn't going to let Ash go again so easily.

G'kaan returned to the imager. *"Ready, Rose? I want you to tell me instantly if you think this is a ruse."*

"You got it."

Rose stared intently into the imager. G'kaan was on

one side, but there was space on the other, an odd split image. Then a fuzzy form appeared. A woman in white.

Rose leaned closer as her face came into focus. She looked like an Alpha, but then again, Bariss were very similar to Alphas.

"Rose? Is that you?" The woman on the screen shifted as if she was having trouble seeing as well.

"It's me," Rose agreed, still unsure of who was on the other end of the channel. "Who're you supposed to be?"

"It's Gandre Li! You don't know what a relief this is. . . ."

Rose pulled back. "You don't sound like Gandre Li. Gandre Li's never been glad to see me before."

G'kaan looked worried on the other side of the imager.

"I don't have time for your games, Rose!" The woman in white slammed her hand down on the terminal. *"For once you're going to listen to me!"*

"Now, that sounds more like Gandre Li," Rose told G'kaan.

"Do you want to get blown to spacedust by a Fleet battle squadron?" Gandre Li threatened.

"What battle squadron?" G'kaan demanded.

"Who's that with you?" Gandre Li asked from her side.

"That's Captain G'kaan of the battleship *Endurance*," Rose explained.

"I hope you have more than one battleship," Gandre Li warned. *"Because there's two Fleet battleships coming to Sol along with six patrolships."*

"At last," Rose breathed.

G'kaan gave her an odd look. *"I'm not so sure I believe such an opportune warning."*

"Just ask Vitality. *Some of Rose's old crew are on board the raider."*

Rose started to stand up, she was so surprised. "My crew! Who?"

"How should I know?" Gandre Li responded irritably. Someone moved in closer on the same side as Gandre Li. *"Trace says it's Dab, Whit, and . . . Mote."*

"No!" Rose exclaimed in disbelief.

Stub was also standing up, looking from her to the imager. "Is it really true?" He laughed in delight.

Rose sank back in her seat as G'kaan began questioning Gandre Li about the Fleet battle squadron. Meanwhile she checked the specs on the larger ship. It did look like the raider that had stolen her old cargo ship, from what she had been able to see out the portal. It even had the modular laser array attached on the bottom.

When G'kaan appeared satisfied, Rose told him, "We should check this with Mote."

Gandre Li lifted her hands in a familiar gesture of resignation. *"All I'm asking is that you don't attack my ship by mistake."*

Gandre Li disappeared from the imager and only G'kaan was left looking at her. *"If your people confirm this, you know what we have to do."*

"Yes, we have to defend Earth."

G'kaan sighed as he ran one hand through his hair. *"The Fleet has double our weapons capabilities and trained crews. We don't stand a chance. We planned the evacuation for this contingency."*

"We can beat them!" Rose insisted. "We've got surprise on our side. We can ambush the Fleet like we did with the other ships, only this time we'll destroy them."

G'kaan was shaking his head. *"We would sustain heavy losses even if we won. And make no mistake about it, Rose, we will lose Sol. The Domain will send enough ships to take it back eventually."*

"Maybe, but how can you tell unless we try? Besides we know exactly when and where the Fleet are coming. How often does that ever happen in battle?"

G'kaan had to admit, *"It does present certain opportunities."*

"We can divert the Fleet's attention from Qin a while longer, if nothing else." Her tone got harsher, but she didn't care. The Qin had made it clear from the start that they were doing this for their own reasons. Only G'kaan had tried to claim he shared their interest in freeing Sol.

G'kaan was looking to his right, probably at M'ke. *"We can lay down the mines between here and Jupiter on their most likely course as part of the ambush. Our ships could stay at maximum weapons range so we can disengage after the initial salvo and retreat to the slip. That way we can inflict maximum losses with minimum risk."*

"You can cut and run any time you like." Rose had other plans, but he didn't need to know that.

"I'll tell the moonbase to evacuate all but the Solian demolition team. They can blow the base once it's clear we're departing." G'kaan's combat teams had finished rigging the moonbase for demolition. The only thing that would be left intact were the slave cubes holding the crews of the various ships they had captured along with the base personnel. They were sitting in a large hangar that had its own emergency environmental unit.

Rose didn't care if the Fleet ever rescued those people. They were the ones who enslaved the Solians. If she'd had her way, they would all be dead. But Free Sol was making the decisions for Earth and the moon, not her.

"Patch me through to that raider," Rose suggested. "We'll find out for sure if Gandre Li is telling the truth."

G'kaan gestured to M'ke, and the imager split again. There were a couple of people on a much darker command deck.

"Mote?" Rose asked. "Are you there?"

"Rose!" It wasn't Mote's voice, but it sounded familiar. *"Mote's right here."*

Someone joined the two on the screen, peering closer at the static. There was an unmistakable bright red patch at the top of that long, thin body. *"Is it really you, Rose? Dab said you were in Sol, but I couldn't believe it. What happened?"*

"Long story. Tell me quick if it's true. Is the Fleet coming?"

"That's what Captain Grex says," Mote replied. *"He would know better than anyone."*

"We're coming to help you," Dab agreed. *"I figured another laser couldn't hurt at a time like this."*

Rose grinned. "Dab, that's exactly what I wanted to hear!"

G'kaan had to rush to get everything done before the Fleet battle squadron came through the Saturn-Jupiter slip. They gathered up the remote comms, leaving only one in stealth orbit around Earth that would be downloaded by the underground. It would provide a permanent way for a ship within rage to communicate with the Solians on Earth. The two interstellar transports headed in the opposite direction across the system, toward the Wolf-Sol slip, to wait at the rendezvous coordinates for them.

M'ke and R'yeb had agreed that tactically they

couldn't pass up an opportunity to ambush the Fleet assault force. Yet even their ambush plans were heavily weighted toward evacuation. Enzo and Margarita were busy dismantling the various working components from the moonbase and transporting them to their Free Sol bases on Earth. They would have several hours to finish the job, since G'kaan had taken his motley fleet nearly all the way to Jupiter to ensure they caught the Fleet soon after they emerged from the intrasolar slip. They would have to catch the Fleet before they could make a course change in their approach to Earth.

To do so would require the ultimate test of their stealthing methods. The three patrolships had been altered to allow polarization of the hull plating. That created an irregular surface that was read by scanners as inert meteoroid material. They had disabled the safeties that prevented all systems from shutting down, but had practiced the restart sequence only a couple of times.

R'yeb and Rose were currently powered down, moving in a drift and a slow roll at maximum missile range. G'kaan had kept Chad's patrolship near his ship on the opposite side of the Fleet's projected course. The raider *Vitality* stayed stubbornly near Rose's ship, despite the fact that G'kaan had reservations about the raider's ability to mimic their stealth methods. There was nothing he could do about it, because Captain Grex had chosen to deal solely with Rose rather than G'kaan.

"They'll be lucky not to shoot each other," L'pash muttered irritably.

G'kaan gave her a sharp look. None of the other command crew had heard except for M'ke. He kept his voice low. "I need your support, L'pash, not your pessimism."

"There was a time when you valued my input," she retorted, her voice rising. "I think this is a serious mistake, risking our people to defend a planet that doesn't belong to Qin."

"Your objection is duly noted. Return to your duties." G'kaan kept his eyes on her until she finally looked back down at her terminal.

M'ke glanced over at G'kaan, his expression approving. He couldn't allow insubordination to go unchecked in his crew.

"I'm picking up a grav burst," M'ke announced. They were close enough to the intrasolar slip to pick up the distortions.

G'kaan bared his fangs. "Here they come."

M'ke counted off the bursts as they came through the comm. It was exactly as Gandre Li had reported: six patrolships and two battleships.

Fen looked up. "That's it! Eight grav bursts."

"Good," Rose said. "Battle alert!"

Fen leaned down to her internal comm and softly passed the order. The Fleet ships were already well within scanner range, but the ambush team had shut down all operations to avoid detection. Everyone was locked down in their seat or wearing grav boots to compensate for the lack of internal gravity.

G'kaan had insisted on going over their evacuation plan twice. Rose wasn't stupid; she knew that they would have to run for it if they got trounced. But their plan was solid, and she hoped to inflict some serious damage on the Fleet, then move in for the kill.

The mines were laid out in a dispersal pattern that should place the maximum number in a direct course between the slip and Earth. Better yet, these mines had

been improved since S'jen had tested them on the battleship *Conviction*. Rose had watched them go off in front
of the Fleet battleship without doing much damage.
G'kaan assured her that the R&D teams had fixed the
frequency problem in the penetration unit. They were
designed to pierce the shields of a ship and allow their
explosive charge to detonate directly against the hull.
Rose hoped the mines were as good as advertised, since
they had spread them in a fairly wide net.

Meanwhile, their missiles would take advantage of the
chaos caused by the minefield. The raider wasn't within
laser range, but Rose had other plans for Dab's crew.
She was very pleased with how Dab had taken control
of her situation. She planned on telling her that the first
chance she got.

"The countdown begins," Rose told her command
crew with a grin. "It's payback time."

G'kaan watched the formation in the imager, a thing of
deadly beauty. Three wedge-shaped patrolships took the
lead in the lower quadrant, with two immense battleships following in the middle quadrant, and three more
patrolships in the upper rear guard. It obviously maxi-
mized their scanner and weapons capability. They were
close enough for the *Endurance* to read them on passive
scanners. They maintained course, indicating that they
hadn't picked up the rotating ships drifting within missile range. They couldn't get close enough to use their
lasers or the Fleet ships would detect them.

The Fleet battle squadron was heading straight for
the minefield. Unfortunately, the battleships were following the lead patrolships and would have time to react
after they struck the minefield. But G'kaan had already

ordered his ambush team to manually lock on to the Fleet battleships with their missiles.

"Targets are approaching coordinates for missile launch," M'ke announced.

G'kaan pressed the internal comm. "Prepare to launch missiles."

Acknowledgments came in from the key battle stations. G'kaan watched the scanners with M'ke, instantly passing the order. "Fire!"

The weapons system powered up instantly, and all six missile tubes emptied. A second barrage immediately followed. It would take time to reload the chambers. G'kaan sent another two rounds, then held his fire to see what the Fleet ships would do after they were attacked.

Chad's *Tranquillity* also flushed its tubes, sending a salvo of three missiles followed by another two in rapid succession. G'kaan checked the trajectory on Chad's missiles with the passives, and saw they were right on target. Rose and R'yeb should have done exactly the same thing on the other side of the Fleet battle squadron. They could only use passive scanners in their powered-down mode.

"Missile impact imminent . . ." M'ke warned.

G'kaan was caught between watching the rapidly falling numbers and the tiny replicas of the Fleet ships in the imager. Then a sparkling of fire burst through the lower quadrant of the imager as the three lead patrolships plowed into the minefield. They skewed hard, breaking formation as they tried to avoid the mines. A gush of torn hull and bulkheads showered from the front end of one patrolship after the rainbow bubble of its shields fell.

The battleships were altering course, apparently having

detected the incoming wave of missiles before they impacted. The imager flashed as the powerful shields on the two battleships fluctuated under the stress. They split apart instantly, curving to face the threat on either side as dozens of missiles exploded against their shields.

"Power up!" G'kaan ordered. "Firing the converter."

L'pash instantly complied. "Systems coming online."

"Scanners in active mode," M'ke added, giving G'kaan the vital information he needed to make his next decision. G'kaan felt a leap of righteous fury when he saw the battleship *Persuasion*, the ship that had destroyed the Qin colonies and killed hundreds of thousands of his people.

"Targeting *Persuasion*," G'kaan decided, routing the information. M'ke passed the order to the *Devotion*. "Prepare for launch!"

The acknowledgments were curt this time. Right on their heels, G'kaan ordered, "Launch!"

Two more six-missile salvos spat at the battleship. After a few moments, Chad's ship followed suit, also sending a dozen missiles toward their target. R'yeb would coordinate her side of the attack.

The lead patrolships spiraled away, with two apparently so damaged they couldn't engage weapons and the third wallowing without engines. But the rear three patrolships moved into position between the battleships. Scanners indicated that there was minimal damage to the battleships.

G'kaan watched as their missiles reached their targets and the shields of the battleships once again flared with the discharge of energy. Another three missiles got through, and one of the battleships lost its starboard missile tubes. But other than minor damage to various systems, the Fleet ships were still more than battle-ready.

G'kaan couldn't help uttering a curse under his breath. M'ke shook his head grimly. Their ambush hadn't inflicted serious damage, but Rose was right to insist they try. The battleships released several rounds of missiles in return, aiming unerringly at their now-exposed ships.

"Evacuate!" G'kaan announced.

"Relayed to all ships," M'ke acknowledged.

G'kaan knew Rose would be bitterly disappointed, but at least they had accomplished something. Now he would have to relay the order back to Earth to blow the moonbase—

"That can't be right," L'pash exclaimed.

"The *Relevance* and *Vitality* are on an intercept course with the battleships!" M'ke exclaimed.

G'kaan quickly checked his navigational scanners. His battleship and Chad's patrolship were heading away, with R'yeb's ship retreating on the other side. But Rose and her raider friends were heading directly toward the Fleet battle squadron.

"Open a channel to her!" G'kaan ordered. He didn't have to say who "her" was.

Rose appeared in the imager. Her eyes were blazing. *"It's time to fight, not talk!"*

"Rose, it's suicide! We haven't done enough damage—"

"I'll show you damage!" she retorted, then cut the channel.

G'kaan stared at M'ke. His advisor looked up from his terminal. "She's not responding."

"She's heading right for them," G'kaan said through

gritted teeth. "Changing course to intercept the battle-ships."

"No!" L'pash exclaimed. "We'll all be killed!"

He took one look at L'pash's expression and de-cided he wouldn't stand for one more moment of in-subordination. "Don't make me replace you, Ops," G'kaan warned, his voice hard and loud enough for everyone to hear.

L'pash wavered, defiance in her eyes, but her years of training won out. She stared down at her terminal.

"Prepare for launch," G'kaan announced to his crew as he headed into the maelstrom. They would last at least long enough to get into laser range.

"The *Endurance* is turning!" Fen shouted out. "Chad's with him. They're coming back to help."

"Well it's about time." Rose altered course to avoid the bulk of the Fleet's first round of missiles. She fol-lowed the *Vitality*, as they had agreed, since the raider's automated point defense used lasers to pick off the mis-siles. At this range, none got through.

"The *Devotion* is right behind us," Fen added.

Rose didn't spare a thought for R'yeb, knowing the Qin captain hadn't turned to help them until G'kaan made his move in support. But at least G'kaan was mak-ing the right choice now. She had to give him that.

"Entering optimum range," Fen warned.

"Launch missiles," Rose ordered. Her missiles shot out in three satisfying salvos.

On the patrolship *Tranquillity*, Chad exclaimed, "Has Rose gone mad?" His navigational scanners showed Rose's ship plowing directly toward the defensive formation that the Fleet had created. To his trained eye, it looked like a highly efficient defense formation . . . but he was heading toward it along with G'kaan and everyone else in this crazy outfit.

"Rose must know what she's doing," his ops officer put in nervously. "Doesn't she?"

Chad took a deep breath. Rose was always in over her head. Acts of desperation wouldn't work every time. But he couldn't let his own crew know his doubts. Not in the middle of battle.

"Sure she does," Chad said instead. "Rose is a miracle worker."

"The *Relevance* took another hit on their fuel cells," M'ke said quietly. "The port tank is about to blow."

G'kaan winced as his own ship shook. Only a very large impact could impart that much force. But damage control said they had only lost two missile tubes, and there was a breach in the pinnace bay, which was contained. That would change now that they had dropped into laser range.

"Firing lasers!" he called out.

No sooner had he fired than the Fleet battleships retaliated, giving him back twice the kick. For a moment, his terminal froze from the overload. He actually felt his ship skew out of control. As soon as he got the helm back, he would have to break off their attack.

Rose couldn't believe the amount of energy slashing through space as the raider joined G'kaan in striking the battleships again and again with their powerful lasers. But the two Fleet battleships seemed to shrug off their attack and shot back purple fire.

Her own ship handled like a tiny sailboat on the ocean during a violent storm. Then the *Persuasion*'s lasers struck out at them, hitting her shields like a ton of bricks. Alarms went off on every deck. She had to break away. Her last missile was sent out, and she had nothing left to fight with. But those big dark ships hung there, taunting her.

As the *Relevance* curved away, the Fleet battleships finally began to move. They were closing in on G'kaan's floundering battleship.

R'yeb started to retreat along with the *Relevance*. It had been a poorly planned and executed attack, resulting in minimal damage to the battleships while their own ships had been hit hard.

But the Fleet battleships were heading after *Endurance*. In one flash, R'yeb knew that Qin couldn't afford to lose G'kaan and his battleship.

"Evacuate!" R'yeb screamed through the internal comm. "Abandon ship!"

There was one stunned moment as everyone stopped in the midst of the fizzing conduits and blaring alarms, then they fled. R'yeb plotted her course, driving the patrolship as fast as its damaged converter would take it.

"What about you?" her comm officer cried out.

R'yeb pushed him away. "Go! Get out *now*!"

The *Devotion* suddenly lunged at the Fleet battleship. "R'yeb!" G'kaan called out as her ship rapidly closed the gap.

Both battleships reacted with their lasers. The *Devotion* dodged a dozen desperate bolts, deflecting them off the shields, shuddering under the impacts. The ship twisted up and around before slamming into the side of the battleship *Persuasion*.

The patrolship seemed to dent the shields before jamming into the hull, bending the brilliant forcefield until it ruptured. An explosion ripped out, engulfing the patrolship as it crashed into a boiling ball of fire.

"R'yeb!" someone cried out. A scattering of lifepods had ejected from the patrolship.

Felenore stared at the imager, her hands clutching the arms of her chair. "What happened to *Persuasion*?"

"One of those renegade patrolships crashed into its starboard side," the Alpha-captain of the *Subjugation* replied incredulously.

Felenore turned back to the imager in time to see one of her own patrolships explode. She wasn't even sure how.

Another one of the enemy patrolships was heading directly towards *Subjugation*.

"Incoming ship!" the Beta at the comm warned. "On a direct intercept course—"

"Evade!" Felenore ordered.

The captain at helm jerked at if he had been shocked. He sent a surge through the converter, curving away from the attackers as his ship leapt to high speed. Only three of their Fleet patrolships followed, with one trailing badly behind.

"Course?" the Alpha-captain requested, his voice still unusually high and tight.

"Back to the intrasolar slip," Felenore said reluctantly. "If this is how they fight, we'll need reinforcements."

* * *

Rose couldn't believe her eyes as the remaining Fleet battleship changed course and sped away. Chad's patrol-ship was actually in pursuit for a few minutes. It looked bad, like Chad was going to follow R'yeb's example and use his own ship as the ultimate weapon.

As her insides twisted, Rose cried out, "No!"

Then the battleship increased speed, with the rest of their damaged battle squadron rushing after them. Chad's ship peeled away and returned to their location. In the midst of her overwhelming emotions, Rose hardly knew why she was so concerned about Chad. Maybe it was because she had finally found a common ground with him. She couldn't lose him now.

Fen looked up at Rose, her eyes wide in shock. "G'kaan is hailing us."

Rose was so unnerved that she couldn't say a word. Her crew were staring at her, waiting to take their tone from her as usual. But she kept searching the imager as if expecting the *Devotion* to magically reappear. When she had destroyed a patrolship full of people coming into Sol, she hadn't felt like this. When she had watched the riots and massacres on Earth, it hadn't affected her this way. Maybe it should have.

"Rose, are you okay?" Fen asked in concern.

"How many lifepods ejected from the *Devotion*?" she asked roughly.

"I only read three. Some were destroyed."

Not enough! Not nearly enough for all the Qin and Creh onboard.

Stub was looking stunned, too. "Rose, we almost tanked! Our port fuel cell was about to blow."

"G'kaan is hailing us again," Fen added quietly.

"Respond," Rose said with an energy she didn't feel. For once she knew she deserved his anger.

G'kaan was standing up, leaning uncomfortably close. His blue eyes practically bulged out of his head. *"You disobeyed my orders! R'yeb's death and those of her crew are on your head, Rose! You are responsible for this."*

Rose swallowed. "I didn't know she would turn kamikaze—"

"Thank the ancestors that she did! My ship would have been destroyed with all hands, along with yours. " Rose's mouth opened but G'kaan rushed on, *"You know it's true! With the damage you sustained, you would never have gotten away. You and your crew should be dead, not R'yeb and my own people!"*

Maybe that's why she couldn't seem to catch her breath. In spite of all of her harebrained schemes and close calls, she had never brought herself face-to-face with death before. She couldn't seem to get her bearings. The cocky retorts she relied on seemed light-years away.

"You should have broken off your attack, and we would have all escaped," G'kaan cried out bitterly. His own pain was clear, as was his fury with her. *"I trusted you as an ally, Rose, and my crew members are dead because of it."*

Behind his words, L'pash was in the background ranting, *". . . endangering our corpsmen to protect some backward planet! You must be insane! You should be stripped of command—"*

"Silence!" G'kaan bellowed.

A hush fell over both ships. For once, Rose wasn't eager to take center stage. But there was nothing left but to do it. "You're right," she admitted quietly.

Her crew held their breath in surprise. Since her first words in the cargo container onboard the *Purpose*, Rose had done nothing but try to pound them into trusting her. She had acted as if she could do anything, and pulled off things that defied imagination. She could have argued that they had beaten the Fleet back once again, but suddenly she felt it in her bones that sometimes the price *was* too high for victory.

Had her mother paid too much? That would be the question that would never leave her. She had tried to ignore it, tried to pretend it didn't matter. But she knew that both her mother's loving face and R'yeb's defiant one would be with her until she died.

She looked into G'kaan's eyes. "I've never given up without a fight before, and I just didn't . . . know."

G'kaan's mouth worked, his fury fighting with his own sense of guilt about joining her hopeless battle and drawing in R'yeb. Rose knew she had hurt him as much as he had ever hurt her. And she didn't even know until now that she cared so much.

G'kaan reached out and closed the channel without a word. Somehow, that made it even worse.

She looked up at her crew, expecting them to spit on her for being so wrong. But sympathy was already flowing. Stub got up and stumbled over to her, putting his arms around her and burying his face in her hair. Fen was sniffling and repeating, "It's okay, Rose. It's okay."

For once, Rose let them take care of her.

25

—⁂—

Heloga Alpha refused all comms and requests for interviews. Dyrone was still recovering from his laser wound, and he had sent word that the MIF could be repaired within a decnight. Heloga had ordered him to proceed, if only so she wouldn't have to look at herself. She was even tempted to brazen it out and use the MIF in public again. But she couldn't face them. Every person she met had the horror in their eyes. They knew.

Heloga hadn't left her home since Winstav had forcibly removed her illusion of beauty. She couldn't bear to have anyone search the folds of her veil with morbid curiosity.

The terminal beeped, indicating there was an urgent message awaiting her. Heloga had shut down her comm implant that linked her to Waanip, so the standard comm lines were the only way a message could get through. It must be something important to be routed here rather than her office.

Heloga was so sluggish she could hardly force herself to turn toward the terminal, and say, "Message accepted."

Winstav Alpha appeared on the monitor. His flightsuit

was the newest fashion, complete with frogged clasps from neck to crotch. Heloga had known smarmy power-seekers like Winstav before, especially when she was a subcommander in the Antares region. Alphas like him aped the regents in order to gain their favor and win plum assignments.

The recorded message began to play. *"I'm leaving with the* Allegiance.*"* Winstav omitted the necessary honorific of "Regional Commander." *"I'll rendezvous with Felenore and the battle squadron before we proceed to Qin. But I wanted to let you know that you've lost."*

Heloga felt a painful tug in her cheek as she tried to sneer at the image of the little man.

Victory gleamed in his expression as the message continued, *"By the time I return, a new regional commander will have Canopus well in hand. You can expect her to bring an order for you to be sent to a retirement colony, where I'm sure you'll have a great deal in common with the other living corpses."*

Heloga ignored the damage to her skin as she slammed her fists down on her thighs. They couldn't downrank her—

"What else did you expect?" Winstav asked, exactly as if he could see her reaction. *"You let an enemy invade Domain territory. The regents don't want another war coming through their back door when they have the Kund to deal with. So your services are no longer needed."* Winstav smiled blandly. *"I wanted to be the first to tell you."*

The arrogant man stared from the screen, drawing out his satisfaction. Heloga started to say something to cut the comm, but Winstav beat her to it. He was evil incarnate, but he would never have won if her own body hadn't given out.

She looked down at her hand clutched convulsively on her thigh. Even encased in protective layers, her fingers were knobby and drawn into claws. She could imagine everyone—her staff, assistants, and enforcers, the little people who had jumped at her word for decades—watching as she was led away. She would be forced to reveal herself. They would stare at her body after she was dead, laid out cold with all her flaws exposed in unforgiving, harsh light . . . preserved on holos for the private enjoyment of Winstav Alpha and his cronies.

Heloga shuddered, sinking down to her knees with her arms wrapped around her sagging flesh.

Her decision was made. She was already dead; it was only a matter of how she would live her final hours. Some people might treasure the contemplative time before nature closed their eyes, but for Heloga, it wasn't the way she intended to live. She wouldn't let the weakness in her body betray everything she had accomplished for her line.

She pulled herself to her feet, wrapping her veil around her face and neck even more securely. The one-way fabric was black, like her mood, and didn't allow a scrap of light to illuminate her face.

Her personal enforcers leaped to their feet when she opened the door. Her Beta-commander was nowhere in sight, which suited her. Ignoring their scramble to cover her, Heloga marched down the corridor and up the lift tube to the landing pad.

Her armored aircar rested on the pad, ready to depart at a moment's notice. She got inside as the driver ran out of the control room, shrugging on his uniform jacket. He skidded to a stop when he saw her in the driver's seat.

Heloga didn't bother to say anything. Her last words weren't going to be to her underlings. The last words they would remember would be her taunt at her party— *"I rule this region!"*

At a touch, the doors of the aircar sealed for vacuum and the autotakeoff sequence lifted it from the pad. Heloga input her destination and gave the order, "Delete safety overrides by order of Regional Commander Heloga Alpha."

After that, it was a matter of waiting patiently as the autopilot maneuvered through the atmospheric traffic on Canopus Prime. Their path curved away from the main lanes to the orbital starport. The autopilot showed that her aircar was queried by local and then planetary traffic control, but they quickly retreated when the ID on her car was triggered. Heloga didn't have to lift a finger. She could go anywhere she wanted to, because she was regional commander.

As Canopus Prime sank away, the huge gas-giant planet swam into view. It was striped deep turquoise and purple, absorbing most light, making it nearly indistinguishable against the starfield. She could have ordered the aircar to dive into its deadly gas atmosphere. Likely she would end up sinking to the depths of the boiling planet. But there was always a chance the aircar could be located and retrieved, and Heloga didn't want anyone shifting through her remains.

So instead, the aircar circled the planet and headed toward a disc that looked like it was the size of her fist. It was one of the binary suns in the system. It was far away, but large and hot enough to brighten Canopus Prime. That was her final goal.

Serene, now that she had finally stopped fighting her fate, Heloga sat back and thought over her long life with great pleasure and satisfaction. She had risen high for her line. She wondered if any of them had lived a life like hers. She had possessed everything she ever desired, using her own hands to build a region out of nothing but stars and empty space.

Since she still held her rank at death, her work would continue to bolster the other rare and precious Helogas. Surely they would become regents soon, and she had helped them by doing an outstanding job in a difficult frontier region for nearly a century. Her achievements wouldn't be overshadowed by recent events. To date, she hadn't received so much as an official reprimand for the loss of Spacepost T-3. It would be her greatest stroke of success to die now, before her reputation could be tarnished by those spiteful strategists. She had beaten Winstav by this one act.

That's when she realized the source of her extraordinary calm. She wasn't going to die. Not really. She was immortal because of all the Helogas who lived now and would come after her. In essence, she would go on. She had retained everything she had worked for in life, and would pass it on to the other Helogas, surviving the death of this one insignificant body. What mattered was the success her line achieved. This was the ultimate strength of the Alphas, the interconnected, immortal web they created as their clones became better and better.

It took a few hours before the sun began to grow larger, erasing the stars with its brightness. Eventually the radiation alarms went off, sounding until Heloga overrode them. It also began to grow warmer. But Heloga lay back on the seat, feeling a smile even if her mouth couldn't form one anymore, remembering everything she had seen and done. She had lived gloriously. And she would never die.

26

————~m————

With one smooth motion, Rose maneuvered the aircar into place against the airlock and snapped on the magnetic seal. "Door-to-door service," she tossed over her shoulder.

"You've gotten good at that since the last time I saw you dock," Mote replied. "Remember Spacepost T-3?"

Rose grinned at the redheaded woman. Of all the good things that had happened in Sol, this was the best. Mote was back! Reliable, steady, cautious Mote. Rose had depended on her almost as much as on Ash. Until a few hours ago, Rose believed that Mote was dead.

"Practice makes perfect." Rose smacked Mote's slender butt as she stood up. "Get in there, I know there are lots of people who want to see you. I've got to take Nip here over to the *Solace* for a visit."

Mote was still smiling, but her smile was bittersweet. "I don't understand why Whit didn't come back. At least it makes sense with Dab. I think she's really starting to love Grex."

"She's smart," Rose retorted. Dab was going into a partnership with Grex, forming a powerful team. Rose was glad to have another ship, a laser-capable one at that, on her side.

Nip offered from the back, "From what I saw, Whit seems happy there."

Rose snorted. "Yeah, maybe he realizes a hijacked patrolship is a big, fat target for the Fleet."

Nip swallowed and sat back, while Mote wrinkled her nose at Rose. "Then I guess you'll need me to do the worrying for you."

"As long as you take care of your pet, I'll be fine." Rose glanced at the large fuzzy cat that Mote had brought home with her.

"I should have brought five," Mote assured her. "Shard will be thrilled, I promise."

Rose laughed as Mote left the aircar. She knew something about cats from living in Tijuana, and where there was one, there were a hundred. "Make sure the airlock is closed, will you, Nip?"

There was the sound of fumbling as Nip adjusted the hatch. "Okay. . . ."

Rose knew nothing would ever change Nip. She wondered why Gandre Li had asked that Nip come with her to the *Solace*. The story of his affair with Trace, including Gandre Li's resentment over it, was known in every intimate detail among the Solians. But maybe Trace trusted Nip and wanted him to be the one to deactivate her collar.

Rose disengaged from her patrolship, pulling out to check the close formation that orbited Earth. They had quite a number of ships now, though most needed reconstruction or were being dismantled for parts. G'kaan's battleship was crawling with repair bots, as was her own patrolship. Once her damaged fuel tank was repaired, she could refuel from the one of the wrecked Fleet patrolships and reload her missile magazines. Chad's *Tranquillity* and the raider had less serious damage.

Despite the likelihood that repairs would bring them back to full power, Rose knew her desperate attack on the Fleet had bought Earth little time, perhaps only a few days. Now she understood why G'kaan kept insisting they couldn't hold Sol. She had been blown away by the powerful attack from the Fleet, and she knew if R'yeb hadn't given her life along with half of her crew, things would have turned out very differently.

It had been too easy to capture the smaller patrolships. In every fight she'd seen between Qin and the Fleet, the Qin had won. But Rose knew she wouldn't be able to sacrifice herself and the *Relevance*, so she couldn't expect to repeat their last success. Chad had refused to answer when she asked if his attack run had been real or a bluff.

The next time the Fleet returned, they would undoubtedly fly straight through the system rather than use the intrasolar slip. With surprise on their side, the Free Sol Flotilla would have barely six hours warning and no choice but to run for it.

But Rose knew better than to despair. Hadn't she proved that she could beat anything they threw at her?

"Prepare to dock," she warned Nip.

Rose pulled up to the *Solace* with her usual swoop and slide. Nip held his breath as the curved hull of the courier rapidly closed.

"No sweat!" Rose laughed.

Nip wiped his brow with a shaky hand as Rose locked down the aircar. By the time she got to the airlock, the other side was open.

"Your girlfriend is waiting," Rose told Nip over her shoulder. His cheeks flushed red, but he came forward eagerly.

Rose avoided the happy reunion while she was busy sealing the airlock behind her. Trace greeted him with a cheerful glee that made boyish Nip seem practically old.

"Hey there, Trace," Rose tossed off. On closer examination, Trace didn't look so good with her haggard face and dark circles under her eyes. "Where's Gandre Li?"

"Up in the lounge. We've got a problem."

"There's always a problem," Rose agreed. "Lead on."

Up in the lounge, Gandre Li was standing near the cabins, while her three crew members were sitting on sofas in the middle. Rose nodded to them, noticing that Takhan had her arms crossed tightly, as if she wasn't happy.

"I saw you dock, Rose," Gandre Li said quietly, the irritation clear in her tone.

Rose grinned. "You need something, Gandre Li?"

Gandre Li pulled herself to her full height, towering over Rose and Nip. Rose responded by slouching and smiling even more. She had paid Gandre Li back in full for services rendered. There was going to be no pulling rank in Sol.

Trace put her arm around Gandre Li's waist, looking anxiously up at her. "It's Herntoff Alpha. We have him tied up in the guest cabin."

"Kinky," Rose said approvingly.

"Stop it, Rose!" Gandre Li exclaimed. "Herntoff is an InSec operative who was planted on my ship. InSec must have connected us to your escape from Archernar shipyard."

That was different. "They must have seen Kwort go into your ship."

"That was always the biggest risk," Gandre Li agreed.

Trace looked miserable. "It's my fault. I brought Kwort on board."

"No, I told you to get him," Nip chimed in.

"Hey," Rose cut through the dreary blame-sharing. "If it hadn't happened, we'd still be slaves."

"It doesn't matter who's responsible," Gandre Li agreed. "What do we do with Herntoff?"

Takhan spoke up from the sofa. "I say kill him."

Gandre Li silently shook her head while Jor and Danal looked concerned. Trace's expression was interesting, to say the least.

"Got a problem with murder?" Rose asked.

"Yes!" Gandre Li glared at her.

"Okay, I'll take him down to the moonbase and put him with the others." Rose waved one hand in a dismissive gesture. "We've got hundreds of hostages, what's one more?"

Takhan stood up and came closer. "That means Herntoff will be freed once Fleet returns to Sol."

That was the kind of statement that used to crawl right up Rose's spine. But now she knew it was no more than the truth, so she nodded. "Yep."

"InSec knows about us already," Gandre Li told Takhan. "Now that I've skipped out on my assignments and Herntoff's disappeared, they'll mind-strip me first chance they get anyway. Nothing's gained by his death."

"He knows about Trace," Takhan insisted.

Rose glanced over as Trace put her hands to her stomach. That one gesture was enough. "You're pregnant!"

Trace's astonishment showed, along with every other person in the lounge.

"How did you know?" Trace exclaimed.

Rose went over and gave her a big hug. "I'm from Tijuana, honey. I've seen plenty of ripe women. Congratulations!"

Nobody seemed to know what to do with her reaction. Maybe it was a cultural thing, but in her part of the world, babies were cause for celebration. That was the Domain for you. Even new life was something to be feared.

Nip, on the other hand, looked like his guts had fallen out. "Is it possible?" he finally squeaked.

Trace smiled at Nip. "Do you mind being a father?"

"You mean . . . it was . . ." Nip reeled back. *"Me?"*

"Apparently you both beat the odds," Gandre Li said flatly.

Rose slapped Nip on the back. "My opinion of you just went up a few notches, Nip."

"How is it possible?" he repeated in a dazed voice.

"I'll give you a disc when we get back to the ship," Rose said under her breath. "Go give the girl a hug like a real man."

Nip stumbled forward, as awkward as usual. But Rose was glad to see that he and Trace were finally talking. She stepped over to Gandre Li. "So that's why you had to run from the Domain."

The Bariss crossed her arms. "That was a big part of it. I realized Herntoff was an operative, and then we had no choice."

Rose nodded, perfectly serious for once. "I don't blame you one bit. But now what are you going to do?"

"First we'll have to change the *Solace's* ID. Captain

Grex says he can show us where to get that done safely, which is a *big* load off my mind. After that, there's a good number of settlements outside the regional border, up near the Elaspian sector. We'll go there first."

"We were thinking that would be a good place for the Free Sol Flotilla to base our operations. I have a feeling that Qin also isn't going to be a pleasant place for a while, and they certainly don't want any help from *Solians*."

"Looks to me like the Qin did a lot for you, Rose."

She nodded, glancing down. "Yeah, G'kaan went out of his way. But he's done all he can. I'm on my own from here on out."

"So are we," Gandre Li admitted.

Rose looked around the gorgeous lounge. As far as taste and elegance went, it beat her ship hands down. But she preferred the merry confusion on board the *Relevance*. Takhan was talking to both Trace and Nip. It sounded like the bot tech knew a thing or two about babies having grown up on a family ship. Rose was glad they seemed to have come to terms with Gandre Li. They had made the right decision about the Alpha. These people didn't need murder on their hands. It was a heavy burden to bear . . . she should know.

"All right," Rose said, smacking her hands together. "We've got an Alpha to move."

It was much later before Rose returned to her berth. First they had to deactivate Trace's collar, so she could never be shocked again. But Trace had kept the silver ring around her neck, since it would deflect suspicion. Rose suspected it also had something to do with Trace's devotion to her mistress, but that was their own business.

Then the transfer of Herntoff Alpha into a slave cube had been amusing, but time-consuming. He had resisted being stripped of his flightsuit and was reduced to pathetic hysterics by the time the bot sealed the cube shut. It reminded Rose of the people who had been abducted along with her, except that many of them had died, while these parasites would eventually be rescued by the Fleet. Her only consolation was that some of them might expire before then. Herntoff seemed like a puny specimen, and he claimed to have serious health problems that might solve Gandre Li's problem for her.

Back on board the *Relevance*, Ash was waiting in Rose's berth, reclining on the cushion-filled bunk. S/he had gotten in the habit of stopping by before bedtime, and Rose found it more comforting than she liked to admit. When she was a little girl, her father would sit on the edge of her bed, talking to her about what she had done that day. He was usually too busy to see her except for that nightly chat.

"You're later than usual," Ash told her.

"Nip is staying on the *Solace* overnight so I had to fetch his things." Rose would prefer to have everyone back in their proper place. The Fleet battleship could be heading insystem right now, but at least the redistributed remote comms would warn them. "I don't want to lose my best helmsman."

"Does he intend to stay with Trace?" Ash asked. "He talks about her a lot."

"I hope not. I don't think Gandre Li would like it." Yet if Nip wanted to, she wouldn't say a word if he moved in with Trace and their baby. Still, that was Nip's news to tell, not hers. "I'd like everyone where they belong before we leave Earth."

"Are we leaving Earth?" Ash sat up straighter, putting aside the pillow in hir lap.

"When the Fleet comes back, we'll have to go."

"You never said that before."

Rose lifted her chin. "Free Sol will keep on fighting. That's what's important. They'll build more ships and will help us fight the Domain."

"How?"

"We're taking it to the stars, Ash. We've got to reach all those pleasure slaves out there and teach them to defy the Domain. Once they start standing up for their rights, then the Alphas will know what Solians are really made of."

"Rose . . . you make it sound like it can really happen."

"I'll make it happen."

"Yes, you always do." Ash stared at Rose for a few long moments. "Can you bring my memory back, Rose?"

"What? I'm no doctor."

"You can do it, if anyone can." Ash leaned forward to take Rose's hand in hirs. "I hate remembering how I let Rikev go. It's even worse than forgetting my past. I feel so useless, so wrong with every step I take—"

"Ash, don't beat up on yourself." Rose clasped hir hand in both of hers. Ash rarely ever reached out to her. "You're a survivor. It was the first thing I saw in you."

"Tell me more," Ash begged.

Rose realized that she should have talked to hir like this before. "I think you're so incredibly tough because you've got tons of experience, but you exist in the moment better than anyone I've ever met. You're not selfish or manipulative at all, and that's why I trust you."

"But I . . . I'm so unhappy. . . ."

"You've always been unhappy. I've never known anyone more hurt than you. Sometimes I watch the others talking to you, tiptoeing around your feelings like you're an open, bleeding wound. But everyone goes to you with their problems because you understand pain. You can make it better somehow."

Ash's eyes were bright. "It feels right . . . but I can't remember!"

"I wish I could help you."

"D'nar says I'm afraid of the truth. That I won't remember until I accept what happened."

Rose brightened up. "I know how to make you tell the truth to yourself." She reached over to one of her shelves to pick up the serneo-inhibitor that G'kaan had finally sent over. "I planned to use this on Bolt."

"That's the Qin truth serum?" Ash asked.

"Yeah, I wanted to find out if Bolt was responsible for my abduction." She turned the injector over in her hands. "But I already know. He's guilty, even if he didn't know the *policía* were going to show up that night. He was working with them to save his own hide, like everyone else. Like I lived off my mother even though I knew the civs were sucking the *barrios* dry."

"What are you going to do about Bolt?" Ash asked.

"I guess I'll have to let him go. I can't keep him locked up in my brig forever. And it's hard to blame him when so many other people did worse. And suffered worse vengeance."

"I like Bolt."

Rose looked at Ash. "Haven't you visited enough prisoners?"

"Shard took me to see him."

"Oh, well, then. That must make it okay." Rose had

to laugh. "If Shard's adopted Bolt, I'll never get rid of him."

Ash gestured toward the serneo-inhibitor. "Jot says the Qin used that on me."

"Yeah, when we first got to Po Alta. You saw the attack on Spacepost T-3 and they wanted to make sure you were telling the truth. But you hated it. I could tell because your hand was shaking."

Ash's hands were shaking now, and s/he stared with morbid fascination at the injector. "I can't remember. . . ."

"Then S'jen used it on you after she kidnapped you. She wanted to know more about Rikev Alpha."

Ash's hand jerked. "I have to remember!"

"Do you want to try it?" Rose asked.

"Yes."

Rose considered Ash. What if she hurt her friend? But Ash had been injected many times before by S'jen, and there had been no problems.

"Okay, lean back," Rose ordered. "You'll feel very relaxed when it starts to work."

Ash reclined on the cushions, hir expression scared. Rose smoothed back hir hair with a smile. "Turn your head toward me."

Ash looked over, exposing hir neck. Rose checked the injector to make sure there was only one dose inside. D'nar had sent along a datarod with instructions on what to do, as if they were too stupid to use a medical injector.

"Okay," Rose said lightly. "Here it comes."

The injector sprayed the serneo-inhibitor into Ash's neck. Hir eyes closed briefly as if s/he was dizzy. Rose patted hir hand, watching to make sure s/he didn't become too flushed. D'nar had given her the antidote in patches, so it would be easy to administer. Rose got one ready to open and slap on hir arm in case of a reaction.

But Ash opened hir eyes. "Rose . . ."

"Do you remember anything?" Rose checked her eyes, noting the dilation of hir pupils. That meant the serneo-inhibitor was in hir bloodstream and should be pumping into hir brain.

Ash looked confused.

"Do you remember coming on board the *Relevance* a few days ago?" Rose asked.

"Yes!" Ash said. "Shard took me to my berth and Jot was waiting there for me. They had fixed it up with Indian blankets, like the ones I saw at Margarita's house that I liked so much."

"Good, so you must remember going down to Earth to the barbecue."

"Yes," Ash agreed. "Enzo and Manuel were there. And Kwort ate so much he got sick. Last night he gave me some enchiladas he programmed into the transposer, but they aren't as good as Margarita's. He says he'll figure out the right balance of ingredients soon enough."

Rose grinned, ready to go for broke. "Good. Now . . . do you remember being in the cargo container on the *Purpose* when I first met you?"

Ash's mouth opened. "I do! Shard was there. And Nip. And Chad, and Jot! We jumped the Poids and took off their flightsuits. They looked a lot smaller naked."

"Good, so you must remember being on Spacepost T-3 with me when we were salvaging. The spacepost was broken in half, and Nip got hurt—"

"On the jagged bulkheads," Ash put in. "The blood spurted out. . . ."

Ash sat straight up, swaying slightly.

"Is something wrong, Ash?"

"Blood . . . so much blood," s/he whispered. "I remember everything. . . ."

"What about Rikev Alpha?" Rose asked.

"Oh!" Ash put hir hands to hir face. "How could I be so stupid! How could I have trusted him?"

Rose said nothing. There was nothing to say.

Ash was dazed, as if too many things were flooding hir at once. "I was on the spacepost with Rikev Alpha. Then I got away after S'jen attacked . . . and on Archernar shipyard Rikev used me again . . . he beat me awfully . . . I remember it now."

Rose reached out to comfort Ash, moving closer. "It'll be okay—"

Ash clung to Rose with both arms as if s/he was afraid of slipping away. Rose hugged hir back as tightly as she could, as Ash cried out, "Oh, Rose, I remember it all!"

27

Repairs were nearing completion on the *Endurance* when G'kaan received a comm from Rose. She was wearing her brown Fleet flightsuit, which was starting to look strangely normal on her. Her expression was somber. *"We're calling a conclave. Meet us in the moon-base with your advisors."*

L'pash slapped one hand on her terminal. "I protest! We should pick up our remote comms and leave. We can't waste time talking to a bunch of Solians!"

G'kaan growled at her, "Silence at ops!"

The command deck went very still, then someone snickered near the rear. L'pash's head whipped around, trying to see who'd done it. But the three corpsmen were apparently occupied with repairs on the data relays.

G'kaan told Rose, "We'll be there shortly." Then he cut the comm. At least Rose hadn't returned a shot at L'pash. Maybe she had learned something from their latest battle. Maybe she realized how important allies were in this fight.

Meanwhile L'pash glared at G'kaan with hatred in her eyes. She was worse than S'jen, who simply ignored him unless interaction was necessary. But L'pash had been the butt of snide comments ever since the rumors spread about her shared lust with a Solian herme. L'pash had come to G'kaan's cabin last night, raging mad at the open gossip. She claimed he had undermined her authority with the crew, who now considered her a "freak." G'kaan had held his temper as long as he could, knowing that L'pash had provoked the crew's petty retaliation because of her assumptions of authority as the captain's mate. When her criticisms against him became personal, questioning his manhood, G'kaan had snapped, "Now you know how I've felt all these years, faced with Qin prejudice! I can't help it that I finally found acceptance among the Solians rather than Qin." She had flounced out and refused to speak to him unless it was to acknowledge an order or to make an official request. Her first official request had been for immediate transfer from the *Endurance*, accompanied by similar requests from her two clanmates.

So G'kaan had lost a trusted advisor. "M'ke, you're with me to the moonbase."

"What about me?" L'pash demanded. "If you're going to make any tactical decisions, I have to give my advice regarding the ship's systems and crew."

G'kaan wished he could refuse. L'pash could easily disrupt their already strained relationship with their Solian allies. But technically she was correct. "Will you join us, L'pash?"

She had already signaled for her replacement. She stood up without answering and went through the door.

G'kaan glanced at M'ke, hoping he could assist in restraining L'pash. Indeed, on the way down to the moonbase in the pinnace, M'ke quietly discussed his analysis of the Domain's strengths and weaknesses with L'pash. Her voice rose occasionally, emphasizing certain points of risk they now faced, but for the most part she tried to remain professional with the older Qin. M'ke apparently had found L'pash during lust crying hysterically near the airlock, and G'kaan felt a stab of guilt every time he thought about it.

They were greeted by Enzo and Margarita. The only other Solians on the base were the demolition team. They would be the last ones to leave before blowing the moonbase and the two laser cannons.

Rose, Chad, and Ash were waiting in the tactical command room. Everything of value had been stripped from the walls and terminals. Dangling conduits marked where equipment had been removed. Only a few lights illuminated the oval table in the middle. Even the corridors had been ripped open to salvage materials that were now being used by the Solians to develop weapons and ships. The entire base was empty and echoing.

L'pash stopped short in horror when she saw that Ash was there. G'kaan loudly greeted the Solians to cover up her reaction, ordering, "L'pash, have a seat here next to M'ke."

Disgust emanated from L'pash as she forced herself to sit down at the same table. M'ke murmured a few soothing words to her, but she refused to look up.

Ash stared at them. She seemed different, not so timid or confused. Her eyes narrowed at L'pash's evident rejection.

"We'll make this quick," Rose told everyone. "We all need to talk about what to do next."

"*Now* what do you want from us?" L'pash exclaimed irritably. "The complete destruction of our battleship?"

"L'pash!" G'kaan exclaimed, while M'ke also tried to shush her.

L'pash shook them off and defiantly faced Rose across the expanse of shiny black marble. "Maybe if every Qin dies trying to save Sol from its *inevitable* fate, then you'll be satisfied. As far as I can tell, nothing less will do. But I know that Qin needs us more than you—"

G'kaan finally demanded, "Silence!" When L'pash snapped her mouth shut, he added, "We are serving Qin by protecting Sol. Every ship we destroy here is one less to invade our territory. If we must die to complete our mission, we *will*."

L'pash refused to back down. "I'm speaking on behalf of corpsmen who were successful in lust. They've requested an immediate return to their clans where they can be protected. That outweighs all other considerations."

"Not in war," G'kaan retorted. Then he caught sight of Margarita's face. She wasn't angry or upset with his corpsman's display of temper. Her dark eyes were sympathetic.

Rose spoke for all of them. "We agree, L'pash. It's time for Qin to leave Sol. You've done as much as you can here. You've done more than anyone had a right to expect, including me."

L'pash sat back slowly, realizing that Rose meant what she said.

G'kaan looked at Rose in disbelief. "You've been fighting every step of the way to keep us here."

Rose cleared her throat. "It was Ash who set me straight, as usual." She smiled at hir, and Ash's face lit up in a way that G'kaan hadn't seen in a long time.

"Ash, you've recovered," he realized. "Do you remember again?"

"Yes, Rose did it for me."

L'pash grimaced, but she didn't say anything.

Ash didn't seem bothered by L'pash. "We've decided the most important thing now is to protect the Solians on Earth."

"Remember Balanc," Chad quietly declared.

"And Jenuar, Impelleneer, and Atalade," G'kaan had to agree. "I understand. You don't want the Fleet to retaliate against your people." The memory of those ravaged Qin colonies would haunt him forever. He certainly didn't want a similar fate for Earth.

Ash nodded. "Rikev Alpha is somewhere in this system, watching us. Right now, he probably thinks that you Qin are controlling the Solians, since he's seen me on board your ship. We want to make sure the Alphas don't start thinking Solians are a threat."

G'kaan could see hir point. If the Qin battleship was gone and Earth was defenseless, the Fleet would assume that Qin was the threat. Alphas would certainly rather not slaughter pleasure slaves, so if the Solians were quiescent the Fleet would simply set up their slave export operations again.

Rose, of all people, pointed out, "The Fleet knows we're here now and they know our status. They could be sneaking up on us, remote comms or not. We'll be outnumbered and outmaneuvered when they return. We have to get out so we can fight another day. Free Sol can wait until after the Fleet battleships have left for Qin, before striking back."

L'pash snorted at that, but G'kaan thought it was only fair. He had used Sol to distract the Fleet from

Qin. Now Sol would use Qin to distract the Fleet from them.

Margarita leaned forward earnestly. "On behalf of Sol, we thank Qin for your assistance. We have truly taken the first steps toward freedom because of you."

G'kaan realized their mission was coming to an end. "Consider it a small payment for what Qin owes Sol. And trust the Qin that we are today, not the Qin that we were. We have a common enemy, and must stand strong together in the face of the Domain." This last he said with a look at Rose.

Rose nodded, and her dark eyes seemed deeper, less challenging. He could tell they were even now. They would work together again, and perhaps become friends. It would be a long time before Rose would trust him, which was more than he had left with L'pash. She would never forgive him and would undoubtedly make his life difficult within the Armada.

Yet G'kaan would never regret choosing Rose. He was resigned to his destiny to be forever star-crossed with his lovers.

Ash stood as the Qin prepared to depart. M'ke spoke a few kind words to congratulate hir on hir recovery. G'kaan said he was also very glad to see hir returned to life. That's how Ash felt—as if s/he had awoken from a walking dream.

L'pash marched straight to the door without a glance at any of the Solians. Ash felt bad that the first sex partner s/he'd ever voluntarily chosen wouldn't speak to hir. But s/he was glad nonetheless that L'pash had needed hir during lust. Now Ash knew what real sex was like. S/he had been freed from hir past during hir amnesia, and could truly feel hir affection for hir Solian friends, as well as enjoying lust with L'pash. Now s/he knew what it felt like to crave someone's touch, and to wallow in the good feelings that sex could give hir. Now s/he was shyly eager to try it again with someone who cared about hir.

Ash smiled as L'pash disappeared, knowing s/he would never see the arrogant Qin again. There were plenty of Solians who were ready to share hir bunk, from Shard to Kwort. Indeed, Kwort was a happy man when they told him it was time to leave Sol. On recovering hir memory, Ash was amazed at how thoroughly he had settled into the crew. He had become a leader among them, and his most constant companion was Clay. Kwort had assured hir yesterday that he had been more than amply rewarded for helping the former slaves. He said he had finally had found a place he belonged.

That's how Ash felt. And there was only one thing s/he needed. Hir best friend and partner, Rose.

S/he reached out for Rose's hand. After a surprised moment, Rose returned hir squeeze. She clearly wasn't used to Ash's newfound comfort with touching, but Rose responded to every overture with interest. Ash knew that more would come in time, now that they were developing their relationship.

Rose's good-bye to G'kaan was strained, but there was none of that awful animosity between them anymore. Ash knew all about Rose's sexual spree with G'kaan, while he had continued to conceal the Qin's culpability in the slave trade. Rose was not one to forgive easily, but she seemed to be letting go of her resentment of G'kaan. It was a different story with Bolt.

Despite Shard's pleas, Rose had refused to let Bolt stay on their ship. But Chad had agreed to let Bolt join his crew. Rose had grumbled that Chad would no doubt regret it, but by now the two were comfortable with their disagreements.

Ash gave G'kaan a happy grin in farewell. "Thanks for taking care of me for so long. But it turns out I did belong with Rose."

G'kaan looked as if he envied hir. "Yes, you do." One hand raised in salute. "Freedom for all."

The Qin left to return to their battleship, and there were only Solians on the moon. They would coordinate their departure with the *Endurance*, heading toward the Wolf-Sol slip to make it appear that they were controlled by Qin and were returning to their territory. But then the Solian ships would circle back around to the Elaspian sector to set up shop for Free Sol.

Margarita and Enzo prepared to go next. Chad said gruffly, "I hate this. It feels like we're abandoning you!"

"You know it's the best thing for everyone," Enzo assured him. "We would still be living in ignorance if you hadn't returned. We will never forget any of you."

"We'll be back before you know it," Rose declared. "Meanwhile we'll start harassing the Canopus region. Maybe we can distract them from Sol for a bit. The strategy worked for the Qin, why not us?"

"Do your best," Margarita told Rose, giving the younger woman a hug. Ash noticed that Rose's hands clenched around Margarita. Rose had haltingly confessed to Ash that she was having nightmares about the death of her mother. Ash had patted her on the back to comfort her, and was fiercely glad s/he could finally do so. The wall that had held hir away from others was finally broken. For that, s/he would always be glad s/he had lost hir memory. How else could s/he have learned to touch anyone with love while the horror of the slave trade was fresh in hir mind?

"We'll tell the demolition team to arm the explosives," Margarita said, as she and Enzo joined hands to leave. Ash was sure their precautions would work, and they would continue to coordinate the revolt with the Free Solians on Earth. "Freedom for all."

Then it was only the three of them.

"Time to go," Chad said sadly. "I knew it would be hard."

Rose went forward a few steps, looking down at the schematic of Earth etched into the black floor. She rubbed one boot against the blue and white image. "Just one second more. Standing here on the moon, it's almost like being home."

Ash reminded her, "Home is where your friends are."

"Okay," Rose said with a laugh. "You've got me. So, let's get out there and get on with the revolt."

In spite of the danger ahead, Ash linked arms with Rose, perfectly happy to go anywhere she did.

About the Author

Susan Wright grew up mostly in Arizona and has lived in New York City for more than fifteen years. She has written nine Star Trek novels: *Dark Passions* 1 & 2, *Gateways: One Small Step*, *Badlands* 1 & 2, *The Best and the Brightest*, *The Tempest*, *Violations*, and *Sins of Commission*. Susan also writes nonfiction books on art and popular culture, including *New York in Old Photographs*, *UFO Headquarters: Area 51*, and *Destination Mars*. Susan received her master's in art history from New York University in 1989. Her website is www.susanwright.info.